THE PRESIDENT'S DAUGHTER

'Propulsive, exhilarating, and unnervingly believable. You won't just read *The President's Daughter*, you'll devour it'
Karin Slaughter

'A rollicking ride combining Clinton's insider knowledge of the top echelons of US power with Patterson's snappy pacing and forensic prose'
Independent

'Even better than their first . . . A rattling roller coaster of a thriller'
Daily Mail

'Deftly interweaves action scenes and family dynamics'
Sunday Times

'Highly entertaining'
N

'I loved this book

'A really propulsive and
Irish Independent

'Full of glorious details into the inner workings of the White House, this is action all the way in a fast and furious tale'
Sun

'Superb thriller, expertly told. Read it in two days. More please'
Piers Morgan

'Legendary author James Patterson has teamed up with ex-US president Bill Clinton to write this chilling crime novel'
Sunday Express

'An absolute rocket . . . Clinton and Patterson are simply the best in the thriller business'
Robert Crais, bestselling author of the Elvis Cole series

'Clinton and Patterson's novel puts their respective expertise to good use'
Time

'A page-turning, painfully human thriller that reveals the human hearts that beat inside those corridors of power'
Tony Parsons, bestselling author of *Your Neighbour's Wife*

'Brace yourself for a thriller with inside secrets and riveting excitement'
Walter Isaacson, internationally bestselling author

'A smart, taut, utterly fantastic roller coaster that had me holding on for dear life'
Chris Bohjalian, bestselling author of *The Flight Attendant*

ALSO BY THE AUTHORS

The President is Missing

BILL CLINTON

AND

JAMES PATTERSON

THE PRESIDENT'S DAUGHTER

PENGUIN BOOKS

PENGUIN BOOKS

UK | USA | Canada | Ireland | Australia
India | New Zealand | South Africa

Penguin Books is part of the Penguin Random House group of companies whose addresses can be found at global.penguinrandomhouse.com.

First published in the UK by Century in 2021
Published in Penguin Books 2022
001

Typeset by Jouve (UK), Milton Keynes

Printed and bound in Great Britain by Clays Ltd, Elcograf S.p.A.

The authorised representative in the EEA is Penguin Random House Ireland, Morrison Chambers, 32 Nassau Street, Dublin D02 YH68

A CIP catalogue record for this book is available from the British Library

ISBN: 978–1–529–15721–5
ISBN: 978–1–529–15722–2 (export)

www.greenpenguin.co.uk

Robert Barnett, our lawyer and friend, convinced us to collaborate on The President Is Missing. *That worked out pretty well. Then—and maybe we should've known better—he talked us into* The President's Daughter. *We're so glad we listened a second time to Bob. You did a fine job, Counselor.*

Even as he sheltered in place at home in New Hampshire, Brendan DuBois was with us throughout all the research, every outline, and more drafts than we care to count. Brendan was our rock—and occasionally the hard-ass that we needed.

PART ONE

CHAPTER 1

Two a.m. local time
Gulf of Sidra, off the coast of Libya

Aboard a Night Stalkers Special Operations MH-60M Black Hawk helicopter code-named Spear One, Navy chief Nick Zeppos of SEAL Team Six checks his watch. Five minutes ago, he and his crew departed from the USS *Wasp* amphibious assault ship outbound to their high-value target this deep dark night. If he and his crew—along with other SEAL fighters aboard a second Black Hawk helicopter, code-named Spear Two—are fortunate, they will track down and kill Asim Al-Asheed well before the sun rises.

Zeppos spares a quick glance at his team members, packed in tightly around him in two crowded rows. In the loud, vibrating helicopter's interior, they're mostly silent, some sipping from plastic water bottles, others leaning over, hands tightly clasped. Up forward, the Night Stalkers pilot and copilot from the famed 160th Special Operations Aviation Regiment Airborne are flying at low altitude, about ten meters above the choppy water, instruments glowing green and blue. Zeppos knows that every SEAL team member inside the dimly lit helicopter is going over the upcoming mission, thinking about their training, then clearing their minds for what's ahead:

Killing Asim Al-Asheed.

It's been a long-range goal of the American intelligence agencies and military. Tonight, after four years of preparation, Zeppos hopes they will hit the jackpot.

SEAL teams and Special Forces have gone after terrorist leaders before—notably Osama bin Laden and Abu Bakr al-Baghdadi and their many deputies and allies, leaders who stayed in the shadows, issuing the orders, not getting their hands soiled beyond making grainy videotapes and flowery promises of death and revenge.

"We're coming up on feet dry!" comes the call from the Night Stalkers crew chief, indicating that they're about to cross over from the sea to the land of Libya, one fractured and squabbling nation, a perfect place to incubate or shelter terrorists like Al-Asheed.

But Al-Asheed is not like other leaders of terrorist organizations.

For the past several years, videos have appeared documenting his group's actions, each showing Al-Asheed in the center of the bloody chaos, depending on a well-planned and well-hidden network of supporters who would only appear to assist him at the last moment and then disappear.

Asim in a crowded shopping mall in Belgium, holding up a trigger device and calmly pressing the button, the hollow *boom!* echoing through the concourse, causing the camera to shake, but not enough to hide the billowing cloud of smoke, the screaming shoppers running by, blood trickling down their torn faces and fractured arms.

Asim walking down a street in Paris, cameraman following him, as he unlimbers an automatic rifle from under a long raincoat, shooting into crowds of pedestrians, aiming especially for the women and children, until a white van picks him up and drives him safely away.

Asim standing behind two sobbing female aid workers from the United Nations in the Sudanese desert, their legs and arms bound, as he calmly goes from one to the other, wielding a large sword and beheading both of them, their blood spattering his clothes.

Navy chief Zeppos stretches his legs, draws them back. Twice before he's been on raids—once into Yemen and once into Iraq—where the intel indicated a good probability that Asim was there, but good wasn't good enough. Both raids had come up empty, with no results except for wounded SEALs, shot-up helicopters, and frustration all around.

But Zeppos hopes that the third time will be the charm.

There are other video recordings too gruesome to be released to the public. A woman schoolteacher in Afghanistan, chained to a rock, doused with gasoline, and set afire. A village elder in Nigeria, held tight by men from Boko Haram, as Asim goes down a line of his family members, slitting their throats.

And Boyd Tanner…

Zeppos spares a glance through the near porthole—he wants not to think of Boyd Tanner, whose cause of death is a closely kept secret among the Special Forces community—and sees the bright glow of light on the horizon marking the rapidly rebuilding port city and capital of Tripoli. The Chinese—in their program called the Belt and Road Initiative—have been pouring in development investments here and in other poor countries around the world.

Publicly, the Chinese government says it's just a way for them, as a growing world power, to share their good fortune and knowledge. Privately, Zeppos and others have received classified briefings depicting the Chinese's real goal: securing resources, allies, and possible future military bases so China can never again be isolated and humiliated as it so often has been in its long history.

The glow on the horizon fades away. Spear One and Spear Two are now over the rolling Libyan deserts where decades back the Germans and British desperately fought, and where their rusted-out tanks and trucks still remain in the unforgiving sands.

Before them, the Italians were once here, and now the Chinese, Zeppos thinks.

Big deal.

He starts to recheck his gear.

The crew boss comes back on the intercom.

"Chief, we've got incoming traffic for you," he says.

Zeppos toggles his mic. "Who? JSOC?"

"No, Nick," the aviator says. "Definitely not JSOC."

Shit, he thinks. Who would dare bother him now?

"Patch it through," he says, and there's a *crickle-crackle* of static, and a very familiar voice comes through, one he's heard scores of times over the radio and TV.

"Chief Zeppos?" the man's voice says. "Matt Keating here. Sorry to bother you, I know you're busy, you don't need me to waste precious seconds. But I wanted to let you know that there's nothing I'd want more than to be riding with you right now."

"Ah, thank you, sir!" he says, raising his voice so the president can hear him.

Keating says, "I have full faith in you and your team that you'll get the job done. No worries on this end. I've got your back. Now you squids body-bag that son of a bitch for the country, the SEALs, and especially for Boyd Tanner. Keating out."

"Yes, sir," Zeppos says, part of him in awe that the man would call him personally, part of him touched by his sincere words, and yet, he hates to admit to himself, Zeppos is pissed off that he'd call right now, in the middle of an op!

Shit, he thinks. *Politics sure can screw up a man.* Then he cuts the president some slack. Keating had been one of them. And he knew about Boyd Tanner.

From SEAL Team Two.

Only a few were supposed to know how he died, and it was not, as his grieving wife and kids were told, in a training accident.

Captured last year after a brutal firefight in Afghanistan, wounded and barely alive. Asim Al-Asheed and his fighters had stripped Boyd Tanner of his gear, his clothes, and taken him to a courtyard, recording it all the while.

Whereupon Asim—using a hammer and spikes—had crucified the Navy warrior on a gnarled tree. The video captured the agonizing hour that Tanner hung there before the captors grew bored and slit his throat.

A couple of guys down the length of the Black Hawk are laughing. Zeppos leans over, sees one of his crew—Kowalski—holding up what looks like a wooden spear with a metal tip.

Zeppos calls out, "What the hell is that thing for?"

Kowalski laughs and flourishes the spear. "Asim Al-Asheed," he yells out. "Once we ID his remains, we should take his head off, put it on this pike, and bring it back to the Oval Office! Don't you think the president will love that?"

More laughter, and Zeppos settles back into the uncomfortable seat, grinning.

Yeah.

It's a good night for him and his fellow warriors to avenge the deaths of so many innocents, and to finally come face-to-face with Asim Al-Asheed, give him a few seconds to recognize who's before him, and then put two taps in his chest and one in his forehead.

This darkened Black Hawk helicopter and its shadowy companion speed into the night.

CHAPTER 2

Two fifteen a.m. local time
Embassy of the People's Republic of China, Tripoli

It's damn well late at night—or early in the morning—in the ground-floor reception room for the Chinese Embassy on Menstir Street and Gargaresh Road, and Jiang Lijun, who's listed on the embassy guest list as a vice president for the China State Construction Engineering Corporation, is stifling a yawn.

This supposed party was to have ended more than an hour ago, but the special guests from this blasted country still won't leave. The political leaders, the tribesmen, and the military officers—gaudy in their uniforms, stripes, and medals, like little boys playing dress-up—are still smoking, drinking, and talking to their patient hosts in various corners of the room.

Jiang sees that the local representatives from the Great Wall Drilling Company, CNPC Services & Engineering, China National Petroleum Corporation, and so many others are valiantly standing in for *zhōng guó*—the Middle Country—by smiling, laughing at the stupid attempts at humor, and otherwise entertaining their peasant guests.

And what barbarians! Even after the lights were dimmed, the near-empty food platters were taken away, and the liquor and bottles of beer—Carlsberg, Heineken, Tsingtao—were removed, these peasants didn't get the message that it was time to wander back to their flea-infested hovels. No, they stayed and gossiped, and some even pulled flasks of liquor from their coat pockets, even here, in this supposedly Muslim country. When he was an exchange student at UCLA, in California, and then at Columbia, in New York, a young Jiang thought he would never encounter a more childish, reckless, and ignorant group of uncouth people, but these Libyans make the Americans seem like honorary Han.

He takes out a pack of Zhonghua cigarettes and lights one. He's standing by himself near two large potted plants, seeing who is talking to whom, which members of the embassy staff look drunk or impatient, and observing the groupings of Libyan guests. A very fragile cease-fire and reconciliation government arose last year, but Jiang still wants to see which tribe members stay away from their alleged fellow countrymen, perhaps setting the stage for a future breakup or civil war.

Good information to have ahead of time.

A slim, bespectacled embassy worker wearing an ill-fitting black suit comes in from the far side of the banquet room. He scans the crowd as he hurries across the polished floor. Ling—that's the boy's name. Jiang takes one last puff of the cigarette, stubs it out in the dirt of the nearest potted plant, and waits.

The worker comes to him, bows slightly, and says, "My apologies, sir. Your presence is requested in the basement. Room twelve."

Jiang nods, starts walking across the room, whereupon a heavyset bearded man, swaying drunk and wearing typical tribal garb of billowing white blouse and black slacks, abruptly steps in front of him.

"Mr. Jiang!" he calls out in accented English, grasping Jiang's shoulders, and Jiang keeps a wide smile frozen on his face, trying not to choke from breathing in the alcoholic fumes coming from this dirty peasant. "Are you leaving? Are you?"

Jiang pats the man's worn hands, gently tugs them off his shoulders. "I'm sorry, my friend, but you know how it is," he replies, also in English, the lingua franca of diplomacy in so many parts of the world. "Duty calls."

The man—Jiang can't recall his name, only knows he's the leader of one of the 150 or so tribes in this barren land—sways again, belches, and says, "Duty, yes." Tears come to his eyes. "I must say this…I must…but your duty, your presence here, it has brought so much to our land. The Italians, the French, the British, the Qataris, the damn Egyptians…they have all tried to rule us, take our resources…Who would think the yellow race would travel halfway around the world to shower us with your wisdom and knowledge?"

At this very moment, Jiang wants to slap the man hard in the face, spin him around, twist and break his neck—*Yellow race, indeed!*—and drop him on the floor.

Instead, mindful of who he is and what he must do, Jiang keeps smiling, squeezes the man's filthy hands, and says, "When I next return to Beijing, I will make sure that your words of thanks are passed along to our president."

And with that, Jiang briskly walks away, feeling the need to go to a washroom and scrub that peasant's stench and dirt off his hands, but instead he presses on.

Duty.

He walks past two unsmiling embassy guards with partially hidden earpieces and pistols barely covered by their suits, and he meets up with Ling, standing by the entrance to the lift. Ling is holding the door open for him and Jiang ignores him, taking the stairs to the basement, moving fast. The electricity in this alleged country still has its sudden blackouts, and even with the building's backup generators, Jiang isn't going to risk being stuck between floors.

He opens the door to the basement, going past another embassy guard, going down an ill-lit hallway, until he comes to a heavy steel door equipped with a palm-print reader mechanism. Jiang presses his right hand down, there's a brief flare of light, and the steel door swings open.

Jiang steps inside, the door swinging shut and locking behind him. The room is pleasantly cool and comfortable, and he's now craving a smoke, but there's no smoking allowed in here, in the embassy operations center for China's Ministry of State Security, staffed around the clock.

The night-duty officer, Liu Xiaobo, wearing black-rimmed glasses, casually dressed in black pants and white open-collared dress shirt, is typing on a keyboard in front of a large computer monitor. "How goes that party upstairs?" he asks. "Lots of camel dung on the floor?"

"Not yet," Jiang says. "What's going on?"

The small room is jammed with filing cabinets, counters, computer monitors, television screens showing CNN, the BBC, and CCTV-13, the China Central Television news channel, as well as plasma screens depicting North Africa, the Mediterranean, and the Gulf of Sidra. Eight other members of the Ministry of State Security are also at work this early morning.

Liu says, "The Americans are up to something."

"Aren't they always? Those dog whelps. What is it this time?"

"They have an amphibious assault ship in the Gulf of Sidra, about twenty kilometers off the Tripoli coast," Liu says, pointing to a reference map on his large video screen. "Thirty minutes ago, they launched two UH-60 helicopters, Black Hawks. They're heading in this direction"—a nicotine-stained finger traces a path on the glowing screen—"and have violated Libyan airspace and are now about…here."

Jiang stares at the screen, at the little triangles marking towns and villages, the geography so flat and nearly featureless until—

"They are heading to the Nafusa Mountains," Jiang says.

"Yes," Liu replies. "They appear to be flying straight and level—no evasive maneuvers—and based on the fuel consumption of their helicopters, there is barely enough fuel to get there and return back to the *Wasp*. To me, that says they are going after something very important in those peaks, something worth the risk of running out of fuel."

A stinging bee, Jiang thinks. *What kind of fools name a warship after an insect?*

He focuses again on the video display.

Liu cautiously says, "Don't you have…an interest in the Nafusa Mountains?"

From long practice and years of work, Jiang keeps his face impassive, his breathing regular, his body still. One does not succeed or get promoted by showing emotion. "Anything else?" he asks.

"No," Liu says. "I just wanted you to know."

Jiang gently clasps the man's shoulder. "That is appreciated, comrade."

Liu appears to enjoy the attention from a man higher up than he is. "May I do any other service for you?"

Jiang nods. "Yes. You have a worker here named Ling, correct? The one who came to fetch me?"

Liu's voice is cautious. "Yes."

"Get him on the next transport home," Jiang says. "Ensure he ends up working for the largest pig farm in Liaoning. Earlier, when he came to me, he nearly ran across the room, practically shouting at me, telling anyone with a brain larger than a pea that I was someone of importance, and not just a typical technocrat. He needs to be punished."

"Very well," Liu says.

"Good," Jiang says. "Now it's time to return upstairs, to see if the camels have arrived, and if the peasants up there are tossing lumps of dung at each other."

Liu laughs at that, returns to his large screen. Jiang walks away and uses a hand scanner to depart the operations center, going back into the empty hallway. If he were to turn left, he would go back to the upward staircase to the reception.

Instead, he turns right, walking quickly to his office at the other end, where Jiang Lijun is not a vice president for the China State Construction Engineering Corporation but a senior officer with the Ministry of State Security.

What the hell are the Americans up to?

CHAPTER 3

◆

Two thirty a.m. local time
Nafusa Mountains, Libya

Aboard Spear One, the crew chief yells out, "Two minutes! Two minutes to target!"

Nick Zeppos holds up two fingers in acknowledgment, and the other team members each hold up two fingers in response. They take off the helicopter's comm gear, put on their helmets with NVGs, which they quickly lower. Zeppos switches on the goggles, and the interior of the modified and stealth Black Hawk comes into sharp, ghostly green view.

Two minutes.

One hundred and twenty seconds.

The voice of Spear One's pilot comes to Zeppos: "Target in sight, at about two o'clock."

Zeppos quickly recalls one other horrific murder that Asim Al-Asheed committed, two years ago, when in front of his followers he and his group executed a Syrian family they thought had betrayed him, and they broadcast a video of the killing to the world. A simple execution, the family had been herded into a steel cage, doused with gasoline, and Asim had struck the match.

The last clear image on the videotape, before the billowing smoke obscured the lens, was the crumpled form of the mother among the flames, desperately and futilely covering her dying son's body with her own.

"Thirty seconds," the pilot announces.

The helicopter's crew chief unlatches the side door, slides it open. Zeppos gives his gear one last check. Cold air rushes in. Zeppos stands up and calls out, "Stick close, move fast, let's get this done."

Nods of acknowledgment and thumbs-up from his team members, all looking like the proverbial bug-eyed monsters, with gear, weapons, and helmets with the four-lensed NVGs. Zeppos leans out the open doorway, takes in the buildings quickly coming into view. Three small buildings to the left, one larger building to the right, set back by itself.

That's Asim Al-Asheed's home, where he is at this very moment, based on all the streams of intelligence gathering that came together to send Zeppos and his team out here tonight.

The structures are all one story. Built of rock and stone. A goat corral in the distance. And that's it. Not even enough buildings to make it a village.

The Black Hawk helicopter flares out, hovers less than a meter above the rocky ground, and in seconds Zeppos is first off, his Oakley combat boots touching ground in the western mountains of Libya, near the border with Tunisia. He's carrying about fifty pounds of gear, along with his Heckler & Koch 416 with extended magazines, but whenever an op like this kicks off, Zeppos feels light and trim.

* * *

Through his night-vision goggles he sees the shapes of the other SEAL members, dropped off by Spear Two, as they move forward in the well-practiced bounding overwatch attack, with sections staying behind, providing cover to those in the lead, and then leapfrogging ahead to take point. Nick takes the lead, head moving back and forth, back and forth, seeing thin lines of the infrared laser sights moving around in the cold and dark air through his NVGs.

Still quiet.

He moves up the slope to the little compound, looking, evaluating, scanning.

Nobody's made contact yet?

No emerging target on the roofs of the three small buildings?

Too damn quiet.

His team is spread out in their roles, weapons at the ready, heads moving back and forth. Their advance should have encountered resistance by now.

"Breach team," Nick whispers to the men next to him. "Go."

With his NVGs, he sees the infrared laser designators flickering around as he keeps on moving. The breach team moves around the larger building, goes to a side window. Chances are the main door is booby-trapped.

He feels a slight thump through the soles of his boots, a brief flare of light.

Movement of his team into the building.

He and the others keep up their silent movement.

Through the earpiece to his PRC 148 MBITR radio, he hears one of his team, Ramirez: "Nick."

"Go."

"We're in the target house."

"Yeah?"

"It's empty," says the disappointed voice. "Nobody's here."

CHAPTER 4

Seven thirty p.m. local time
White House Situation Room

It's crowded in the Situation Room this tense evening. I'm at the head of the table, watching the raid on Asim Al-Asheed's compound unfold. It's tight quarters, with Vice President Pamela Barnes sitting in the near corner, staring at the video screens, and with Admiral Horace McCoy, head of the Joint Chiefs of Staff, sitting at my elbow. Next to him are a Navy captain and an Army colonel, tapping away on their secure government laptops, whispering information for McCoy to pass on to the crowd in this historic room. Funny thing that doesn't get reported much is that there's more than just one room in here, the others full of staff serving and processing information from around the world.

Besides the vice president, the other officials in here are Jack Lyon, my chief of staff; the members of my national security team; and a White House photographer.

The two most important are a stern Black woman with

long, braided hair, Sandra Powell, the national security advisor, and Pridham Collum, secretary of defense, a smooth-faced bespectacled man who looks younger than his forty years.

Sandra is both a defense and foreign policy expert and the author of several policy books that are actually easy to read. Pridham was appointed because of his mastery of the Pentagon's massive, complex budget and his extraordinary ability to cut through the regulatory and procurement jungle to get needed weapons systems off the design software and into the field. He also has important defense experience from his previous job, as a deputy assistant secretary for International Security Policy.

Though the media refers to them as President Keating's security team, they're largely my predecessor's team. I just haven't had the time to evaluate them and decide who I want to stay on as my term ends its first full year, which began six months ago, when my predecessor, President Martin Lovering, died of an aortic aneurysm that ruptured while he was fishing on the Columbia River in his beloved Washington State.

Admiral McCoy says, "Spear One and Spear Two are thirty seconds out from the target."

I nod, looking up at the ghostly infrared images displayed on the large center screen, showing the two modified stealth Black Hawk helicopters approaching the small compound where Asim Al-Asheed and his band of followers are supposed to be hiding. One of those helicopters is carrying Navy chief Nick Zeppos. I guess I shouldn't have called him a few minutes ago, but the temptation was too great. I really did want to wish him well, and I really wished I could have been on this raid, where the objectives are clear and one's enemies are out in the open, unlike in the Washington political scene, where motives are murky and adversaries disguise themselves within power suits and smooth rhetoric.

My right hip aches in muscle memory at seeing the SEALs

fly in, remembering my own missions, and that helo crack-up years ago in Afghanistan that shattered my hip and ended my Navy career. Later, at loose ends, I opted for a fresh round of danger and peril—I entered politics, and the good people of Texas's Seventh Congressional District sent me to represent them on Capitol Hill.

The helicopters halt in their flight, and ghostly figures emerge from both, advancing in the bounding overwatch attack I'm so very familiar with.

A faint snap, and I realize I've just broken the pen I'm holding.

No one seems to notice except my vice president, who gives me a cool, appraising glance, and then goes back to watching the screen.

They say politics is the art of the compromise, and the last tumultuous year has been full of it. When then senator Martin Lovering was on the edge of getting enough delegates to win our party's nomination two years ago, there was a push to balance the ticket and enhance his national security creds by picking…me, someone who hadn't been in Congress very long, and certainly hadn't been in what's known as the race for the White House.

That calculated political move angered a lot of the party's more dovish members, including Florida governor Pamela Barnes, who had run a close second to Senator Lovering in the campaign, and who understandably thought she should have been asked to serve as vice president with Lovering.

Well, that dream did eventually come true for her. A month after I became president because of President Lovering's sudden and unexpected death, I nominated her to the job. She was the third person to become vice president in this way since the Twenty-Fifth Amendment gave us a process to fill a vacancy in that office. I chose her because I wanted to unify our party, hoping that we could accomplish more as I served out the rest of my predecessor's term. But if Barnes was happy or grateful to get to her current spot, she's never once showed it to me.

Meanwhile, flanked by my national security team, I'm doing something that's hard for me: keeping my damn mouth shut.

Waiting.

On the screen I see the shapes of the SEALs moving briskly and efficiently, and I fight off my own memories of being on missions just like this one. With your team, breathing hard, weapon in hand, every sense in your body heightened, on the move, following the rehearsed plan, ready at a moment's notice to open fire.

I've been there before, in Iraq, Afghanistan, Yemen.

In all of them, the constant factor was being out at night exposed, with your best friends and fellow warriors around you, ready to cry havoc and let slip 5.56mm ammunition and grenades at our nation's enemies. Like these men now in Libya, nearly five thousand miles away, their every movement and action being noted here, in this room.

Being here, instead of there, feels strange. Adding to the unreality, just a short walk away from this intense meeting is my wife, Dr. Samantha Rowell Keating, working on a paper for some prominent archaeological journal, and our daughter, Melanie, whom we always call Mel, holding a party in the family quarters with some of her classmates from Sidwell Friends.

I'm happy for both of them. It's not easy to maintain any sort of normal life in this very unnormal place.

I'm looking at the screen again, seeing the figures move, see three enter a building.

That's all.

No flares of light, no tracer rounds, no frantic movement of armed men rushing out to attack the invaders.

Admiral McCoy clears his throat. "Sir…"

"I know," I say. "The raid's a bust. Asim Al-Asheed isn't there."

CHAPTER 5

Two thirty-five a.m. local time
Embassy of the People's Republic of China, Tripoli

In his secure and dull basement office marking his role as the senior officer of the Chinese Ministry of State Security for all of North Africa, Jiang Lijun sits at his desk, smoking another Zhonghua cigarette, thinking. The room is spare, with only one bookshelf and three heavy-metal locked filing cabinets. A photo of the Great Helmsman is on the wall, next to one of the current president. On his desk are two photos: one of his wife, Zhen, and the other of his late father. Jiang was only five years old in 1999 when he and his weeping mother stood on the tarmac at the Beijing Capital International Airport, awaiting the cremated remains of Father after the Americans killed him along with two others in the basement of the Chinese Embassy.

The May 7 raid had occurred during the NATO bombing campaign to halt the Serbians from doing what was their destiny: to control their territories and conquer their enemies. The West had been using that tactic for centuries, but because the

Serbs were "the other," they were blamed and bombed for doing the same as all the great powers.

Father had been working at the Chinese Embassy on Augusta Cesarca Road as a communications officer when four bombs from an American B-2 Spirit hit the embassy, supposedly by mistake, although no one in China believed such a tale. Everyone knew it was a deliberate attempt by the West to punish China for standing with the Serbians.

Later, as Jiang grew older and attended school, he learned that the bomber that killed Father had come from the famed American Air Force 509th Bomb Group, the same that had dropped the atomic bombs in 1945, incinerating tens of thousands of civilians.

That unit, he thinks, has experience in killing innocent Asians.

He gives a quick glance at the photo of Zhen, taken during their honeymoon in Hawaii. Right now she's in Beijing, visiting her ill father. She works at the ministry's headquarters at 14 Dongchangan Avenue as a personnel manager.

Jiang's grandfather—Jiang Yun—had been an illiterate peasant until he joined the Red Army, fighting both the Japanese and the Kuomintang and then becoming a quiet yet powerful party functionary in Shanghai. He had lived long enough to see how successful his son had become, and Jiang feels a pang of regret that the Americans prevented his father from seeing his own son's success.

Jiang touches Zhen's photo for a moment. He has vowed many times that their future child will grow up in a peaceful and strong world, a global community recognizing the proper place and strength of China.

Whatever it takes.

He opens the center drawer of his desk, takes out a detailed map of Libya, and goes to the cold, carpeted floor, where he spreads it out. There are hundreds of high-quality digital maps available for him here in the secure ministry computer system that can show an individual flower in the White House Rose Garden, or the upturned faces of American sailors on the bridge of a nuclear armed ballistic missile submarine, departing Kitsap in Washington State.

But accessing such maps leaves digital traces for others in his ministry and elsewhere to see.

He is skilled at not leaving any traces.

A finger moves from the Gulf of Sidra to the mountains of Nafusa. Jiang looks at the legend at the base of the map, marking distances in kilometers. He goes to his desk, returns with a metal ruler, places it on the map.

He wishes he knew the exact location of that American Navy ship—named, he still cannot believe, after a stinging insect—but asking that question would raise too many others later down the line.

The night-duty officer here—Liu Xiaobo—is correct. The Americans will be very shortly landing in these rugged mountains without much of a fuel reserve. Oh, they can get refueled midair, but in Libya there are plenty of electronic eyes and ears from the Middle Country, Russia, Iran, and others. Curious eyes and ears that can cause a lot of questions to be raised.

He rubs the little triangles of the marked villages. Liu is doubly correct: Jiang does have an interest in someone living there, and now he wonders what to do.

He leaves the map and ruler on the floor, goes back to his desk. He removes a thin chain from around his neck that holds a small rectangular digital key and inserts it into the lower right-hand desk drawer. A faint *click,* and he opens the drawer. This device came directly to him from Schlage—avoiding the ministry's supply system—and he is certain that this drawer cannot ever be tampered with or opened without his permission.

Among papers, thumb drives, notebooks, and other possessions is the latest limited-edition satellite phone, made by Iridium, an American company, and it's special in that it can be used inside a building. The West is finally beginning to learn that all those cheap electronics they purchased from the Middle Country over the decades contained spyware and electronic back doors for his employers, and Jiang needs a secure way to make phone calls without being tracked by his own people.

A small notebook comes out, with certain numbers written inside.

He powers up the satellite phone, waiting a few seconds to calculate his next move.

Kill Americans, he finally decides, as the phone blinks to life.

What he has been destined to do, ever since that May night in 1999.

CHAPTER 6

❖

Two forty a.m. local time
Nafusa Mountains, Libya

In the clear and cold mountain air, Nick Zeppos holds up his closed fist, signaling to everyone within eyeshot to keep quiet. Fury builds inside of him. *Shit, not again.*

The third time isn't going to be the charm.

He scans the small buildings, sees a stone-strewn path leading up to a rise. He stares at it, knowing that their rides home are out there, circling in the distance, waiting to take them back to the *Wasp,* hopefully carrying satchels full of intelligence info and a body bag holding the warm remains of Asim Al-Asheed.

But their hands are empty of such prizes. And Spear One and Spear Two up there are going to be empty of fuel soon enough.

Decision time.

He's reaching for his mic, ready to send out the recall request, when he thinks he hears a bell.

What?

He starts up the path.

The tinkling noise grows louder.

He knows the fuel tanks of the two Black Hawk helicopters are getting emptier.

But he keeps on moving.

CHAPTER 7

❖

Seven forty p.m. local time
White House Situation Room

In the increasingly tense atmosphere of the Situation Room, Vice President Pamela Barnes speaks up for the first time.

"Why aren't the SEALs leaving?" she demands. "Isn't the fuel running low for their transport? Wasn't their time on Libyan soil limited…and their presence illegal, I might add?"

I want to respond but I keep my mouth shut. Years ago, when I was a member of the teams, BUD/S (Basic Underwater Demolition/SEAL) Class 342, I could answer her question within seconds.

But I'm no longer a SEAL.

Just POTUS.

Others will have to answer her inquiries.

At my side, Admiral Horace McCoy, head of the Joint Chiefs of Staff, says, "Madam Vice President, the situation still remains…fluid. I imagine the SEAL teams are exploring and exploiting the situation, to see if there are any possible targets within their vicinity."

I say, "Any other questions, Pamela?"

She glares at me, and I stare right back at her. She does a good job as vice president, did a fairly good job as governor of Florida, and nearly got to the Oval Office as a candidate two years ago, but she's reactive and doesn't know much when it comes to the military. My vice president thinks SEAL members and others are windup toys that, once dispatched, go in one direction, follow their orders, and quickly return.

And if they get broken or destroyed along the way, well, so what? There are plenty more where they came from.

"Sir," Admiral McCoy says. "Look at the screen."

I turn away from Vice President Barnes and look at the ghostly moving images coming in from our overhead drone assets. The white shapes of the SEAL fighters are stretched out in a skirmish line, and the drone follows their movements.

Other buildings come into view.

Along with an enclosure with small animals milling about.

Other ghostly white shapes begin to show up on the roofs of these new buildings, weapons in hands.

Admiral McCoy says, "I think the situation is evolving, sir."

I say, "Good."

CHAPTER 8

❖

Two forty a.m. local time
Nafusa Mountains, Libya

Once they approach the crest of the small rise, Chief Zeppos's attack force, acting as one, flattens out on the rocky soil and clumps of stunted grass and shrubbery, so as not to be silhouetted against the night sky. Zeppos peers over, his HK416 assault rifle firm in his gloved hands, the ground cold against his body.

He whispers, "I'll be damned."

Over to the left is a small stone corral, with goats, some with bells around their necks.

A louder *tinkle-tinkle* reaches him.

But what really gets his attention is the layout of this compound.

It's a mirror image of where they landed several long minutes ago.

A mapping error.

What a goddamn surprise.

A whisper in his headphones from one of his team members, who uses the word for terrorists: "This is Blake. Two tangos in sight at building to the southwest. Engaging."

"Roger that," Zeppos says, his whole mood and attitude changing, thinking, *Yes, here we go, we're at the right spot. Asim Al-Asheed, we're coming for you.*

A muffled *pfft pfft pfft* comes from the area of the smallest building to the left. Two men carrying AK-47s crumple to the ground.

Not a peaceful tribal compound now, is it? An element of surprise is gone, if it ever was really there.

Semper Gumby, he thinks. *Always flexible.*

He gets up from the rise, and the platoon quietly, quickly, and efficiently moves into action, moving as one combined unit, none of the yelling and shrieking of "Go, go, go!" you see in bad video games. Just a tightly knit group moving as they were trained, getting the job done with as little drama as possible.

A man, also armed, runs out of the closest small building and Zeppos takes him down with two shots, and as he moves quickly by the motionless form, he puts two more into the man's chest.

Closer now to the larger building, and Zeppos thinks that with drones and other intelligence assets overhead, every move, whisper, and shot fired in this small compound is being witnessed by personnel at the combined Special Operations center at Bagram, in viewing rooms at the Pentagon and Langley, and in the White House Situation Room.

He hates to admit it, but he feels just a bit of pride and pressure at knowing that the president of the United States is watching their progress tonight from thousands of miles away. After all, the former vice president and Texas congressman had once done this same work, having served in the teams years ago, just after the Twin Towers came down.

We won't let you down, sir, Zeppos thinks.

"Breach team," he whispers. "Go."

Two of his SEALs peel off and approach the larger building. It's in view more clearly now, and Zeppos feels himself becoming cool and composed. In another minute or so, there'll be a dynamic entry, and any male person in there is going to get two taps to the chest and one to the forehead. Photos will be taken of the target corpse, the body will be measured and fingerprinted, and DNA swabs will be taken later for positive analysis.

Asim, he thinks, *we're coming for your ass.*

The two SEALs are at the door.

Zeppos sees that the door is heavy metal, padlocked.

It's going to take a bit longer if the windows are similarly secured.

They move around to the side, seeking an opportunity.

Another whisper from Miller, another team operator: "Tango engaged."

Pfft, pfft.

The SEALs are at a window at the larger building, their target, and they begin their work, and—

The light and sound of the explosion knocks Zeppos back—hard!—on the ground. He coughs up blood and dirt and rolls, getting to his knees, HK416 in his hands, blind.

He blinks, flips up the night-vision goggles, shades his eyes from the sudden light with his hands.

The target building has collapsed from an explosion, flames and smoke billowing.

Gunfire rattles out from the other two buildings.

Zeppos flattens his position, starts returning fire.

"Status," he says. "Status."

No answer from his SEAL members.

He fires twice more.

"Status," he calls again, louder. "Status."

Rounds come whining in and about him, striking nearby rocks.

"Shit, shit, shit," he mutters, switching out an empty magazine with a full one for his assault rifle.

Sorry, sir, he thinks, firing again at the winking lights on the closest building, *we failed.*

CHAPTER 9

Seven forty-five p.m. local time
White House Situation Room

Admiral McCoy says, "Contact. The SEALs are engaging armed men in the second compound. It looks like the other landing site was a mistake."

I just nod.

What else could I do?

There's a thought in the back of my mind.

Is this going to be a Carter moment?

Or an Obama moment?

Unlucky Jimmy Carter, learning in April 1980 that the bold plan to rescue the Iranian-held hostages has ended in a flame-filled debacle in the desert.

Or lucky Barack Obama, learning in this very room that the bold plan to kill OBL in May 2011 has ended in triumph with the words from Abbottabad, *"For God and country—Geronimo, Geronimo, Geronimo. Geronimo EKIA."*

The corner of the large video screen briefly flashes with the image of the helicopters due in minutes to pick up the SEALs, hopefully uninjured and carrying out loads of computer hard drives, papers, thumb drives, cell phones, and—

A large flare of light appears in the upper right of the screen.

Some people in the room murmur, and Vice President Barnes calls out, "What just happened?"

I pick up another pen, hold on to it.

All I can do.

It's out of our hands, it's out of all of our hands, and like so many times before, a carefully planned military operation has failed upon contacting the enemy.

The bad guys always get a vote, I recall from my Navy days.

Admiral McCoy says, "Something's gone wrong."

"I can tell," I say.

"The target building... we all saw it. It just exploded."

Vice President Barnes says sharply, "Was it the SEALs?"

"No, ma'am," the admiral says. "The explosion seems internal. It wasn't caused by our forces on the ground. Nor by any of our air assets in the area."

More whispers to him from the Navy captain and the Army colonel.

I say, "Understood."

Up on the screen, the collapsed building comes into better view. More ghost figures move around. One, and then two, fall.

Our nation's finest, falling on foreign soil, wounded or killed.

Sent in by me.

McCoy says, "The SEALs are returning fire, sir. And... three have entered the destroyed building. To examine... to see what's going on."

I just nod.

The faces of the other people in the Situation Room seem drained of blood, of any thoughts. We are all just waiting.

Waiting.

I say, "Are the helicopters still safely on station to exfil?"

Whispers at my side, and the admiral says, "Yes, sir. Do you—"

"No," I interrupt. "The guys on the ground. It's their call."

"Yes, sir," he replies.

I wait.

The vice president is staring at me, her face stern, her short blond hair perfectly styled and in place.

McCoy clears his throat. "Sir…the SEALs are preparing their exfil. They…uh, we have casualties, sir."

"How many?"

"Two KIA, at least three WIA."

Two dead and three wounded.

Shit.

"And Asim Al-Asheed? What's his status?"

No answer. A huddle once more.

I drop the pen and slap my hand on the conference room table. "Admiral! What's the status of Asim Al-Asheed?"

CHAPTER 10

Two forty-five a.m. local time
Nafusa Mountains, Libya

His lower left shin is hurting and Chief Zeppos glances down, sees the torn fabric of his fatigue pants, now feels blood trickling down.

Fuck it, he thinks as he works with the other SEAL team members to get control of this screwed-up goat wrangling. The large building that exploded a few minutes ago is partially collapsed, smoke trails going up, small fires burning. They are still taking fire from the near ridge, but it's undisciplined and random, and Lopez, the best sniper in his platoon, is calmly taking the gunmen out, one by one, with his MK 13 Remington bolt-action rifle.

Goats who were spooked to shit by the explosion are now milling around their stone corral, looking for some human caretaker.

Long friggin' wait, goats, Zeppos thinks. One of his guys, Herez, comes to him and says, "We've got the wounded stabilized, Nick."

He nods. The wounded just might make it, and the heavy cost of two dead just might be the only high price paid tonight.

Prudhomme is dead, a good guy from New Orleans, who was the shittiest cook in the unit, despite his last name and Cajun heritage.

And Kowalski.

Who wanted Asim Al-Asheed's head on a pike, a trophy to bring back to the Oval Office.

Three other men are coming out of the collapsed building, coughing and moving quickly in his direction.

Picabo is at Zeppos's side. "No military-age men, no computer drives, no filing cabinets…not a goddamn thing! Just bedding and stoves and canned food."

There are seven dead terrorist fighters in and around the compound, and an earlier quick examination showed that none of them was Asim Al-Asheed. Zeppos spits on the ground, sees his three guys being treated, and sees Wallace standing guard over the still forms of Prudhomme and Kowalski.

"Anything else?"

Picabo coughs. "Shit, Chief, sorry. We got dead civilians in there."

"Fuck," Zeppos says.

The fire up on the ridge seems to have ceased. His wounded leg is still aching. The target building—with nothing inside worth this trip or his wounded or dead—still smolders.

Picabo says, "Shitheads knew we were coming."

"Yeah."

"Time for exfil, Chief?"

Zeppos toggles his radio mic. "Yeah," he says. "Time to get the hell out of here."

CHAPTER 11

Seven forty-nine p.m. local time
White House Situation Room

On the display screen I see the flames and smoke trails coming up from the large building that was the SEALs' target this disastrous evening. The shot of the compound widens some from the local viewing platform, allowing us to see the two specialized stealth MH-60M Black Hawk helicopters descend to pick up the team. I intently watch as the shadowy white figures make their way to the helicopters, some walking with assistance from their teammates.

Two sets of SEALs are moving slower, burdened by carrying their dead comrades between them.

"Sir," says Admiral McCoy.

"Go," I say.

"Asim Al-Asheed wasn't there," he says, and I hear a few people in the room sigh with disappointment. "Seven terrorists were killed, they were closely examined, and none matched his description."

The room is quiet, all eyes on me.

This crowded facility is now a very lonely place.

"Were they able to retrieve anything of value?"

"No, sir," he says. "A few jihadi pamphlets, identification cards from the dead terrorists. That's it. No computer drives, no thumb drives, no cell phones."

I see the helicopters lift off from the compound. Soon the screen is clear except for the smoke and the death.

"Will the helicopters have enough fuel to get back to the *Wasp*?" I ask.

"Not sure," Admiral McCoy says. "But they'll get there safely. The *Wasp* can maneuver in closer to shore, or we can set up air refueling once they get their feet wet."

I stare at the screen, where a few minutes ago there were hard determined men fighting for a goal, for our country, for me…and now there's nothing.

"Admiral," I say.

"Sir."

I glance at him, at the somber faces of my team. I'm sure they were all looking forward to seeing me announce on television that Asim Al-Asheed was killed or captured, and I've no doubt that some would later have told friends and family what it was "really like" to be next to the president of the United States on such a momentous occasion.

"Civilians," I say. "Were there any civilians killed?"

To his credit, McCoy doesn't hesitate. "Yes, sir. A woman and three young girls. It seems from what documentation the SEALs recovered that they were the wife and three daughters of Asim Al-Asheed."

Oh, damn, I think.

"Killed by us," I say.

"Killed when the building exploded," McCoy says.

"And it exploded because we were there," I say. "From cross

fire striking an IED, somebody dropping an RPG round and cooking off a pile of munitions—something like that."

The room is briefly silent.

To no one in particular I say, "Can someone kill that goddamn video feed?"

In about a second, the screen goes black.

At least something has gone right tonight.

I catch the attention of my chief of staff, Jack Lyon. He's heavyset, with round horn-rimmed glasses, brown hair slicked back. He's been a party pro for years and was my predecessor's first appointment, and I've kept him on because he knows how to open doors and make the right phone calls to the right people, which is worth more than gold in this city.

"Jack," I say.

"Sir," he says.

I check the clocks. We're closing in on 8 p.m. Too soon.

"Contact the networks and cable news stations," I say. "I'm going to make a public announcement at 9 p.m. The SEALs should be safely back at the *Wasp* by then."

With a murmur of voices and heads turning to me, my chief of staff says, "The major networks might be reluctant to cut into their programming unless I can give them information on what you plan to say, Mr. President."

"And have them leak it within sixty seconds of you calling?"

He says, "At least a five-minute warning. Give them that, Mr. President."

I nod. "Fair enough. Tell them that at 9 p.m., I plan to inform the world of tonight's military action against Asim Al-Asheed and explain that it did not meet its objectives."

Don't say fail, I think. *Americans don't like the word* failure.

National Security Advisor Sandra Powell says, "Mr. President, I think you should pause, wait until all the facts come in and—"

I lift my hand.

"No," I say. "Not tonight. We screwed up. We killed civilians. That's not who we are. It was by accident and in the fog of war, but I'm not going to have this administration duck and weave and issue weasel-worded statements on how we're not going to say anything until all the facts are in. To hell with that. We all saw what happened. The SEALs went in—under my orders and authority—and performed their mission. It didn't go well. And in the process, innocents died. That's our responsibility."

The room stays quiet.

Secretary of Defense Pridham Collum clears his throat. "If I may, Mr. President, the troops in the field might not appreciate your remarks."

At that moment I snap. "Pridham, who do you think knows more about how the troops feel: a veteran, or a graduate of the Sloan School at MIT?"

I instantly regret the words.

The secretary of defense's face reddens, and he looks down at his notepad and papers.

I look around at my advisors.

Keep it together.

"Tonight I'll explain the goals of the mission, and repeat the intelligence reports of the crimes Asim Al-Asheed has committed over the years," I say. "I'll say that I ordered in the SEALs based on the best information and intelligence we had, and I'll express my personal regrets as to what happened in that compound."

Chief of Staff Lyon quietly asks, "An apology, Mr. President?"

"With the responsibility comes the apology," I say. "It's the right thing to do."

National Security Advisor Powell presses me. "Mr. President, if I may, this will be a grave mistake. You'll be undermining our standing and authority in that part of the world. Our allies—

while publicly praising us—will secretly wonder if we're going weak."

I gather up pen, papers, and legal pad and stand up. One of the perks of being president is that when you stand up, the meeting is over.

"If being weak is taking responsibility for your mistakes," I say, "then I'm all right with that."

A few more of my people try to say something as I go out the door, but Vice President Pamela Barnes, sitting in the corner and just looking at me, is not one of them.

CHAPTER 12

Nine oh six p.m. local time
Vice president's residence, US Naval Observatory

After a long, steaming-hot shower in her private quarters at the US Naval Observatory installation, Vice President Pamela Barnes is wearing a plain blue terry cloth bathrobe that has accompanied her from the governor's mansion in Tallahassee to here in Washington. As she tries to do most nights after wading through the swamp of DC politics, she's relaxing in a comfortable chair, a tumbler of Glenlivet and ice in hand, her husband, Richard, at her feet.

He's leaning against a footstool, rubbing moisturizing lotion into her cracked and sore feet, which have been a constant irritant ever since she stood up for herself and others and entered politics years back.

The luxurious living room—stuffed full of antique furniture and oil paintings—is dimly lit, and on the large-screen television before them, the president of the United States seems to be wrapping up his announcement.

"…through the offices of the International Red Cross in Geneva, I've directed the State Department to begin the process of offering financial compensation to the families of those accidentally killed tonight by our military…"

The vice president's husband snorts, his strong hands working in the lotion. "Fool. Might as well just hand that terrorist fella a blank check. Hasn't he figured out that whatever money goes to that man's relatives will slip through and go right to Asim Al-Asheed?"

Barnes takes a satisfying sip of the harsh whiskey, the one little vice she allows herself each night. One drink, and one drink only. She spent enough time in Tallahassee to see how many promising careers were wrecked over too much booze and too little judgment.

She says, "Treasury says they can work around that. Set up some sort of fund that can only be accessed by certain people, traceable so it can't be used to buy plastic explosives or ammunition."

Richard reapplies some of the moisturizer into his strong weathered hands. He was a cattleman in Osceola County and made his living through that and by selling a chunk of his land for a casino years back. She met him when she was a Florida state senator and he was a representative, and she was initially attracted to his beefy frame—he was no pretty boy state rep in a nice suit—and sharp political mind.

It was due to his strategizing that she had gotten to the governor's mansion in Tallahassee and just a handful of goddamn delegates away from becoming president, a goal that had been so tantalizingly close to being realized.

Damn that man, she thinks, taking another sip, recalling that unctuous and oily senator from Washington State who hadn't had the goddamn decency to croak before the convention was over and chose Matt Keating as his veep, leading her to take the nomination by acclamation. Now there were talks already about naming schools and highways after the dead damn fool who hadn't given her the job that was rightfully hers.

"...the actions tonight of the Naval and Army forces of the United States were done under my orders, and they carried out my orders with their typical excellence and bravery," Keating says. "If there is any blame associated with tonight's military action, and the resulting civilian deaths, it is mine, and mine alone. The Army and Navy performed admirably and did all that was asked of them."

Richard goes back to work on her feet, and damn it, she does so enjoy his strong hands at work down there. "Bullshit," he says. "They screwed the pooch, and you wrapping yourself in a flag ain't gonna help you, Navy boy. The voters don't like fuckups, and they sure as hell don't like the United States apologizing...not to mention handing out money while they do."

"Richard, please..."

He stops and looks up at her with his hard gray eyes, his thick brown hair trimmed and styled. "Pamela, you listen, now, and listen good. And please don't interrupt me."

Another sip of her drink. "All right, go on."

"It's like this," he says. "You and I both know that while Keating is doing okay in the polls right now, his support is soft, especially in the party. There's a lot of good people out there, people with long memories and deep pockets, who think you got screwed over at the convention in Denver. If Lovering had the balls to do the right thing and had picked you as veep, then you'd be in the Oval Office, not that Texas cowboy. And you and I both know that you sure as hell wouldn't be on national television apologizing for anything."

The warmth of the whiskey is seeping through her, and her feet are feeling fine, and she says, "Ancient history, Richard. All done and past."

He wipes his hand on a small white towel, stands up. "History is what we make of it, Pamela. You know what's going to happen. He'll get a little bump in the polls by pretending to be a strong man, but in a while, the stories and the gossip will come out. About how weak he is, how he went on national TV tonight with two of our brave Navy SEALs dead, and how he pissed on their memory and bravery by apologizing like a little schoolboy. And you combine that with how he can't control his bitch wife, Samantha, that snooty college professor—well, in six months, his support will be cratering."

Over the years, Richard's homeboy style and rough way of talking have fooled many a slick and supposedly smart political opponent, and Pamela has learned to trust his instincts.

"And that'll be less than a year until the Iowa caucuses and the New Hampshire primary," she says.

A pleased nod. "You got it, Pamela. Look, let me start poking around, talking to people, see what resources are out there. There are plenty in the party who are ready to drop Keating and back you up when the right time comes. It's our job to make sure there is a right time."

Pamela sees the man on the television screen say, "Thank you, and good night."

The vice president picks up the remote, switches off the television, finishes off her drink.

"Then do your job, Richard," she says.

CHAPTER 13

Four oh five a.m. local time
Embassy of the People's Republic of China, Tripoli

In a small dining room off the main kitchen at the Chinese Embassy, Jiang Lijun of the Ministry of State Security and a handful of other night staff are watching the China Central Television news channel service on a set suspended from a corner of the ceiling.

On the screen, the American president is making a somber speech, explanatory subtitles scrolling. Sitting next to Jiang at a round dinner table, smoking a cigarette and sipping a cup of tea, is Liu Xiaobo, the night-duty officer who alerted him to the American attack. He's taking a morning break.

"Unbelievable, is it not?" Liu asks.

Jiang nods, sipping his own cup of Da Hong Pao tea. "I certainly agree."

Liu shakes his head in wonderment. "Amazing! The fool is actually apologizing for what his soldiers did tonight. Apologize! Can you imagine our president apologizing for anything like that? He wouldn't dare! If he even attempted to do such a thing, the presidium would bring him up short in a moment...perhaps even demote him."

Jiang smiles, takes another satisfying swallow of the hot tea. "In two years, the American voters will have their chance to demote Keating, if they choose to."

The night officer says, "True. And what a gift that would be, eh?"

"Agreed," Jiang says, reflecting on all that's gone on since the former president suddenly died. "Ever since he assumed the office, Keating has been pushing us, pressing us, humiliating us...complaints in the World Trade Organization, lawsuits over patents and copyrights...even running ships and planes over and near our bases in the South China Sea. Like those waters belonged to them, and not us."

Up on the television screen, Jiang watches the humble yet arrogant American president mouth his words of apology. Jiang's tablemate, Liu, is entirely correct. To see their own president on television, groveling and nearly weeping like this American leader...it would never happen.

Never.

Which is why, Jiang thinks, *we will eventually win.*

No apologies.

Just the actions of a world power gaining its rightful place.

Liu taps cigarette ash in his teacup's saucer. "Wouldn't it be something, Comrade Jiang, if, when the time comes for those Americans to vote, this failed raid tonight and his speech full of regrets would cause Keating's defeat? What a happy outcome that would be."

Jiang nods with satisfaction, recalling that single phone call he made less than two hours ago from his secure office in the basement. A call made for his nation, of course, but for his unborn child as well.

"A very happy outcome indeed," he says.

CHAPTER 14

Eight a.m. local time
Nafusa Mountains, Libya

In a remote cave in these historic mountains in Libya, Asim Al-Asheed sits cross-legged on a wool blanket, waiting. His morning cup of chai is nearly finished. The cold air makes the peaks look sharp and hard. Around him he has a special blanket that his Chinese ally gave him years back, one designed to hide his thermal images from the cursed drones that continually fly, snoop, and try to track him down. The color of the blanket is nearly identical to the rocks, meaning that even to a drone flying near the cave's entrance with a strong camera, he's barely detectable.

Next to him is a small rucksack containing his Koran, a change of clothes, food, water. Against the rock wall is a loaded AK-47 semiautomatic rifle, and at his side is a 7.62mm Russian-made Tokarev pistol.

A few meters behind him, deeper into the cave, is the courier who brought him the news of his family's death. Last night in this cave, Asim had dreams of demons and *jinis* tearing apart his wife and little girls, and with the courier's arrival a few hours ago, the dream had indeed come true.

Inna lillahi wa inna ilayhi raji'un, he prays again. *Indeed, to God we belong and to God we shall return.*

The courier doesn't move, doesn't speak. He is wrapped in a swath of blue plastic, sitting up against the rock wall, keeping quiet.

Asim doesn't mind the solitude, the hard rock, the harshness of the plain environment around him. He knows the fine restaurants, hotels, and universities of New York, London, Paris, and Berlin. He has visited these places many times, spreading money to quiet supporters, receiving assurances of future assistance when the time comes. But the life of the West, with all its seductions, tempted him and his brothers and sisters to a life of fat, godless leisure.

He looks to his hands, rough, worn, and scarred. Years ago, when he was just a student, these hands were soft and smooth, and he dreamed then of becoming a surgeon. Through the generosity of a rich aunt who lived in neighboring Tunisia, he was able to spend nearly a year at the Université de Tunis El Manar, studying medicine. There he had gotten drunk, had whored, but he also studied hard, and a life in the West beckoned to him…until the call of jihad became too strong to ignore.

Asim rubs at his rough hands.

A long time ago.

It's been only a little while since the sun has risen, and he sits and tries to stay at peace, remembering how more than a century ago Omar Mukhtar, peace be upon him, fought the Italians for years in this nation, Asim's home country. That blessed man lived and fought in mountains such as these, against the colonialists and Europeans and the West, which tried for millennia to conquer these lands and people.

Asim has always taken inspiration from him.

His lands, his people, his family.

Movement down below.

Asim picks up a set of German-made Zeiss binoculars, focuses on what's coming up the barely visible mountain trail.

There.

A male and female, walking carefully up the narrow and stone-strewn path even as they laugh and talk with each other. The bright red knapsacks they carry stand out against the harsh land they are casually strolling through. The man looks strong, young, his long blond hair a similar shade to the woman's. A score of meters below Asim, they pause, still talking.

The man helps the woman take off her knapsack. Her fleece jacket is tight against her chest. The man takes off his knapsack, laughs again, and starts coming up the trail, closer to Asim and the cave.

Asim grasps the Russian-made pistol.

Up in the bright blue sky of these mountains, a falcon appears, riding the morning thermals.

The blond-haired man pauses at the cave entrance, turns and waves and shouts at the blond woman below him, and she waves back at him. The man steps into the cave, ducking his head, and when his eyes adjust to the darkness, he smiles and says, "*As-salaam 'alaykum,* my cousin."

To his cousin Faraj, Asim says, *"Wa 'alaykum as-salaam."*

The man sits cross-legged beside him.

A few minutes of silence pass.

Asim says, "Who is the whore with you?"

"A student from Denmark. I met her at a club in Tripoli. She is backpacking across here and into Tunisia, looking at Roman ruins. I told her there were remote ruins hidden in these mountains, and she agreed to come on a trip with me. I used the fine words I learned at college upon her. It was easy."

"And she believed you?" Asim asks.

Faraj touches his long, fair hair. "She's a young stupid woman. She'll believe anything."

Remembering his own life as a student, Asim nods in acknowledgment.

Faraj says, "Cousin, when can I dye my hair back to brown? I feel like an *'ahmaq,* a fool."

"When I say so," he says. "That colored hair and that whore are keeping you alive while you walk through these mountains. No American operating a drone will think two blond-haired hikers are enemies to be tracked or killed."

"Yes, cousin."

"But you did do well, choosing that whore to go with you. Quite smart."

"Thank you, cousin."

Asim sits quietly for a while longer, and Faraj says, "Pardon me, cousin, but…is that Ali, behind us?"

"Yes," Asim says.

"He's dead."

Asim says, "He brought me the news of my Layla and our three girls. He couldn't answer any of my questions. I asked about Layla and then Amina, Zara, and Fatima. He could not answer. He became…angry at my questioning."

His voice chokes for just a second.

Strength, he thinks. *Oh, Allah, give me strength.*

He says, "I could not stand for that. I cut his throat."

Faraj says, "I understand, cousin."

Gaining strength—*my thanks, Allah*—Asim says, "Tell me what you can."

"The Americans came in six hours ago. It seems our fighters were warned. A battle ensued. The main building containing munitions and supplies for our upcoming Tripoli action exploded. Your women…they were later laid out beside the building, with shrouds." Faraj spits out the cave's entrance. "Like the dogs were trying to pay respect."

Asim clasps his hands together. "When a day or two has passed, go back and make an inspection, bury our dead, mark the graves of my wife and girls. Someday I shall visit them, *inshallah.*"

A woman's voice carries up the thin mountain air. "The whore becomes impatient, cousin," Faraj says. "I need to leave. Can I be of any other help?"

"The American president—Keating. He has a daughter, does he not?"

"He does."

"I will think upon that."

"Do you—"

"No, not now," Asim says. "We need to be patient."

Faraj stands up, reaches down, and pulls up Asim's right hand, which he kisses. "I mourn for your women, Asim."

"Thank you, cousin," he says. "They are… *were* a blessing and a joy to me."

Asim stops talking. His throat is constricted.

Faraj heads to the cave entrance. "Shall I kill the whore now?"

"No," Asim says. "It's not her time. Killing her will raise questions, concerns. But when you reach home, you may return your hair to your natural color, Faraj. You have served me well."

"As you wish, cousin."

Faraj leaves and Asim waits, not bothering to watch him return to the woman student, who should pray to her God with deep thanks for the rest of her life, because she came oh so close to being sent to her heaven today.

He waits.

The smell from Ali is growing stronger. At some point he will need to leave.

But not now.

His family, his wife, his girls. All gone. Allah has willed it, but still…

The ache burns inside of him.

He watches the falcon at play, moving so slowly and innocently, but hunting and hunting, being so patient to strike at the right time.

Asim prays for such patience.

CHAPTER 15

Inauguration Day
The Oval Office

I can sense the tension from Samantha this morning as a group of photographers take the very last shot of President Matthew Keating and his adorable family, about four hours from when I become former president Matthew Keating. My left arm is around her and my right arm is around our daughter, Melanie, and while Mel's shoulder feels like it belongs to a typical teen girl waiting to squirm away from dear old Dad, my wife's shoulder feels like it's been carved out of granite.

Then one of my assistants from the White House press office raises her hand and says, "Thank you, thank you very much, we've got a busy day ahead of us," and she does the gallant job of moving the press pool out of the Oval Office, doing a fair imitation of herding cats.

It's supposed to be photos only, but for decades the White House press corps has prided itself on pushing the boundaries and stretching the rules as much as possible, and this historic day is no exception.

"Mr. President, did you leave a note in the Resolute desk for the president-elect?"

"Any final thoughts on the last day of your administration?"

"How do you feel about being the only president in American history to lose reelection to his vice president?"

Samantha's hard shoulder tenses up even more, and I keep a fixed smile on my face as the gaggle is pushed through, past the Secret Service agent, and the slightly curved door is closed behind them, leaving just the three of us.

Mel moves away and says, "Jeesh, I thought they'd never leave. They just couldn't pass up one more chance to be assholes."

She's wearing a green dress and a soft yellow jacket, and her blond hair—which is usually a frizzy mess—is nicely styled for this historic day. A set of eyeglasses with clear acrylic frames outlines her pale blue eyes, which, unfortunately, are doubly affected: with myopia and astigmatism.

"Mom, Dad, all right if I give my room one last visit before we go?"

"Looking for any lost treasures?" I ask.

A little roll of the eyes. "Dad, please, yeah, I'm looking for my favorite Barbie doll."

"The one with the kung fu grip or the matched set of Colt revolvers?"

Another, larger roll of her eyes. "Dad…okay, I'll see you both in a bit."

Samantha gives a knowing smile to our teen daughter. "No tricks or funny stuff today, okay? We've got a tight schedule."

"Sure, Mom."

"And if you can, find those eyeglasses you lost last month."

"Mom!" Mel protests. "You make it sound like I lost them on purpose."

With a smile, my wife says, "Go, then. Just don't be late."

Mel leaves the Oval Office, passing by the Secret Service agent on guard, who whispers into the microphone in his shirt cuff—probably saying, "Hope is en route to the family quarters"—and I take a breath, trying to ease the tight band constricting my chest. It's been a grim and rotten six months since Vice President Pamela Barnes defeated me at our party's convention in Chicago and I graciously conceded and urged the party to unite behind her.

Ever since Chicago, I've felt like I've been serving a jail sentence. After the convention ended, I was a lame duck and couldn't accomplish much of anything while she went on the campaign trail. She never asked for my help, so I spent too much time reliving the primaries. Though I narrowly won the total vote, she swept the caucuses and won more superdelegates and won the nomination fair and square.

Under the shrewd guidance of her ruthless husband, she used the failed Libyan operation and my honest account of it to make me look both too weak and too warlike. It was a neat trick, playing well to the political press and to younger voters always looking for something new.

I should have been able to figure out how to win anyway, but I couldn't. Unfortunately, I went into a tough presidential campaign with more experience as a Navy SEAL in battles overseas than in political wars at home. And I was still angry about it, so angry I was tempted a couple of times to resign and let her have the damn office before she rode to victory in the November election.

But I couldn't do it. No current or former SEAL would ever give up before the job is done. And no president should, either.

Samantha lets out a sigh. She has on a burgundy dress and her black hair is styled luxuriously. Around her neck is a simple gold chain. She's a beautiful woman who captured me when we first met near San Diego, where I was training and she was a Stanford graduate student in anthropology researching pre-Columbian Native American settlements.

Her tanned skin is flawless, and I've gently teased her over the years that she had both the looks and brains to have been a model, and she's always said no, her nose was too large. And I've always sweetly disagreed.

"You think we can trust Mel to come back in time?" she asks.

"She never likes to be left behind," I say. "So I'll say yes."

Samantha asks, "How much longer?"

I check my watch. "About five minutes before we have to shove off."

"Can you do something for me?"

"Sure," I say. "I'm still the president for another four hours. You want me to bomb Albania?"

"Can you make it the tenure committee at Stanford?" she asks, familiar steel showing through her smile for an old grudge that my dear wife will never, ever forget.

"Give me the GPS coordinates and they're yours," I say.

She takes my hand and together we have a seat on one of the two matching cream-colored couches, and I think of all the people I've hosted here in the Oval Office over the years—from the prime minister of Israel to a Girl Scout delegation including the top Girl Scout cookie sellers in the nation—and I say, "I suppose in my official role I can't order you to change your mind."

She strokes my hand. "You couldn't even do that when you were in the Navy, Matt. But good try."

"When?" I ask.

"Sooner than I thought," she says. "Boston University promised me the midyear opening in their archaeology department, and it came through this morning. Full professor. It starts within a week. And I've accepted."

Lots of thoughts come to the fore, but I choose the easy path, saying, "Congratulations. I know that means a lot to you. And you'll do a great job."

"They also said that you could—"

"Thanks, but still not interested," I say. My smart, educated wife's sharp mind is earning her professorship and research opportunities. I'm not about to take some real instructor's place to lead seminars about politics or democracy or some other damn thing.

Sam is heading to Boston, and I'm heading to a remote New Hampshire lakeside home. She is calling due a bill I had prepared in our short White House term, always saying while I was president that someday she'd make her schedule and time her own, and Sam, being the smart woman that she is, is doing just that. Setting her own place in the world.

I slide my hand over hers and give it a squeeze. "The media is going to love the news of my taking this BU position," Samantha says. "A First Lady who never really fits in abandons her husband and child to go off and dig in dirt when his term ends."

"To hell with them," I say.

"Oh, they had a point, Matt," she says. "We both know I never really fit here in DC, fulfilling the traditional roles of traditional First Ladies. But the prospect of running more negative stories will make them rub their hands in glee."

"Tell them you're heading to Oak Island," I say. "That might shut them up...except for the History Channel. They'll think your project is more important than being First Lady."

She squeezes my hand back. "If I'm lucky." Samantha takes a long look around the Oval Office and says, "Forgive me, Matt, but I've never liked this place, this office. Seeing you at work here...it was like you were a museum docent, playing a part."

"According to my party delegates, I wasn't doing a very good job of it," I say. "Still, it was a hell of a ride, Sam, wasn't it?"

Samantha kisses me on the cheek. "You promised me adventure and travel after we got married, Matt, but never this."

"That's your man, under-promising and over-delivering."

"You also promised that you would make history, and that I would discover history. My part didn't quite work out."

It surely didn't. Lots of schools offered Samantha teaching positions after she abruptly became First Lady, but she turned them all down for one good reason: they wanted her title and publicity, and didn't want to give her the opportunity to do real academic work.

Samantha says, "Think you're facing a hard adjustment to being former president Keating?"

"Won't miss the 3 a.m. phone calls," I say.

She stands up. "Oh, I think at some point you'll miss it, Matt. Not being in charge. Seeing the news coming out of here in the upcoming months and thinking, *I could do a better job.* But I won't miss being First Lady Samantha Keating. No offense to all those official visits I've done over the years, but I'm looking forward to getting back to teaching and getting my hands dirty."

The curved door to the Oval Office opens. My chief of staff, Jack Lyon, pokes his head in. "Mr. President, Mrs. Keating, it's time."

She starts walking ahead of me. "It certainly is."

We go ahead, and I know what the Secret Service agent at the door is whispering—"Harbor and Harp are moving"—and as we go out into the hallway, I take Samantha's hand and whisper in her ear, and she laughs out loud, and I know that Jack Lyon and other members of my nearby staff are wondering what I've just said.

They'll never know.

But Samantha does.

There's still time to take care of that tenure committee.

CHAPTER 16

Manchester Airport, New Hampshire

Ten hours later I'm now former president Matthew Keating, a one-term president known to history as the first to lose my job against an insurgent vice president. While she and her husband are enjoying themselves, dancing at one of the ten or so inaugural balls in the District of Columbia, I'm standing in the opening of a remote hangar at Manchester Airport in New Hampshire, watching January snow flurries whip across the near runway. The lights are blurred yellow from the snowflakes. Samantha is a few yards away, checking her iPhone. Several of my die-hard New Hampshire supporters have shown up with welcome signs.

Mel is at the other end of the hangar, bundled in a blue down jacket, getting coffee from two New Hampshire state troopers and a young female Secret Service agent. She's trying to smile and laugh it up with the three law enforcement officers, but it's just an act. I don't think she's used to the fact that Dad and

Mom—while not officially separating—are going to lead separate lives for the foreseeable future. My plan is to unwind after these brutal years in the Oval Office, and Sam's is to go back to her first love: teaching and doing research. Just temporary, we say to each other and to Mel, and I hope we're right.

With Samantha checking her iPhone and Mel getting coffee, I'm standing by myself, with one Secret Service agent behind me and another one on station by the door. Adjusting to my new status is going to take a while, I know, but one thing has remained: my constant Secret Service protection, which for the rest of my life will be at my side, along with my code name—Harbor.

But I'm not missing one individual: the male or female officer who had been at my side since the day I was sworn in, the one carrying the heavy thick satchel known as the football, with the codes and communications devices that gave me that horrible power to launch nuclear weapons.

During my term, that burden gave me lots of nightmares, riding shotgun with those harsh and loud dreams of my combat missions when I was in the teams.

That officer slipped away at about noon today to take Pamela Barnes's side, and the new president can have him.

Samantha looks up from her iPhone and says, "It's all set, then."

"Is it, then?" I ask.

She smiles. "I meant my condo in Boston. The lights and heat are on."

Samantha walks over to me, looking out at the snow. It seems to be coming down heavier. A while ago, our Air Force transport—no longer Air Force One, of course—took off ahead of the arriving snow.

I'm at a loss for words. What to say at a moment like this?

Ask her to change her mind?

No.

Not that she's now about to regain her former life as a college professor and archaeologist, the life she had while I was in the teams and later Congress. But then came that awful day of President Martin Lovering's passing, when his deputy chief of staff and a local US Court of Appeals judge carrying his Bible abruptly entered my office at the Old Executive Office Building and changed her life along with mine.

Once Samantha has made up her mind, a mere mortal like me is powerless to change it.

Besides, as much as I hate to admit it, she's right.

It's her time.

Samantha says, "What are you thinking?"

"I'm thinking you've got better driving conditions than I do," I say. "Mostly highway to Boston—lucky you."

"You can come along for the ride."

I say, "I'll take a rain check. Or snow check."

It's her time, but it's also mine. There's a rural retreat waiting for me and I'm so looking forward to the absence of cities and tall buildings and bright lights. The quiet will be a blessed change.

All right, I will have our daughter Mel with me, but I've learned to sleep in temporary quarters in the mountains of Afghanistan, so I'm sure I can adjust to a teen girl underfoot who'll be finishing her Sidwell Friends education from a remote location.

I hope.

"Any reporters around?" Samantha asks.

"I think they're hiding out in the terminal," I say. "The A-list journalists are back in DC and Georgetown, toasting the Barnes Administration at inaugural balls and parties. Not interested in seeing a former president rejected by his party slink off into the snow and woods."

"Their loss," she says, coming close for my hug and kiss,

and then she whispers, "You did your best, Matt. You're not a professional politician or a desperate office seeker. You were put into a tough situation and you did your best. History will recognize that."

"I'm not holding my breath."

Lights move at the other end of the runway, and she gently breaks our embrace. "Matt, you could have done so much more if the entire system hadn't been crippled long before you entered the Oval Office. From Twitter mobs to focus groups, nothing can get done anymore. Not your fault."

I say, "You mean I was too good for the American people?"

Another smile, a quick peck on my cheek. "Not so fast, sailor boy. It's complicated, just like you. The real people are still there, with their problems and potential, hopes and dreams. It's just hard for them to make good decisions when their brains are filled, and their spirits broken, with so much crap. I'll call you when I get to Boston. And I'll come up next weekend to see what, if anything, you've actually unpacked. Come March, I'll be up with you and Mel during BU's spring break."

Other lights appear.

One black Chevrolet Suburban pulls up. A plainclothes New Hampshire state trooper is driving, with a second in the passenger seat. As was her right, Sam has refused Secret Service protection, and as a courtesy, these troopers will take her to Boston.

Another Suburban rolls in, followed by two others, escorted fore and aft by New Hampshire State Police cruisers, lights flashing. At least my position as a former president rates a bit flashier and more secure transport to my new home up north.

Mel walks toward me, holding two cups of coffee in her hands, one for her, one for me.

Samantha gives her a quick hug and kiss and whisper, and then walks to her ride to Boston. She gets in and the Suburban glides out across the snowy tarmac.

Our daughter Mel hands me a cup and wipes at her eyes.

I put my arm around her. "How's it going, kiddo?"

"Sucks," she says.

"Sure does," I say. "Congrats again on your early acceptance from Dartmouth. Chosen a major yet?"

"Nope."

"A school?"

"No again," she says. Mel stays within my grasp, and I'm cherishing this special quiet moment with her.

I say, "Anything you feel like studying?"

"Not yet," she says.

I give her a gentle squeeze. "How about things you don't feel like studying?"

She laughs and sips at her coffee. "Political science, Dad. Sorry. And definitely not journalism. Or anything to do with TV."

I feel an old spike of anger. A few days after I gave my speech accepting responsibility for the death of Asim Al-Asheed's family, *Saturday Night Live* did a skit with an actress depicting Mel—wearing Coke-bottle-thick glasses—hitting bull's-eye after bull's-eye at a shooting range, the joke being that at least one member of the Keating family knew how to shoot straight.

That was a rough weekend, and it took months for Mel to bounce back from public humiliation in front of an audience of millions. The producer of *SNL* eventually apologized for including my daughter in such a mocking way, and after that he cast actors who played me as a clueless military robot. I was fair game, and they were funny. I accepted his apology and the head of NBC felt he could safely go outside again.

"How about the military? Follow in your old man's footsteps?"

"Dad?"

"Yes?"

"You've jumped out of aircraft lots, right?"

"Yes. And helicopters, too. But always with a parachute."

"You think I'm really gonna like to do that?"

"Well, I can always hope."

Mel says, "Let's go, okay?"

"You got it, kiddo."

The two of us walk into the flying snow, as the promised possibilities and real achievements of the presidency of Matthew Keating finally come to an end.

PART TWO

CHAPTER 17

The post-presidency of Matthew Keating, year two
Lake Marie, New Hampshire

I yell out, "Come on, David, make the Secret Service proud! I'm going to kick your ass!"

We're paddling identical dark green Old Town canoes across Lake Marie, and his is trailing mine by about two feet, his strong face emoting a mix of amusement and grim exertion as he vies to take the lead.

I'm shirtless on this hot June day, but David Stahl, special agent in charge of my Secret Service detail, is wearing a loose black T-shirt that conceals both his strength and whatever weapons and communications gear he's carrying. This race across the dark blue waters is a daily event to keep us both in shape, although he's about ten years younger than me and probably doesn't need the extra exercise.

Past the dock where a single-engine pontoon boat is moored is the old-fashioned large lake home I purchased during the interregnum between Pamela Barnes's election and her inauguration. It's two stories, dark brown, with a wraparound enclosed porch and three outbuildings, a detached two-car garage, a shed for my workout gear, and a small refurbished barn for the Secret Service detail. Pine trees and white birches are scattered around the grounds, which have conservation land on either side, meaning no nosy neighbors.

"Just a few more yards, David, c'mon, dig in!" I yell. "Don't wimp out on me now! Do it, c'mon, do it!"

Unfair, I know, but I'm feeling a thrill knowing that even though he's younger than me, and in better shape, I am going to kick his ass indeed, and he knows that I won't stand for him slacking off so that I can later brag about a win.

This is a canoe race, not a golf match, and it's impossible to futz with the results, like using handicaps or mulligans. It's straightforward, win or lose, no excuses.

I like that clarity.

I hear the harsh scrape of my canoe bow striking sand first and I let out a whoop of joy, and I clamber out into shin-deep water as Agent David Stahl keeps on pushing and comes in second. My right hip, crushed in a helo crash in Afghanistan a long time ago, barely aches this morning. A good thing. I drag my canoe a couple of feet up our little beach and see David, his short black hair sweated through, right behind me. He gasps, "Pretty good, sir, pretty good."

He slops through the lake water and I help him drag his canoe from the dock to the small open structure that serves as a boathouse. As we put up our paddles and PFDs, I hear a woman's voice: "Mr. President, got a moment?"

There's a cooler at my feet and I open it, pull out a bottle of water, pass it over to my lead Secret Service agent, and then take one for myself.

Coming down the flagstone path from the house is Madeline Perry, my chief of staff while I'm still getting used to my post-presidency. She's about my age and, as *Glamour* magazine would say, big-boned, with shoulder-length black hair and very fair skin that can't tolerate the sun. She volunteered to join me in my New Hampshire exile, when most others on my White House staff stuck around to find jobs with the new Barnes Administration or elsewhere in DC. Today, Madeline has on her standard uniform of black slacks and flowing pastel blouse.

I twist off the cap of the water bottle, take a long cold swallow. Madeline comes closer and says, "I'm heading off to the Manchester office, sir, and then I have a flight to Manhattan."

"Safe travels," I say.

"I'm sure it'll be safe," she says, "but what would make it a memorable trip is for you to say yes."

"Yes to what?" I ask, though I'm teasing her. I know what she's looking for. At least four publishing companies have expressed interest in my autobiography. Now I have to agree to write it.

Her thin lips press together, and I hold up a hand in surrender. "Maddie, Maddie, okay. Not today, but soon. All right? Promise."

She shakes her head. "Mr. President, the longer you're out of office, the quicker the window closes on you telling your story. The interest will start to fade away, and publishers will go find other projects."

Another nice swallow of cold water. "You make that sound like a bad thing."

Madeline makes her way back up to the house, her head turning back to me. "It *is* a bad thing, if all you want to do is barely make enough money for you and your family, much less starting the foundation to help all your fellow vets who have problems a lot bigger than your election loss."

Ouch, I think, and I turn to Agent Stahl for reassurance or sympathy, but, smart guy that he is, he's moved back to the boathouse to tend to the canoes, pretending not to hear my little exchange with Maddie.

I watch my chief of staff go behind the garage, where her Volvo is parked. I know I shouldn't be so rough on her. Hers is a thankless and anonymous job, managing my post-presidency. My first year out I got about a hundred thousand letters, most handled by volunteers, and now that's gone down to about twenty thousand, and Madeline rides herd on that and so many other tasks, from speech requests to folks wanting me to tell the real truth about what's being hidden in Area 51 and whether Roswell was an alien encounter.

Some days I'm envious of the carefree time after Eisenhower's 1953 inauguration when Harry Truman and his wife, Bess, hopped into their car and drove themselves home to Missouri. I'm not yet ready to give up the enjoyment of just being a person and a dad.

Up at the house, a screen door slaps closed, and Mel comes bounding down the porch stairs, yelling, "Hey, Dad, I'm getting ready to head out with Tim. Who won the race?"

I call back, "Who do you think?"

She laughs. "That's ten in a row, right?"

Agent Stahl says, "Hey, it's nine. Let's keep the numbers straight."

"Whatever you say, Dave," Mel replies, grinning. "You need anything at the store?"

I take a moment to admire my daughter as she moves quickly down the flagstone path, eyeglasses firm on her face, her blond hair still damp from her morning shower. She's wearing a dark green knapsack on her back, climbing boots, khaki shorts, and a light gray sweatshirt on which is printed DARTMOUTH. Mel's nineteen, smarter than I ever was at her age—my interests were beers, girls, guns, and horses, while Mel scored in the upper 1 percent on the SATs.

I say, "What do you mean 'at the store'? You're not due back until tomorrow."

She stops in front of me, perfect white smile wide. "I know. But I also know you love those maple square pastries at Cook's General Store. You want me to pick up a box when I come back home?"

Ah, Cook's General Store. I remember with a flush of shame the first day I went shopping there, two years back, and could not believe how much a gallon of milk cost. Nearly four bucks? For real? When did that happen?

That's when I knew I had been in a bubble for way too long.

I shake my head, give Mel a hug and a kiss on the cheek. "I'd love that, but my cholesterol level won't. Thanks for the offer."

Mel gives me a quick hug back. "You let me know when your cholesterol level surrenders, okay?"

"Okay," I say. "And have fun with your Tim, all right?"

A little eye roll. "*My* Tim…okay, Dad."

"And call me tomorrow when you get your cell service back, all right?"

A laugh. "Sure, Dad. You can trust me! I'll be safe and sound. Look, gotta run. He's picking me up on the access road. He should be there by now."

My daughter whirls and goes up the flagstone path, between the house and garage, and I watch until she's out of view.

Agent David Stahl says, "What's your schedule, sir?"

"Oh, nothing major. Second cup of coffee, read the morning newspapers, first shower of the day, and then clearing some saplings and brush out by the old stone wall. Exceptionally exciting, eh?"

"And Mel?"

Mel was no longer eligible for Secret Service protection once I left office—the cutoff age for children of former presidents is sixteen—and since those professional guardians have left her side, it's amazing how much she's relaxed and opened up. But still, Agent Stahl likes to keep up with what our daughter is doing and seeing, and I like knowing he's doing that.

"A hike with Tim Kenyon, her friend from school," I say. "Going up to Mount Rollins, spending the night at a hut owned by the Dartmouth Outing Club, and then coming back tomorrow."

"The weather's great," he says. "They should have a good time. How do you like him?"

"Tim?" I reply. "Mel likes him, so I do, too. She told me he even considered taking ROTC up at Dartmouth so that's points in his favor. A bit nervous when we first met, but he's been fine ever since I gave him a little pep talk."

"What did you tell him?"

I smile at Agent Stahl, still worn and sweaty from our canoe race. "I told him that I had a 9mm pistol and a shovel, and I knew how to use both. See you later, David."

CHAPTER

18

Near the American-Canadian border

Lloyd Franklin is driving his battered black Ford F-150 pickup truck and his cousin Josh is riding shotgun when Lloyd spots two figures emerging from the deep woods along this narrow dirt road five miles south of the Canadian border.

Josh is sleeping, his bearded face drooping and nearly touching the stained Boston Bruins T-shirt covering his beer gut, and Lloyd nudges him with his elbow and says, "Wake up."

Josh coughs, wipes at his eyes, and says, "Trouble? What? Border Patrol?"

Good question, because secured under a worn blue tarp in the rear of Lloyd's truck are ten cases of Marlboro cigarettes—five hundred cartons total—heading to their smuggling partner in Ontario. Bought at forty-eight dollars per carton at a number of stores in and around Lebanon, New Hampshire, Lloyd and Josh charge eighty dollars American in Ontario.

Even with the cost of gas and the payoff to their Canadian partner, Lloyd and his cousin are going to clear over fifteen thousand dollars in this quick trip on this narrow dirt road that's one of the many illegal crossings in and out of their northern neighbor. Jobs that Lloyd and his cousin could do up here have been fading away, and food stamps and surplus cheese and oatmeal just ain't making it.

Lloyd peers through the dirty windshield. "Don't know who the hell they are. Dressed all in white."

"Priests, maybe?" Josh asks.

"I—ah, you asshole!"

The two strangers come out in the middle of the dirt road, the taller and older of them holding up a hand. Lloyd brakes—he feels the grinding underfoot; with the cash they'll be getting, he can finally afford to get the rotors replaced—and stops about four feet away from the two guys.

"Look at that, will you?" Lloyd says, thinking, *Yeah, they're wearing white jumpsuits and they look pretty weird out here in the middle of nowhere.*

Josh breathes heavily, reaching under the seat, pulling out a holstered .357 Ruger revolver. Josh unholsters the revolver, holds it in his plump lap, and says, "If these two don't get out of the way, I'll handle it."

Lloyd lowers the window as the taller and older man starts walking toward them. "Lighten up, Josh. Probably just a couple of freaks, lost in the woods. Looking for their yoga partners or something."

"You lighten up," Josh snaps back. "Goddamn Citizens Bank is about to foreclose on my house, kick me and Lisa and the kids out, and I'm not going to let that happen. Don't care if these two are starving or been lost for a month: we're not helping, and we're getting to the handoff on schedule."

The man comes up to the driver's side, smiling, dark skin,

bushy eyebrows, and says in an accented voice, "Sorry to bother you."

"What's the problem?" Lloyd asks. "And why are you wearing those... hazmat suits, right?"

The man continues to smile, an odd look in his eyes. "That's correct, you smart fellow. And there's no problem. We just need your truck. Now."

There's a light amusing tone to the man's voice, but fright creeps up the back of Lloyd's neck, and Josh says, "Screw this. Get moving, coz."

The man says, "Ah, yes, screw this. I bet we are interrupting you, the two of you. Ready to pleasure each other?"

Lloyd throws the truck in Park and Josh says, "You two...," and Lloyd slams open the door, hitting the guy. He and Josh have done roofing, house framing, logging, and have ridden for years with the North Mountain Boys motorcycle gang, and these two creepy shits are about to get tuned up. He and Josh have at least a good half foot on both of them, and about forty or fifty pounds.

This is going to be fun.

Josh slides his revolver into his waistband and goes to the younger, smaller guy, grabbing him by the collar. He says, "You think this is funny? You think we're fags or something?"

Lloyd is moving onto the first guy but pauses, wanting to see Josh get the first hard punch into the little guy, and—

The small guy squirms, doing something fast with his hands.

Josh yelps.

Spins around, pretty quick for a big and heavy guy.

Josh's hands are around his throat.

He stares at Lloyd.

Josh gurgles.

Coughs.

Blood sprays out from between his fingers, trying to hold

his severed throat together, and he stumbles two steps and falls down heavy on the dirt road.

Lloyd panics, seeing the first guy coming toward him, still smiling, and he realizes with sharp horror why the two are wearing hazmat suits—so they don't get soaked with blood—and he turns and has started running when there's a hard punch to his back.

His legs fold up underneath him.

He hits the dirt hard, tasting it, and then he's rolled over by the first man, who's holding a sharp skinny knife in his hand. There's a bright red drop of blood on the point of the knife. Lloyd stares at it. His breathing slows down.

The man says, "I've severed your spinal cord between the L3 and L4 lumbar region. I learned the technique in medical school, years ago in Tunisia, and practiced it many times in combat across the world. You will never walk again." Then he laughs. "But the time period of 'again' is flexible, isn't it?"

The other man joins him, also smiling.

Lloyd whispers, "Why?"

"Why not?" he says as the knife comes down for the last time.

CHAPTER 19

Lake Marie, New Hampshire

An hour or so after Mel leaves, I've showered, read the newspapers—just skimmed them, really, for it's a sad state of affairs when you eventually realize just how wrong journalists can be in covering stories—and have had my second cup of coffee while chewing on a leftover venison sausage link from breakfast.

Last November this venison was a buck scrambling along a ridge on the other side of the lake before I took him down with a single shot from a scoped Remington .308 rifle. The sharpness of my shooting skills pleased me, and my Secret Service detail was pleased that their protectee had gotten his kill for that year's deer season and could go back to the safety of his compound without being out in the open with other hunters.

After finishing my post-breakfast snack, I take up a handsaw and a pair of pruning shears and head off to the south side of our property.

It's a special place, even though Samantha has spent less than a month here in all her visits. Most of this land is conservation land, never to be built upon, and those people who do live here almost all follow the old New Hampshire tradition of never bothering their neighbors or gossiping about them to visitors or news reporters.

Out on the lake is a white Boston Whaler carrying two fishermen who are really Secret Service. Last year the *Union Leader* did a little piece calling the agents the unluckiest fishermen in the state, but since then, the press has pretty much left them alone.

As I'm chopping, cutting, and piling up brush, I think back to two famed fellow POTUS brush cutters—Ronald Reagan and George W. Bush—and how their workouts never quite made sense to a lot of people. They thought, *Hey, you've been at the pinnacle of fame and power; why go out and get your hands dirty?*

I saw at a stubborn pine sapling that's near an old stone wall on the property. To save the wall, I need to uproot the sapling. The work keeps my mind occupied, busy enough to avoid continual flashbacks to my three-and-a-half-year term and the way it ended.

There were so many long and fruitless meetings with congressional leaders from both sides of the aisle, me talking with them, arguing with them, and sometimes pleading with them, at one point saying, "Damn it, we're all Americans here. Isn't there anything we can work on to move our country forward?"

And constantly getting the same smug, superior answers. "Don't blame us, Mr. President. Blame *them*."

I also spent a lot of late nights in the Oval Office, signing letters of condolence to the families of the best of us, men and women who died for the idea of America, and not the squabbling and revenge-minded nation we had become. Three times I came across the names of men I knew and fought with, back when I was younger, fitter, and with the teams.

And I spent other late nights as well, reviewing what was called, in typical innocuous bureaucratic fashion, the Disposition Matrix database, prepared by the National Counterterrorism Center, but was really known as the kill list. Months of work, research, surveillance, and intelligence intercepts, coming up with a list of known terrorists who were a clear and present danger to the United States. And there I was, sitting by myself and, like a Roman emperor of old, putting a check mark next to those I decided were going to be killed in the next few days. That's something I'm glad I don't have to do anymore.

The sapling finally comes down.

Mission accomplished. Almost. I'll do the final uprooting tomorrow when I need more distraction.

I look up and see something odd flying in the distance.

I stop, shade my eyes. Since moving here, I've gotten used to the different kinds of birds moving in and around Lake Marie, including the loons, whose night calls sound like someone's being throttled, but I don't recognize what's flying over there.

I watch for a few seconds, and then it disappears behind the far tree line.

And I get back to work, something suddenly bothering me, something I can't quite figure out.

CHAPTER 20

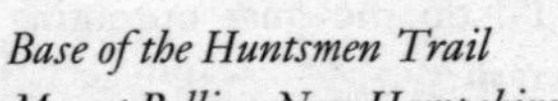

Base of the Huntsmen Trail
Mount Rollins, New Hampshire

In the front seat of a black Cadillac Escalade, the older man rubs at his clean-shaven chin and looks at the video display from the laptop set on top of the center console. Sitting next to him in the passenger seat, the younger man has a rectangular control system in his hand, with two small joysticks and other switches. He is controlling a drone with a video system, and they've just watched the home of former president Matthew Keating disappear from view.

It pleases the older man to see the West's famed drone technology turned against them. For years he's marshaled their wireless networks, cell phones, triggering devices to create the bombs that shattered so many bodies and sowed so much terror.

And the Internet—which promised so much when it came out, to bind the world as one—ended up turning into a well-used and safe communications network for him and his warriors.

After they hid their stolen pickup truck this morning, they took the Cadillac they're sitting in from a young family in northern Vermont. There's still a bit of blood and brain matter on the dashboard, and in the rear an empty baby's seat, along with a flower-print cloth bag stuffed with toys and other childish things. If they keep the car, they'll have to clean the blood off.

"Next?" the older man asks.

"We find the girl," the younger man says. "It shouldn't take long."

"Do it," the older man says, watching with quiet envy and fascination how the younger man manipulates the controls of the complex machine that projects the drone's camera-made images onto the computer screen.

"There. There she is."

From a bird's-eye view, the younger man thinks, staring at the screen. A red sedan moving along these narrow, paved roads.

The older man says, "And you are sure that the Americans, that they are not tracking you?"

"Impossible," the man next to him says with confidence. "There are thousands of such drones at play across this country right now. The officials who control the airspace, they have rules about where drones can go, and how high and low they can go, but most people ignore the rules."

"But their Secret Service..."

"Once he left office, his daughter was no longer due the Secret Service protection. It's the law, if you can believe it...under special circumstances, it can be requested, but no, not with her. The daughter wants to be on her own, going to school, without armed guards near her."

He murmurs, "A brave girl, then."

"And foolish," is the reply.

And a stupid father, he thinks, to let his daughter roam at will, with no guards, no security.

The camera in the air follows the vehicle with no difficulty and the older man shakes his head, again looking around him at the rich land and forests. Such an impossibly plentiful and gifted country, but why in Allah's name do they persist in meddling and interfering and being colonialists around the world?

A flash of anger sears through him.

If only they would stay home, so many innocents would still be alive.

"There," his companion says. "As I earlier learned…they are stopping here. At the beginning of the trail called Sherman's Path."

The vehicle pulls into a dirt lot still visible from the air. Again, the younger man is stunned at how easy it was to find this girl's schedule: by looking at websites and bulletin boards of her college, from something called the Dartmouth Outing Club. Less than an hour's work and research has brought him here, looking down at her, like some blessed spirit overlooking all.

He admits, though, that going through that college's campus brought him a yearning he thought he had snuffed out years ago, a yearning about being a student and not worrying over anything except friends and grades.

He is no longer so innocent.

He stares at the screen once more. Other vehicles are parked in the lot, and the girl and the boy get out. Both retrieve knapsacks from the rear of the vehicle. There's an embrace, a kiss, and then they walk away from the vehicles and disappear into the woods.

"Satisfied?" his companion asks.

For years, he thinks in satisfaction, the West has used these drones to rain down hellfire upon his friends, his fighters, and, yes, his family and other families. Fat and comfortable men (and women!) sitting and sipping their sugary drinks in safety, killing from thousands of kilometers away, seeing the silent explosions but not once hearing them, or the shrieking and crying of the wounded and dying, and then driving home without a care in the world.

Now, it's his turn.

His turn to look from the sky.

Like a falcon on the hunt, he thinks.

Patiently and quietly waiting to strike.

CHAPTER 21

Sherman's Path
Mount Rollins, New Hampshire

It's a clear, cool, and gorgeous day on Sherman's Path, and Mel Keating is enjoying this climb up Mount Rollins, where she and her boyfriend, Tim Kenyon, will spend the night with other members of the Dartmouth Outing Club at a small hut the club owns near the summit. She stops for a moment on a granite outcropping, puts her thumbs through her knapsack's straps.

Tim emerges from the trail and surrounding scrub brush, smiling, face a bit sweaty, bright-blue knapsack on his back, and she takes his hand as he gets to her. "Damn nice view, Mel," he says.

She kisses him. "I've got a better view ahead."

"Where?"

"Just you wait."

She lets go of his hand and just takes in the rolling peaks of the White Mountains and the deep green of the forests, some of the trees shadowed a darker shade of green from the overhead clouds gently scudding by. Out beyond is the Connecticut River and the mountains of Vermont.

Mel takes a deep cleansing breath.

Just her and Tim, and nobody else.

She lowers her glasses, and everything instantly turns to muddled shapes of green and blue. Nothing to see, nothing to spot. She remembers the boring times at state dinners back at the White House, when she'd be sitting with Mom and Dad, and she'd lower her glasses so all she could see was colored blobs. That made the time pass. She really didn't want to be there, didn't really want to see all those well-dressed men and women pretending to like Dad and be his friend so they could get something in return.

Mel slides the glasses back up, and everything comes into view.

That's what she likes.

Being ignored and seeing only what she wants to see.

Tim reaches above the knapsack and rubs her neck. "What are you looking at?"

"Nothing."

"Oh, that doesn't sound good."

Mel laughs. "You goof, it's the best! No staff, no news reporters, no cameras, no Secret Service agents standing like statues in the corner. Nobody! Just you and me."

"Sounds lonely," Tim says.

She slaps his butt. "Don't you get it? There's nobody keeping an eye on me, and I'm loving every second of it. Come along. Let's get moving."

Some minutes later, Tim is sitting at the edge of a small mountainside pool ringed with boulders and saplings and shrubs, letting his feet soak, enjoying the sun on his back, the sweet quiet buzz of the joint he and Mel just shared. He's thinking of how damn lucky he is.

He was shy at first when he and Mel—her identity was no secret on the Dartmouth campus—shared a history class on Africa last semester. He had no interest in even trying to talk to her until one day in class Mel mentioned the importance of microloans in Africa, and a few loudmouths started hammering her about being ignorant of the real world, being privileged, and not having an authentic life.

When the loudmouths took a moment to catch their respective breaths, Tim surprised himself by saying, "I grew up in a third-floor apartment in Southie, my dad was a lineman for Eversource, my mom worked cleaning other people's homes and clipped coupons to go grocery shopping, and man, I'd trade that authentic life for privilege any day of the week."

A bunch of the students laughed, Mel caught his eye with a smile, and after class he asked her to coffee at Lou's Bakery. That's how it started.

Tim, a scholarship student, dating the daughter of President Matt Keating.

What a world.

What a life.

Sitting on a moss-covered boulder, Mel nudges him and says, "How're your feet?"

"Feeling cold and fine."

"Then let's do the whole thing," she says, standing up, tugging up her gray Dartmouth sweatshirt. "Feel like a swim?"

He smiles, still slightly buzzed. "Mel…someone could see us!"

She smiles right back and shrugs, revealing the tan sports bra under the sweatshirt, and then starts lowering her shorts. "Here? In the middle of a national forest? Lighten up, sweetie. Nobody's around for miles."

After she strips, Mel yelps as she jumps into the pool, keeping her head and glasses above the water. The water is cold and sharp. Tim takes his time, wading in, shifting his weight as he tries to keep his footing on the slippery rocks, and he yowls like a hurt puppy when the cold mountain water reaches just below his waist.

The pond is small, and with three strong strokes Mel reaches the other side, then swims back, the cold water now bracing, making her heart race, everything tingling. She tilts her head back, looking up past the tall pines and seeing the bright bare blue patch of sky. Nothing. Nobody watching her, following her, recording her.

Bliss.

Another yelp from Tim, and she turns her head to him. Tim wanted to go Navy ROTC but a bad set of lungs prevented him from doing so, and even though she knows that Dad wishes he'd get a haircut, his Southie background and interest in the Navy scored Tim in the plus side of the boyfriend column with Dad.

Tim lowers himself farther into the water, until it reaches his strong shoulders. "Did you see the sign-up list for the overnight at the cabin?" he asks. "Sorry to say, Cam Carlucci is coming."

"I know," Mel says, treading water, leaning back, letting her hair soak, looking up at the sharp blue and empty sky.

"You know he's going to want you to—"

Mel looks back at her Tim. "Yeah. He and his buds want to go to the Seabrook nuclear plant this Labor Day weekend, occupy it, and shut it down."

Poor Tim's lips seem to be turning blue. "They sure want you there."

In a mocking tone, Mel imitates Cam and says, "'Oh, Mel, you can make such an impact if you get arrested. Think of the headlines. Think of your influence.' To hell with him. They don't want me. They want a puppet to get news coverage."

Tim laughs. "You going to tell him that tonight?"

"Nah," she says. "I'll tell him I already have plans for Labor Day weekend."

Her boyfriend looks puzzled. "You do?"

She swims to him and gives him a kiss, hands on his shoulders. "Dopey boy, yes: with you."

His hands move through the water and are on her waist, and she's enjoying the touch just as she hears voices. Mel looks up.

For the first time in a long time, she's frightened.

CHAPTER 22

Lake Marie, New Hampshire

After getting out of the shower for the second time today (following a spectacular tumble in a muddy patch of dirt) and drying off, I'm idly playing the which-body-scar-goes-to-which-op game when my iPhone rings. I wrap a towel around me and pick up the phone, knowing that only about twenty people in the world have this number. Occasionally, though, a call comes in from "John" in Mumbai, pretending to be a Microsoft employee in Redmond, and I've been tempted to tell John who he's really talking to, but I've resisted the urge.

This time, however, the number is blocked. Puzzled, I answer.

"Keating," I say.

A strong woman's voice comes through. "Mr. President? This is Sarah Palumbo calling from the NSC."

The name quickly pops up in my mind. Sarah, a former Army brigadier general and deputy director at the CIA, has been the deputy national security advisor for the National Security Council since my term. When Sandra Powell returned to academia, Sarah should have been promoted to director, but President Barnes filled the position with someone to whom she owed a favor. Sarah knows her stuff, from the annual output of Russian oil fields to the status of Colombian cartel smuggling submarines.

"Sarah—good to hear from you," I say, still dripping some water onto the bathroom's tile floor. "How're your mom and dad doing? Enjoying the snowbird life in Florida?"

Sarah and her family grew up in Buffalo, where lake-effect winter storms can dump up to four feet of snow in an afternoon, and she chuckles and says, "They're loving every warm second of it. Sir, do you have a moment?"

"My day is full of moments," I reply. "What's going on?"

"Sir…"—the tone of her voice instantly changes, worrying me—"sir, this is unofficial, but I wanted to let you know what I learned this morning. Sometimes the bureaucracy takes too long to respond to emerging developments, and I don't want that to happen here. It's too important."

I say, "Go on."

She says, "I was sitting in for the director at today's threat assessment meeting, going over the President's Daily Brief and other inter-agency reports."

The jargon instantly transports me back to being POTUS, and I'm not sure I like it.

"What's going on, Sarah?"

The briefest of pauses. "Sir, we've noticed an uptick in chatter from various terrorist cells in the Mideast, Europe, and Canada. Nothing we can specifically attach a name or a date to, but something is on the horizon, something bad, something that will generate a lot of attention."

Shit, I think. "All right," I say. "Terrorists are keying

themselves up to strike. Why are you calling me? Who are they after?"

"Mr. President," she says, "they're coming after you."

I manage to get dressed while the deputy national security advisor goes on via my phone's speaker. "The chatter and email intercepts are proving hard to crack, but your name keeps coming up, along with numerous phrases expressing a desire for revenge, for loyal jihadists everywhere to rise up and kill you. It's serious enough that the information warrants passing along to Homeland Security and the FBI, but that can take time...which is why I've called. To let you and your Secret Service detail know right now."

I wipe at my damp face with a towel. "Thanks, Sarah. I appreciate that...but going outside of channels could get you into a lot of trouble."

She says, "Mr. President, I didn't like the way you were treated when the vice president took you on. That campaign...it made me sick to my stomach. And I wasn't going to sit on this information without warning you."

"I didn't like the campaign much myself," I say. "Thanks for the warning."

"Be safe, Mr. President."

I find Agent Stahl sitting on the large wraparound porch, pounding the keys on a black government-issue laptop, away from the refurbished barn that serves as the detail's headquarters. I give him a quick briefing, and he hangs on every word, his face serious.

I say, "I want you to get word out to your Portland office or the Maine State Police. Get coverage on my wife. She's at a BU dig site in...Hitchcock. Yeah, that's the place. Hitchcock, Maine. She'll put up a fight, but see if they can quickly get her someplace safe until we find out just what the hell is going on."

He nods, slams the lid of his laptop closed. "Got it, sir."

"Then I want you to fire up the Suburban," I say. "You and I are going to get Mel. Maybe take along another agent and as much firepower as we can carry."

He stands up and puts the laptop under his arm, hesitates for a second.

"I'm sorry, sir, I need to advise you, in the strongest terms, not to do that," he says. "It's not safe."

"The hell with that, David! A serious terrorist threat coming after me means both Samantha and Mel might be in danger as well. You know that, David. We're going to get into the Suburban, drive to that mountain trail, and best as we can start running up that path. Scoop her up and bring her back."

He's troubled. "Mr. President…the Suburban we have isn't armored up, nor does it have the same level of protection as the presidential limo. It's too risky."

"Don't care," I say, feeling a pressure beginning at the base of my neck.

"*I* care, sir, and that's my job," he says. "The threats that are out there…maybe they want you to leave the compound, get yourself exposed with only an agent or two to assist you. There might be a team of attackers waiting for you to drive out."

"Then round up the day shift, and we'll all go. Strength in numbers."

"Mr. President, please," he says. "We need to protect you and defend the compound. I can't strip this place of agents to have them head to the mountain and get Mel. And even if we took every vehicle we have, none of them are armored. A couple of automatic weapons from roadside terrorists could destroy each vehicle and kill whoever's inside."

"David…"

He looks strained. "Sir, I'll contact the New Hampshire State Police, the Grafton County Sheriff's Department, Fish and Game, get some personnel up to the mountain, soon as I can," he says. "They can protect Mel, bring her back here."

"Not enough," I snap.

He shakes his head. "Sir, I'll also contact our field office in Burlington, have a couple of agents hook up with those personnel going to Mount Rollins," he says. "We'll take care of your wife, and we'll take care of Mel. It's the best I can do, based on your…status."

I know what he's saying, and Agent Stahl is too polite to say it out loud.

If I was currently POTUS, I'd have an army of agents at my beck and call, and there'd be a helicopter loaded with armed personnel going up to Mount Rollins to pick up Mel and immediately bring her back. Members of the Secret Service's Counter Assault Team would be roaming the compound, and there'd be heavily armed checkpoints at each road within miles of the place, stopping and examining traffic. Snipers and bomb-sniffing dogs would be prowling the woods and back roads.

But I'm not POTUS anymore, and the level of protection for me and my family is not nearly what it was when I was at 1600 Pennsylvania Avenue.

"Sir," Agent Stahl says. "Please, let me make the calls. Right now. I'll let you know once everything is secure. And I'll start working on getting more personnel to staff the compound."

I just nod, turn away, knowing Agent Stahl is right.

CHAPTER 23

Sherman's Path
Mount Rollins, New Hampshire

Mel breaks away from Tim's sweet touch and yes, it's all wrong. The two men are smiling but there's no friendliness or humor in those gazes. And the slacks, dress shoes, and button-front shirts they're wearing, with no knapsacks or even water bottles, are all wrong for being up in the mountains.

Tim looks to the two men and then to Mel, and whispers, "Guess we got caught, huh?"

She slowly treads water and whispers, "Tim, get the hell out of here. Now. Get to the other side of the pool, get into the woods. Run."

Tim is confused. "Mel, what's the problem?"

The two men are coming closer, still smiling.

She knows.

When Dad was first running for Congress and some Rotary Club guy was speaking at a Bonefish restaurant, a newspaper reporter covering the event asked a bored Mel what she thought, and she said, "He talks too much."

Which was true. But it got her into trouble with Mom at the time. Mel always had a knack for seeing people for what they really were.

And these two aren't hikers.

They're killers.

The taller man stops. "Mel Keating, please get dressed and come with us. And your friend as well."

Tim says, "Who the hell are you guys? Why should we go with you?"

The other man pulls out a pistol.

Oh, God, Mel thinks, and the water feels so much colder.

"Does that answer your question?" the nearer man asks, still smiling.

Mel raises her voice, trying to be strong in front of Tim. "Don't you want to avert your eyes as I get out?"

He shrugs. "Oh, Mel Keating. I've seen much worse."

Besides registering a fear that's making her legs and arms quiver, Mel Keating is rip-roaring 100 percent pissed off at herself as she climbs down the mountain with the two armed men and Tim, hair still wet, feet damp in her boots. When they suddenly appeared, Mel knew right away that something wasn't right, even beyond their lack of proper outdoor clothing.

It was their faces.

Smiling and open, but Mel caught their eyes, saw the eyes of hunters. Growing up in Texas, she knew that most of her family were hunters, and when Dad was in the Navy and some of his buddies came by for a visit, just before they were about to go off on a mission, she saw that same look.

Always moving, flickering, evaluating, ready to strike out.

If they hadn't been in the water—her suggestion!—and had

been on the trail, she would have shoved Tim into the woods and they would have started running, taking advantage of the tangled brush and trees to escape.

But in the water, there had been no escape. Just the humiliation of climbing out of the pond, getting dressed under the men's stares, and being forced back on the trail, and then taking a separate path down the mountain.

Tim is in front of her, his face pale whenever he turns to look back at Mel, and in front of him, quickly descending the trail, is the younger man. The older man is right behind her, and as the younger man slows down and gently negotiates a stretch of broken boulders, Mel says to the older man, "Why are you doing this?"

The man smiles, and his accent isn't as heavy as before. "You know."

"But my dad…he isn't the president anymore! If you're looking for—"

"Mel Keating, you have no idea what I'm looking for, now, do you?"

"But you don't have to do this," she says, thinking furiously, and Tim looks back, eyes wide with fright, and she goes on and says, "Just let us go."

"Allah wills otherwise, I'm afraid."

Thinking hard, Mel says, "Please. Islam is a religion of peace, isn't it? Prove it. Let us go. If you have a message, a concern, or a complaint, I'll pass it along to my dad. He can see it gets to the right people."

The man doesn't say a word, and then bursts out laughing. "Oh, you young ignorant girl. What you don't know about me and Islam could fill a container ship. But I have been a patient teacher for many, many years…and you and your father have so much to learn, and I have so much to teach. I have been waiting a very, very long time for this."

He gently caresses her neck with the muzzle end of the pistol.

"Now, please move," he says. "All of this discussion is quite interesting, but I have a feeling you're trying to…what is it? Stall. Yes. Stall in case we meet other hikers coming up this trail. As you hope for a distraction or an escape. Please. We did not plan this much and travel this far to allow a stray hiker or two to delay us. Melanie Keating, do start moving."

Tim is still staring at her, fear-wide eyes filled with moisture, and Mel wants to take a moment and say, *Sorry, Tim, dating the president's daughter didn't turn out the way you hoped, now, did it?*

Another shove from the pistol.

She starts down the trail, slowing her pace, and that's instantly noticed.

The older man says, "Move quicker, Miss Keating, or I will lose patience and leave your head on a trail sign."

CHAPTER 24

Huntsmen Trail
Mount Rollins, New Hampshire

The minutes slip by quickly, and with each footfall, Mel knows it's up to her to get herself and Tim away from these men. If she were stuck in a snowstorm in these mountains, or washed up ashore on a deserted Maine island, there's no one she'd rather have at her side than Tim.

But this is different.

She thinks of all the hard young men—and some women—she met when Dad was in the Navy, and later, when he campaigned for Congress. She heard the tales, sometimes eavesdropping when she should have been in bed, and she learned a lot about what was really out there beyond the borders and oceans. She'd trade anything to have one of those campaign volunteers here now instead of sweet, innocent Tim.

Hell, her mom—who was at Dad's side from the beginning and worked in the nasty backstabbing world of higher education—would be thinking like Mel right now, looking for options, a way out.

The woods thin.

The trail widens.

The dirt parking lot comes into view and she looks and looks—

Damn.

Just one vehicle on this trailhead, a couple of miles away from where Tim parked his car.

A black Cadillac Escalade.

Oh, if only there were two or three cars here, full of hikers, maybe some rough, strong football or rugby players from the college.

It's still up to her.

"Step faster now," the older man behind her says.

They're on the dirt surface of the parking lot.

Tim stops, and he takes two steps to her, whispering, "It's gonna be okay, I promise."

Tim tries to keep things together as he looks over the two armed men, thoughts roaring through his mind at the speed of Class IV rapids. Like being in a fast-moving and dangerous river, you observe the conditions and think through the best survival options.

Damn it, he thinks. He should have listened better to Mel back in the pool, gotten up and raced away. Sure, running naked through the trees would have hurt like hell, but at least he could have eventually found someone, maybe someone with a cell phone, to put out the word that Mel Keating was being kidnapped.

Back at the pool, Mel was the president's daughter, sensitive to danger, and not Mel, the typical Dartmouth student.

Mel steps forward and says, "All right. Look. Whatever you

want, whatever you need, it all comes down to me. Not my friend here"—she points to Tim. "Take me. Leave him behind."

Tim can't believe how brave and calm Mel seems to be, and he takes in her words, and thinks, *All right, maybe we can do something here.*

In a side pocket of his knapsack is a folding knife that he can quickly unclasp. Back at the pool, putting the knapsack on, he had quietly unzipped the pocket. If he can get these two to let him take the pack off, he could get into that side pocket and—

The older man lowers his pistol and says, "You would want that? To leave your companion behind? And go alone with us?"

Mel nods as the younger man moves closer to Tim.

Might work.

Keep on talking, Mel, he thinks. *Keep on talking.*

He says, "Hey, guys, my back is aching. Mind if I take my knapsack off?"

Mel says, "Yes. That's what I want. Leave Tim behind. I'll go with you."

Tim starts to loosen his straps. Desperate, but if he can get the knapsack off, he can toss it at the guy with the gun, and then go after the other guy with the knife. Slice him or stab him, anything to hurt him, and Mel and he can start running through the woods.

Mel says, "What do you say, sir? Will you do it? Doesn't it make sense?"

The older man says, "It certainly does."

Tim is thinking, *Okay, let's do this thing.*

"Young man," he says. "Do you promise to stay here if we leave? Do you?"

Tim thinks, *Jesus, it's going to work. This guy is letting his guard down.*

"You bet," Tim says. "I promise."

* * *

Mel thinks, *I'm making an impression. Maybe he'll do just that. Let Tim go, and in a while, he'll be with the cops and giving them a description of these two armed guys, the Cadillac, and what direction they were headed…this just might work out.*

To her shocked surprise, the older man asks Tim if he would promise to stay behind.

Tim looks relieved. "You bet. I promise."

The older man says something quick—Arabic, perhaps?—and then in English says, "Very well, we will leave you here."

Thank you, God, Mel thinks. *It's going to be all right.*

The younger man steps over, sticks the end of his pistol in Tim's left ear, and Mel watches in horrified silence as Tim tries to squirm his head away from the touch of the metal, and there's a loud report.

A spray of blood.

Tim grunts, collapses upon himself onto the dirt parking lot, shudders, and quickly dies.

CHAPTER 25

Huntsmen trailhead
Mount Rollins, New Hampshire

It took some talking on his part and spending money for a day babysitter, but Clem Townsend is one happy guy this morning, with his wife, Sheila, by his side as they drive up the dirt road to the Huntsmen Trail, which leads up to Mount Rollins. Ten years ago to this day, the two of them hiked up here and he popped the question on the summit, holding a nice engagement ring he had bought at the Walmart over in West Lebanon. Of course she said yes, and this mountain and this trail have always had a special place in their memories, and every anniversary, they make it a point to repeat the climb. Ten years and three kids later, Sheila still looks pretty good, even with a few extra pounds, and Lord knows, he thinks, he's added a few more himself—

"Clem, look out!"

He wrests the steering wheel of their old Subaru Forester to the left as a large black SUV roars down the narrow dirt road, coming within inches of sideswiping them on the right side. He calls out "Jerk!" as the Subaru's left wheels drop into a shallow drainage ditch. Sheila holds on to the dashboard as their car goes *thump thump thump* and then manages to get back onto the dirt road.

He stops, breathing hard.

"Christ, that was close," he says. "You okay, hon?"

Sheila nods. "What a clown. He came so close I thought he was going to rip off the side-view mirror."

Clem eases up on the brakes and drives slowly for another minute or so, and they come out into the dirt lot for the trailhead, and as Clem parks near the wooden trail sign with yellow lettering, Sheila says, "Oh, look at that. Those idiots left a pile of trash behind. No wonder they were in a hurry."

He looks over and freezes. He and Sheila own a little gas station and convenience store in the nearby town of Spencer, where he's a volunteer firefighter-EMT. He knows what he's seeing, and it's not trash.

Clem switches off the engine. "Sheila…get your cell phone out. See if there's service up here."

Sheila fumbles in her purse as he gets out of the Subaru into the cool late morning. At the start of the trail is a crumpled form, and he quickly walks over, saying, "Hey, you okay? You okay?"

Young man, eyes open in surprise, wearing khaki shorts and a Patriots T-shirt, crumpled up on his side, knapsack secured to his back and the side of his head a bloody, oozing mess.

Sweet Jesus, Clem thinks.

Sheila is next to him, her shaking hands holding her Galaxy cell phone, and she says, "Clem, we got service."

"Call 911. Tell the dispatcher where we are, and there's a man killed here."

She makes the call and Clem stays away from the body, knowing what to do, what not to do. The young boy is dead and there's nothing to do for him. No reason to go up and check the body, now, is there? Leave the boy be, along with any evidence the police will find. He hears Sheila on the phone, her voice even and calm. Good strong woman, he thinks. Lucky to have her.

But something else is odd.

Another knapsack dumped on the ground about six feet away.

Another hiker? The shooter? Was this guy on the ground trying to steal that knapsack, a tussle, and then somebody took out a handgun?

Sheila says, "Hear that?"

A faint sound of a siren.

"Somebody's moving fast," he says.

Sheila says, "Dispatcher managed to get ahold of Donny Brooks, out of Troop F. I bet that's him."

Clem is pleased. This part of the state has little or no town police departments, meaning the state police and the county sheriff are often the first responders. Because of their little store, he and Sheila know every sheriff's deputy and state trooper within a fifty-mile radius.

Like the trooper driving a dark green Dodge Charger coming into view, light bar flashing as the cruiser comes to a skidding halt. Donny Brooks is at the wheel and Clem sees him use his cruiser's radio to sign off at the scene. He quickly steps out in the standard trooper uniform of dark green shirt and tan trousers, and his face is wound up with concern and energy as he comes up to them, putting on his round campaign-style hat over short blond hair. He's in his late twenties, bulked up around his shoulders, and he moves in a hurry.

Donny gives the body a quick view, staying a few feet back. "Clem," he says. "When did you find the boy?"

"About ten minutes ago, Donny," he says. "Sheila and I were coming up here for a hike—"

"Anybody in the area? See or hear anything while coming up here?"

Sheila says, "We almost got run down by a big black SUV. Son of a bitch nearly ran us off the road."

Donny is still staring at the body. He pulls a small notebook out of his left shirt pocket, along with a pen, and starts taking notes. "How long from when you saw the SUV and when you found the body?"

Sheila says, "About three minutes."

"What kind was it?"

Clem says, "I don't know."

Sheila says, "Cadillac Escalade, that's what it was. Damn thing nearly hit me, nearly ripped off the side-view mirror."

Donny says, "Did you get the license plate?"

"No, I didn't," Sheila says. "Sorry to say, I didn't see what state it was."

The state trooper checks his watch, and from observing troopers and other cops working over the years, Clem knows what Donny is doing: estimating how far the Cadillac has gone since the two of them nearly got hit.

Donny toggles his shoulder radio mic and says, "Dispatch, one one four. Put out a BOLO for a black Cadillac Escalade, departing the area, heading to Upper Valley Road. Possible witness or suspect. Alert departments in Purmort, Montcalm, Spencer, Monmouth, and Leah on the BOLO as well. Contact Sergeant Wagner. Have him report here."

There's more radio chatter back and forth, and when there's a pause, Clem says, "See that extra knapsack? Dumped there? Don't you think that's odd, Donny?"

The young trooper nods. "Yeah. Noticed that right after I rolled up."

"Gonna take a look at it?"

"Should wait for my supervisor to show up but...shit, might be helpful."

Donny circles around the knapsack, and then puts on a pair of latex gloves, squats, opens it up. Clem eases up to see what might be in the pack, and out comes a water bottle, two granola bars, a dark blue sweatshirt, a pair of wool hiking socks, and a tan wallet.

"That's something," Clem says.

Sheila is next to him, close enough for him to hear her breathing.

The trooper opens the wallet, pulls out what looks to be a student ID, and Clem peers closer and is stunned at the photo and the name of a pretty young blond woman.

MELANIE R. KEATING

"Oh, shit," Donny says as more sirens sound off in the distance.

Sheila says, "That...that's President Keating's daughter!"

Clem can't say a word.

This is going to be one anniversary to remember.

CHAPTER 26

Northwestern New Hampshire

Mel Keating is trying to ease her rapid breathing, which is hard to do, since her arms and legs are bound by duct tape, her head is covered by a cloth hood tied around the base of her neck, and her mouth is taped and filled with a wadded-up piece of cloth. Luckily, her glasses are still secure on her face. Part of her is quaking in deep horror and shock at seeing Tim shot dead in front of her, snuffed out before he was even old enough to drink, blasted away in a dirt parking lot by two terrorists.

Tangos, she thinks, her eyes streaming tears, using the familiar military slang for terrorists. *Killers. Scum.*

The kind of people Dad fought when he was in the teams, and later, when he was president.

Mel is stunned at her college classmates' ignorance and apathy about the real world, and she's learned to keep her mouth shut during late-night hangs, when her fellow students would drone on and on about how the real roots of terrorism were poverty, despair, and inequality.

One night she pointed out that Osama bin Laden had come from a wealthy Saudi construction family and was certainly not penniless or oppressed, and boy, she never made that mistake again after putting up with an hour of listening to how ignorant, unfeeling, and privileged she was.

The hood is canvas, smelling of grain. She still fights to keep her breathing steady, and she is desperately trying to listen in on her two captors as they speed along.

Her.

They wanted her.

The president's daughter.

But why?

Dad's been out of office for nearly two years. No power, no influence, no way to pick up a phone and meet their demands.

Shut up, she thinks.

Focus.

A minute ago, the SUV she's in got off the dirt road and swerved left, onto a paved highway.

Think.

Listen.

On a paved road.

Damn it, she thinks, *you should have been paying attention.*

Toughen up, girl.

Keep calm, keep breathing through your nose, stay relaxed.

Don't think of sweet Tim, don't think of his being murdered, don't think.

Listen.

The hum of the tires on a paved road.

They're still going on pavement, Upper Valley Road.

Pay attention.

The SUV stops.

Backs up.

Back on a dirt road.

Start counting.

One thousand one, one thousand two, one thousand three…

She's being transported, taken to a hideout, a remote place for her kidnappers to keep her secure and send out a ransom demand. By counting and keeping track, she can retrace her travel at some point and—

The SUV stops.

Moves around.

Back on a paved road.

Okay, how many seconds was that?

Ten, eleven?

The SUV goes in a circle, stays in a circle, circling and—

Back on a dirt road.

Now a paved road.

Tears come to her eyes.

Those guys up there, they're good, confusing her, making sure she can't keep track of shit.

The tears come faster.

Mel thinks, *Okay, you two are good.*

But I'm pretty good myself.

She takes a deep cleansing breath, remembers paved road, dirt road, paved road, dirt once more, and she starts counting again as her kidnappers speed along the smooth pavement.

If they think they've kidnapped some typical college kid who's going to demand a pillow and safe place, Mel is relishing the chance to prove them oh so very wrong.

CHAPTER 27

Northwestern New Hampshire

Sometime later, Mel feels the SUV stay on a dirt road for a good length of time, and she resumes counting one more time, going *one thousand one, one thousand two,* and keeping focused.

The tears have stopped. No time for tears. Her legs and arms are cramped, her mouth is dry-raw with the cloth stuck inside, and she's wondering how long it will be before Tim's body is found.

The sudden shot of a pistol, the look of shock on Tim's face, the spray of blood out in the air…

Her ears pop.

Going up in altitude, then.

The SUV slows.

Stops.

Right at sixty-three seconds.

Remember that.

The forward doors open and shut.

Murmur of voices. The rear hatch opens and she dimly senses sunlight through the cloth bag. Hands grab her and she's lifted up with ease, and she fights not to moan, groan, or flail around. She won't give the bastards the satisfaction of seeing her squirm in fear.

No.

She won't give them that.

She's moved around, and she senses she's in a house because she can hear the footsteps of her two captors, and the squeak of a door opening, and now they're on steps.

And—

Mel is gently lowered onto a bed.

Hands move across her and she recoils at the touch, but they are brisk, formal, tearing away the duct tape and using…a razor? scissors?…to cut through and remove other swaths of tape.

The bag is last.

It comes off and she blinks her eyes through her glasses several times, and then the younger guy comes to her, and he's got something in his hands, a little bottle of…

Vegetable oil?

He smears a bit on the edge of the duct tape across her mouth, and then gently tugs, and repeats the procedure several times, until the tape is removed without much pain.

For real? They kill Tim and kidnap her, and they're concerned now about hurting her?

The guy's older companion looks on, staring.

The tape is gone, and she works at the cloth with her tongue, but the guy who pulled the tape off, he does the same with the wad of cloth, and she says, "Ugh," and then he offers her a drink of bottled water.

She swallows, swallows, and then spits out a stream on the guy, catching him right in his smug face.

"You bastards!" she yells out. "You miserable, evil killers. You will—"

The older man with the bushy eyebrows steps closer, and something about his dead eyes stops her. She takes a breath, now really scared. Not wanting to look at him, she gives the room a quick glance.

A concrete cube, with no windows and the only exit a heavy metal door. She's on a small made bed. There's a lamp in the corner. Small table and chair bolted to the floor. A chemical toilet.

That is it.

The older man says, "Here you are, Melanie Keating, and here you will stay, unless your father agrees to my demands."

She wants to spit at him again, but she doesn't have the saliva. "My dad is tougher than you think. Don't you idiots know that? Do you think he's going to give in to your demands?"

The older man smiles a weary smile, gestures to his companion, who goes to the door and unlocks it.

He says, "He may be a tough man, as you say."

He gently pats her on the head, like a prized pet or toy.

"But is he a tough father?"

He quickly leaves the room, the door closes behind him and is locked, and Mel is the loneliest she's ever been in her life.

Mel curls up on the bed, hugging herself, praying.

God, please have Dad get me out of here.

Please.

A few minutes pass, and then she stops the prayers, stops hugging herself.

Mel sits up, wipes at her eyes.

All right, she thinks. *You've had your cry.*

Maybe Dad will find her.

Maybe not.
But no more crying.
Time to start thinking, and planning.
Mel thinks, *If I'm getting free, it's going to be up to me.*
Nobody else.

CHAPTER 28

Lake Marie, New Hampshire

After my phone call from Deputy National Security Advisor Sarah Palumbo and the grim and unsatisfactory discussion with Agent David Stahl, I'm trying to vent my frustrations on my late-morning chores.

Not much else an ex-POTUS can do in these circumstances. Earlier, David gently recommended that I stay inside for the day, and I equally gently told him no.

Well, maybe not so gently.

What I'm looking to do is clear out the brush and saplings and old growth that's strangled this old stone wall, set here probably two centuries ago. It'll look nice, especially after I get the land rototilled and plant some grass. I stand up, stretch my back, try to enjoy the view, try to quiet the concern in my mind. Hard to believe with all these forests, but these trees are relatively young. Centuries ago, most of the trees here were cleared out by the earlier settlers and farmers, and then, when cheaper and more fertile land opened up in the West (after the Native Americans were nearly wiped out, of course), many farms were abandoned, and the trees reclaimed their birthright.

And why New Hampshire?

I grew up in Texas, lived for a number of years wherever the Navy sent me, returned to Texas, but decided to lay my head down here, in the Granite State, which threw me a lifeline after I got my ass kicked in the Iowa caucuses by my rebellious vice president, Pamela Barnes. The people here gave me a solid victory in the famed first-in-the-nation primary.

I like—and honor—loyalty.

I fumble for my iPhone, check the time, and do a quick selfie video with my recent work in the background.

"Hey, Sam, here's my daily update," I say. "Making progress. In a couple of months, it'll all be cleared away. Hey, maybe you and your crew can come here and do a dig. Who knows what you might find? Love you. Will call you tonight."

I switch off, send my daily selfie to Sam's email account with its bu.edu address, and look forward to getting back to work. In the time Sam's been at BU, we've made it work, with us spending time together, usually every other weekend, and for longer stretches during the summer. Holidays, of course, and a few events at Dartmouth with our daughter Melanie.

It's an odd relationship, I know, but the Ozzie and Harriet family of the 1950s is long gone.

I go back to the stone wall and a figure emerges from behind the rough rocks, wearing camouflage clothing, black gloves, a sniper's veil, and holding an SR-16 CQB 5.56mm assault rifle.

My muscle memory kicks in and I grab at my right hip, where there is—

Nothing.

No weapon at all.

Damn chatter is right after all.

I'm about to toss the handsaw at the figure when it suddenly lowers the weapon, tears off its sniper's veil, and the sweaty face of a young blond woman is revealed—

Secret Service Agent Stacy Fields holding an agency-issued weapon

—and she speaks into her wrist microphone: "This is Fields. I've got Harbor at the old stone wall. Repeat, Harbor is at the old stone wall."

I swivel to the sound of a racing engine.

The Boston Whaler is rushing in my direction, the two agents no longer carrying fishing poles but carrying weapons, and there's a flow of water at the bow, and I flash back to my Navy days, recalling, *That boat is sure moving fast. It's got a bone in its teeth.*

Something is seriously wrong.

That chatter warning from Deputy National Security Advisor Palumbo is right on the mark.

Another engine roars louder, and a bouncing mottled-green Yamaha four-seater UTV is racing toward me, Agent David Stahl at the wheel, wearing a Kevlar vest, and two other Secret Service agents—Ron Dalton and Paula Chin—are riding with him, also wearing Kevlar vests and holding out their own SR-16 CQB 5.56mm assault rifles.

The UTV skids to a halt and Agent Fields grabs the waistband of my shorts and the collar of my T-shirt and says, "Sir, we've got to get you to safety. Now! Please!"

The Boston Whaler swerves to shore and the two armed agents jump out of the boat, quickly push through the water, kneeling down on the shoreline, looking out to the lake with weapons at the ready. I drop the handsaw, and Agent Fields propels me to the open rear seat in the UTV. I'm bundled in and buckled and the UTV roars in a half circle as I'm pushed down, and a Kevlar bullet-resistant blanket is tossed over me, and I've barely adjusted to my cramped position when the UTV's engine roars with speed.

Something is seriously wrong.

I bounce and rattle and then the engine roars louder, and there's a quick, skidding halt, and the heavy blanket is tugged off me, and I'm unbuckled from the rear seat, and I'm practically carried to the two-car garage adjacent to my lake house. The left garage door is lifting up, revealing a reinforced concrete bunker with a heavy metal door in the center.

My lake home's safe room.

There's a blur of motion and orders of "Go, go, go," and the door is opened from inside by Secret Service agent Nicole Washington and I'm carried and propelled, with the other armed agents around me.

I'm pushed inside.

Agent Paula Chin brings up the rear, standing at the door, SR-16 CQB assault rifle up to her face, blocking any outside view or aimed weapon as the heavy door is closed, and I think that this is what they mean by that simple phrase *putting one's life on the line.*

The door closes.

She steps back.

I sit down on a plain black leather couch.

"David," I quickly say. "What's wrong? What do you know?"

This room was built before I moved in, and it's designed to keep me and Mel—and Sam, if she's here—protected in case of any external threat. There's a self-contained air system, food, stored water, and a tiny bathroom, and about the only thing that could breach this little cube inside my garage is a tactical nuclear weapon being dropped on the roof. There are couches that fold out into beds and a small dining area, with a refrigerator and a stove, and it's about as cheerful as a prison cell.

“David!” I call out again.

There’s a communications console set up at the other side of the room, with CCTV screens monitoring various parts of my property. From one screen I see the end of our dirt access road. The omnipresent New Hampshire State Police cruiser has shifted position to block the entrance, and two state police troopers are kneeling behind the cruiser, automatic weapons in hand.

Agent Nicole Washington is seated at the console, earphone and mic on her head, and Agent Stahl is standing behind her, speaking quietly but firmly.

“Contact the field offices in Burlington, Concord, and Boston,” he says. “We need more bodies here, stat. Then get on the secure line to DC. We need to alert them, and we need the FBI to—”

I yell out, “Agent Stahl, what the hell is going on?”

He quickly turns to me, and he no longer looks like the happy subordinate from earlier, after his defeat in our canoe race.

His face is hard-set, full of fury and concern, and it’s the look of a man with a mission, a man in charge, despite having a former president sitting before him.

His words come out, each one hitting me like a hammer blow to the gut.

Stahl says, “I’m sorry to tell you this, Mr. President. Your information about the threats was correct. Mel has been kidnapped.”

CHAPTER 29

Lake Marie, New Hampshire

Secret Service agent David Stahl is originally from Bakersfield, California, and after serving in the Marines—three tours in Afghanistan—he joined the Secret Service, and over the past ten years he's worked his way up to the Presidential Protection Detail.

But despite all the training, all the simulations, all the practice drills, he feels as though the entire weight of the Secret Service and Homeland Security is on his shoulders as he reacts to the evolving situation and makes decisions that he knows years from now will be examined, critiqued, and second-guessed.

So the hell what? he thinks.

This is what he signed up for.

And job one at this very moment is to keep Harbor in place before the ex-SEAL operator in front of him grabs a weapon and breaks out of here to hunt for his daughter on his own.

Keating's body is tense and coiled, a warrior who needs to strike out, and strike out now.

David knows the feeling well.

Keating says, "Tell me what you know."

"Sir, I'll make it quick, and please…we've got work to do to locate your daughter and protect you as well."

Keating's face colors. "Don't insult me. I know that. Go."

Stahl says, "Personnel from Fish and Game and the Grafton County Sheriff's Department were en route to Mount Rollins. They just didn't get there in time. Your daughter's knapsack was found at the Huntsmen trailhead. The body of her friend, Tim Kenyon, was found nearby. Shot in the head. No ransom note as of yet."

The former president nods, face pale. David says, "The New Hampshire State Police were the first responders at the murder scene. They've transmitted a BOLO for a black Cadillac Escalade that was seen speeding away from the trail. Roadblocks are being set up and we're asking for airborne units from the Vermont State Police and the New Hampshire State Police to begin an airborne search. We're—"

Keating holds up a hand. "I'm keeping you from your job. Get to it…but is there anything else I should know right now?"

"No, Mr. President," Stahl says.

And to himself, as he turns back to Agent Nicole Washington and the procedures that need to be followed and the notifications that must be made, he admits that he's just lied to Matthew Keating.

Because Mel's kidnapping is Agent Stahl's fault.

And not just because of this morning's warning.

Two months earlier, he is in his small upstairs office in the renovated barn on the Keating property when his desk phone rings. He picks it up—"Stahl"—and Agent Washington is on the other end.

"David, I've got Director Murray on the line," she says. "Are you in or out?"

He rubs at his tired eyes. He's been working on the staffing schedule for the next three months, and as always, he's shorthanded, he's always shorthanded, having to ask the detail here to work mandatory overtime, which is a quick way to burn out good agents and send them to the private sector. He's the special agent in charge of the detail, and he should have a deputy special agent to take some of the burden, but that position's been unfilled for months.

"I wish I was out," he says. "Put her on."

Faith Murray is the deputy assistant director in charge of the Presidential Protection Detail, and she gets right to the point. "Stahl, what the hell are you doing up there in New Hampshire?"

He slowly sits up straighter in his chair. "My job," he says. "What's the problem?"

"The problem is that you're violating both policy and procedure by providing security to Mel Keating," she snaps. "You know how much trouble you're in?"

Stahl says, "We're not providing protection to Mel Keating."

"That's not what I've heard," she says. "Stop the bullshit. What are you doing?"

He rubs at his eyes again, looks out the small window. There's music and laughter and a volleyball net, as Mel Keating is having a cookout with a few friends, Dartmouth students. Right now, Stahl wishes he was their age, worrying only about upcoming lectures and not getting a ball spiked in your face.

There's also a dull ache inside of him from missing his wife, Hannah, who these past five years has been dead from leukemia, leaving him a solitary widower with no time for or interest in reentering the dating pool.

"Field training," he says. "I don't want the detail here to get stale. So we do exercises where we're surveilling and following individuals. It made sense to have them follow Mel Keating."

"Does she know?"

"No, ma'am."

"And her father?"

Again, "No, ma'am."

"Then knock it off," Murray says. "There are approved training modules. Follow them. And Mel Keating is old enough that she doesn't need protection."

"Ma'am, I—"

"What is it?"

He grits his teeth for a moment. "Her father is a former president, and a former SEAL operator. It makes sense that he has a number of enemies out there. Lots of enemies."

"You protect him, and that's it."

"It's not enough!"

"I say it is," she says. "I'm late for a session with the secretary of Homeland Security. Anything else? Make it quick."

He wants to say no, it's not enough, damn it. And if you had worked more in the field, out in the rain and the snow, working long shifts and being alert all the time, you would know. Instead of going to training seminars and retreats and schools, being promoted the bureaucratic way instead of coming from the field, you would know deep in your bones how exposed and vulnerable Mel Keating is.

Hell, he thinks, even this compound is vulnerable. At the homes of other former presidents, operations centers are always at an off-site building so the entire protection detail isn't a single target in one place. But the Barnes Administration and its congressional supporters have hacked and slashed the Secret

Service budget—some DC commentators said it was revenge for President Keating's decision to contest his vice president's election challenge—and the lack of agents and resources here has been the result.

"Not at the moment, Director," he says, and she hangs up on him.

Stahl is looking at the CCTV screens and says, "Get Towler and Wrenn back out on the water. Nobody gets within a hundred yards of the place lakeside. Got it?"

"On it," Washington says as she starts quietly speaking into the microphone, and as they've done before in training simulations and drills, the two of them work in sync, keeping focused on the job and nothing else.

Protect Harbor at all costs.

Even though right now he feels as though he's failed the president and his kidnapped daughter.

CHAPTER 30

Lake Marie, New Hampshire

Inside the safe room, a soft murmur begins as the expensive and classified HVAC system kicks in, pumping fresh air into the space and filtering any biowarfare pathogens that might have been released on the property.

Stahl shakes his head.

Stop whining. Do your job.

"Roll back the outer perimeter," Stahl says. "Set them up at the secondary defensive line."

Phones are ringing, static-filled radio messages are frantically crackling through small speakers. Agent Chin is behind a thick Kevlar and metal mobile barricade, gently lining up spare magazines on the floor for her automatic rifle, a gas mask nearby in case there's an attempt to break through the door.

Mel Keating has been kidnapped. Is that a one-off or the start of something else? Do the terrorists want Stahl to try to evac Harbor now, before reinforcements are in place? Take him out by an RPG or an ambush squad when Keating's on the move?

Or is there an assault team now moving through the woods, heavily armed and with penetrative explosives, to lay siege to the safe house?

Washington says, "The state police SWAT team is responding, going to the preapproved staging location."

Stahl nods. If Keating was still serving as president, Stahl would have a shitload more resources at his fingertips. Armored vehicles, limousines, helicopter and aircraft within driving distance, and the Secret Service's Counter Assault Team, which could take on and win a firefight against any standard army squad in the world.

Washington says, "We've got three agents inbound from Burlington, four from Concord, and eight from Boston."

Stahl says, "Who's in the house?"

"Emma Curtis."

Our sacrificial lamb, Stahl thinks. The bulk of the agents are either here in the safe room or have been pulled back from the Keating property to set up a more defined and local defensive perimeter. But an agent has to be on duty at the main house to receive and brief those agents and other law enforcement officers as they arrive to beef up the compound's defenses, because no one is getting in and out of the safe room until it's time for Harbor to evacuate.

Which isn't happening anytime soon.

But it also means that in the wood-framed and undefended house, if an attack comes, Curtis is on her own.

Washington says, "Vermont State Police is offering their SWAT team."

"Tell them thanks and reach out to Concord."

Another quick second, and Washington says, "Secretary Charles is on the line."

Secretary of Homeland Security Paul Charles, Stahl thinks. Used to run the Florida Highway Patrol before the new president picked him to run Homeland Security, which has had oversight authority over the Secret Service ever since 9/11.

And he's utterly useless.

"Tell him we're busy," Stahl says.

He glances around the room.

Nobody is saying a word.

Everyone is focused on their area of responsibility, sliding into their preplanned and pretrained positions.

Keating is sitting on the couch, jaw set, staring right and hard at Stahl.

Stahl has to look away.

Washington says, "David, we've caught a break from the FBI."

"Nice change of pace," Stahl says. "What is it?"

"Eight members of their Hostage Rescue Team are doing training at Hanscom Air Force Base in Massachusetts," she says. "They can be in the air in five minutes."

Stahl says, "We'll take them."

A low voice that he can barely recognize comes from behind him.

"David."

He turns and Keating is standing up.

"Two points," he says. "What's the status of my wife?"

"Professor Keating is still at the archaeological site in Hitchcock, with about a half dozen grad students and volunteers."

"Has her protection arrived yet?" Keating asks.

"Maine State Police should be there by now," Stahl says. "There's a National Guard armory within two miles of where she is. That's where they'll take her."

Keating nods. "All right."

Stahl is desperate to get back to the task at hand, check the status of the perimeter defense, see if he can get two more agents on watercraft out on the lake, work up a plan to eventually get Harbor out of here and someplace larger and easier to defend.

Stahl says, "Sir, what's the other point?"

"Did I hear right and there's an HRT team coming here? By helicopter?"

"Yes, sir. They'll be here in under an hour."

Keating nods, and Stahl sees the look in the man's face change, from that of a protectee to one now in charge.

"Good," he says. "Once they arrive, we're getting on that Black Hawk and getting the hell out of here."

CHAPTER 31

Hitchcock, Maine

It's late morning in the small fishing village of Hitchcock, Maine, and Boston University professor and former First Lady Samantha Keating is on her sore and aching knees, looking down at what is slowly—oh, so slowly!—being uncovered by two of her grad students from a meter down in the dirt.

She's sweaty, her hands are encrusted with dirt, there are blisters developing along both thumbs, her clothes smell, and she's in her own form of paradise. In so many campaign seasons past, she got trapped at some political event in an ill-fitting gown, eating tough chicken and cold potatoes, attempting small talk with some unctuous man or woman running for office.

But not now, not here.

This is where she belongs, this is where she thrives. Not in that damn plastic and artificial arena of politics but here on the ground, in the dirt, slowly uncovering stories and secrets from the past.

A young grad student, Cameron Dane, is gingerly sweeping away more of the fine soil with a camel hair brush when she says, “Professor, do you see this? Do you?”

An open tent has been constructed over this part of the dig, protecting the uncovered soil and artifacts from the strong Maine sun, but Samantha can easily see what’s coming into view: curved red tiles, made by humans, and from Europe.

“Yes,” she says, her voice rising in excitement. “Yes, I do!”

Paul Juarez, another grad student, says in awe, “Professor, that’s Basque. No doubt about it.”

Samantha’s smile widens. “Nice to know a gamble sometimes pays off, right?”

The students laugh as more of the red tile is revealed.

Jackpot, she thinks.

Despite all the poorly written and distributed books in grade school and high school that talked about the early French and English explorers and settlers to these shores, the real history is more complex and puzzling. Up in Newfoundland and along other provinces in Canada, there are archaeological sites that show that Basque fishermen from the 1400s—long before Columbus stumbled his way into the Caribbean—were fishing the astounding wealth of cod and whales that clustered around these shores.

There were always suggestions and theories that the Basque could have gone farther south, here to Maine, and if any evidence were discovered, it would forever change the history of New England.

Such history has never been found.

Until today.

“Careful there, Paul,” Samantha gently says to Juarez. “These tiles haven’t seen the light of day for more than six hundred years. Another six or so minutes won’t make a difference.”

The Atlantic Ocean’s waves hitting the rough rocks and

boulders provide the predominant sounds here at the site in Hitchcock until the noise of a racing engine reaches her ears.

Big deal. Right now she doesn't care about the twenty-first century and its technology and squabbles, and God, she certainly doesn't care to think about all those wasted hours and days and weeks being First Lady and pretending to care.

This is her time, her place, and she imagines what it must have been like to have been one of the Basque fishermen back in the 1400s, sailing here and finding the rich schools of fish, unbelievable wealth far from their traditional fishing grounds in France and Spain. Not coming here to conquer or make an empire—no, just coming here to work the waters.

One of the site's volunteers, an older gent named Picard wearing jeans and a gray sweatshirt, runs up to the tent. "Professor Keating, there are two men over there looking for you!"

She says, "Tell them to go away. I'm busy."

Samantha continues to stare at the emerging tiles. To find a Basque fishing station here, in Maine...the headlines that would produce, the papers she could write, maybe even a book-length history. Two years ago, *People* magazine profiled her as she started fieldwork here, and since then the news media has left her alone.

But to have them pay attention, to this, now...

The volunteer is insistent. "Professor Keating, they're—"

Samantha holds up a hand. "They can wait. Or go away. Their choice. Paul, you're doing good work there."

In the distance and coming from the small dirt parking lot, she sees two men running toward this tent, running past the two other, smaller tents, the three screen sifters where dirt is checked for artifacts, heading right at her, both wearing dark gray suits with white shirts and neckties, and she slowly stands up.

Both men have shoulder holsters.

It's as though a cold chunk of this Maine dirt has just sunk into her chest.

"Cameron," she says.

"Yes, Professor Keating," the student says, not looking up from the history being unearthed in front of her.

"Something is going on," she says. "Until I come back, you're in charge."

Cameron lifts her head and Samantha walks out into the open sun, and the red-faced man holds out a leather wallet with a gold badge inside.

"Mrs. Keating," he gasps. "Detective Sergeant Frank Courtney, Maine State Police. You've got to come with us."

Matt, she instantly thinks, *oh, Matt, what have they done to you?*

"Let me get my bag," she says, and then the other officer's voice freezes her in place.

"Mrs. Keating, we don't have time. We need to get you out of here," he says.

The briefest and most horrible of pauses.

"Your daughter Mel has been kidnapped."

CHAPTER 32

Northwestern New Hampshire

Mel is not sure how long she's been in the basement cell, but it feels as though it's been hours. She's thirsty, hungry, and cold, and she's untucked a blanket from the bed and has wrapped it around herself. She sits on the bed cross-legged, thinking and listening and looking.

Not much to see. Earlier she explored the small room, and when the door was open, she noticed it has exterior hinges and is secured by a keypad. The bed, chair, table, and lamp are all securely fastened to the floor. The same with the chemical toilet. There's no external power cord leading from the lamp, and the light cannot be turned off. At one point, Mel was tempted to shatter the lightbulb, make the sharp glass some sort of a weapon, but she quickly realized that it would plunge the room into utter darkness, and she shivers at that thought.

She moves on the bed, still trying to think things through, trying not to remember—

Tim's funny way of imitating the host of *The Daily Show.*

Tim sticking up for her that time in the African history class.

Tim's sweet habit, when they were sitting together at lunch or driving or hanging out and studying, of occasionally just reaching out and gently rubbing her neck.

Not in an attempt to get her into bed or get her clothes off—no, just a sweet way of saying, *Hey, I'm here, let me know if you need anything.*

She wipes at her eyes.

Quiet.

It's too quiet.

She gets up off the bed, stands on tiptoe, cocks her head to see if she can hear anything from upstairs.

Nothing.

No footsteps, no talking, no doors slamming.

Her cell is pretty well insulated.

She takes off her glasses because she knows from long experience that for some reason when she removes them, when her bad eyesight is given no corrective, her hearing skills seem to improve.

But nothing changes.

She can't hear a thing.

Mel sits down, takes stock. Her clothes, and that's it. Her hiking boots were taken off back when she was bundled into the SUV, so there's no chance of using the bootlaces to make some sort of garrote to strangle one of the two tangos—like that would happen.

Thin gold necklace around her neck, a gift from Dad on her fourteenth birthday.

And a gold ring on her right hand that once belonged to Mom's grandmother.

She gets up and goes around the room once again. No ventilation system so there'll be no taking off a grille and crawling to freedom like in *Die Hard* or some other movie. A clicking noise, coming from the other side of the door. Mel moves to the bed but doesn't sit down.

No, she thinks, brushing away the tears from her eyes, her thoughts going to Tim again.

She's going to stand up to these two sons of bitches.

The door opens and the older man comes in, followed by his companion. The older man is holding what looks to be a small video camera, and the other man holds out a newspaper.

Both have pistols holstered at their sides.

The older man says, "We will shortly provide you with a meal and water. But this meal comes at a price."

A quick outburst of Arabic, and the newspaper is thrust toward her, a copy of *USA Today*.

Mel keeps her hands at her sides.

The man with the video camera sighs. "This will be quick, and requires nothing on your part, save you hold out the newspaper to prove to your father that you are alive on this day. If you do not cooperate, then my cousin will…encourage you. It will be painful, and at the end, you will still hold up the newspaper."

His words, spoken so well and plainly, like an instructor gently explaining the difference between John Locke and Karl Marx, still hit her cold and hard.

"Is that it?" she asks.

He nods. "Yes. I won't even ask you to speak. Just hold the newspaper for a few moments, and then we will leave, and then you will be fed."

She holds out her hand, takes the newspaper, and blinks back tears, then unfolds the paper and holds it under her chin.

"Very good," the man with the camera says, and he brings it closer and Mel feels her fingers begin to tremble.

The paper is shaking.

She's ashamed and scared, and won't this fool hurry up and finish and leave?

"There," he says, lowering the camera. He reaches over and takes the paper from her hands. "You will soon be fed."

"Lucky me," she shoots back. "What's on the menu? The two of you look like you couldn't even use a microwave."

The older man says, "It will be satisfactory, I promise."

"And after that?"

He moves to the door, his companion right beside him. "Up to your father and Allah. Soon he will receive this video and a message from me."

"What are you asking for?"

He opens the door, smiling. "For something your father will never be able to provide."

The door starts to close, and Mel says, "Wait...just wait. Can I ask a favor?"

The man stops in the doorway, pauses for a moment.

"You may ask."

Mel points to him. "I'm...I'm afraid of guns. I'm sorry, that's just the way it is. The next time you or your friend come in, please, will you leave your guns behind?"

The man smiles and nods.

"No."

He and the other one pass through the opening, and the door is securely locked behind them.

A few minutes later she's back on her bed, cross-legged again, blanket over her cold shoulders, remembering and thinking.

Remembering a time a few years back, when Dad became president and there were those weird couple of weeks when they moved into the White House, and there were meetings and tours and briefings, and there was one Secret Service agent—David Stahl—who pulled her aside and said, "Mel, you're going to have 24/7 protection here and wherever you go, but there may be a time when there's a mistake, a screwup, or an overwhelming assault. You might be on your own. Let's talk about what you can do then."

That was an interesting meeting indeed, and while she was scared shitless at some of the things Agent Stahl said could happen, she was also proud that even though she was only a teenager he was treating her as an adult.

She remembers everything he said.

And now she's thinking of what just happened, and how Mom and Dad are going to react when they see this video released later, and what that terrorist jerk is going to say and demand.

Mel manages a smile.

One thing, though, is that he seemed to accept what she said back then, that she was afraid of guns.

That is bullshit.

Dad taught her how to use firearms when she was in first grade, and since then she's fired everything from a .22 Ruger pistol to a fully automatic M4 assault rifle.

She knows that.

But that jerk doesn't know that.

The little victory heartens her.

CHAPTER 33

Lake Marie, New Hampshire

Agent David Stahl looks pretty pissed and frustrated, and I don't blame him. I'm proposing to violate every piece of procedure and training he's learned over the years, and it's my job in the next few seconds to break through that training.

Trying to keep my voice on an even keel, I say, "If Mel's been kidnapped, that means there's going to be a ransom demand."

Part of me silently breaks out in prayer, thinking, *Please please please let there be a ransom demand. Please let her be alive. Please, God, help me get my girl back.*

Because I know I have enemies out there with long memories, and right now, a ransom demand is our very best option.

I won't let myself imagine anything else.

Stahl says, "Perhaps, Mr. President. Again, this might be a ruse, to get you moving and vulnerable, open to an attack."

I go on.

"Perhaps. But if there's a ransom demand, then the FBI and Homeland Security come in, along with every law enforcement agency in New England. Samantha and I need to know what's going on, what the demand is, what options are out there. Am I right, David?"

His lips are pressed together, his jaw is firm, and he nods. The other Secret Service agents in this safe room are doing their best to ignore us. What a change, what a difference. Last night I barbecued cheeseburgers and hot dogs for this crew, later did my best to beat them at poker, and now that cheery and happy crew has morphed into who they are really: trained men and women ready to kill to protect me.

"That means meetings, phone calls, briefings, and videoconferences." I move a hand around. "Which can't happen in this concrete box. I need to get out of here, David, and now."

"But Mr. President, I—"

I interrupt. "I'm not the president. Pamela Barnes is. I'm just the former POTUS, with no power, no influence, no responsibilities. You and everyone else here are sworn to protect me, and I can't thank you enough. But I'm not going to sit here, wrapped in cotton, and wait."

"Sir, we're getting other assets up here to safely transport you to a more secure location."

"How long will that take?" I ask. "We have a helicopter coming here, crewed by the FBI. Let the HRT team deploy, and with everyone departing the chopper, you and I and maybe another agent or two will slip aboard, and out."

His face is still stern-looking, and I'd hate to be under his supervision and called into his small office in my house for a reaming out.

But one way or another, I'm getting out of here.

We stare at each other.

He breaks first. "Where would you go?"

"Manchester Airport," I say. "From there, Reagan National, and then the Saunders Hotel, over at Crystal City."

"Why the Saunders?" he asks.

"My reelection campaign still has an office there, still wrapping up paperwork and other crap from the FEC. It's already been vetted by your folks. It's across the river from DC."

"How are you getting there?"

I say, "I need my iPhone from the house."

Stahl shakes his head. "Can't open that door, sir."

"Yes, you can," I say. "Get the on-duty agent from the house to bring over my iPhone and my go bag, up in the first closet in my bedroom. I'll make the necessary arrangements to secure a flight."

Another heavy few seconds pass. "This will mean my job," he says.

"I still have some friends in DC," I say. "I'll do my best to help you."

He stares, and without breaking eye contact with me, he says, "Nicole."

"David," the agent at the comm console says.

"Contact Emma," he says. "Get Harbor's iPhone and go bag over here."

"All right," she says.

My face relaxes some, and David's expression seems to lighten as well. David says to Nicole, "Then contact the HRT. Once the team disembarks, they're taking on two to the Manchester airport."

"All right," she says.

I nod.

"All right," I say.

A tiny triumph, a tiny step toward finding my daughter, but I'll take it.

CHAPTER 34

❖

Lake Marie, New Hampshire

Six minutes later I'm in a corner of the safe room while my detail continues to work the phone and other communications systems. There's a lot of calm talk, phones ringing, and more crackling radio messages. I scroll through my contacts list on my iPhone, furiously thinking and hoping, seeing what friends are out there.

Truth is, there are not many.

One thing I quickly learned in politics, and it was one hell of a learning curve indeed, is that there are very few people you meet who will become true friends. Most folks you meet in politics, no matter how open the smiles and how deep the compliments, just want you and your office. And when you're out of office, they fade away.

But a few stick around.

There.

Trask Floyd.

Once in the teams like me, he found a second career as a Hollywood stuntman, and then a third career as a wealthy actor and movie director, and we became friends when I was a congressman and he needed help from the Texas Film Commission.

The phone rings once, twice, and a young male voice answers, "Trask Floyd's phone."

I say, "This is Matt Keating. I need to talk to Trask."

Once upon a time, my name would allow the famed White House switchboard to get me connected with nearly anyone on the planet with access to a telephone.

But no longer.

"Sorry, sir, he's not available."

"Where is he?"

"He's setting up a shot, and we're already behind schedule, so—"

I find my command voice. "Son, you get Trask Floyd on the phone in the next sixty seconds or you'll regret it for the next sixty years of your life. Go."

The phone goes silent.

A few long seconds drag by.

Mel, I think.

Oh, Mel, where the hell are you? Who's got you?

The phone comes to life.

"Matt," Trask says. "I don't know what you just said to Tommy, but he looks like someone just drained a quart of blood from him."

I say, "Where are you?"

"Vasquez Rocks in California," he says. "Getting ready to blow up shit and film same."

California, I think. Damn. I was hoping he'd be closer.

I say, "I need your help."

"You got it, Matt."

Good old Trask. No questions, no demands, no inquiries.

"What do you need?"

"I need an aircraft at the Manchester airport in New Hampshire to fly me and a Secret Service agent to DC."

Trask says, "When do you need it?"

"Five minutes ago."

"Shit," Trask says.

From my phone I can hear voices in the background on the other end. It's sounding like people out there at his filming location want his attention.

"Mr. Floyd—"

"Trask, we've got to—"

"We're losing the sun—"

"Hold on," Trask says. He seems to hold the phone against his chest, and there's a loud muffled stream of curses, and then he returns to the phone and says, "All right, you've got it."

I close my eyes in relief. "Don't you want to know what's going on?"

"No," he says. "I need to make some phone calls, and you need to do what you've got to do. God bless you, Mr. President. I've got your back."

Minutes later I hear the low hum of a nearby helicopter, the noise even penetrating the concrete, and I'm by the door, go bag in my hand, and Agent Stahl is standing next to me, also holding a black canvas bag. In his other hand he holds a SIG Sauer pistol.

From the console Agent Washington says, "The Black Hawk's on the ground."

The door is unlatched, and Agent Chin pulls it open. Agent Stahl goes out first and I'm right behind him, and in front of us, on the lawn going down to a sandy beach at the lake shoreline, a Black Hawk helicopter is on the ground, rotors still roaring.

A line of black-clad, helmeted, and booted members of the FBI's famed Hostage Rescue Team come out, and David and I run by them, heads bowed down from the heavy propeller rush, bits of gravel and dirt hammering at us.

God, so many memories come back to me about boarding helicopters just like this, heading off to dangerous and desperate missions, but none, none are as desperate as this one.

Agent Stahl gets into the helicopter first, helps me aboard, and a crew chief slides the side door closed, and we make our way to the webbed seats and sit down, me across from him.

We both put on headsets though I have nothing to say as the Black Hawk lifts up over the forested peaks of this part of New Hampshire, and I look down, anger and fear pounding through me, thinking, *Mel might be down there. Mel might be right below us.*

What to do?

I shift my go bag so it's within easy reach, knowing what's in there: spare clothes, sneakers, water, energy bars, and cash.

Among other things.

As POTUS, the only weapons I ever came near belonged to the Secret Service or its CAT team.

Yet in my go bag are a SIG Sauer 9mm P226 pistol and a disassembled Colt M4 automatic rifle, with a TAWS 32 thermal sight, and plenty of ammunition for both.

I'm an ex-POTUS now.

And I'm also a father who's willing to go anywhere, and kill anyone involved, to get his daughter back.

CHAPTER 35

The Oval Office
The White House

President Pamela Barnes is having her photo taken with a delegation from the Junior Chamber of Commerce, and she's idly thinking about which face she's using today. Throughout her career in politics, she's secretly noted the different faces she uses for different occasions, from warm and gracious to angry and demanding, and in front of this young group, she's wearing her interested yet very busy face.

She steps in the middle of the huddle as the cameras whir and click, and she nods and ignores the questions the White House press pool is throwing at her like water balloons.

"Madam President, the Speaker says the budget talks are on hold until you…"

"Madam President, how do you respond to the Chinese threats about closing the Straits of Taiwan…"

"Madam President, despite their personal promises to you, it appears the average NATO defense budget is going to decrease again this year..."

She keeps that smile frozen on her face, and one of her young male staffers, checking his watch, says, "That's enough now, thank you, thank you very much," and he holds his hands wide to push out the press pool and the fresh-faced and eager members of the Junior Chamber of Commerce delegation.

One of the adult hosts, a stout Asian woman in a dark blue skirt suit, trails behind and offers a hand that Pamela gives a quick shake.

"Thanks for coming," Pamela says. "I hope you enjoy the rest of the day."

The woman's eyes are brimming with tears. "Thank you, thank you, Madam President...believe me, we're all pulling for you. We all love you. God bless you, Madam President."

Pamela's smile is for real as she reaches out and touches the woman's shoulder. "Thank you, that's quite kind of you," she says, and while she is touched by the visitor's sudden outburst of emotion, she quickly starts thinking, *Well, not* everyone's *pulling for me, especially the House leadership, China, Russia, Iran, a good part of the news media and the Internet, and a very large part of the country who still can't get over calling the leader of the free world "Madam."*

Finally, the group departs the Oval Office, and Pamela's husband, Richard, strolls in, leather-bound folder in his strong and still-weathered hands, and she once again feels that pleasing rush of love and appreciation for her husband as he comes near. He has on his daily uniform of a dark gray suit from Savile Row and a dark red necktie, and before she got where she belongs—here, in the White House—there were nasty remarks about the expense of his suits.

And at the time, Richard said, "Look, I grew up in Osceola County with cow shit all over my clothes, and now you're begrudging me a chance to clean up?"

To the only man she can 100 percent trust in this city, Pamela says, "What's next on the schedule?"

Without hesitation, Richard says, "I've canceled it all."

That knocks her back. After her narrow win two Novembers ago, Richard headed her transition team, and there were howls of outrage when she pulled a JFK (who appointed his brother Bobby attorney general) and named him chief of staff. But her history-making victory tempered those howls, and now there were days like this one, when she wishes she was on day two of her term, riding on so much goodwill.

"What's happened?" she asks, going back to the historic Resolute desk, used by so many past presidents.

The door to the Oval Office closes and Richard sits next to her at the desk. "Mel Keating's been kidnapped."

"What?" She's astounded, horrified. "Matt Keating's daughter?"

She had been preparing herself for a terrorist attack, a military action, the death of someone prominent…but this?

Richard opens the leather-bound binder and says, "Nearly two hours ago. I got a briefing from Secretary Charles at Homeland Security. Mel Keating and her boyfriend were on a hike up in the White Mountains, about a half hour's drive from Matt's home on Lake Marie. The boyfriend's body was found on a dirt parking lot, at a trailhead. He'd been murdered, one shot to the head. Mel's knapsack was on the ground near him."

"What the…where in hell was her Secret Service coverage?"

"Her father's no longer president, and the law says her protection ends when she turns sixteen. Mel Keating is nineteen."

Pamela takes a breath. "Any ransom demands?"

"Not yet."

"Any idea who might be involved?"

Richard says, "Matt's service in the SEALs and his political record means a long list of enemies, Madam President. I'm sure the FBI is running that down at the moment."

"What's being done right now?"

"Local law enforcement is responding, we've got the FBI Hostage Rescue Team on the ground at Matt's home, and the Bureau is sending in every available agent from Boston to Buffalo."

"News media?"

"Just Internet rumors so far that something unusual is going on up there in New Hampshire, but you can bet it's going to break wide open very shortly," Richard says. "We should have you make a statement as soon as possible, get in front of it right away."

Pamela rubs at her eyes. "Shouldn't Lisa Blair take the lead? Won't people want to hear from the head of the FBI?"

"No, ma'am," Richard says with confidence. "If this was any other high-profile kidnapping, I would agree with you. But not the daughter of the former president. You need to take the lead, take control, show the country that you're on top of things."

Pamela nods. Her husband and chief of staff is making sense. "All right," she says. "I want Director Blair over here soonest for a briefing. Get Secretary Charles and the head of the Secret Service here as well, and General Perkins, and Fred Munroe. Full-court press. Oh…and where's the vice president?"

"On an aircraft, heading to South America," he says. "But the Joint Chiefs chairman, and your national security advisor…Are you certain, Madam President?"

"Dead certain, Richard," she says. "What are the chances that Mel was kidnapped for cash by some local yokels? There's going to be a national security and military aspect to this kidnapping, and I want to make sure we plan through all possible contingencies."

"On it, Madam President," he says.

Pamela shakes her head. Years back, she and Richard tried

to have children to no avail, and neither of them wanted to go the grueling and possibly fruitless IVF route. So they lavished attention on their nieces, nephews, and cousins (and amazing how many more cousins came out of the woodwork once she was sworn in!), and she can't imagine the horror of having a child kidnapped.

She says, "I want to talk to Matt Keating."

"Ah, not possible at the moment, ma'am."

"Why the hell not?"

"He's in an FBI Black Hawk, heading to the Manchester airport. I believe from there, he'll be coming down to the DC area to be in close contact for information and developments."

"And Samantha Keating?"

"En route as well."

She says, "Okay, at first opportunity, I want a face-to-face with them both. No press."

"I'll make it happen."

Pamela is thinking: *Who else to get in here?* She has full faith and confidence in FBI director Lisa Blair even though she was appointed by Pamela's predecessor, and there are none better in the world when it comes to resolving kidnappings. Her secretary of Homeland Security, though, is a Florida cop with little imagination, and she'll make sure he shuts up and does what the FBI wants Homeland Security to do. And how about the NSA? The best in intercepting communications, and she'll have to make sure that—

Her husband and chief of staff is still sitting there.

From experience, she knows that's a huge signal.

"What else, Richard?"

He locks her in with his steady gaze and says, "This is a crisis, Madam President. But it is also an opportunity. The past several months haven't been good for us, have they?"

"Richard, it's just—"

He interrupts her. "Pamela, we're sinking. Floundering. Your history-making achievement is in everyone's rearview mirror. Now here's a chance to take control, show real leadership, and make the tough decisions that will impress our people and other countries."

Pamela looks right back at the man who helped put her here, in the most famed office in the world.

"What kind of tough decisions, Richard?"

His gaze is steady and calm. "Pamela, when you find out what they want for a ransom, you're going to say no."

CHAPTER 36

Saunders Hotel
Arlington, Virginia

It's chaos on the fifth floor of the Saunders Hotel a few minutes after my arrival with Agent David Stahl, and I'm doing my best to make it a controlled chaos. We were met at Dulles Airport with two Suburbans and three other Secret Service agents from the field office on 1100 L Street NW, in the District of Columbia. The agent sitting next to me in the rear of the second Suburban was a Hispanic male, and I surprised him by saying, "Agent Morales, how are you? How're the twin boys?"

Amazed, he managed to stammer out, "Very—very good, sir. They're both in first grade, making their nuns miserable."

"Good for them," I said, grateful I had just spent a minute or two thinking of something else besides Mel. Agent Morales spent six months in the Presidential Protective Division when I was POTUS, and when you spend nearly every waking moment with agents like him, you get to know their lives, families, and experiences.

On the fifth floor, Agent Morales is standing watch at the open door linking the suite belonging to my failed reelection campaign to another empty room, allowing us more office space. Both spaces are filled with hotel security staff, managers, workers bringing in more desks and chairs and computer terminals, and I'm paying for all of this with the Visa card issued in the name of the still existing Committee to Reelect Matthew Keating, and I imagine I'm running up one hell of a bill and I don't really give a shit.

Lights are burning brightly, phones are ringing, and a large flat-screen television is muted and tuned to CNN, the worldwide news network that is the United States' unofficial eighteenth intelligence agency for broadcasting breaking news before it reaches the White House or the State Department.

Every few seconds there's a "Mr. President, Mr. President"—questions come my way about getting more secretarial staff, additional rooms for sleeping, what kind of coffee and meals should be ordered—and I'm in the center of this damn storm, longing for the simplicity and organization of the White House Situation Room.

I want at least a minute to myself to find out where Samantha is and ask Agent Stahl if he's gotten any additional news from either the New Hampshire State Police or the FBI, but each time I turn, there's someone else in front of me holding a cell phone or a laptop, asking me a question.

"Everyone! Shut the hell up, now!" says a bellowing voice belonging to a woman. "I don't want to hear another goddamn peep from anybody!"

I turn and nearly sag in relief in the sudden silence as Madeline Perry, my chief of staff, strolls right in, eyes flashing, head turning, as if issuing an open challenge to stand in her way.

She comes to me, gives me a quick hug. "Oh, Mr. President..."

I pull away, blinking at the sudden tears. "Thanks for getting here so quickly, Maddie."

She takes both of my hands in hers, gives them a quick squeeze. "I practically had to bribe my way onto the best flight available from LaGuardia to Dulles. Anything new?"

"Not that I know of."

She drops my hands, spots Agent Stahl on the phone, and says, "David! Huddle up time with me and Harbor. Now."

We both follow her into the nearest empty room, which happens to be the suite's large bathroom. Madeline ushers us in and, before closing the door, says, "Anybody knocking on this door will get their fingers broken, I goddamn guarantee it!"

In the bathroom, Madeline says, "Agent Stahl, what's the latest? Any ransom demand?"

He shakes his head. "Not that I know of. The latest is that the FBI's HRT is still on-site at Lake Marie, every FBI agent that can walk in the Northeast is arriving up there, there's a New England–wide BOLO going out for the Cadillac Escalade we suspect was used in Mel's kidnapping, and right now, all border stations in New England and New York State are being closed."

Madeline says, "Mr. President, have you heard from the White House? FBI? Homeland Security?"

"Not yet," I say. "I've been pretty mobile for the past couple of hours. If I stop answering questions about what kind of phone systems to install, I plan on reaching out, not waiting."

"Good," Madeline says. "Trust me, when we leave this room, you're not going to be bothered." She takes a quick breath. "I haven't seen anything in the news media about Mel's…situation, but that's going to change pretty damn quick. I'll start working up a statement for you to issue." She struggles to contain her emotions. "Oh, that poor girl."

I say, "Agent Stahl, any word on my wife?"

He says, "I was just getting an update when Maddie arrived, Mr. President. Maine State Police and agents from the Portland field office got her on a United flight to Dulles, which landed about thirty minutes ago. We have a detail bringing her in."

Another bit of relief flows through me.

I need Samantha here.

My wife, Mel's mom, and, most importantly, my partner.

I won't get through this and get Mel back without her at my side.

"Good to know," I say. "Maddie, how long before the story is out?"

"Minutes, if that," she says.

I run a hand across my face. "Then this goes global, and every nut with a grudge or psychic with a vision is going to start clogging the phone lines and email accounts of the FBI and Homeland Security and everyone else in between."

Madeline nods. "True, sir. But let's get you out of here, allow you to get to work. Make some phone calls on your own before everything gets clogged with nonsense."

I reach for the doorknob and Madeline says, "No, sir, I'm going out first."

She opens the door and again raises her voice. "Listen up, people, and listen up well! I'm Madeline Perry, President Keating's chief of staff, and any question, request, or announcement comes to me, and me only. Got it? In other words, leave him the hell alone. We're taking the room next door and if you need him, you come through me." Then, to me: "This way, sir."

I follow Madeline to the door leading to the other suite, and her plan immediately falls apart, as the other door opens and Samantha strolls in, sees me, and says, "Matt!"

A few seconds pass and I get in a hard hug with her, feeling her hair against my face, smelling Maine salt air and dirt, and thinking of times past—confirming her pregnancy, me coming home from my first overseas deployment, that horrid day two summers ago when now president Barnes beat me in the California primary—and at each of those times, I didn't want to let Samantha go.

Like now.

But I pull away and kiss her and she's crying and says, "Anything? Anything at all?"

I hold her face in my hands and I'm about to think of what I can possibly say when Madeline Perry calls out, "Turn it up! Turn it up!"

We all face the flat-screen television, where a familiar-looking woman is sitting at the CNN anchor's desk, and there's a bright red-lettered crawl—BREAKING NEWS—and someone finally finds the remote and the woman's voice booms right out into the crowded hotel suite.

"...CNN has learned from two high-level federal law enforcement sources that Melanie Keating, the daughter of former president Matthew Keating, has been kidnapped while on a hike in the White Mountains of northwestern New Hampshire and that her male hiking companion was brutally murdered..."

CHAPTER 37

Monmouth, New Hampshire

Officer Corinne Bradford of the Monmouth Police Department pulls her ten-year-old town police cruiser into one of the reserved spots near the police station and switches off the engine. A few minutes ago, Chief Randy Grambler called her on her cell phone, asking her to come back to the station.

She wonders what's going on that the chief would want her to report in without putting anything out over the regular radio dispatch, and she's hoping it's something to do with the kidnapping of the president's daughter, Mel Keating.

Corinne steps out of the cruiser, metal clipboard under her arm, just as a state police cruiser roars by on Route 3, followed by a Grafton County sheriff's cruiser and two black Chevy Suburbans with flashing lights in the radiator grilles and windshield visors. Two Black Hawk helicopters are flying by to the south, up where Mount Rollins is, only about a twenty-minute drive from her new hometown.

She's still getting used to calling this place home. A year ago, she was living in Brockton, Massachusetts, had a great job with the Massachusetts State Police, until a series of scandals involving her troop—and not her directly, thank God—led to whole-scale reshuffling of the staties, leaving her dismissed and looking for a new job.

Which is now being one cop in a three-person department in the middle of the damn woods and mountains, headed by a local who's apparently been chief since the last ice age.

She walks to the side of the one-story white clapboard building with tall black window shutters; this marks the entire town government and police force of Monmouth, said force being in the rear basement. Corinne opens the sticky door and Chief Grambler is sitting behind a dull gray metal desk, his long legs outstretched. His six-foot-six frame is so gaunt he looks one meal away from fainting. He wears the same kind of dark blue uniform Corinne has, but on his, the knees and elbows are shiny from age.

He scribbles on a slip of paper and passes it to Corinne. Overhead pipes from the town hall's plumbing system rattle as someone on the first floor flushes a toilet. The department's cramped office contains two desks, chairs, filing cabinets, and cardboard boxes filled with old records from last century. There is no jail or holding cell. The few folks Corinne has picked up during her two months here have all been taken to the Grafton County jail over in Haverhill for processing.

"Here," Grambler says. "Go see Yvonne Clarkson, up on Mast Road. Number four. Somebody stole something from her this morning and she's pretty pissed about it."

Corinne takes the paper, thinking, *Are you kidding?* She learned from her very first day that the cops in this small town were called on for everything from a broken mailbox to a dog running loose and chasing someone's chickens.

"Okay," she says. "But why did you call me in? Reaching me through dispatch would have been quicker."

Grambler smiles, puts his hands behind his head, leans back so Corinne can hear both his chair and back creak. "Yvonne's been around for a while. Used to be a selectman and on the planning board. Lots of folks don't like her much, so why give the gossips with police scanners something to talk about?"

She glances at the address, folds the paper in half. "Anything new about Mel Keating's kidnapping?"

"Nope."

"You hear anything from the state police or the county sheriff?"

"Nope."

She squeezes the paper hard in her hand. When she was with the Massachusetts State Police, she twice took part in a security detail assisting the Secret Service during a presidential visit, and she loved the rush and buzz of being part of something bigger, something important.

"We could help with the search, you know," she says. "We could cover areas that—"

"Corinne, go do your job, all right?" Grambler says, picking up a copy of the *Union Leader*. "And your job is seeing Yvonne Clarkson. Go."

Later that day, she's spent twenty minutes in Yvonne Clarkson's cluttered and dusty living room, drinking warm iced tea made from concentrated powder, listening to the older woman's health complaints and political observations, before trying for the fourth time to steer the conversation to the reason for Corinne's visit.

"Ma'am, yes, I'll make sure to remember what you said about Dr. Yahn if I ever have foot surgery over at Dartmouth-

Hitchcock," she says. "But please. Can you tell me what happened this morning?"

The woman appears to be in her seventies, hair dyed black, with equally dark eyebrows, and she's wearing a loose yellow top and khaki shorts down to her wrinkled knees. Her toenails and fingernails are painted a bright red, matching her lipstick.

"Well, it's like this," she says, sighing with apparent frustration. "Monmouth has changed so much since I've lived here, ever since the college and medical center kept on expanding and expanding, forcing good locals out with the high property taxes and rents. Things happen that just shouldn't happen."

"Like what?" Corinne asks for at least the fourth time.

Yvonne Clarkson leans forward, her voice a whisper. "Theft. Actual stealing of one's private property. Used to be you could keep your doors unlocked, your trucks parked in the driveway with the keys in the ignition. No longer."

"And what was stolen?" Corinne asks.

"My morning newspaper, that's what," the woman says. "Can you believe it? Right out of the delivery tube!"

Corinne struggles to keep her face blank. She thinks, *When I was in Massachusetts, I responded to DUI accidents and saved at least two lives by performing immediate first aid. I've done four traffic stops resulting in the seizure of at least a hundred pounds of heroin, and once I provided a shift's worth of backup at an armed hostage situation in Melrose.*

"Your newspaper?" she asks.

"That's right," she says. "My *USA Today*. They've only just started home delivery in the area and those damn thieves took it this morning."

"Thieves?"

A triumphant nod. "I'm an early riser. I saw the little bastard—excuse my French—step out of a black SUV and pull it right out of the newspaper tube, easy as you please."

Corinne scribbles a few notes.

"You sure?"

"Positive," the woman says. "Two shitheads. One driving, one who stepped out and grabbed my paper. You think you can find them?"

Corinne tries not to sigh.

A stolen newspaper, a street value—try not to laugh!—of two bucks.

"Well, I'm sure we'll give it a go, but there's not much to go on. I mean, a guy and a black SUV."

Her lips purse. "You're from away, so you didn't know my uncle Caleb, did you?"

"No, ma'am," Corinne says, once again having to defend herself for the crime of being born in Massachusetts.

"He ran one of the biggest car dealerships in Manchester," Clarkson says. "Double-C Fine Autos. I worked summers there for many years, helping out, from typing to working in the parts department. I knew cars then, and I know cars now. I can tell you exactly what kind of SUV was in front of my house early this morning."

Corinne says, "What kind was it, then?"

A pleased nod. "This year's Cadillac Escalade. Black. With tinted windows."

CHAPTER 38

The Oval Office
The White House

When the curved door to the Oval Office silently opens, President Pamela Barnes gets up from behind the Resolute desk and approaches her predecessor, Matthew Keating, and his wife, Samantha. Both look worn and haunted, and Barnes has a brief memory of when she was governor and met with a delegation of parents who had lost their children to shootings. The two people in front of her have the same look on their wan faces.

"Matt, Samantha," Barnes says, striding forward. "I'm so sorry to hear what's happened to Mel, and trust me, we're doing everything possible to get her back safely."

Samantha Keating looks a bit dazed as she gingerly walks forward, but her husband looks as though he wants to kill someone, his eyes sharp and hard. Barnes remembers a bit of history: back when President William McKinley was assassinated, his good friend and power broker Senator Mark Hanna said about

Theodore Roosevelt, "That damned cowboy is president of the United States!"

Three years ago, she had the same reaction upon hearing of President Lovering's sudden death, and she said to her husband, "That damned sailor is now president!"

She tries to put all that behind her. She gives Samantha a quick hug, squeezes Matt's hand, leads them both to the two couches in the center of the Oval Office. Accompanying them are Lisa Blair, the director of the FBI, and Paul Charles, secretary of Homeland Security, along with Barnes's husband, Richard, and a young aide, Lydia Wang.

Matt and Samantha sit together on the couch across from Barnes, tightly holding hands, and she says, "I'm so sorry for what's happened to Mel, and I promise you both that the full strength and resources of the federal government are responding to safely locate her."

Yet the words her husband and chief of staff told her earlier stab at her:

Pamela, when you find out what they want for a ransom, you're going to say no.

Samantha nods at her soothing words but Matt gets right to it.

"Tell me what you're doing," he says.

Direct and to the point, without a single ounce of courtesy or politeness—*which is why this is my home now and not yours,* she thinks.

"Director Blair?" she says. "The latest?"

Blair sits forward on the cream-colored couch, hands clasped in front of her. "We're flooding the zone, Madam President, even pulling in agents from field offices in Canada. Our investigation is currently moving along two tracks. The first is talking to Mel's fellow students, friends, teachers, and dormitory residents, to see if anything unusual has been going on in the last few weeks.

Strangers hanging around the campus, asking questions about Mel, break-ins or unusual occurrences."

Barnes says, "What's the second track?"

"Trying to find her," Blair says. "We've taken the lead and we're working with the New Hampshire State Police and every local law enforcement agency up there, including Fish and Game personnel. Roadblocks are being set up on every minor and major road near Mount Rollins, and every home and business within a twenty-mile radius of the kidnapping scene is being investigated, residents and business owners being interviewed. We also have K-9 units moving along the more popular hiking trails in the area."

"How many border crossings into Canada are there?" Matt asks.

Homeland Security secretary Paul Charles seems surprised to be asked a question, and Barnes once again regrets the political deal that put him into his position. Like an old-time cop, he pulls out a tattered notebook, flips to a page, and says, "There's twenty-four between Maine and Canada, one in New Hampshire, and fifteen in Vermont. Our, uh, Border Patrol units are on alert. There's a tremendous backup in traffic leaving the States and going into Canada. I'm sure there won't be many complaints now, but Madam President, there's going to be a huge squawk if, um, we don't lighten up on those restrictions. And soon."

Before Matt can speak, Barnes says, "Not now, Paul, not now. What's the status of the Secret Service?"

He shrugs. "Not much." He tries a smile. "I mean, the proverbial horse is out of the barn, am I right? I mean, Mr. and Mrs. Keating are right here, their residence on Lake Marie is being protected, and Mel...well, I just want to make it clear now, before we go any further, that the Secret Service wasn't responsible for Mel Keating's protection. She was nineteen, and—"

Matt's voice, low and as cold as granite, says, "Nobody's blaming the Secret Service for anything. Madam President, may I?"

Barnes says, "Of course, Matt, go ahead."

"Madam President, there were recent court decisions impacting information sharing between the FBI and the NSA," he says. "Getting the NSA officially on board to assist the FBI will take time. Would you consider issuing directives and contacting General Winship at the NSA to immediately get their cooperation?"

Director Blair turns on the couch, looks at Barnes, nods. "That could save us some important hours, Madam President."

"Consider it done," she says, and continues, "Director Blair, can we—"

The door to the Oval Office quietly swings open and Felicia Taft, a young Black woman and deputy chief of staff, comes in, holding an open laptop in her hands.

Everyone in the room turns to her, and Barnes says, "What's going on, Felicia?"

She quickly comes to the center of the room, puts the open laptop on the coffee table.

"Madam President, we've just received a news alert from Al Jazeera," she says, nearly breathless. "They've received a ransom demand for Mel Keating, and plan to air it in one minute."

CHAPTER 39

The Oval Office
The White House

I'm still holding on to Sam's hand, but back in this familiar room, I feel slipped out of time, out of place. The last time I was here was a year and a half ago, in the waning hours of my presidency, and now I'm back, not as POTUS but as one angry and frightened father, half listening to the woman before me—a polished politician who's always found the proper meaning and phrasing to climb that slippery pole of political advancement—make the standard promises and vows.

I want to believe her, but I'm too experienced, too suspicious.

The men and women out there now, in the field, doing their very best to find Mel—I trust and believe in them.

But their superiors, the directors and bureaucrats with clean fingernails and stained consciences?

Not so much.

Out there in those government buildings are deals to be made, grudges to be maintained, and in this emerging crisis,

I know that some hard-hearted souls will be seeing this as an opportunity for their own advancement, and nothing else.

The laptop swivels around and I look at the screen and there's a male television anchor who's blabbing about Mel's kidnapping and the horror of it and the pain Sam and I must be feeling, and I ignore him, willing some producer out there in Doha, Qatar, to hurry the hell up.

Sitting on this couch with me are Sam and Lydia Wang, an assistant to the president. Across from us are the president, Director Blair, and Secretary Charles. The president's husband is standing behind her.

The anchor's face disappears.

A blue screen appears.

A clean-shaven man with an olive complexion and black hair appears in a white shirt neatly buttoned up to his neck. He's apparently sitting in front of a black cement wall. (*Good tradecraft,* the old operator in me thinks, *not giving out any identifying details from the background.*) The man nods, his face determined, his dark eyes sharp as flint, and his first sentence hits me like an M4 buttstock to the gut.

"I am Asim Al-Asheed, a warrior of Allah, and this is for you, Matthew Keating," he begins. "I have your daughter Melanie in my control."

Sam squeezes my hand and moans. "Oh, Matt, it's that..."

"Yes," I say. I'm not really thinking; the word comes out automatically. "That's the terrorist whose wife and daughters were killed because of me."

And that old operator voice whispers to me again.

No matter what is said or promised, you will never see Mel again.

I stare at the screen, keeping focused.

He pauses, and I know the bastard is doing so to stretch out the torment for Sam and me.

I stare, and it's like he's staring right at me.

"Your daughter is alive," he says. "She is well."

Then his voice lowers. "Unlike my dead girls, killed under your orders, your direction. Can you imagine the pain of a father, knowing that not only is his wife gone, but his girls as well, his cherished offspring?"

He seems to move his hands below the screen and then holds up three small color photographs showing young smiling girls with dark hair and curls, wearing bright clothes, and he says, "These are my loved ones. Amina, Zara, and Fatima. The ones burnt, crushed, and dismembered by you, Matthew Keating. Any reasonable father would seek revenge, would he not? Revenge for the death of his daughters?"

He brings up another photo, a woman in a black chador, but her plump and smiling face is visible.

"And my wife, Layla," Asim says. "A wonderful and pious companion and mother. You, Matthew Keating, you are fortunate: your wife is still alive. Sitting next to you at this moment, I am sure."

He lowers the photo.

He seems to take a breath. "As I have said, revenge would be a logical path, would it not? A reasonable one? But your daughter, Melanie, she is alive. I will prove it now."

The video dissolves into several seconds of a scared Mel, staring at the camera, eyes red-rimmed behind her glasses, hair disheveled, holding a copy of *USA Today.* I stare, make sure she's breathing, she's alive. All I see is her frightened yet defiant face and the paper under her chin.

Next to me Sam is sobbing.

The video dissolves back to Asim Al-Asheed.

"There. With today's newspaper, you can see she is currently alive and well. You, Matthew Keating, you killed my wife and my daughters. Here, I have proven to you that your daughter,

Melanie, is still alive. Tell me now: who is the true terrorist? The true killer? The true barbarian?"

Another pause.

The fucker is taunting me.

"You, Matthew Keating, have until noon tomorrow to fulfill the following demands."

I hear Richard Barnes whisper, "Oh, shit, here it comes," and Asim says, "By noon tomorrow, Eastern time, I will release Mel Keating, safe and unharmed, if these conditions are met.

"One. The release of the three fellow warriors who are currently being held in barbaric and inhumane conditions at your so-called super-max prison in Florence, Colorado: Ayaan al-Amin, Nawaf al-Khattab, and Arda al-Hadid."

Warriors, I furiously think and remember. Cold-blooded and happy killers who slaughtered scores of innocents across Europe and North Africa.

"These three men will be released from Florence and flown to an abandoned airstrip in Libya, coordinates twenty-eight degrees, twenty-four minutes, twelve seconds north, and thirteen degrees, ten minutes, and twenty-six seconds east. Any attempt to follow them or impede their journey will result in the death of Melanie Keating. This includes surveillance from your drones.

"Two. A ransom in the amount of one hundred million dollars in bitcoin to be paid within the next thirty-six hours. You will access a Tor browser and enter the following letters and numbers in its browser window"—Asim rattles off a series of letters and numbers—"and follow the instructions that appear. Failure to pay the ransom will result in the death of Melanie Keating."

I can feel Sam's body next to me, trembling and shaking.

"Three. A complete and full pardon from President Pamela Barnes for any and all crimes I may or may not have committed against Americans in the United States or abroad."

He gives a knowing and pleased smile at that last one.

"If the pardon is not made and published, you certainly know what happens next."

He pauses, staring right into the center of the camera lens.

"Matthew Keating," he says. "Now, at last, you have a hint, the briefest taste of what you did to me years ago."

He smiles. "Until we perhaps meet, Matthew Keating, *ma'al-salāmah.*"

The video goes blank. The Al Jazeera anchor reappears. The Oval Office is silent, and I break the silence.

"That damn fool," I say. "He's just made a huge mistake."

CHAPTER 40

The Oval Office
The White House

All in the Oval Office turn to me, and I see the barest look of irritation on President Barnes's face because this is her space, and now everyone's paying attention to me.

"Matt," she says. "Go on."

I say, "He just made it easier for us to find him, by a magnitude. Where would we be if he had just sent out an email listing his demands, with the photo of Mel attached? We wouldn't know who he was, who was behind the kidnapping, or anything else. Now we do. Director Blair and every other intelligence agency of ours can start walking back the cat. Am I right, Director Blair?"

The FBI director says, "Absolutely right, Mr. President."

President Barnes says, "Explain what that phrase means, please," and her husband and chief of staff adds in deference, "Just to ensure we're all on the same page."

Director Blair says, "Walking back the cat means that now

that we know who's behind Mel Keating's kidnapping and he's supplied us with a photo, we can reexamine message traffic, photos, border crossings. Pick up his trail. Find out who his associates are and where they're located. Start running down leads. Mr. President, Madam President, this is very good news."

There's a murmur of voices and Director Blair says, "Mr. President, I need to ask you and your wife some questions."

Samantha nods and I say, "Go."

"Have either of you received threatening notes or phone calls recently?"

"No," I say.

"No," my wife says.

"Any unexpected visitors or strangers at your lakefront home?"

"No," I say.

Director Blair is about to resume speaking when I say, "Ask the same question of my wife."

"Sir?"

In a bleak voice, Samantha says, "For the past few months, I've been in Hitchcock, Maine, conducting an archaeological dig. No one's bothered me, there've been no threatening notes or emails, and no unexpected visitors."

I can feel her trembling.

Director Blair says, "If I may, Madam President, I need to get back to my offices. We're setting up a task force there and at our field office in Manchester."

"Director, whatever you need, whenever you need it, you call me and you'll get it," Barnes says.

The FBI director starts moving away from the couches, joined by a quiet Secretary Charles, and I say, "What about your daily brief, Madam President?"

She stares right at me, her gaze hard and cold, just like it was the day in this very office when she told me she was going to challenge me in our party's primaries.

"I don't know what you're talking about, Matt."

I try to be cautious, stepping through this minefield. I've just embarrassed the leader of the free world in front of others, and that's just not acceptable.

"I received word this morning that the daily brief was going to contain information about an increase in terrorist chatter, indicating an attack was in the planning stages," I say. "An attack against me."

Barnes's husband and chief of staff doesn't hesitate for a moment. "Who told you that?"

I say, "At this point, Richard, that doesn't matter, does it? What matters is that the intelligence agencies received indications of an attack upon me. That should be something that Director Blair is made aware of."

The president says, "Agreed. I'll make sure it happens."

Director Blair says, "Thank you, ma'am," and heads to the door, followed by Secretary Charles, Lydia Wang, and Felicia Taft, holding the laptop. Then a voice surprises me, and I think it surprises everyone in the room.

"You fools," my wife, Samantha, says. "It's staring you right in your collective faces, and you can't see it. Every one of you is wrong, including you, Matt."

I'm struck by her sharp words and know enough from experience to keep my mouth shut.

But Chief of Staff Richard Barnes never learned the lesson.

"What the hell do you mean, *wrong?*" he demands, hands on the back of the couch where his wife is sitting. "What can you possibly see that no one else can?"

A few times I've sat in on Samantha's classes, and I observed that there's a color to her face and a set to her jaw when she's about to cut someone off at the knees.

Like now.

"Everything, you damn fool," she says, strong voice not wavering. "You're all looking at this like it's some goddamn standard terrorist kidnapping with a standard terrorist demand." She takes a breath. "Idiots. Asim isn't making demands of the United States government. Replay the message. Asim is making demands of Mel Keating's dad. He's putting incredible pressure on my husband because he wants to make Matt suffer, he wants Matt to overthink, and most of all he wants Matt to be fearful. He wants to give Matt a taste of what it's like, knowing you're powerless to defend your family."

The Oval Office is silent, and even Director Blair and Secretary Charles have halted mid-stride across the light yellow carpet with the president's seal in the center; they're paying attention to my wife.

Samantha looks around at each and every one and says, "He wants Matt to be afraid. Not just afraid of what Asim might do to"—Samantha's voice breaks for a moment—"our daughter. No, he wants Matt to also be afraid of his government, the people he now has to trust explicitly to fulfill these demands to get Mel released. Matt is no longer the president. He has no power, no authority. So my question to all of you fine people in this room…Should Matt be afraid of you as well?"

CHAPTER 41

Monmouth, New Hampshire

Less than a half hour after the hostage tape for Mel Keating was released, Officer Corinne Bradford finds her boss sitting in a booth at his second office, Karl's Diner. His long legs extend to the middle of the tiled floor, and as Corinne approaches him, she sees that he's holding court with two older women and an older man. The three booth mates are Monmouth old-timers and are, respectively, a selectman, a planning board member, and a stringer who writes copy for the statewide *Union Leader* and a couple of local weeklies.

They smirk and smile as Corinne gets closer, and she briefly wonders what kind of stories about her Chief Grambler passes along to the townies, because folks from away are always good fun for those who can trace their families back to the first settlers who reached this valley in 1785.

One of the women stands up, taking one big messy slurp from

her coffee, and says, "Chief, looks like Corinne's pretty hair is on fire. Guess we'll leave her be with you."

There are murmurs of "Thanks" and "See you later," and Corinne sits down across from the chief. "Hungry?" he says.

"No, not really, Chief," she says. "I found out—"

"Coffee?" he asks. "There's always room for some caffeine. Mary! A fresh mug over here, okay?"

Corinne grimaces, again hating those Massachusetts State Police officers who screwed the pooch so hard that it propelled her here to a job with a third more hours and half of her pay and working for a chief who thinks progress in policing ended in 1932.

"Chief, did you hear the news about the ransom message for Mel Keating?"

"Damn," he says, glancing back at the television hanging from the stained ceiling over the lunch counter, always turned to Fox News. "All I've heard about the last hour is about that bug-eyed little brat. A day from now, you'll see that it's all been a setup. A hoax." A fresh cup of coffee is placed before him by a teen waitress, her pregnant belly nearly bursting the buttons on her pink uniform.

Chief Grambler takes a sip, nods in pleased satisfaction, and says, "In other words, fake news."

Any other time, Corinne would shoot back at the chief's ignorance, but this isn't any other time. She pulls out her iPhone, flips through a couple of screens, and rotates it in front of his red fleshy face. "See?" Corinne asks. "That's the photo of Mel Keating that her kidnapper released today, her holding the current *USA Today.* And before that was announced, I was over at Yvonne Clarkson's house, just like you wanted. And she told me that early this morning, her *USA Today* was taken from her newspaper delivery tube by a guy driving an Escalade."

The chief takes another sip of coffee, looking bored. "Dear me."

"Chief, don't you see it? There's a nationwide BOLO out for a black Escalade, and the guy who steals Yvonne's newspaper, he was driving an Escalade!"

"Gosh, Corinne, that sure sounds like what we in law enforcement circles call a *clue*," he says cheerfully, and then his mood changes. "So what? You start working this, going down this rabbit hole, putting in for OT while ignoring your real duties, how would that look to the selectmen? And you think anybody from the Feds is gonna step up to compensate the town?"

"But Chief, at least we could—"

A firm shake of the head, another sip from his coffee. "And no, you're not going over my head to call the FBI or the Secret Service. They always ignore us or call us rubes when we look for their help. Screw 'em."

Corinne's face feels as though it's burning, and she's hoping no one in the near booths can see or sense her humiliation.

"But this is what you can do, and what you're gonna do," he says. "Get in your cruiser and go park at the old Esso station lot just off Exit 16. Lots of flatlander reporters and Feds are screaming up I-89 to get to this part of the world. Run radar. Nice chance to grab some ticket revenue and make me, the selectmen, and the taxpayers happy. Got it?"

Corinne doesn't bother to argue, knowing that this thick piece of granite sitting across from her won't change his mind.

"Yes, Chief," she says.

"Good," he says. "About time you got some more real police work under that wide belt of yours."

Later that day, after driving past Yvonne Clarkson's house and the Huntsmen trailhead a few times, Corinne Bradford is driving along the Upper Valley Road, keeping an eye on things, knowing she's about fifteen miles away from Exit 16 and not really giving a shit.

Here the Upper Valley Road merges onto Route 113, and up ahead is what locally is considered urban sprawl: a McDonald's, a Burger King, an Irving gas station, and a Citizens Bank branch, with a drive-up window parallel to the road.

Corinne makes a sudden decision and pulls into the bank parking lot.

Nine minutes later she's in the office of Jackie Lynch, the branch manager, who's sitting at her desk while the two of them watch CCTV footage from the bank's drive-up window.

Jackie is slim and hard-faced, with closely cropped blond hair. Each of her ears bears about a half dozen small earrings, and she's wearing a charcoal-gray suit. She rubs on the surface of her shiny desk with one hand and says, "You know, I'm really putting my job on the line here by not going through the proper channels and having you come back with a warrant."

Corinne says, "I know, Jackie, and it's all on me. The department appreciates your cooperation. But I'm running down a tip concerning the kidnapping of Mel Keating. Time is of the essence."

"Well…I guess that makes it all right."

Corinne is staring at the black-and-white images of the drive-up window, seeing a Volkswagen Beetle pull up, the drawer slide out, an English springer spaniel crawling over the male driver's lap, seeking a treat and—

She's ignoring all that.

Looking at the road.

Not much traffic.

A white van speeds by.

A yellow school bus.

Quiet.

Pickup truck, followed by another pickup truck, and—

Corinne nearly shouts, "Stop the recording, right there. Now!"

Jackie's fingers hit the keyboard.

Freezing in place a black Cadillac Escalade with tinted windows passing by.

She checks the time.

Assuming the newspaper was stolen by the men in the Escalade, they headed north to Huntsmen Trail, kidnapped Mel Keating, and now—newspaper and Mel in their SUV—they continued north.

The timing makes sense.

Corinne's heart seems to seize up with excitement.

"Jackie," she says, "can you print this screenshot out for me?"

Jackie's fingers move again on the keyboard. "Is this something, Officer Bradford?"

Corinne says, "I think so. I certainly think so."

CHAPTER 42

Chinatown
New York, New York

Jiang Lijun of the Ministry of State Security, who has been officially accredited with his government's mission to the United Nations, is sitting on a bench in Columbus Park off Mulberry Street. Next to him is a heavyset and sweating associate professor at John Jay College of Criminal Justice, and Jiang is in the process of destroying this pathetic man's life and enjoying every minute of it.

Jiang's wife, Zhen, has a distant cousin who is a performer with the Chinese Acrobatic Theater, and Jiang has always been fascinated with the man's expertise on a tightrope. Although he would never say it aloud to Zhen, Jiang has always thought the two of them—Jiang and her cousin—were similar in their professions: walking carefully high in the air, balancing themselves against abrupt changes or gusts of wind.

And that's what Jiang is doing at this moment: walking high in the air, with no safety net. His meet with this large man is supposed to be a negotiation about him passing along information about his classmates during his future attendance at the FBI's National Academy.

But Jiang is taking a gamble, squeezing this man, going further than his precise instructions. Maneuvering and working one's way at the ministry takes an iron will and the resolve to gamble at the right time, and in the sunlight in this small New York park, Jiang knows it's time.

The associate professor of law, police science, and criminal justice administration used to be a deputy police commissioner in New York, and he wrings his large hands together again, his thin brown hair damp with sweat and pasted to his large forehead, his oversize tan suit ill-fitting.

"It was an accident, that's all," he says for the fifth time. "After I broke my ankle, I just couldn't stand the pain…and with the opioid crackdown…I didn't mean for it to get out of hand."

Jiang gingerly pats the man's strong shoulder, feeling as though he's petting a dumb ox, and says, "Of course you didn't want it to get this far. But you paid big money for other sources, illegal sources. To the point of nearly one hundred thousand dollars. One hundred thousand dollars you embezzled from those Department of Justice grants you received."

The associate professor groans and says, "Please, please stop reminding me."

That's my job, you fool, Jiang thinks. He says, "But you've agreed to my proposition, right? We arrange for you to confidentially receive funds so you can make amends, and you can blame the temporary funding gap on an accounting error. In exchange, when you attend the FBI academy in Quantico, Virginia, this fall and get briefed on that new software program called MOGUL, you'll pass on all of that information to me or an associate. And my superiors in Taipei will be very grateful."

The former NYPD cop looks up at him, tears in his eyes. "But why can't you get that information through regular channels?"

Jiang smiles. The stupid fool next to him thinks Jiang is an intelligence operative with that damn breakaway province, Taiwan. Which is why he always meets his contacts in Chinatown: even though all deny it, to the officials of the CIA and FBI and the NYPD counterterrorism division, all Chinese look the same.

Even to this former NYPD cop.

Jiang says, "Beijing has a hold on this nation and the UN and so many of its states. We're small, only miles away from millions of Communists, and we must do what we can to protect ourselves. You do understand, right?"

A slow nod. "Yeah. I do. My granddad, he lost a foot at the Chosin Reservoir, fighting off those damn Chicoms. I understand real well."

Such understanding. Jiang's uncle Bohai is a commander with the Ministry of Public Security in Beijing and a student of Daosim, and when Jiang was younger, Bohai taught him the teachings from *Sage Emperor Guan's Book of Enlightenment.* For one, "It is through filial piety, sibling harmony, dedication, trustworthiness, propriety, sacrifice, honor, and sense of shame that we become fully human."

This blubbering man next to him, once a prominent police official for this city of more than eight million, definitely never learned the subjects of propriety, honor, or even trustworthiness.

Which is why Jiang has found it so easy to control him.

For he is not fully human.

Another pat to this ox's shoulder as Jiang's iPhone vibrates in his jacket pocket. Jiang stands up and says, "I'll be in contact with you at the right time. In the meantime…you're a smart man. I don't need to explain to you what will happen if you back out of our agreement. Right?"

He starts to say, "But it was all a mistake, I didn't mean to…"

But Jiang is strolling away from the pathetic man, checking the text on his iPhone, seeing the simple message.

PLEASE DON'T BE LATE FOR LUNCH

He quickens his steps.

To get from Columbus Park to the Permanent Mission of the People's Republic of China to the United Nations, located on East 35th Street, is normally only a fifteen-minute taxi ride, but it takes Jiang nearly an hour to get there due to the various bits of tradecraft he uses known as the SDR (surveillance detection route). During those nearly sixty minutes spent traveling to East 35th Street, he has shed his jacket, put on a baseball cap with a long bill, and wiped off some makeup that darkened his face.

Now he is in the basement office of his superior, Li Baodong, in a concrete cube with no windows and no outlets that would allow any sort of entry from any intelligence agency or corporate security service looking to gain information. The room is warm and carpeted, with fake plants, locked filing cabinets, and Li, who is well over 250 pounds and seems to thrive in this environment.

He wears a white shirt—sweated through at the armpits—a red necktie, and black trousers, and his chubby face is plump and full, highlighted by slicked-back black hair and gold-rimmed glasses.

Among the other intelligence personnel at the mission,

Li is known as *Pàng mógū*—fat mushroom—because of how much he thrives in the basement, but his fat and happy face conceals a razor-sharp mind and attitude that has sent several underperforming intelligence officers to exile in Chad or upper Canada.

He says, "How did your meet go today?"

Jiang sits in a cool leather chair before Li's desk, steeling himself for what his boss may say next. "The man was crumbling. I decided to push him."

"How?"

"I took a gamble. I told him that we would give him the money to pay for his embezzlement, and in return, he'd give us information on that new software program, MOGUL."

Li slowly blinks behind his glasses. "That's not what you were supposed to do."

Jiang stares at him, thinking, *One of these days, I will have your job because you're too fat to be out in the field and doing what has to be done to protect the Middle Kingdom.*

Jiang says, "There was an opportunity. I took it. It will pay off for us."

"But what if he goes to the FBI and confesses all?"

"The jackass thinks I'm working for the *tái bāzi,* and if he confesses—which I entirely doubt, sir—any blowback will be against Taipei. Not us."

Li says, "That was dangerous."

"The odds are in our favor."

"Perhaps," Li says. "You are certainly one for *bào dàtuǐ,* I will give you that."

Bào dàtuǐ, Jiang thinks, *to cling to someone's lap.* In other words, to curry favor.

But Li is wrong.

Jiang is not currying favor with his boss.

He's setting him up to be replaced at the right time.

Li says, "Any other place, comrade, I'd be reprimanding you for exceeding your authority, but I don't have the time. Something has broken in the news today that will involve you. The daughter of the president has been kidnapped."

Jiang says, "I thought the old bitch was barren."

Li shakes his head. "No, not her. The previous president. Keating. His teen girl was kidnapped."

Jiang is confused, a feeling he hates. "How does this involve me?"

"The thug taking credit for kidnapping the girl is Asim Al-Asheed," Li says, peering down at a sheet of paper on his desk next to a secure computer terminal. "He was an asset of ours for a period of time in Libya, correct? And controlled by you?"

Asim, Jiang thinks. *A capable warrior who gladly accepted assistance from foreigners, but who was a devil to control.* There are several achievements in his life that Jiang is proud of, and getting out of Libya and not having to meet face-to-face again with that barbarian is one of them.

Asim is only a tool, that is it. Also, definitely not fully human.

"Yes, of course," Jiang says. "He helped us settle differences among various tribes for a number of our pipeline projects and drilling expeditions. Where there was competition and chaos, Asim brought peace in the district so our work would not be interrupted."

His superior purses his fat lips. "'Settle differences.' Fine choice of words. Well, he has a difference with President Keating and kidnapped his daughter this morning, somewhere in their province of New Hampshire, near that college. Dartmouth."

Jiang stays silent. He has nothing to offer, so there is no chance he will say anything troubling.

Bùzuō bú huì sǐ. You will not get into trouble if you do not seek trouble.

Li sighs. "Do you have means of contacting this Asim Al-Asheed?"

Jiang thinks furiously. The easy answer would be to say no, for he dreads the thought of once again entering that barbarian's world, where a slight or a difference in religious thought could result in a slit throat, but Jiang hasn't gotten this far by doing the easy things.

Avenging Father and hurting the nation that killed him means taking risks, and this is only the newest risk to face.

"Yes," he says. "I do."

Li nods, turns over a sheet of paper. "Then do so. Negotiations and other talks with the Americans over trade, technology, and military relations are frozen. Beijing is seeking any chance or opportunity to break this jam with the Americans and gain an advantage. Every bit of pressure and counteraction against them hasn't produced the results Beijing wants. Working to secure the former president's daughter's safe return will do just that. It will make us heroes in the eyes of the world and, most importantly, to their simple people."

Jiang says, "I see. I am to contact Asim Al-Asheed and do what I can to get the daughter released."

Li's fat face flushes. "No, you will not. You will meet *personally* with this Asim creature, and convince him one way or another to release that girl. Understood? Beijing demands it. And so do I."

With years of practice, Jiang keeps his face emotionless and bland. He is thinking of these orders but is also remembering something else. Being on that windswept runway as a child back in May 1999 with his mourning mother, receiving the formal box containing the ashes of Father, killed by American bombs, and vowing then and there to dedicate his life to opposing the Americans.

Even if it means disobeying a direct order like this, and

not lifting a finger to prevent the death of the former president's kidnapped daughter. Anything to hurt and embarrass this nation.

"I do understand," Jiang smoothly lies, getting up from his seat. "I'll get right to work."

CHAPTER 43

◆

The Oval Office
The White House

After the curved door to the Oval Office closes, leaving the four of them alone, Samantha Keating looks at the angry faces of President Barnes and Barnes's husband, the chief of staff, and says, "Well? Anybody want to answer my question? Do Matt and I have anything to fear?"

With anger in his voice, Richard Barnes says, "Mrs. Keating, with all due respect, I can't believe you've just said that!"

"Richard," she says, feeling her face warm, "you and I and everyone else in this room have gone through the fires, the double-talk, the betrayals, to get here. We all have a lot more in common than we like to admit. There are no innocents here. What I asked was a legitimate question. Can you answer it?"

She takes a breath. The memories of her time in this horrid place, the compromises, the arguments, the betrayals, are coming up to the surface. She tried so very hard to bury it all when she walked out of here two Januarys ago. Before her are the man and woman who years back chose to betray the trust of her husband, and to force him out of office.

It all comes back.

Samantha continues, "For the past year and a half, I've been back in the real world, working with students who worry about their loans, their grades, and how they'll get a job after they graduate. It's been refreshing as hell, being among people who don't care about polls, focus groups, and who's up over someone else. I can trust them. Can Matt and I trust you?"

President Barnes leans forward and, with a soft voice, says, "Samantha, please believe me when I say this: the entire force of the federal government is going to work as one to find Mel and bring her back safely."

Matt squeezes Samantha's hand but stays quiet.

Samantha says, "All right, then." She keeps her voice controlled. "Despite my detours into politics, at heart I'm just a college professor. I don't deal with speculation. Only facts. And I wanted it out here, in this room, that, despite the efforts of that son of a bitch Asim Al-Asheed, Matt and I have nothing to fear from this administration."

The president's husband and chief of staff says, "No bullshit, Mrs. Keating. You and your husband should have no concerns. We have this. We won't let you down. I give you my word."

She nearly has to bite her tongue, and then shakes her head. "Your word." She looks up at him. "All right, Richard. Your word it is."

Something in his eyes tells her she's struck home, and a memory from more than two years ago comes to her, like an old nightmare that just won't die, even in the middle of a sunlit day.

At that time, she was working late in her offices in the East Wing when an unexpected visitor came by, ushered in by her chief of staff, June Walters, whom Samantha knows was secretly rooting for Matt's vice president to defeat him at the upcoming convention. Her visitor had made himself known at a Secret Service kiosk at the northeast gate, and once his name had been passed along to Samantha, she made the necessary arrangements.

She smiled at seeing the familiar young man come in, dressed casually in jeans, dark green T-shirt, and short leather jacket. Samantha got up from behind her disorganized desk—she had been trying to juggle her own schedule and the ravenous needs of the Committee to Reelect Matthew Keating—and offered a hand.

"Carl," she said. "What a nice surprise."

"Thanks, professor," Carl Sanchez said, taking a chair after giving her hand a brief shake. When she was teaching at Stanford, he had been one of her smartest and most capable grad students, and she had written one of her best letters of recommendation for him when he graduated.

Samantha waved a hand and went back to her desk and said, "Not a professor at the moment, Carl. I'm the First Lady of the nation…and most days, I wish I was back in California. And you? Please tell me you're at some school, teaching freshmen and overseeing a dig somewhere."

Carl shook his head. "Didn't work out, professor…er, Mrs. Keating."

"Please," she said. "Enough time has passed. It's Samantha."

A knowing shrug. "You know how it is. Too many applicants, too few openings, colleges cutting back on salaries, pouring money into administrators and fancy dining halls. Taught a few semesters as an adjunct, and at my last job, I was living in the back of my car and taking showers at the gym. Decided then to make a career change and started working for my uncle. He runs a security firm. Good pay, nice bennies, some travel."

Samantha recalled the great papers and projects Carl had

produced back at Stanford, focusing on the forgotten history of overlooked Native American tribes from Siskiyou County, and she thought, *What a shame.*

"And now?"

He said, "I won't waste your time, profess…er, Samantha. It's like this. A few months ago, I was in Macau, overseeing the update of a security system my uncle's company had installed at a new hotel and casino there, the Golden Palace Macau. Very high priced, designed for what they call whales, high rollers."

Samantha saw a nervous flicker in Carl's eyes, but like a good teacher who knew her student was about to say something important, she kept her mouth closed. "Go on," was all she said.

Carl rubbed both hands on his legs, drew a deep breath. "I was working in the security ops center at two in the morning, drinking lousy coffee, trying to debug a system, and keeping an eye on some of the CCTV feeds. I mean, those whales and others that can afford portable jamming systems don't know their systems don't work with what the Chinese have in their back pockets."

Samantha said, "What did you see?"

"Someone I shouldn't have seen."

"Who?"

He glanced around her cluttered office, as if he couldn't look her in the eye.

"The vice president's husband. That cowboy from Florida. The one who sold some of his farmland a while back for a casino."

"Richard Barnes?"

Carl looked down at the carpet. "Yeah. But he wasn't alone…it was, uh, well, okay, I don't want to say it aloud. He wasn't by himself. Do you see what I mean? Something…that's illegal in most countries."

Samantha felt as though all the coffee she'd drunk to keep her awake was about to crawl out of her churning stomach.

Carl stood up. "He's…I don't like him. And I don't like his wife. And I don't like what they're both doing to your husband. That's not right."

He reached into his pocket, took out a small rectangular piece of black plastic, gently put it on top of a pile of papers. "This is for you."

Samantha stared at it as if it were a scorpion or some other stinging insect.

"What's that, Carl?"

He started to leave her office. "That's a thumb drive, with a recording of the vice president's hubby over in Macau, thousands of miles away from his wife and his country, thinking he can't possibly get caught…and Professor Keating, use that video at the right time, and your husband can't lose. I erased the source recording, so the Chinese don't have it. Only you."

He slipped out of her office and she didn't say a word, just stared at that little piece of metal and plastic.

Outside the Oval Office, she's walking with Matt down one of the historic and well-furnished hallways in this place that was once their home, and she says, "Matt, I'm sorry I lost it back there."

Matt takes her hand, holds it tight. Around them are Secret Service agents, staff members to this administration, and as she stiffly walks down this familiar corridor, she whispers, "Oh, Matt…where is she?"

One thing she learned a long time ago is to never, ever let them—including your own staff—see you sweat or lose your cool in public because gossip and leaks can get out there to the media and the ravenous blogs. Nevertheless, she wipes at her eyes with her free hand and the tears just erupt.

Within a second, Matt is hugging her hard, and she buries her face in his shoulder, and the tears really flow as she's thinking that her daughter—their girl!—is being held by a monster who can kill with such ease and pleasure.

Matt whispers, "Thousands of people across the country, Sam, are looking for Mel right now. We're not alone. We're going to get her back. I promise. We're going to get her back."

And she slips and whispers, "Oh, Matt, it's my fault... my fault."

He gently breaks free, strokes her hair, kisses her forehead, and says, "Sam, it's not your fault. How can you say that? It's not your fault."

She bites her lower lip and peers over his shoulder, noticing the staff and Secret Service doing their best not to look at them, and thinks, *But it is my fault, Matt. I had the key to your reelection win in my hand, the thumb drive with Richard Barnes's perversions recorded, and I didn't use it.*

I couldn't use it.

And I wouldn't use it.

Samantha wipes at her eyes, tries to smile at her strong and troubled husband.

"I know, it's just... so much."

But she's thinking, *No, back then, Matt, I didn't want you to win. I wanted to leave this horrible town and build a new life for us, and it's my fault you didn't win reelection. If you had won, we'd still be here in the White House with all the protection, and Mel would be safe.*

"All right?" Matt asks with concern.

She nods, tears still in her eyes. "Enough. Let's get back to the hotel."

CHAPTER 44

Northwestern New Hampshire

Mel Keating is sitting on the edge of her well-made bed in her concrete cell, ready to escape, ready to humiliate her kidnappers.

Her first meal of the day was some sort of chicken and rice dish, served on a paper plate with a spoon and a red plastic cup of water.

But when she sipped the water, she found that her kidnappers had accidentally given her two plastic cups, one nestled in the other.

She slipped out the spare cup and hid it under her bedding and was sitting politely and quietly when the younger man—called Faraj—came in to pick up the dishes.

A mistake.

They gave her something extra, and she is going to use that to her advantage.

She remembers again the briefing she received from Agent

Stahl during those weird busy few weeks when she and Mom and Dad moved into the White House.

Secret Service agent David Stahl was sitting in a plain wooden chair in her new bedroom at the White House and said with a quiet yet firm voice, “And another thing, Mel. If you’re kidnapped, the first hours are the most important.”

“Why’s that?” she asked, still trying to grasp that this was all real, that she was no longer living at the Naval Observatory with Mom and Dad, that Dad was really the president, and now she was living in the White House.

Unbelievable!

Agent Stahl said, “The first few minutes, the first few hours—it’s a time of flux. Your captors will be nervous, high-strung, trying to adjust to what they’ve just done. That’s when you should grab any chance to escape. A day or two later, they’ve settled into a routine, they’ve set up the watch schedule, you’re their prisoner. It’ll be too late by then. The first few hours…that’s your gift. Use it.”

She nodded, scared by what he was saying but still trying to take it all in.

She was now the president’s daughter.

“Mel,” Agent Stahl said. “Any questions?”

“No,” she said. “Not now.”

He smiled. “Don’t worry. The chances of this happening are infinitesimally small. But it’s good to be prepared.”

She wanted to laugh or joke at the thought of being kidnapped, but the hard look in that Secret Service agent’s eyes—so much like Dad’s!—kept her mouth shut.

Mel hears the door being unlocked, takes a breath, takes her glasses off with one hand and again rubs her eyes hard, pinches at her cheeks, gets the tears rolling.

The glasses go back on with her free hand.

Be prepared, she remembers.

The first few hours... that's your gift. Use it.

The door swings open and it's the younger of the two again, Faraj. He steps in, holding a yellow plastic tray with a covered dish and another red plastic cup. He's dressed in jeans and a checked flannel shirt, and a holstered pistol is at his right side.

He steps toward her, and Mel coughs, chokes, and does her best to start crying, saying, "Please... I'm so scared... Won't you let me free? Please? I'll make sure my daddy gives you a reward!"

Faraj sneers at her, and Mel thinks, *Just two more steps, two more steps, and I'll wipe that damn sneer off your face, jerk.*

Faraj Al-Asheed comes closer to the weeping little baby girl and thinks, *What a spoiled brat, what a fool.* Her entire pleasured life is ahead of her and she cries like someone who has lost a dolly. Her life has been pampered and safe, no worries of missed meals or thirst or ragged clothes or the sudden explosion of a bomb falling from the sky.

And for him? Once, years ago, Faraj had a chance to escape the squabbling militias and tribes around Tripoli, and he went to Paris and through luck and connections actually spent two semesters on scholarship at film school, at the École Internationale de Création Audiovisuelle et de Réalisation, learning filmmaking and special effects and wanting to create movies and—

Faraj says, "Stop crying, little girl. Your—"

She stands up and tosses some liquid in his eyes, burning them.

Mel yells, "I'm not a little girl!" as she tosses the foul liquid in the red plastic cup, a mixture of the chemical fluid in the toilet and—ugh!—her own pee, at the creep's face, but the stuff works, as the man yelps and drops the tray and stumbles back. Mel doesn't hesitate and tosses a hard kick right into the kidnapper's crotch.

He yelps something sharp in Arabic, doubles over, and Mel tugs the 9mm pistol out of his holster.

"Don't move!" she yells as she tries to go around him to that beautiful open door, but the jerk moves forward, trying to block her.

I warned you, she thinks as she pulls the hammer back on the pistol and smoothly and quickly pulls the trigger.

CHAPTER 45

Northwestern New Hampshire

The click of the hammer snapping down on the pistol stuns Mel, and with practiced ease, from many trips to the range with her dad, she quickly works the action of the pistol, trying to clear any possible jam, and once again—

Click.

Faraj stands up, grinning, eyes half closed, and he tugs at the hem of his flannel shirt, brings it up to wipe at his eyes, and Mel throws the useless pistol at that smiling bastard, slips past his hands, and—

Bumps right into Asim Al-Asheed.

He seizes her throat with a strong right hand, starts squeezing.

Mel can't breathe.

Can't scream.

She flails at his arms and strong chest and face, and he comes back into her cell, pushes her down on the bed.

Mel gasps, chokes, and brings her hands up to her pained throat.

A bout of coughing doubles her over, and the fake tears from earlier are replaced by real ones.

Asim stands over her and, in a slow and menacing tone, says, "Stupid child, do you really think I would allow my cousin in here with a loaded weapon? Do you?"

Faraj is standing next to Asim, smiling though his eyes are reddened.

Asim says, "We know so much about you, how you were raised, how you were taught. We know you are not uncomfortable around firearms. We know you lied earlier. Having my cousin appear to be armed was a…ploy. Yes, a ploy, to give you hope, to make you feel like you had a chance, and it worked. Now you know, Mel Keating, deep within everything inside of you, that you cannot escape, that you will never escape, and that you belong to us, in life or death."

The tears come quicker, and Mel has to look away.

"Forever," he says.

Asim says a few words in Arabic and Faraj returns with a metal folding chair. Asim sits down, giving Mel Keating a good steady look. He is pleased at how well everything has proceeded, pleased at how well his plan has worked out. At some point she was going to try to grab Faraj's pistol and escape. He's just a bit surprised at how quickly she has done it.

Mel stops weeping, takes her glasses off, rubs at her eyes, and then stares at Asim.

Not with fear.

Or sadness.

But with defiance.

Seeing this young girl's determined face stabs at him, reminds him of his oldest daughter, Amina, who is—was!—nearly this girl's age. There is nothing the same about them, from their hair to their complexions, but the fierceness in their eyes…Amina was a good daughter, and always one to obey her mother and help in the kitchen and with the laundry, but there was always a simmering defiance in those eyes.

Like in those of this young lady in front of him, in his possession.

Asim says, "Why do you think you are here?"

Mel folds her arms. "You like blond chicks?"

He restrains himself, for hearing those words makes him want to slap that face hard, leave a bruise on a cheek, a split lip, blood trickling down.

Asim says, "Because you're a prisoner of war, that is why. A war that has been going on for centuries."

Mel shrugs. "What, you're going to give me a lecture on the clash of civilizations, West versus East, Islam versus Christianity? The works of Samuel Huntington, pro and con? Please. I've heard it before, from professionals who know a hell of a lot more about it than you."

Asim clenches his fists. "Academics. Weak men. Book learners. I knew them well when I was your age and was at university, before jihad called me away. What do they know about war?"

"War?" the president's daughter snaps back. "Some war you've got there. Beheading innocents. Blowing up shopping malls. Taking a machine gun out and shooting up a street in Paris. I'm sure years from now poets will be singing the praises of your courage, facing the unarmed and the crying children."

"What do you know of war?" he says, struggling to keep his voice even.

"Plenty," she says. "Or have you already forgotten who my dad is, and what he did before becoming a congressman?"

"Your father," Asim spits out. "You talk about brave warriors. He and his ilk, heavily armed, connected to the Internet, being able to view a battleground thanks to your satellites and surveillance drones...what chance do any warriors such as myself have against such overwhelming technology and arms?"

The young girl with the reddened eyes doesn't waver. "Setting fire to a day care center, killing children who barely know how to walk and speak. That's some warrior."

Asim says, "Yes, as grim as it is, it is a warrior's action. Look to yourself, look to your father, when he was president. When a drone is fired and misses a target, and obliterates a wedding party, how long do you mourn for the innocents, how much do you demand an investigation into what happened? Or if a scared American soldier in a foreign land faces an approaching van that doesn't stop in time, and he machine-guns the father and mother and children inside, how much do you care? No, Mel Keating, you and the rest of your people just shrug your shoulders, go to your cell phone screens, and don't pay it any attention."

She starts to reply, but Asim talks over her, waving a hand about the concrete cell. "Such a rich, fortunate, fat, corrupt, and godless country. How would you feel, how would you react, Mel Keating, if these lands were so rich yet so weak that powers from abroad felt free to roam this land with ease, installing and deposing your state governors at will, killing civilians all in the name of what they feel is holy? How would you feel?"

There's a waver in her previously strong eyes. Asim feels that finally he is penetrating her smug assurance.

He says, "I'll tell you how you would feel. You would feel oppressed, ground down, and you and your fellow people would take up arms to force these foreigners from your lands. No matter the cost, no matter the blood spilt."

Mel clears her throat. "That's just a simple explanation. That's all."

Asim gets up. "You and your people should have followed the philosophy of your sixth president. He was a wise man."

Mel doesn't say anything.

Asim smiles. "Confused, young girl? You dare to lecture me on my history and beliefs, and yet the mention of your sixth president leaves you clueless? I will help you. He was John Quincy Adams, and he once said, 'Americans should not go abroad to slay dragons they do not understand in the name of spreading democracy.' Understand now? You have traveled and reached across the globe to slay dragons. Don't be surprised when the dragons return the favor."

Mel squeezes her arms tighter. Asim says, "Consider yourself fortunate. At any other place or time, a captor who had attacked my cousin would have been severely punished...in a creative and bloody way. But for you, Mel Keating, the president's daughter, my only punishment is this."

He gestures to the floor, where the spilt food and paper plate and plasticware are scattered. "Here is your evening meal. You will have to eat off the floor, like so many people displaced by your government are forced to do."

Asim turns and walks away, and Mel says, "Please...you said something before. What did you mean? About keeping me...forever. Why did you say that? Didn't you make a ransom demand? Won't you...let me go if the demand is met?"

He types in the keypad code that unlocks the door, turns to her with a wide smile. "You are an educated young lady. I'm sure you'll figure out what *forever* means."

CHAPTER

46

Saunders Hotel
Arlington, Virginia

Thanks to the efforts of my highly skilled and somewhat scary chief of staff, Madeline Perry, my wife, Samantha, and I are keeping watch in the second connected suite at the Saunders Hotel. The room is cluttered with barely touched room service trays of food, CNN is on the TV with the volume turned down, and Samantha is on one of the two beds, curled up, watching silently as the correspondents and experts on the screen talk to each other and the millions of people watching.

I turned down the volume about a half hour ago, after some alleged "expert" on hostage taking and kidnapping smugly said that in all likelihood, our daughter was already dead, and Samantha cried out and it was a race between me and Agent Stahl to turn down the damn TV.

I kept my mouth shut, but I made a note of the man's name, knowing that somehow, somewhere, he and I would have an interesting meeting one of these days.

I'm pacing around the large suite like the proverbial caged animal, and it's the damn helplessness that's killing me. When I was in the teams, there was training, planning, more training, and then execution. As a congressman, vice president, and then POTUS, I at least had the illusion that I could make decisions and choices, and most times, they were followed through with as they filtered down through the bureaucracy.

Now?

I'm dependent on other people for the safety of my daughter, and I'm hating every dark and frightening second. I see my go bag in the corner and nearly laugh at the pathetic black canvas case. Inside are weapons and ammunition, ready for... what? To fly back to New Hampshire and blindly go into the woods and start hunting?

I can hear phones ringing and muffled voices from the other attached suite, where Madeline Perry is keeping a tight control on matters, and I need to continue to trust her. She will come in here if there's a development or if a decision has to be made.

I look to my wife. Her eyes are closed. She seems to be dozing.

Agent Stahl is working on a laptop.

Me?

Apparently useless.

I let a second or two pass, and then whisper, "Man up, buttercup."

If any of my past team members could magically be here, they would be shocked at what I'm doing.

Which is nothing.

The drapes are pulled, and I look over at the screen, and CNN is broadcasting a shot of traffic backing up at some checkpoint on a rural road in New Hampshire.

Time to change that equation.

I go to a corner of the large suite where there's a work

area with a table and chairs, and I take out my iPhone and get to work.

First call is to Sarah Palumbo, the deputy national security advisor for the National Security Council, who warned me hours and a lifetime ago about the President's Daily Brief that indicated I was the target of increased terrorist chatter and interest.

Sure.

Like many intelligence analyses, it was generally accurate but not specific enough.

They were coming for me, all right.

By kidnapping Mel.

The phone rings once, then rings and rings and goes to voicemail.

"This is Palumbo," says the familiar voice. "You know the drill."

I say, "Sarah, Matt Keating here…please call me back when you can. Thanks."

I disconnect the call.

Who next?

I could call others I know in DC law enforcement and the military who are going all out in trying to find Mel, but what would I accomplish, except for distracting them from their work? And maybe angering President Barnes and her people at a time when I can't afford to do that?

Time to go overseas.

I check the time, surprised to see we're now in the morning hours.

But I really shouldn't be surprised. When I was with the teams, in the middle of planning or conducting an op, I could easily get by on four hours of sleep a day, and Lord knows I'm in the middle of one right now.

* * *

I have two calls to make and decide to make the hard one first.

As a congressman, vice president, and president, I met scores of foreign leaders, military and intelligence personnel, and assorted aides and advisors to the same. Most I met for a grip and grin in my office, or later the Oval Office, and that's it, but sometimes there's a connection, a quick realization that you could do business with this man or woman in a foreign government who knows matters and knows how to get things done.

That leads to back channels, unofficial lines of communication, and negotiations with men and women you trust aren't bullshitting you.

Like the man I'm dialing right now.

The phone rings once and is picked up. "Yes?"

I'm dreading this call, but I have to admit, I'm happy it was answered.

"Ahmad? It's Matt Keating."

A sigh from the other end of the call, somewhere in either the deserts or the air-conditioned high-rises of Saudi Arabia.

"Ah, Matt, my sympathies," Ahmad says in his cultured voice with a hint of a British accent. "You know I give my best wishes to you and Samantha for the safe release of Melanie."

"Thank you," I say.

For a few seconds, time passes slowly as Ahmad, also known as Major General Ahmad Bin Nayef, former deputy director of the General Intelligence Directorate of Saudi Arabia, makes me wait. Some years ago, when I was a simple congressman from Texas, I heard that one of Ahmad's sons, receiving flight training at Sheppard Air Force Base in Wichita County, was getting more than the usual hazing as the clichéd furriner.

I put an end to that nonsense with one phone call to the base commandant and another to the secretary of the Air Force.

"Ahmad, please," I say. "I'm looking for any help you and your associates can give us."

"*Us* meaning you, Matt, or *us* meaning the United States?"

I clench my iPhone harder. "Whichever can get my daughter back."

"Ah, well, that's posing a difficulty, as I'm sure you know," he says. "President Barnes and her secretary of state are not particularly liked in the Kingdom. Their insistence that we change our government and way of life to what is seen in your Palm Beach County has not been well received. The CIA station chief and our FBI liaison have officially asked for our assistance, but many here in Riyadh have long memories and insulted pride. I'm sorry to say, that will impact just how far we will go."

I close my eyes, rub at them. As that wily old Henry Kissinger once said, "America has no permanent friends or enemies, only interests." And since FDR agreed back in 1945 to provide military assistance to Saudi Arabia, that rich and troubling place has been one of our biggest interests in the Middle East.

Do I and other previous presidents agree with everything they do? Of course not, especially when it comes to human rights. But they have a wide-ranging intelligence service, and although some in the Kingdom have funneled money to terrorists around the world, others there, friends of the West, have funded important covert missions from us to the British or to the French to keep ahead of those who like to maim and kill innocents.

Like Asim.

And when it came to bloody fights like the one to contain and crush ISIS, the Saudis were a vital and quiet ally.

"I know, Ahmad," I reply. "And where I can, I've done my best to temper the Barnes Administration's demands and proposals, but there's only so much I can do. I'm a former president, and I know what it's like to be ignored and belittled by the current administration. Ahmad, please: father to father, I'm seeking your help."

And just like that, Ahmad says, "Then you will receive it, my friend. I've already made inquiries, but so far it's not been encouraging. This…creature, Asim Al-Asheed, he is even feared by our most hardened men in the Kingdom. He takes too much pleasure in the killing, using the blessed words of the Prophet as a shield. He has many friends and assets in a network around the world. But I will tell you this, something that is troubling me."

"What is it, Ahmad?"

He says, "Your CIA and FBI, they have not pushed back where we have been taking our time, delaying. It's like they expected our resistance and decided that was just fine. And that, Matt, frightens me for you almost as much as Asim Al-Asheed."

CHAPTER 47

Williams Pond
Leah, New Hampshire

Jiang Lijun of the Chinese Ministry of State Security yawns again as the sun starts to make itself known through the peaks of this state's White Mountains. He waits in his rental GMC sedan in this dirt parking lot adjacent to a wide body of water in the northern part of this New Hampshire state.

It took nearly every free second to plan and make this trip after meeting with his boss, Li Baodong: Jiang Lijun drove out to Newark and then took a flight to Montreal, and then drove a rental to Sherbrooke and then another rental to here, this small town. At the border crossing in Vermont, the line of cars and trucks going into Canada was at a crawl, as uniformed men with dogs seemed to search everybody and everything.

On the ride down here, Black Hawk helicopters and other aircraft were a constant presence in the air, and twice he pulled over for roaring police cruisers coming up behind him with flashing lights and sirens.

But now he waits for Asim Al-Asheed to arrive.

By slipping past his watchers and illegally traveling to Canada, and then illegally reentering the United States, Jiang has violated numerous American diplomatic protocols for Chinese representatives, and he would be immediately expelled if caught. But so what? Just another trip across the tightrope.

He yawns again, thinks of his wife, Zhen, and how upset she was that he had to leave so unexpectedly. Zhen is a smart woman, knows of Jiang's work, is employed at the mission as a clerical staff supervisor, and with their daughter, Li Na, in her arms, she said, "Do you really have to go?"

At any other time, Jiang would have abruptly dismissed her, but the little form of their daughter and her sweet innocent eyes…oh, that touched him.

Maybe being a father was changing him.

Was fieldwork like this still in his future?

Earlier, Jiang had reached out to Asim and was pleased to see the despicable man's quick reply. The system to do so was simple and nearly untraceable. Years ago, when Jiang was controlling Asim in Libya, he had set up an anonymous email account through a Swiss-based company that offered the world's best secured encryption, and he shared the address and password with Asim. Using this shared account, they could leave messages in the email system's drafts folder without anyone, from the NSA to Great Britain's Government Communications Headquarters, having a hint of what they were doing.

Every six months or so he would contact Asim, just to keep that line of communication open, but the last email was the important one: it set up this meet.

On the dashboard is a pack of Marlboro cigarettes. Time for a smoke. He smokes only Zhonghuas in his office at the New York embassy. He gets out of the car and takes a good look at the pond and the small park. Already there are visitors, mostly fishermen and children. Two men are hunched over a picnic table, with cups of coffee and breakfast pastries. Farther away, at another picnic table, children are squabbling with their parents.

Filial piety, for these barbarians?

Never.

Ugh. To live in such an empty and wooded place.

Years ago, dear Mother cried when he left for his schooling in America. She thought he would never return, but she had nothing to worry about. At UCLA and then Columbia, where he got his master's degree in international affairs, he found the Americans lazy and unfocused, and while they droned on and on about freedom, the only freedom he and his fellow Chinese students experienced was the freedom of the Americans to lecture them.

One day at lunch at the Ferris Booth Commons in Lerner Hall, an earnest woman grad student from Cambridge—the one in Massachusetts, not England—started lecturing him about Tiananmen, and she only shut up when he asked her if she had ever heard of the slaughters at Kent State and Jackson State.

A black pickup truck rattles in and parks nearby. An old man, hunched over and holding a fishing pole, slowly steps out of the cab. He wears baggy jeans and a dirty yellow jacket, and a black knit cap is pulled over his head. Jiang reads the bumper stickers on the back of the truck: REGISTER CRIMINALS, NOT GUNS. MOLON LABE / COME AND GET IT. I FEAR MY GOVERNMENT.

Jiang shakes his head. How this undisciplined rabble of a people got anything done is still a mystery to him. His own country only strode onto the world stage when the party took control in 1949. One party, one rule, one strong leader. That's how his grandfather went from being an illiterate soldier to a respected party official who even made it unscathed through the Cultural Revolution.

Jiang checks his watch. Asim is late. Of course. The men

from the Middle East he has dealt with over the years can kill children, blow up airliners, and slaughter customers at a shopping center but they are unable to tell time or keep—

The old man limps by and turns and shoves against Jiang's side, dropping his fishing pole.

Something hard is digging into Jiang's ribs.

"Hello, my old Chinese friend," Asim Al-Asheed says.

Asim smiles in pleasure at seeing the shocked look on the Chinaman's face. Asim respects the man's money and weapons, but that is about it. He is a smooth-handed and smooth-faced functionary, that is all. Definitely not a warrior who has had to wash the blood of his enemies off his clothes.

And Jiang barely noticed Asim when he drove up in the smelly pickup truck, the one he and his cousin took two days ago, after killing the cigarette smugglers in the woods over in Vermont State. With old clothes, pebbles in his shoes to make him limp, a stretch of tape across his shoulders to make him hunchbacked, and a smear of color across his eyebrows to make them look gray, he fooled this "intelligence" officer.

Asim pulls his pistol back. "I am here, Jiang Lijun. Don't look so surprised. And don't waste my time. What do you want?"

The Chinaman quickly recovers, smiles, lights up a cigarette without offering one to Asim, who ignores the insult. Jiang says, "Congratulations, Asim. One professional to another, this has been one impressive operation. It must have taken years of preparation. Quite admirable."

"Thank you," Asim says. "My contacts and networks are well paid, well prepared, and have been in place for years. And they always respond to my requests, whether it's for weapons, money, or transportation."

"But what now, Asim?"

"You know of my demands."

Jiang shrugs. "Nonsense, and you know it. If you get your demands and release the girl, the Americans will chase you down to the ends of the globe and kill you. And if you don't receive your demands and you kill the girl, they will do the same, only quicker. The Americans are a softhearted and softheaded bunch. Killing a girl will only enrage them."

The Chinaman takes another drag of his cigarette. "Well?"

Asim says, "My plans are mine. And what are yours?"

Jiang drops the cigarette on the ground, grinds it with the heel of his shoe. "Officially, I'm here to ask you—as a courtesy and favor—to release the girl to me. It removes a dangerous burden from you, and it assists my government in improving relations with the United States. In return, we'll be quite generous in rewarding you and your cousin. A nice cash payment, and relocation to any safe place on the globe. Even China."

Asim smiles, shakes his head. "Would you transport us, then, to Xinjiang Province? Where we would live among our cousins, the Uighurs? Would we then be placed into camps, reeducated, forced to work in slave labor factories?"

The Chinaman remains quiet, stoic. Asim says, "You said... *officially*. Is there an unofficial position?"

Jiang looks out across the quiet pond. "Yes."

"And?"

A long pause, as though Jiang is considering what to say next. His voice softens.

"I want you to succeed, whatever you're planning to do," Jiang says. "I can provide you with funds, means of transportation, weapons. Some intelligence on what the Americans are up to. Whatever it takes for you to humiliate this nation. I am on your side."

Asim ponders this. "Why would you do this for me?"

"My business," Jiang says. "And I have put my career and

life in jeopardy by making this offer to you. Remember that, because I won't forget."

Asim picks up the fishing pole, starts back to the truck. "I will remember your exposure, and I will consider your generous, and unofficial, offer. Thank you for the visit, old friend. Let us remain in touch."

Jiang opens the door to his car. "Yes. Let's."

Ten minutes later, Jiang is driving along the country road when he rounds a corner and approaches a police roadblock. There are police cruisers and a wooden barricade painted orange, and officers in black jumpsuits and helmets, with automatic weapons.

Jiang slows down his rental GMC, lowers the window.

Two men approach. One comes up to the door, the other stands back, covering him with an automatic rifle.

"License and registration, sir," the closer man asks. His face is flushed, eyes red-rimmed, as if he has worked too many hours without rest.

"Absolutely, sir," Jiang says.

He hands over the car's rental paperwork and his license.

The officer gives it a good look. "You're a Canadian citizen, Mr. Yang?"

"I am."

"Do you have your passport with you?"

"Absolutely," Jiang says. "A moment, please."

He hands over his dark blue passport, its cover emblazoned with the seal of Canada, along with PASSPORT / PASSEPORT in bright yellow letters.

The officer says, "Your business in New Hampshire, Mr. Yang?"

"I'm traveling to Boston," he says, thinking he's on that tightrope once more, and all is well. "I work for Resolute Forest

Products in Montreal and I'm making sales calls to a number of businesses in Manchester and Boston. Would you like to see my business card?"

A shake of the head, and his passport and paperwork are returned. "Not necessary. Could you open the trunk, please?"

"Of course."

He releases the toggle to the trunk and some other officers inspect it. The armed man near him produces two photos and says, "Have you seen either of these two men in your travels? Please look closely."

Jiang keeps his face bland as he looks over the color photos of Asim Al-Asheed and his cousin Faraj, one of them with a beard, one of them clean-shaven.

A thought comes to him.

He could tell these men that he saw Asim in that pickup truck, provide them with the license plate, and within minutes, a cordon would be drawn up and then hundreds—if not thousands—of police, government, and military searchers would flood this area.

And Asim would be captured, and the girl would be freed, and Jiang would have accomplished his mission.

His official mission. He would be congratulated, receive a promotion and citations, and perhaps relations would improve between his homeland and this unvirtuous country.

But his unofficial mission is more near and dear to him. *For you, Father,* he thinks, *and for you as well, daughter.*

He smiles. "No, sir, I have not seen these two men."

"Very well," the officer says, stepping away, motioning for Jiang's trunk to be shut and the barrier to be moved. Other cars have lined up behind Jiang. "You're free to go."

"Thank you," Jiang says, and to himself he says, *cào nǐ mā, you and this entire foul place.*

CHAPTER 48

❖

Saunders Hotel
Arlington, Virginia

After I disconnect my call to Saudi Arabia, I wait for a minute before attempting my second overseas phone call. Samantha—bless her—still seems to be sleeping, and I quietly walk over to Agent Stahl, typing away on his government-issue laptop at a round table on this side of the suite.

I need him to check something out.

Keeping my voice low, I say, "David."

"Sir?"

"Tell me, do you have contacts in the Treasury Department?"

David lifts his head. His hair is in disarray, face pale, eyes swollen and tired. "Certainly, sir."

"There's that fund in the Treasury Department…the Judgment Fund," I say, drawing on my memories as a congressman serving on the Financial Services Committee. "It's a quick and easy way for the president to transfer funds, like bitcoin, for the payment for Mel's ransom."

"Sounds familiar, sir," Agent Stahl says, stifling a yawn.

"Reach out to your contacts," I say. "Find out what progress is being made to prepare the bitcoin payment."

I check my watch, my heart feeling like lead. Just seven more hours before the ransom deadline.

David says, "On it, sir."

I go back to my work area, check on Samantha.

Still sleeping.

I hope she won't remember whatever dreams she might be having.

I go to my iPhone, dial another number, and it goes to voicemail.

"This is Palumbo," says the familiar voice. "You know the drill."

Yes, I think, *I certainly know the drill.*

The deputy national security advisor for the National Security Council isn't answering my calls.

The next call goes more smoothly and is answered on the second ring.

"Mr. President," says the voice, with an accent that has a touch of Brooklyn and Hebrew. It belongs to Danny Cohen, the retired head of Israel's Mossad. "I was expecting your call. How are you and your dear wife holding up?"

"As well as can be expected," I say. "We're in a hotel suite across the river from DC, trying to keep on top of developments. And Danny—how's retirement treating you?"

A soft laugh. "Nice, in a way, when your biggest problem of the day is getting a replacement pump for your irrigation system so your orange grove doesn't dry out. But…you've not called to check in on my retirement. What can I do for you, Mr. President?"

"First, call me Matt," I say. "And second…I know there are official communications and information sharing going on between Langley and Tel Aviv, but is there anything you may be hearing unofficially that can be of use? I…I just can't sit back and just hope everything works out, Danny."

Danny says, "Asim Al-Asheed has always been a tough man, Matt."

"I know," I say. "A freelance terrorist with no ties to a nation-state, like one of those evil types Ian Fleming used to come up with back when things were simpler, but with a worldwide network of supporters."

"A good analogy, Matt," Danny says. "Our people are working very, very hard to come up with anything solid, trying to see if we have anything that traces Asim's travels to the United States and your home. But he and his cousin, they work diligently, using cutouts and false identities. They are cold and cunning, with quiet allies across the world. But the work still goes on from Tel Aviv, I can promise you that. Many favors are being called in, and pressure is being applied."

I nod. Mossad is legendary for its intelligence work and operations for good reason. From the beginning, a precondition of Israel's survival has been knowing what their neighbors are up to. Then, as more and more Jews came as refugees and migrants to Israel from countries like Russia and Kazakhstan, Morocco and Ethiopia, the US and Canada, Israel was able to develop back channels and direct information-gathering networks, not just in its region but in nations across the world, including those publicly wishing for its death.

If any intelligence agency can catch a scent of Asim Al-Asheed's travels, it will be Danny Cohen's old haunt.

"Thank you, Danny," I say. From the other side of the room, I hear Agent Stahl talking to someone via his phone.

"I wish I could do more, Matt," Danny says with sympathy,

"and I wish you could have done more when you were in the White House. You inherited a tough situation. But I believe you would have accomplished a lot more in a second term, which your vice president's betrayal denied you."

Danny is being overgenerous. Presidents before me have tried to settle the thorny issues dividing Israelis and Palestinians, and future presidents will keep trying. The formula for success sounds simple: land for peace—land for an independent Palestinian state, security guarantees for Israel. It's like the old joke about how to make elephant stew. Step one, boil a large pot of water. Step two, get an elephant.

Though the violence between Israel and the Palestinians has been reduced, the possibility of peace that once seemed so close has dimmed: the continued expansion of settlements in the West Bank leaves less land for a Palestinian state, and the rise of Iran and its so-called Shia crescent stretching across parts of Iraq, Syria, Yemen, and Bahrain has driven Israel closer to the Sunni Arab states, which care more about their economic and security relationships with Israel than about solving the Palestinian problem. These factors, plus the iron grip of Hamas on the Palestinians in Gaza for more than a decade, will bedevil whoever occupies the Oval Office.

Danny knows all of that better than I do, of course.

"I did what I could with the time I had," I say. "Which wasn't much. One of these days, if peace does break out, I'll be just a footnote. If that."

Danny knows that, too. What matters to him is that he was sure of my commitment to Israel's security. With the current administration, he isn't so sure. He really wants to help.

"You are a good man, Mr. President, and bless you and Samantha and Mel," Danny says. "I will contact you if I learn anything, anything at all."

As I disconnect the call with the old Mossad leader, I

hear a muffled curse behind me and turn. Agent Stahl is at his laptop.

"The bastards. The coldhearted bastards," he whispers.

I go over to him.

"David?"

Tears are in his eyes. "Nothing," he says, voice rising. "Nothing! There's no movement, no plans, no procedures in place to get that bitcoin ready to be transferred. Nothing, Mr. President!"

A sob comes from behind me.

I turn.

Samantha is sitting up on the bed, hand to her face. "I was right! Matt…I was right! They're not going to get our daughter back, are they?"

I try not to lose my temper. "No, they're not."

There are tears in her eyes but her voice is strong and firm. "Matt, what are we going to do?"

I look to Agent Stahl, and then to my duffel bag filled with arms and ammunition, and I'm fully alert, aware, all senses tingling, like I'm about to step into a Black Hawk in the middle of the night, ready to strike at whatever enemy is out there.

"Whatever it takes," I say. "We're getting Mel back."

CHAPTER 49

Monmouth, New Hampshire

Officer Corinne Bradford is lying on her stomach in a copse of woods and low brush, keeping view on the large house below her, about a hundred feet away. The ground is cold and moist against her chilled skin as she brings up the binoculars again, scanning the quiet yard.

It's a cold morning and she's hoping against hope that this little thread, this little clue, will work out.

The previous several hours were spent going up and down Route 113, stopping at every farm stand, service station, and little shop, showing off the photo of the Cadillac Escalade snapped from the Citizens Bank CCTV system, and telling everyone it was a confidential investigation so word wouldn't get back to her idiot chief. At RJ's Hardware, at last, she got a hit.

"Sure," Bing Torrance, the store's manager, said an hour ago. "I saw something like that go up the dirt road to the Macomber place the other day. I know they've been renting it, off and on, for years, but I thought it was weird to see a strange vehicle there, 'cause they haven't rented their place in over a year."

So here she is.

Cold.

Thirsty.

What she wouldn't do for a coffee and a breakfast sandwich from McDonald's.

Or two.

Corinne checks her watch.

In an hour she's due to report to work at the police station.

Should she go to work and tell Chief Grambler what she's found out?

Sure.

Some hardware guy thought he saw a Cadillac Escalade go up to this house. And I've kept watch on it for a couple of hours, and haven't seen a light, a person, or anything.

And Chief Grambler will probably fire her cold ass for insubordination.

Corinne brings up the binoculars again. An impressive two-story wooden house, dark brown, with a detached three-car garage. Pricey. Behind the house the well-mowed lawn goes down to a large, isolated pond, and there's a fixed dock going out into the water.

Another check of the watch, and Corinne thinks, *Damn it, no matter what, I'm not moving. I'll call in sick or something, but nope, I'm staying right here.*

Corinne lowers the binoculars again, rubs at her tired and cold eyes.

Hot coffee.

Why in the world didn't she come up here prepared, with a thermos and maybe—

The sound of an engine snaps her right out of it.

The binoculars are back in her hands.

Her heart is slamming right along.

There's an open stretch just before the garage where there's a good view, and something is coming up the dirt road, engine getting louder.

"Damn," she whispers.

Not a Cadillac Escalade.

A battered old black pickup truck. Ford.

"Damn," she whispers again.

All this time, all this waiting, her clothing soaked through and cold, just to see an old black Ford pickup truck.

The middle garage door quietly slides up, and the pickup truck goes into the empty bay.

Hold it.

Hold on!

She tries to steady her breathing, the shakes starting in her wrists and hands.

In the left bay of the garage is a black Cadillac Escalade.

The hardware guy was right!

She waits.

Takes deep breaths.

Movement.

A man comes out of the garage as the door slowly descends behind him. He has a dull yellow coat over his arm, and he's rubbing at his forehead with a cloth, and when he lowers the cloth, Corinne almost gasps.

It's the terrorist kidnapper.

Asim Al-Asheed.

Right here in front of her.

Corinne picks up the binoculars, slowly moves back down into a thicket of trees, pulls out her phone.

NO SERVICE

Damn it all to hell!

That's one thing that she hasn't gotten used to: the many areas up here where there is no cell-tower service. It's as if she's been cast back into the 1990s.

Corinne looks back at where she's come from.

Her 9mm SIG Sauer is holstered at her side.

She's convinced, deep in her bones, that the president's daughter is up at the house.

Should she try to rescue her?

Now?

Corinne hates herself, but no, that would be suicide.

She's got to contact...

Who?

Chief Grambler?

No.

That idiot would argue, dismiss, and pooh-pooh what she's found out.

Time to think of someone else. And pray that she gets cell service.

A few minutes later—praise the Lord!—she gets cell service, and she searches through her contacts until she finds the listing for Clark Yates, who used to be with her in the Massachusetts State Police and who lucked out by jumping over to the New Hampshire State Police before the great purge began.

The phone rings.

Rings.

Rings.

"Pick up, pick up, pick up," she whispers.

"Hello?"

She sags in relief. "Clark, it's Corinne Bradford."

"Corinne... damn, it's early. I mean—"

"Clark," she interrupts. "You've got to help me. I know where the president's daughter is located. I've found the kidnapper and seen his vehicle."

"Corinne…are you sure? And why are you telling me? Shouldn't you—"

"Yeah, I know," she says, glancing around at the trees, exposed granite boulders, and underbrush. "But my chief is an idiot. Look, consider this a solid tip. In northern Monmouth, on a dirt road marked with a wooden sign that says *Macomber,* off Route 113, just past RJ's Hardware. At the end of the dirt road is a two-story country-style house, with a large pond at the rear."

"Corinne…"

"I saw him! I saw the damn terrorist kidnapper, Clark. And the Cadillac Escalade. Honest to God."

She hears something rustling out there, probably the wind moving the tall trees back and forth, rubbing against each other.

Clark says, "Okay. Got it. I'll start making calls. I hope to God you're right."

"Me, too," she says. "Me, too. Bye for now. Don't let me down!"

Corinne disconnects her call and there's a snap, like a stick being cracked. She looks behind her, at the man she saw outside the garage, coming toward her with a knife in his hand, smiling with quiet confidence.

CHAPTER 50

Northwestern New Hampshire

Mel Keating rolls over on the bed and sits up as the door to her cell grinds open. She's not sure what time it is, not with the light still glaring at her, and she's confused and sleepy, and she knows this is part of their process, to weaken her. Mel has heard stories from Dad and his buds in the teams about SERE training—survival, evasion, resistance, and escape—where they learn to survive being a POW. And part of SERE includes either sleep deprivation or screwing around with your sleep patterns.

The younger one, Faraj, comes in, and Mel feels a sharp cold jolt of fear.

His hands are empty.

Isn't it time for breakfast?

Why is he here?

He's smiling, his eyes still slightly reddened from her attack yesterday, and Mel stands up, not wanting to remain seated, a scared victim ready for whatever's coming her way.

If the son of a bitch plans to assault her, she's going to make sure he either fails or pays for it with scratches, bruised testicles, or a gouged eye.

He steps forward, nods.

"Are you hungry?" he asks.

Mel says, "Is this a trick question?"

"A trick… what?"

"A question that's a taunt. Or an insult. Not a real question."

He nods again, smiling. "No, it is a real question. Nothing else. Are you hungry?"

The truth is that her stomach's been growling at her for a while, and she's not sure how long it's been since she scooped up the cold vegetable soup from the concrete floor with her hands and ate it like—

Like a frightened, hungry refugee.

Just as Asim wanted.

"Yes, I am."

"It is breakfast time," Faraj says. "What would you like?"

"To have breakfast at Pope's Diner, over in Spencer. You two could come if you'd like."

That amuses him, and his smile is wider. "That is not possible. Tell me your favorite breakfast. What is it? I shall do my best to prepare it."

Mel replies without thinking. "Pancakes. With butter. And real maple syrup, not that cane sugar crap they sell in supermarkets. And bacon. Extra crispy. Orange juice. Coffee."

Faraj listens to her and says, "You seem to know what you want."

"That's…" Her voice catches. "Dad likes to make me breakfast on Sundays. And for the Secret Service at our house. And…sometimes he goes around to the nearby towns, helps the local churches when they have Sunday brunches for their congregations."

"I had not heard of that," Faraj says.

Mel crosses her arms, wills her eyes to stop watering. "Because he doesn't promote it, doesn't allow press coverage. He just…does it."

Faraj says, "You're a lucky girl."

"I'm not a girl," she says. "And yes, I know I'm lucky. And if you're going to give me a lecture on how lucky I am, because I live in the West, because I have no fears of going hungry or getting sick without treatment, shut up already. I've heard it already."

Faraj's face tenses. "No, that's not what I was going to say. You are wrong."

Mel says, "Prove it."

Her kidnapper says, "Do you know of a prison in Tripoli? Called Abu Salim?"

"No," Mel says, wondering, *Why the embarrassment? Why the mocking? Just get on with it.*

"The most famed and evil prison in my country," Faraj says, voice soft. "That stray dog, that boy colonel, that costumed fool, that's where he imprisoned those who opposed him, or insulted him, or just because he had a whim that this man should be punished. In 1996, the prisoners revolted, and more than twelve hundred were massacred. And after the bodies were dragged out and the blood was washed away, it remained open."

Mel sees the young man's face change before her, from what he was—a terrorist, killer, and kidnapper—to a son burdened by memories.

"I never knew my mother," he says. "My father, Hassan, ran a tea shop in Tripoli…and I remember him feeding me sweets at the end of the day, those that he couldn't sell. And when I was five or six, he was taken to Abu Salim and never came out."

Mel wants to say something in the silence that follows in her concrete cell, but she can't think of a word.

Her captor briefly shakes his head, as if he's trying to bring himself back to the moment.

His voice is still soft. "When I said you were lucky, it was because you know your father, and you still have your father."

Turning, Faraj says, "Your breakfast will be here shortly."

Mel is pleasantly surprised at the breakfast she's just eaten because it's exactly what she ordered, and, desperately hungry from having eaten the cold meal from the floor hours ago, she eats every bit of it.

Placing the tray on the floor, she suddenly yawns. She's so damned tired.

Mel sits back on the bed, yawns again. Why shouldn't she be tired? She's been running on shock and adrenaline since the kidnapping and seeing Tim get murdered...

She lies down on the bed. Thinks things through. Again remembers Agent Stahl and his briefing back there at the White House.

Mel slowly slides the gold band from her right ring finger, holds it up to the never-ceasing bright light. The old initials are still visible within: FROM ST TO KM 12/10/41.

A gift from Mom's granddad to his fiancée, who would become his wife—and Mom's grandmother—after he enlisted in the Navy, shortly after the attack on Pearl Harbor.

She grips the ring tightly in her fist.

So very tired.

CHAPTER 51

The Oval Office
The White House

To the secretary of Homeland Security and to the director of the FBI, President Pamela Barnes says, "It's 8 a.m. Four hours away from the noon deadline set by Asim Al-Asheed. What's the latest?"

Secretary Paul Charles starts to speak, but FBI director Lisa Blair rolls right over him and says, "We've got at least a hundred agents in the field around Mount Rollins, with more flying in and driving in with each hour. They're working with local agencies in setting up roadblocks, interviewing travelers, and running down possible leads. Our current challenge is that this area of New Hampshire and nearby Vermont is heavily wooded, very rural, with lots of isolated homes, cottages, and hunting camps, not to mention hiking trails and unmarked dirt roads that don't appear on maps or on GPS. There's a lot of driving, door knocking, and interrogating drivers, but so far, no real leads have developed."

In addition to these two, the only other person in the Oval Office is Barnes's husband and chief of staff, Richard. As he said earlier, this was not the time to have aides or notetakers leave a paper trail of the sensitive topics under discussion.

Richard says, "What about the vehicle spotted leaving the kidnapping scene? The black Escalade?"

Blair and Charles are sitting in leather armchairs in front of the Resolute desk, while Barnes's husband is sitting at her left, legs crossed, leaning forward impatiently.

Director Blair purses her lips in anger. "That was a lead that we were hoping to keep confidential. But someone up there leaked it to a local weekly newspaper, and that report was picked up by the Associated Press bureau in Concord, and the word quickly spread."

Barnes says, "Why's that a problem, Director?"

The FBI head says, "Because every concerned citizen, crank, or nut up and down the Connecticut River Valley has been clogging the tip line of every police agency from the Canadian border to Long Island Sound, saying they've seen that black Escalade drive by, or go into a parking garage or apartment building parking lot. Each and every one of those leads has to be tracked down, Madam President. It's a hell of a chore."

"I see," Barnes says. "And inter-agency cooperation?"

"As well as can be expected," Blair says. "The CIA has been working its sources overseas, and the NSA is going through its phone and email records. The challenge is that the CIA works in a wilderness of mirrors and mazes…Is the information they're getting the real deal, or are they being played by someone with an agenda? How valid is any intelligence they're receiving? As for the NSA, they have thousands of terabytes of recorded information to sift through. And we know from painful experience that Asim Al-Asheed, his cousin Faraj, and their supporters are extremely careful with their communications."

Richard says, "So no good news, then."

Director Blair says, "It speaks for itself, Mr. Barnes."

"Anything else to add?" the president asks.

Director Blair says, "We've pre-positioned one unit from the Hostage Rescue Team at a regional high school outside of Spencer, about five miles away from Mount Rollins, where Mel Keating was kidnapped. Another unit is en route to give them support. The unit there has both air and ground transport to respond immediately if we get any actionable intelligence. In addition, we have access to DOD resources as well, and there's an NSA representative at the scene there to provide support."

The president looks to her rumpled and overwhelmed secretary of Homeland Security and regrets once again naming him to that post after her election. But as head of the Florida Highway Patrol and as a political operator, Paul Charles helped swing a lot of support to her when she started her insurrection against Matt Keating.

She should have asked for his resignation yesterday, but firing him would be a hell of a sign of weakness at this time.

"What do you have, Paul?"

"We're working as best as we can with our FBI friends"—his voice is tinged with contempt—"and we're bringing in two units of our Counter Assault Team from the Secret Service to provide support to the HRT."

"We don't need it," Director Blair snaps.

"Well, you're going to get it," he says, grinning.

"Enough," Barnes says. "Anything else, Paul?"

"The border crossings," Charles says. "We really need to take a hard look at the situation, Madam President. The backup of traffic crossing into Canada—"

Barnes says, "No."

Her Homeland Security secretary says, "With all due respect,

Madam President, the chances that the terrorists are going to cross the border into Canada with Mel Keating in their control is very, very remote."

"But that remote chance is there, isn't it?" she says. "Keep the inspections going."

"Yes, ma'am."

"Anything more?" she asks.

Charles looks to Blair and then shrugs and says, "Er, I guess I'll have to be the one to ask the question that everyone's thinking about. The ransom."

"What about it?" Richard asks.

"Er…is it going to be paid?"

Barnes crisply says, "No. We don't pay ransoms to terrorists."

"But," Charles goes on, "it's Matt Keating's daughter."

"Yes," she says, "and I'm keeping the both of you from finding her. Get to it, Director Blair and Secretary Charles. Go find her. You've got just four hours."

When she's alone with her husband, President Barnes leans back in her chair, rubs at her forehead.

"God, Richard," she says. "Am I doing the right thing?"

"Absolutely," he says.

"But Mel Keating might be dead by the end of the day."

"And whose fault is that?" her chief of staff demands. "I'll tell you. It's Asim and his butcher cousin. And it's the FBI and Homeland Security, for not doing their jobs. And it's one more person."

"Who?"

"You're not going to like it, Pamela, but it's Matt Keating's fault."

"Richard…"

He shifts his chair so he can better look at her. "I mean it. You have a former president, a former SEAL member, who has a number of enemies around the world. He didn't protect his girl. That's on him."

"But Mel Keating wasn't eligible for Secret Service protection after she turned sixteen."

Richard presses on. "Then he should have done something about it. Restrict her movements. Move someplace more public. Hire private security. Or ask you for a presidential directive, a special exemption for his daughter, so she could get Secret Service protection. Matt Keating did none of that."

Richard gets up and says, "Standing firm against Mel Keating's kidnappers—no matter the pressure you're getting—is going to gain you respect and admiration across the world, including from a lot of bad actors in North Korea, Iran, Russia, and our constant-pain-in-the-ass competitors, the Chinese. In the long run, that's going to save a lot more lives than one kidnapped girl."

"I see what you mean, Richard, but it doesn't mean I have to like it."

He goes to the door leading to the main corridor outside the Oval Office and says, "In an hour I'll have a statement for you to give to the press about your disappointment that the deadline has passed, and that Mel Keating has not been located."

"But what if she's found alive in the next four hours?"

Her husband just shakes his head and opens the door.

President Barnes rubs at her forehead again, trying to remind herself why she wanted this job so much.

Heading to the White House's lobby after leaving the Oval Office with Secretary of Homeland Security Charles, Director Blair remembers the time years back when she came into this building to be interviewed for her current job by President Matt Keating. He was ready to submit her name to the Senate for confirmation, and that meeting was the last and most important step. She had been prepped to talk about her Army Criminal Investigative Division career, her years as head of the Kansas Bureau of Investigation, and her later job as assistant deputy director of the FBI.

But the interview lasted for about five minutes. While pouring her a cup of coffee from a small table in front of the couch they were sharing, President Keating said, "The FBI's gotten too politicized in the last few years. I want the agency to return to its law enforcement roots, stay away from politics as much as possible, and get shit done. What do you think?"

"I agree, Mr. President," she said.

"Good. The job is yours."

Confused, Blair said, "Is that all?"

Keating smiled, passing over the coffee cup. "You want to go over to Quantico and see who does better in Hogan's Alley?"

She recalls that simple and direct order with melancholy. Blair would never admit it aloud, but she misses reporting to Keating.

In a low voice, Blair says, "God, days like this I hate this city."

Secretary Charles says, "What did you say?"

But she ignores him.

Her phone is vibrating hard against her hip.

CHAPTER 52

Saunders Hotel
Arlington, Virginia

I'm pacing the floor of my suite at the Saunders Hotel with such anger and violence I'm convinced that the cooks in the basement kitchen can hear me. I go to the door connecting to the other suite, fling it open, and yell out, "Maddie!"

She emerges from a huddle of Secret Service agents, hotel staff, and some of my own folks from what remains of the Reelect President Keating campaign. She comes over to me, hair in disarray, eyes red and puffy, and says, "Sir?"

I say, "You have a connection with the Federal Bureau of Prisons, right? A...sister? Cousin?"

"Niece, sir," she says. "My niece Sharon."

"Can you call her?" I ask. "Find out if there's been any movement in getting those three prisoners out of the super max. The ones that Asim Al-Asheed wants freed as part of his ransom demand."

The barest pause, and I think, *You've gone too far, you've pushed her too much,* but before I can take it back, Maddie says, "Yes, of course, Mr. President. I'll get right to it."

I go back into the suite. Agent Stahl is talking in a low voice on the phone, and Samantha is sitting cross-legged on the suite's bed, hugging a pillow in her lap, and I say to her, "I'm working on it. We're getting her back."

Sam says, "I know," and her eyes, while moistened from an earlier burst of tears, are filled with anger as well as contempt.

She says, "They lied to us, back in the Oval Office."

"No," I say. "The president and the chief of staff will tell us later that they told us the truth while we were there. When we left, facts on the ground changed, there were new developments, news they couldn't pass on to us because of time constrictions."

"Like what?"

"I'm going to find out," I say. I go back to my little work area, try again to call Sarah Palumbo, deputy national security advisor for the National Security Council, and once again, the call goes to voicemail.

What message to leave?

I say, "Sarah, guess we're all having a bad day. Right?"

I hang up and there's a knock at the door.

"Come in," I call out.

My chief of staff, Maddie, comes in, face drawn and worried, and she says, "Sir…I've talked to Sharon. My niece. From the Federal Bureau of Prisons."

The look on her face says it all.

"Nothing, am I right? No movement of those three prisoners from the super max."

She nods and says, "I'll…I'm going back to work, Mr. President."

"Thanks, Maddie."

It's time to call President Barnes.

* * *

Unlike what bad novels and even worse movies portray, former presidents and current presidents rarely make phone calls to each other, for the nation has only one president at a time, and now her name is Pamela Barnes and she lives at 1600 Pennsylvania Avenue. And if there is a phone call, it's usually from the current president to the former, not the other way around.

But I still need to talk to her, and it's going to be a chore to get past the phone operators and gatekeepers. There is a private number that goes through the White House switchboard so friends and family members of POTUS can be connected without delay, but that number is changed every time a new administration moves in.

So I call the main White House switchboard—202-456-1414—and after it's picked up after the first ring by a brisk young man saying, "The White House," I say, "This is Matt Keating. Could you please connect me with Felicia Taft?"

Felicia is the deputy chief of staff, and there's a moment of silence, no doubt as the operator checks in with her to see if she'll accept my call, and then Felicia comes on the line and says, "Good morning, Mr. President. What can I do for you?"

From the unmade bed, Samantha is giving me a good hard look, and I feel like I am back at BUD/S training, being given a cold unflinching evaluation by an instructor who's judging my every step and utterance.

I say, "Felicia, I need to talk to Richard. As soon as possible."

"Ah, may I ask what this is about, Mr. President?"

"Do you really have to ask, Felicia?" I say, and I immediately regret my tone because I've put her in a terrible bind and she's the gatekeeper who's going to decide whether this call goes any further, but she's a professional and says, "Hold on, Mr. President. I'll see if he's free."

"Thank you," I say, and I sit down, rub my face, think of Mel out there, a captive, tired, hungry, wondering if her dad is going to find her, and then the familiar voice comes on the line.

"Matt, Richard Barnes here."

I say, "Richard, I need to talk to the president."

"Ah, Matt, that's going to be a challenge."

"Richard, whatever you said to Sam and me yesterday is so much bullshit, and you know it," I say. "There's been no action to get the bitcoin secured for the ransom, and those three prisoners that Asim Al-Asheed wanted free are still in solitary at the super max. What's going on?"

"Matt, you know as well as I do that circumstances change and—"

"Richard, I want to talk to the president. Now." I look at my watch. Good Lord, is it really nearly 9 a.m.?

"I'll see what I can do. She's quite busy."

"In three hours, we hit the deadline," I say. "What the hell are you doing?"

"Our jobs," he says. "Along with the FBI, Homeland Security, the Secret Service, every—"

I say, "Don't you dare insult me like that, Richard. I'm getting my daughter freed, with or without you."

A cold pause. "What the hell do you mean by that?"

"I still have a few friends in the DC media," I say. "How do you think they'll react when I tell them that you're playing games with my daughter's life? That for whatever reason, you're dragging your feet, and you have no intention to pay the ransom?"

"Matt, don't you dare."

"Then don't you dare ignore me, Richard, because I'll make it happen," I say, my voice rising in anger. "And if the deadline expires and Mel's not released, her blood is going to be on your hands, and on the hands of your damn wife!"

I lost it.

I shouldn't have lost it.

Richard's voice is tight. "The president is a very, very busy woman. Your daughter is only one of her concerns. The world's a big, nasty, and dangerous place. You know it just as well as we do. And we're leaving it up to the professionals to find her, and if you leak some crazed story that we're not doing anything to find your girl, this administration and I will come down on you like a ton of cement. Got it?"

I say, "Find my daughter, Richard."

"We're working on it," he says. "And if she can, I'll have the president reach out to you later today. But don't hold your breath."

I disconnect the call and exhale loudly. I stand up, pace some more, and Agent Stahl is looking at me and so is Samantha, and it's time to go full DEFCON 1.

I get to my phone, start scrolling through my contacts, knowing I'm about to violate about a half dozen laws, social compacts, and unofficial DC ways of doing business, but I don't care about any of that.

Mel.

That's it.

I told Samantha I'm getting her back, and there's no stopping now.

There.

I find a private cell number, press it without hesitation, and it rings, and rings, and is answered by a woman, near breathless.

"Director Blair," she says. "Who the hell is this?"

Realizing that her caller ID is registering UNKNOWN, I quickly say, "Lisa, it's Matt Keating."

"Oh, Mr. President, I—"

"Lisa, I don't have time for pleasantries," I quickly say. "What the hell is going on?"

"Mr. President, I—"

"Lisa, tell me they're not dragging their feet. Tell me the bitcoin is being prepared, tell me the three prisoners are being prepped for transport to Libya. What the hell is going on over there?"

"Mr. President—"

"Lisa—"

She nearly snaps my head off through the airwaves. "Mr. President, shut your damn mouth!"

I pause mid-stride, breathing hard.

"Director," I manage to say. "Go on."

Then the universe seems to contract to nothing but my phone and the FBI director's excited voice.

Lisa says, "I'm trying to tell you, sir. We've gotten good intel from New Hampshire. We think we've found your daughter."

CHAPTER 53

Eastfield Regional High School
Eastfield, New Hampshire

In the gymnasium of Eastfield Regional High School, near banners hanging from the rafters honoring the Eastfield Explorers' achievements in basketball and lacrosse, FBI special agent Ross Faulkner, team leader of the FBI Hostage Rescue Team, is doing his very best not to punch out the New Hampshire State Police major standing in front of him, nearly toe to toe. Ross is a ten-year veteran of the FBI's most elite unit, and before joining the FBI, he was a Marine gunnery sergeant, having served three tours in Iraq. He has experience negotiating with various tribes and militias in northern Iraq, but this local cop is really starting to piss him off.

Major Harry Croteau of the New Hampshire State Police is dressed in a black jumpsuit and boots, like every other man in this guarded gymnasium, and his fleshy face is red with anger as he says, "I'll tell you again, Agent Faulkner, you don't have jurisdiction here."

"I say otherwise," Ross says. "It's a kidnapping."

Croteau raises his voice. "It's only a federal offense under certain circumstances, like a minor child being taken, crossing state lines with the victim, or the crime taking place aboard an aircraft. None of these fits in this situation. It's a state crime, and we're taking lead."

Ross says, "With all due respect, Major, I don't have time for this bullshit. We're here, the president's daughter is out there, and a known terrorist is holding her. That's all I need, and that's all it's going to be."

"The hell you say."

Phones are ringing, other members of Ross's twenty-member team are around the gym, their weapons and gear scattered on large folding tables, their vehicles parked outside in spots marked FOR TEACHERS ONLY. They've been here for nearly a day, after departing Marine Corps Air Facility Quantico in a borrowed Air Force C-17 Globemaster transport aircraft and landing at nearby Lebanon Airport. The HRT prides itself on being only four hours away from any location in the United States, and this trip has been no different.

Ross says, "Yes, the hell I say, along with the FBI director and the attorney general. This is our op and—"

"Ross!" is shouted from the other side of the gym. "Over here, now!"

He says, "Major, get the hell out. Before I arrest you on suspicion of income tax evasion or some damn thing."

Ross goes to a table where one of the HRT members, Gus Donaldson, swivels in a folding chair, communications gear and telephones behind him, and holds up a sheet of paper with writing on it.

"Ross," Gus says, voice tight with excitement, "we've caught a break. A good one."

Other HRT members gather around. "Go," Ross says.

"Early this morning, a local cop spotted a black Cadillac Escalade entering the garage of a large vacation home at the end of an unmarked dirt road, near a pond, isolated. The dirt road is off Route 113, marked with a sign that says *Macomber*. Near an RJ's hardware store. She saw the driver step out of the garage. She's positive it was Asim Al-Asheed."

"Did she make the call to us?"

Gus says, "No. She reached out to a sergeant she knows in the NH State Police, he kicked it over to his superior in his local troop, and that got pushed up the ladder. He vouches for her, says she's a straight shooter. No bullshit artist."

"Where is she now?"

"Out of contact," he says. "Cell phone coverage is pretty spotty around here."

"Tyler!" Ross calls out to another HRT member. "You copy that location info?"

Tyler is the team's research pro, and right now he's stationed before two large terminals. He says, "On it," and starts tapping away. Ross heads over, and in the very few seconds it takes to approach Tyler, the researcher says, with joy in his voice, "Got it! It's in Monmouth, near the border with Spencer. Property owned by a Dan Macomber, from Salem, Massachusetts. Here's the tax map."

Again, the HRT members cluster around, staring at the right-hand screen. Not only does the online tax map from the town's assessor's office have a floor map of the residence, but there's even a photo.

Two-story wooden house. Detached three-car garage. Front door and side door to the house. Large bay window to the right of the front door. Standard window to the left of the door. Windows on the second floor.

The floor map shows two large bedrooms and a bathroom upstairs. Bathroom downstairs. Large living room and small bedroom off to the right of the front door, kitchen and dining room to the left.

Thanks to his years of training and on-the-ground ops, Ross is quickly running through deployment options, seeing where he should post the initial squads. He says, “Sniper recon team, go. Split up when you get there, one squad to the east, the other squad to the west. I want eyes on target soonest. Check in when you’re secure…and head out quiet, like you’re making a Dunkin’ Donuts run. There’s so many reporters out there that we don’t want a goddamn media escort.”

As one, the team members scramble to the tables, picking up their weapons and gear, racing to a rear exit of the gym, their booted feet echoing loudly in the space. Ross feels tired, tense, wired. In any other hostage situation, there would be time to build a full-scale mock-up of the target house to allow the HRT assault teams a chance to practice their dynamic entry, over and over again.

But the time is slipping away. This is going to be a fast-moving op.

He goes down the line of tables, stopping at the end, where there’s a young red-haired woman with black-rimmed glasses. She’s wearing a T-shirt for some rock band Ross has never heard of. She sits in front of a set of complex keyboards, staring intently at a terminal streaming rows of letters and numbers.

“Ma’am,” he says, forgetting her name for the moment, knowing only that she’s from the National Security Agency and says she volunteered, “did you hear our update?”

“Uh-huh,” she says, chewing on her lower lip. “That I did, thanks. I’m doing data harvesting now.”

Next to the NSA representative is a skinny young Black man in Air Force fatigues with the bars of a first lieutenant, name tag COLLINS, and he’s murmuring to himself as he works a joystick. On the large monitor before him is an aerial view of a forested peak, and rows of numbers run along the bottom and side. Then a pond comes into view, and then a house.

The target house, Ross thinks. *There you are.*

Are you in there, Mel Keating?

Ross asks, "Any chance whoever's inside might hear or see you?"

Collins says, "Only if they have next-gen thermal imaging and acoustic detection equipment that even the Chinese and Russians don't have yet. Kestrel is pretty rad and good at what she does...we're about ten thousand feet up, damn near invisible...and here we go."

Ross is used to the high-quality equipment the DOD has and sometimes lends to the FBI, but this drone footage is so crisp and clear he feels as though he's hovering above the house. This equipment is so secret he and his fellow HRT members had to sign documents kicking up their classification levels so they could see what it can do. He can even make out splotches of lichen and moss on the edges of the shingles on the house's roof.

The camera zooms in even more, dipping and yawing, and the home looks empty. Nobody on the front lawn or rear lawn. Small dirt beach empty. No boats tied up to the dock.

Collins says, "We got fresh tire tracks in the dirt driveway."

Ross checks his watch. How far from this staging area to that dirt road? How many more minutes before the first teams there report back?

"Hey, Mr. FBI!"

He turns to Claire—yes, that's her name, Claire Boone from the NSA, one tough-looking young lady, even with the T-shirt and torn jeans—and she says, "The local electric company is called Liberty Utilities. I've accessed their system and got a real-time read off that home's electrical meter, which is one of those smart meters. It was pretty flat for the past three months but there's been a fifty percent uptick in kilowatt-hour usage in the past three days."

One of Ross's HRT guys approaches him and says, "Somebody's moved in."

Collins says, "All right, Agent Faulkner, let's see if we can sneak a peek inside."

The Air Force lieutenant works the keyboard, and in a quick moment, the overhead view of the house changes over to a black-and-white spectral ghost image reading thermal heat sources from inside.

Three fuzzy blobs of white appear.

Two seem to be together, in the kitchen area.

The third blob is fainter.

Ross says, "Lieutenant, what are we seeing?"

Collins says, "Kestrel is showing two people in the kitchen of the target house. Based on their location, it seems like they're around a table or something. Maybe having a late breakfast. I'm also seeing a faint heat signature from what appears to be a stove."

Ross is trying to keep focused, steady, but his heart rate and breathing are quickening.

"And the third image?"

"Pretty faint," Collins says. "Like the person is in the cellar below the two other persons."

"Gus," he quickly says to his communications officer. "Get the word out to the director. We've got a good hit, and we're responding."

Ross raises his voice. "Assault teams, saddle up! We're going to get the president's daughter!"

CHAPTER 54

Saunders Hotel
Arlington, Virginia

I open the door connecting the two suites in time to see FBI director Lisa Blair come in via the hallway door, with four agents following her, two of them carrying large black hard plastic cases. They pass Madeline Perry, my chief of staff, and other Secret Service agents and the skeletal staff from my failed reelection campaign from two years ago.

"Mr. President," Lisa says, approaching me. "Sorry I snapped at you back there."

I open the door wider.

"I deserved it," I say. "What do you have?"

Agent David Stahl stands up from his desk and laptop, and my wife gets off the bed, her face lightening up, hands clasped in front of her, and Blair's four agents—two female and two male—come in and quickly get to work, unpacking the hard plastic cases, pulling out keyboards, computers, and terminal screens. Madeline Perry comes in as well, her hands clasped, like she's uttering a silent prayer.

Lisa says, "A sighting came in from a police officer who located a black Cadillac Escalade in a garage at a remote home, next to a pond, at the end of a long dirt road. Isolated. The police officer says she saw Asim Al-Asheed walk from the garage to the house a few hours ago."

My fists instinctively clench.

Got you, you slippery bastard.

"Has it been verified?" I ask. Sam comes next to me and I put an arm around her waist.

Lisa says, "Our HRT section is based at a regional high school near the town of Monmouth. It has reps from the NSA and the Air Force. The NSA has retrieved utility records from the target house. The kilowatt-hour usage was pretty flat until recently. The house should be empty. It's being used."

"And the Air Force?" I ask. "What do they have?"

On the table I was working from earlier, agents are setting up a thin terminal screen and plugging in a power plug and cables to black boxes and keyboards.

"Give me a second and we'll show you," the FBI director says. "Cynthia, show us the latest feed from the target house."

"Yes, ma'am," a slim FBI agent says.

To the FBI director I say, "Lisa...don't get me wrong. I appreciate this more than you know. But why aren't you back at the White House, or at the Hoover building?"

She gives me a hard glance. "This is where I want to be. This is where I belong, Mr. President."

"Ma'am," says Cynthia, the FBI agent. "Here's the current video feed from Monmouth."

I instantly recognize the kind of black-and-white footage that pops up on the screen, the overhead view of a good-sized house, the numbers along the side and bottom indicating altitude, time, and date, the longitude and latitude of the spot the drone is hovering over. But what really catches my attention are the three white shapes in the house, two brighter than the third. I think I know what I'm seeing but I don't want to guess.

Lisa takes control, tapping a finger on the little white shapes.

"Thermal imaging. The Air Force liaison officer says the two brighter shapes are people in the kitchen. The third, fainter shape is someone in the basement."

Samantha gasps and brings a hand to her face.

Maddie, standing next to her, grabs Sam's hand, gives it a comforting squeeze.

A chubby male FBI officer—a random thought comes to mind: How did he pass the Bureau's grueling physical requirements?—wearing a headset with a mic says, "Ma'am, I've got Special Agent Faulkner on the horn."

"Let's hear him," she says, and to me she adds, "He's the HRT section leader in New Hampshire."

A hiss and crackling sound comes from the terminal's speakers, and Lisa says in a louder voice, "Agent Faulkner, this is Director Blair. Do you read me?"

"Five by five, ma'am," says a strong male voice, and it's a type of voice I've heard before. It belongs to an experienced and sharp-edged operator, in his zone and ready to get the job done.

God, do I wish I was there with him and the others.

Lisa says, "I've got President Keating and his wife with me, with others, and we're getting a visual feed from the Air Force asset. What's your status?"

"Ma'am, we've got four sniper/observers who are at the property. They're currently getting into position and will be giving us a report shortly. We're rolling an assault team and other units to that location now."

In a soft voice I say to the FBI director, "Ask Agent Faulkner if we could get the drone imaging to zoom out. I want to see more of the property."

"Agent Faulkner," Lisa says. "Could you have the Air Force liaison zoom out the current imaging to get a wider view of the target area?"

"Roger that, ma'am," he says.

Slowly the black-and-white image on the screen zooms out, revealing a pond, a dock, and what looks to be a dirt driveway, and then I see what I so desperately want to see.

Four thermal images, two on each side of the driveway in the woods, slowly approaching the house.

As Agent Faulkner promised, four FBI scout snipers are closing in.

I reach for Sam's free hand and she leans into me. Maddie is still holding on from Sam's right side.

"Sam, look," I whisper. "We're getting our girl back."

CHAPTER 55

Macomber residence
Monmouth, New Hampshire

FBI special agent Chris Whitney is a three-year veteran of the HRT, and even though he's been on hundreds of training missions and half a dozen real ops, he is working hard to stay focused and work with the team to get this job done, to free President Keating's daughter, and not act like an FNG getting the shakes.

No shakes today.

Get the job done.

Get the president's daughter out safely.

He is firmly hidden in a line of trees and low brush that's about twenty meters away from the dirt driveway, with a good view of the front of the three-bay garage and the near house. He's wearing a camouflage Nomex jumpsuit, ballistic helmet, and a MOLLE vest with a Springfield .45-caliber pistol holstered to it, along with a .223 HK416 automatic rifle and spare ammunition for both guns.

The three other sniper/observers are similarly armed, and prior to their coming here, Chris and those three guys came to an unofficial understanding. The normal rules of engagement are that they're not to open fire unless one of the two terrorists inside—either Asim Al-Asheed or his cousin Faraj—are holding weapons.

Screw that. Chris and other HRT operators know of Boyd Tanner from SEAL Team Two, and how he was nailed to a tree in Afghanistan by the bastard inside that house and his friends. So if Chris or anyone else gets a good shot at Asim, even if he's just holding a kitten, a .308 full-metal-jacket round is going to separate his brain stem from his spine, and to hell with any Monday-morning quarterbacking.

Chris slowly moves a bit closer, still getting a great view of the front side of the house. Fellow sniper Javier Delgado is up by the garage, and Henry Fong and Tom Plunkett are on the other side of the house.

From the earpiece snug inside his right ear come the quiet professional words of his fellow snipers.

"Delgado is on scene."

"Fong on scene."

"Plunkett on scene."

It used to be that these transmissions would be in code, like Sierra One or Hotel Four, but years of experience showed that clear names and clear language reduced the chances of miscommunication.

Chris toggles a switch. "Faulkner, this is Whitney. All on scene, eyes on target."

The voice of the HRT team leader comes through. "Roger that. Immediate Action Team is on station at the end of the road. They're en route."

Chris maintains eyes on target, his customized Remington model 700 bolt-action rifle firm in his grasp. He's looking through a Leupold Mark 6 3-18x44mm telescopic sight. In every week of training, he and the other HRT operators fire more than a thousand rounds of ammunition at various targets.

He's hoping he gets a chance to add one or two more to that total today.

"Whitney, this is Delgado," he hears through his radio earpiece.

"Go," he says.

Javier says, "Got a quick peek into the garage. Apparently empty of people. But I saw a black Cadillac Escalade inside."

"Roger that," Chris says. "Faulkner, you copy?"

"Affirmative," the HRT team leader says. "Immediate Action Team should be at your location in sixty seconds."

Chris takes a moment to check his watch. Nearly noon.

Surprise, surprise, Asim, he thinks, *your demands are going to be answered in less than a minute.*

With love and good wishes.

A flicker of movement.

Two groups of three armed black-clad men burst from the near tree line, and in seconds, they are at the bay window in front of the house and at the side door.

Chris is looking through the scope sight, his finger near the trigger, needing only a few ounces of applied pressure to fire off a round.

C'mon, Asim, he thinks.

Come to me.

CHAPTER 56

White House Situation Room

President Pamela Barnes is at the head of the table in the Situation Room, her husband, Richard, at her left, and Gary Reynolds, deputy director of the FBI, at her right. Other White House Situation Room staff are in the room, along with two female FBI agents accompanying the deputy director. In normal circumstances, her vice president—Oregon senator Coleman Pelletier—would be here, but thankfully, he's on a ten-day goodwill tour in South America, far away from the White House media and from Richard, who despises the man. A while back, Richard said, "That fool helped us get into the White House, but to call him an empty suit is an insult to quality fabric."

Three large video screens are on the wall at the other end of the table. One is off. The screen on the left shows the end of a dirt road that intersects with a paved road, and that little juncture is filled with New Hampshire State Police cruisers, Humvees, and black Chevrolet Suburbans belonging to the

Hostage Rescue Team. A police line with wooden barricades has been set up on the main road, and it seems as though the entire New England press corps is gathering there. Earlier, Barnes received a report that the FAA cleared all the airspace around that part of New Hampshire so no news helicopters will interfere with the unfolding operation.

The third video screen offers a view of the target house, where thermal imaging shows two subjects on the main floor, and a third, fainter image indicates someone in the basement.

Deputy director Reynolds is slim and tense-looking in a dark gray suit, and has a hearing bud in his left ear. He's narrating what is happening, and—*for all that's holy,* Barnes thinks—what is about to happen.

"The HRT team leader reports that the scout snipers are on scene, and that one of them has confirmed there's a black Cadillac Escalade in the garage."

Barnes just nods.

"The assault team is moving into position. They will be breaching the house and entering in less than a minute."

A warm sense of satisfaction and anticipation is beginning to grow within her.

Richard was right. Refuse to pay the ransom, let the professionals do it.

She turns and smiles at her husband and chief of staff, but instead of smiling back, he whispers, "I still call bullshit on FBI director Blair going over to Matt Keating's hotel room. She should be here, not her deputy. That's her damn job."

Barnes whispers back, "It can wait. Let's just get through the day."

That brightens his face. "Told you it would all work out, Madam President. By this time next week, your poll numbers will be up at least twenty points. Then you're going to fire Director Blair and that idiot clodhopper who's running Homeland Security."

Barnes turns back to the aerial view of the road. Astounding how crisp and clear the footage is. It reminds her again of the tremendous waste and resources hidden within the DOD budget, and how it's soon going to be time to take a really good look and squeeze out that misuse, no matter how many military contractors squeal.

Reynolds says, "Assault teams are in position."

The warm feeling of excitement and anticipation that Barnes is feeling grows larger. Richard slides out a piece of paper from a leather folder and says, "Madam President, we'll be having a media availability at 12:30 p.m. in the Rose Garden. Here are your remarks to review when you get a moment."

Barnes raises a hand, her signal to her chief of staff for *Not now; later, please,* and Reynolds says, "Ten seconds, Madam President."

"Very good," she says.

Focusing on the screen before her, she hears Deputy Director Reynolds say, "They're moving now."

And although she's been a guest at training sessions over the years for everyone from the Green Berets to Marine Recon, all showing off how good they are with their high-priced weapons and military toys in an attempt to get more funding, Barnes does have grudging respect for how fast these FBI agents are.

Two groups of three men (and why aren't any women there?) burst from the tree line and go to the house. They split up, and three go to the front, to a large window, and the other three go to the side, where there's another window and a door.

Richard whispers into her ear, "We're going to run this footage 24/7 in our TV spots when you're up for reelection, Madam President."

She smiles.

It's going to be all right after all.

CHAPTER 57

Saunders Hotel
Arlington, Virginia

There's a rush of memories coming at me as I see the clear and crisp color footage from the overhead drone, showing in great detail the HRT team's assault on the house holding Asim Al-Asheed, Faraj Al-Asheed, and Melanie Keating.

I'm still holding my wife's left hand, and Madeline Perry is still on the other side, holding her right hand, and I stare and remember all of my past training drills and ops in Iraq and Afghanistan, remember the cold, calm feeling of doing your job, performing what you were trained for, confident in your skills and those of your team members. Hard to believe that there's no real fear, just the tunnel vision of realizing what's ahead, what's at stake.

I silently say "Go, go, go" as I see the two three-man squads erupt from the tree line, knowing that there are four snipers in the woods providing overwatch and that there are now HRT vehicles racing up the dirt road to join the action.

There are radio-crisp messages coming out of the speakers, and even Director Blair remains silent as the operation unfolds.

The first team reaches the bay window up front, clustered together and working as one, all dressed in camouflage Nomex jumpsuits, helmets, and goggles, weapons and gear firmly strapped to their torsos.

The man in front swings a Halligan tool, smashing the window, raking and clearing the broken glass, ducking down and then moving away as the second man slams a metal ladder against the wall under the window.

I think, *Flash-bang grenades, M84s,* and the operator with the ladder tosses one through the broken window, and there's a brilliant flash of light and a cloud of smoke, and a similar light and blossom of smoke erupt from the other side of the house.

The third operator races up the ladder, followed by his two teammates, and this all takes place in just a matter of seconds as they quickly climb into the house. I think now of the controlled chaos erupting in the house's interior, the armed HRT operators moving sharply, yelling, "Down, down, down, hands, hands, hands!"

The HRT's mainstay in operations like this: *Speed, surprise, and violence of action.*

When I was in the teams, we often trained and sometimes worked with the HRT, and the band of tension around my chest is slightly lightened at knowing the kind of operators who are going in, knowing that apart from the operators in the teams or Delta Force, these are the best at what they do.

From the speakers comes the satisfied voice of the HRT leader. "Assault team reports two men in custody. No shots fired."

Samantha says, "Oh, thank you, thank you," and Maddie wipes at her eyes with her free hand, smiling with relief.

The HRT leader says, "Assault teams proceeding to the basement."

My God, what Mel must be thinking and hearing right now, I think, *the explosions of the stun grenades, the thumping of the feet overhead, the yells,* and I smile through my own tears, knowing our girl is seconds away from being freed.

And how long to get back to New Hampshire? For a reunion of reunions? Will we even sleep in the next twenty-four hours from the excitement and joy?

And will we ever let her leave our compound alone again?

"Team moving into basement."

I smile wider.

"Team in basement."

Samantha leans into me, silently joyful, and then it all ends.

The confident voice of the HRT leader is no longer confident.

"Say again?" he's asking someone next to him from his position in New Hampshire. "Repeat. Confirm that."

Samantha says, "Matt, what's going on?"

I just don't know, and what I hear next nearly makes me stumble back, like a sudden punch in the gut from pure black darkness.

The voice from the speakers: "Assault team confirms, third male in custody in the basement. Repeat, third male."

Director Blair says, "HRT leader, I need another confirmation. Are you saying there's a male in the basement? Not a female? Not Mel Keating?"

A few seconds of static crackling.

"Confirmed, Director Blair," says the weary voice. "Three males in custody. Appear to be locals. No female, no Mel Keating. More information forthcoming, ma'am."

Director Blair's face is pale, and I can just imagine what Sam and I look like.

Terrified and frightened parents, seconds away from receiving the most joyous news of our lives, ready to celebrate and hug and cry at the utter delight of having our kidnapped daughter safely freed and returned to us.

And then falling off a hidden cliff.

Director Blair says, "Matt, Sam…I…we'll find out what happened. Honest. We'll find out in a few minutes. I promise."

I check my watch.

It's 12:15 p.m., fifteen minutes past Asim Al-Asheed's ransom deadline.

Which has not been met.

My wife sees me look at my watch, and she notes the time as well.

Trying to keep her voice steady through the flowing tears, Sam says, "Matt, they didn't pay the ransom. They've killed our girl."

CHAPTER 58

Macomber residence
Monmouth, New Hampshire

HRT team leader and FBI special agent Ross Faulkner walks into the kitchen of the target house, removes his ballistic helmet, takes a look at the scene, his booted feet crunching on broken window glass. A wooden table is on its side, two chairs are smashed, and the air smells of exploded firecrackers; the odor is coming from the magnesium charges in the flash-bang grenades. Four of his team are in the kitchen, and others are fanning out through the house. An evidence-processing squad will be here in just a few minutes to search through every room, closet, and cabinet, as well as the nearby garage.

Three barefoot young men are sitting up against the kitchen wall, shaking, faces red, eyes watery, their arms behind them, flex-tied tight. The one on the right is wearing only a pair of plaid underwear, and the other two are wearing sweatpants and tank tops. The one in the middle's tank top is blue with red letters that say UMASS LOWELL.

All three have large wet spots just below their waists.

Standard procedure is to split up these three characters and start interrogating them separately, but Ross and his team don't have time, and today is definitely not standard. Hundreds of miles away, FBI director Lisa Blair and Matt and Samantha Keating are waiting for answers.

"Who are you guys?" Ross demands. "What the hell are you doing here?"

The one on the left, stockier than the others, with short blond hair shaved high and tight, says, "My name's Bruce Hardy. That's Gus Millet, and that's Lenny Atkins. We go to college down at UMass Lowell."

"You or your parents own this place?"

Bruce protests, "We're not trespassing! Honest to Christ! We're here legit!"

Ross says, "When did you get here?"

"About... an hour ago. Maybe ninety minutes."

"If none of you own it, do you know the owners?"

The one in the middle, skinny, red-haired, with freckles on his face and bare shoulders, says, "We won this place."

"What do you mean, *won?*"

The red-haired guy—Gus Millet—starts coughing and coughing, and at his side, Bruce says, "Yeah. I won it. I got an email from some outfit, saying I had won a week here, for free. Got my name from Facebook. One of those games where you answer the questions about what kind of movie star you are, you know? That's how it worked."

Ross doesn't know but nods otherwise. "Go on. Make it quick."

"The outfit sent me a money order for a thousand bucks," Gus says. "Said there was another thousand bucks in cash waiting for me and my buds when we got here. The place would be open. No need for keys. And yeah, just like the email said, there was a thousand bucks in cash. Ten one-hundred-dollar bills, stuck in the silverware drawer."

To Ross it's all becoming clear in a logical and horrid way; he knows of Asim's expertise in setting up clandestine support networks. He says, "And if you arrived here at a certain time, and if there were three of you, there'd be another payment of a thousand dollars coming your way after the week was done. Right?"

Bruce says, "No. There'd be another two grand. Not one. Sent to me by another couple of money orders. Hey, was this legit? Was it? Shit, if not, I'm not giving the money back. It's mine. I won it, fair and square."

Ross says to the young man on the right, Lenny Atkins, who's wearing just plaid underwear, "And what the hell were you doing in the basement?"

Lenny's face is pale, and he swallows and swallows again, as if he's desperately trying not to vomit.

He says, "Uh, when we got here, I was still pretty hungover from last night. I just needed to sleep it off more. These two kept on talking and yapping and farting around and I couldn't stand it. Downstairs had a bed, and I went down there and crashed."

Ross turns away as HRT team member Neil Spooner comes up from the basement. "There's a cell down there, built against the concrete foundation. Bed, chemical toilet, lamp. Nothing else. Even the bed's been made."

Ross nods and goes out to the main living room, the foul taste of failure in his mouth. He and his team did exactly what they were ordered to do. They managed a perfect breach and entry with only minutes to prepare, and in any other universe, this would be checked off as a successful op.

Sure.

Like that old joke: The operation was a success, but the patient died.

Were Asim Al-Asheed and his cousin Faraj really here? Was Mel Keating?

Behind him, one of the three captives yells out, "Hey! When do we get out of here? I wanna call my dad!"

Ross ignores him.

Shit.

A voice comes through his earpiece. "Faulkner, this is Martinez."

"Martinez, go."

"We've got a dead female on the property, about thirty meters to the east of the house."

Something cold seems lodged in his throat. He checks the time. It's 12:35 p.m., long after the ransom deadline.

Faulkner says, "Is it the president's daughter?"

"No," is the firm answer. "It's a woman in her early thirties, dressed in camos, carrying a holstered SIG Sauer and an ID saying she's a cop with the Monmouth Police Department. Must be the one who sent in the original sighting call. And that's why we couldn't raise her later."

Faulkner sighs. "Roger that. Cause of death?"

"Throat slit. Pretty messy. And I'd say she's been dead just a few hours."

A woman's voice comes to him through his earpiece. "Agent Faulkner, this is Director Blair. Just want to reconfirm what I've been hearing over the traffic. You've got a dead police officer on the property, correct?"

"That's affirmative, ma'am," he says. "We've got evidence-processing teams working the house, seeing what actionable intelligence we might find. But I'd say that with the officer's sighting and her eventual murder, I'm confident that Asim Al-Asheed was here."

The director doesn't reply to his message, but she doesn't have to.

Ross knows they're both thinking the same thing.

Most likely Asim Al-Asheed was here.

But what about Mel Keating?

Where's the president's daughter?

CHAPTER 59

Saunders Hotel
Arlington, Virginia

Secret Service agent David Stahl sits slumped in a chair in the hotel suite belonging to the Keatings, knowing his career and his life are pretty much done. Not that it's anything compared to what's happening to the president and his wife, but it's his, and he owns it. Over the years he and other agents, during drinking bouts and bull sessions, would talk and discuss successful protections—Rawhide in Washington on March 30, 1981—and the agency's biggest failure, Lancer, in Dallas on November 22, 1963.

Now the historians will add Hope to that list, with his name firmly attached.

He thinks of haunted Secret Service agent Clint Hill, who was with the Secret Service vehicle riding behind the presidential limousine on that day in Dallas. Even though he risked everything to jump on the car and shield the First Lady and the fatally wounded Lancer with his own body, he carried a deep guilt for years, thinking that if he had only been a second or two faster, he could have taken the third bullet and saved the president.

With his own guilt gnawing at him, Stahl turns away from the stricken looks of Matt and Samantha Keating and stares at a framed print of some Winslow Homer painting depicting an ocean scene. Even after that horrid day, Agent Hill stayed with the Secret Service, performing with honor, becoming special agent in charge of presidential protection and then assistant director of the Secret Service before his retirement.

Stahl knows he can't do anything like that. He's done with the Secret Service, either this month or next. He should have disobeyed orders, should have maintained discreet protection of Mel Keating via his detail's "training sessions." Or he should have convinced Harbor to spend the money to assign private security to Mel.

Damn it, Harbor wanted to go out and get up that mountain, find and retrieve Mel on his own, and instead of sticking with procedures, Stahl should have taken the gamble, should have joined Harbor on the search with two or three other agents from the detail. Get the job done, screw procedures and policies.

Beat Asim Al-Asheed to his target.

The conversation on the other side of the room among the FBI director, the Keatings, and Madeline Perry catches his attention, with the president saying, "All right, with that police officer's murder, it seems logical that Asim Al-Asheed was there. But that doesn't mean Mel was being held there, right?"

The president's chief of staff says, "There was the homemade cell in the basement."

Keating shakes his head. "Doesn't mean a damn thing. That bastard is good at covering his tracks, putting up red herrings. For all we know, Mel is with the cousin, Faraj."

Stahl finds his voice. "Search the cell."

FBI director Blair gives him a withering look, that of one law enforcement official gazing upon the failure of another. "It's been done."

Stahl sits up straighter, finding his voice. "No. Get an evidence team in there, really search the place. Every nook and cranny, every square inch."

"And what will they be looking for?" she asks, barely veiled contempt in her voice.

He says, "They'll know it when they find it."

She stands there, and the president says, "Lisa, please."

"All right, then," she says, and she contacts the HRT director on scene, and Stahl just sits and waits.

And remembers.

In Mel Keating's bedroom on the second floor of the White House on one of those very busy few days after Matthew Keating was sworn in as president, Stahl said, "Miss Keating, I hope I haven't scared you."

She shook her head, and Stahl thought, *No, she's the daughter of two smart and tough parents. She wouldn't be scared.*

Mel said, "No, I'm fine. I mean, when Dad was in the teams, we were always on alert around the house, in case strangers were hanging around, or if there were hang-up phone calls."

"That's good experience," Stahl said. "But if you're kidnapped, the kidnappers might decide to move you after a day or so. Make sure that after you're aware of your surroundings, you try to leave something behind to help us know you were there. A hidden note. A bit of graffiti. Or some personal item that only your Mom and Dad would recognize. Think you can remember that?"

And Mel looked at him almost with pride. "Of course, Agent Stahl."

* * *

The wait ends about six minutes later.

"Director," says the voice from the computer's speakers. "This is Faulkner."

"Go," Director Blair says.

"We found something."

Stahl stands up. The Keatings and their chief of staff move closer to the computer terminal and its speakers.

Blair says, "Go on."

"It was under the bed, against one of the metal posts holding it in place. A gold ring. There's an inscription inside and it says—"

Samantha Keating speaks up, joy making her voice shake. "'From ST to KM, December 10, 1941.' Grampie Steve gave that ring to my Grammie Kim, just after he joined the Navy when Pearl Harbor was bombed. I gave that ring to Mel on her sixteenth birthday."

Now they're all looking at Stahl, and Director Blair says, "How did you know?"

Stahl says, "A few days after President Keating was sworn in, when the First Family was moving in from the Naval Observatory, I had a meeting with Mel. I explained to her the challenges of living in the White House, and how her Secret Service protection was going to increase, because she was now the president's daughter. Among the things we talked about was what she could do if she were kidnapped. I said even with her protection, something could happen."

Madeline Perry mutters something and Stahl is sure she just said, "That's a goddamn understatement," but he ignores her and goes on.

"I said there would always be a chance that the kidnappers would try to move her from one location to another. I told her that she should try to leave something behind, a scribbled note, a piece of clothing, or jewelry, so that we would know she had been there."

Director Blair says, "Smart and tough girl."

Samantha Keating looks to her husband. "Matt, so she was there. She was there!"

And the next question hangs in the air, taunting all of them.

Where is Mel Keating now?

Stahl's guilt increases.

He has no answer for that, and thinks again, *It's all my fault.*

CHAPTER 60

Family quarters
The White House

President Pamela Barnes is sitting in a comfortable chair in her private quarters on the second floor of the White House, having her daily drink of Glenlivet and ice three hours ahead of schedule. Her husband, Richard, is sitting near her, sipping a tumbler of ice water, his long legs and expensive Lucchese Romia cowboy boots stretched out in front of him.

He starts to speak, and she holds up her hand.

He quickly quiets himself.

One of the perks, she thinks, of having your husband work for you.

Barnes asks, "We haven't heard from Treasury again, have we?"

Richard shakes his head. "No, Pamela. They're trying various options to locate that account, but it's gone."

She remembers those first few frantic minutes down in the Situation Room after the rescue went south, when she turned to Richard and said, "Pay the ransom. Now. Make it happen.

Get those prisoners out of super max, draw up the goddamn pardon. Let's see if we can salvage something from this damn disaster."

But there is nothing to be salvaged. The account that was prepared to receive the ransom via a Tor browser on what was called the dark web has been taken down.

It seems the window for paying the ransom has been firmly closed by Asim Al-Asheed.

She takes a strong sip of the bracing drink, feeling it jolt her, wake her, and considers what's before her.

Barnes says, "That was quite the roller coaster ride earlier, wasn't it?"

"Yes, Pamela, it was."

"The whole bright afternoon and the following days were ahead of us, weren't they?" she goes on, settling back in the chair. "The daughter of the former president rescued. One of the world's most wanted terrorists captured. Superb footage of our FBI in action, not screwing up for a nice change of pace. Lovely news reports about the Keating family being reunited. Perhaps even a meet later in the Oval Office, with me giving awards to the FBI agents who rescued her, complete with the happy Keating family looking on. Smiles and handshakes and hugs all around."

Her husband and chief of staff remains quiet.

Good.

"Our poll numbers reaching the sky," she goes on. "And with all this wonderful news going on, another side benefit is, maybe the macho, red-white-and-blue wing of the party that still worships that Navy boy would finally shut up and get on the team for our upcoming reelection campaign. But that's not going to happen, Richard, is it?"

"No, Pamela."

She rubs the cold glass tumbler against her forehead, sees

the framed photos and plaques and other remembrances from when she was governor of Florida. Up there is an old Florida flag from the late 1800s, showing the state seal against a white background, before that damn red Saint Andrew's cross was added back in 1900. Most historians believe it was added to show nostalgia for the old Confederacy.

One of Barnes's quiet goals as governor was to strip that disgusting red cross from the flag before she left office, but she knew that most of the voters and their representatives in Tallahassee would never go for it.

That's the joy and the scourge of politics. Doing what was right, but also knowing your limitations.

Another strong sip.

She says, "You're going to let slip a story in the next hour to a trusted reporter, high up in the business, and I mean *trusted,* Richard. There can't be blowback on this, linking it back to you, or to me. Especially me."

"Absolutely," he says.

She sharpens her voice. "I mean it, Richard."

He clasps his still-worn cattle rancher hands in front of him, smiles. "A trusted foreign policy advisor for one of your predecessors said that most DC journalists are twenty-seven years old, no real experience except for reporting on political campaigns, and they literally know nothing. That's still true today, fortunately."

"Good," Barnes says. "The story I want to see appear later on the Internet is that the Barnes Administration was led on by an intelligence failure from the top levels of the FBI and Homeland Security. That the Barnes Administration was ready and willing to secretly pay the ransom to free Mel Keating but was strongly advised not to do so by these advisors. President Barnes was told by agencies she trusted that they had a strong lead on the whereabouts of Mel Keating, and, trusting their professional judgment, she let the professionals do their job. That's why the ransom wasn't paid."

Richard doesn't say anything.

Barnes goes on, feeling strength returning to her with every word she speaks. "The story should also say that President Barnes is personally heartbroken over today's failed rescue mission, and that she is ensuring that all federal and local law enforcement officials are redoubling their efforts to find Mel Keating. Got it?"

He nods. "That's...pretty bold."

"What's that old saying: Fortune favors the bold? Or the brave? As you pointed out a couple of days ago, Richard, our fortunes are in the tank. We need to climb out, no matter what it takes."

"There'll be pushback from Director Blair and that moron Paul Charles in Homeland Security. They'll deny everything."

"Fine," she says. "There were no aides or notetakers with us during our last meeting. The FBI can deny all they want, and Paul Charles won't see that he's getting played. He'll leak out to his own pet journalists that he agreed with me, to pay the ransom, and he'll say that it's all the FBI's fault. The fool won't see that by defending himself, he'll just be confirming our position."

Her husband says, "Impressive. When do you want it?"

"Now," she says, and Richard gets up from his chair. Before he steps away, she says, "Oh, one more thing."

"Yes?"

Barnes holds out her empty glass tumbler. "It's been a bear of a day. Get me another drink."

He takes the glass from her hand. "Absolutely, Madam President."

CHAPTER 61

Saunders Hotel
Arlington, Virginia

Samantha Keating is sitting on a chair in the hotel suite, staring out the window. She can't stand looking at the large-screen television, even with the sound off, seeing video of the failed rescue mission repeated over and over again, and seeing the various talking heads debate, discuss, and argue over whether her girl is still alive.

To hell with them all.

Matt is talking with FBI director Blair, and Agent Stahl is in the conversation as well. Next to her, sweet Maddie Perry is staying quiet, holding a Gideon's Bible in her hands, silently reading and praying for Mel.

Samantha closes her eyes, seeing again the overhead view of that damn house and the pond nearby, and she's not sure why, but there is a nagging feeling of déjà vu, as if she's seen that house, as if she's been to that house, and she knows it can't be true.

It's impossible.

But still the feeling remains.

She's a doctor and a professor, she believes only in evidence and, especially when it comes to archaeology, solid evidence. No research or digs stemming from legends of Druids or Irish monks landing in North America—only facts. That is what propelled her in her Basque research. The facts of their voyages to North America were true and were signposts for her eventual research and digs and that lovely discovery of a previously unknown Basque settlement in the Americas.

She wishes she could remember the sheer innocent joy of discovery that happened days back in that coastal town of Hitchcock, before those two Maine State Police detectives raced up to tell her that her life was broken.

More talk over there in the corner with her husband and the FBI and Secret Service, thrashing out options, where to go next, and *how* to go next. One big question is how the world's most wanted terrorist and his cousin were able to slip Mel out of that house through such a tight law enforcement cordon.

For Samantha and everyone else are certain that Mel was there.

The gold ring, carefully hidden, proves it.

Maddie continues her silent reading.

The three over there continue their chattering.

And that memory returns, of being at that house, over the water and—it comes to her.

Nearly two years ago, Samantha was contacted by a friend of hers from the University of Maine, in Orono, who said an elderly uncle claimed to have some Basque pottery he had recovered while working on a fishing trawler. The uncle was convinced by his niece to turn over the pottery to Samantha, but the problem was that he had left his life as a fisherman and gone full prepper, moving to an isolated lake in the Great North Woods in upper Maine.

Getting there meant driving for hours over dirt roads, or—

"Matt," Samantha says, getting up and going over to him and Agent Stahl and FBI director Blair.

"Yes?"

"That small pond...the one adjacent to the house where Mel was kept. How big is it?"

"What?" Matt asks, confused.

"How big is it? The longest stretch?"

Director Blair says, "I don't see why—"

Matt says, "David, you know how to work Google better than me. Find out."

"On it, Mr. President." Agent Stahl goes to the keyboard and Blair still looks confused, but Samantha sees a look on Matt's face that shows he understands what she's looking for.

"Got it, Mr. President," Agent Stahl says. "Long Pea Pond. Its greatest length is...just over three thousand feet."

Samantha says, "Floatplane. That's how they got out without being noticed...a floatplane came in and took the three of them away."

Director Blair says, "How do you know?"

Tears are coming to her eyes as she remembers that sunny day, a peaceful and pleasant day, no real worries, remembers flying over forested lands and peaks, glimpsing ponds and lakes below, eagerly looking forward to seeing what that old fisherman found.

Which turned out to be a Sears and Roebuck soup bowl, circa 1930.

Samantha says, "A Cessna T206 floatplane with a load of four passengers can take off and land from a body of water that's two thousand, nine hundred and thirty-two feet in length. I know that because I flew on one two years back. That's how they did it. Flying low to the ground, getting in and out, and then..."

Her husband says, "If he or she is a good pilot, flying low to the ground to avoid radar…it could work."

Director Blair steps away, gets on her phone, starts speaking quickly and firmly to whoever's on the other end.

Agent Stahl does the same.

Matt looks at her, obviously tired and anguished but nevertheless conveying his loving respect. Any other time or place or situation, Samantha would relish the look.

"Good job," he says.

Samantha says, "I know how they got her out. I don't know where she is now, Matt. Not good enough. Not by a long shot."

CHAPTER 62

Saunders Hotel
Arlington, Virginia

Following Sam's insight, some busy minutes are spent on the phone, and then Director Blair says, "Mr. President, Mrs. Keating, I'm sorry to do this, but—"

I give her a weary nod. "You've got to go. Back to your office. I understand. And probably take a nasty phone call from the president's chief of staff."

She gestures to the chubby male FBI agent from before. "Special Agent Burke will stay here, will be my personal liaison to you and your wife. I'll keep you apprised of any developments. And getting nasty phone calls from Richard Barnes is all part of the joy of the job."

"Thanks, Lisa."

Blair goes to Samantha, pauses, and gives her a hug, and then gives me one as well. Totally unprofessional and unnecessary, but I find it comforting.

She says, "We'll get her back safe. Honest."

"I know you will," I say, but Samantha stares at the carpeted floor and says nothing as Director Blair and three of her agents depart.

Madeline Perry, my chief of staff, says, "I'll get back to work in the other room, sir. I'll send up some food for you all. What would you like?"

"Anything," I say. "Nothing."

At some point, there's a thick silence in the room that matches the smell of sweat, despair, and uneaten sandwiches and cheeseburgers. Sam is on her side of the bed, dozing, and FBI special agent Burke is sitting back in his chair, arms crossed against his plump chest. Agent Stahl is in his own chair, on the other side of the room, and he's sleeping.

About the only development came hours ago, when three witnesses in the area of Long Pea Pond said that they saw a light gray floatplane flying nearby earlier this morning, flying low, hugging the tree lines and peaks.

One witness is certain that the aircraft flew north.

Another is equally certain that it went west.

And the third has no concept of direction, and could only vaguely say, "It was up there somewhere. I'm sure of it."

I go over and open the door to the adjoining suite. It's quiet in there, with staffers and others dozing in chairs or on the floor, but Madeline Perry is staring intently at her computer screen.

"Maddie?" I say.

She seems startled and glances over at me. "Oh, sorry, sir. You surprised me. What is it?"

I say, "It's quiet now. I need to do something, something I should've done hours ago."

"What's that?"

"Talk to Tim Kenyon's parents," I say. "Can you arrange it?"

"Certainly, sir."

* * *

Less than fifteen minutes later, Madeline Perry comes into the second suite and hands over her phone.

"Bill Kenyon, sir," she says. "And his wife, Laura."

I take the phone, take a breath. When I was president, I made similar calls to the fathers and mothers, husbands and wives, of personnel who had been killed in the line of duty. None of the calls were easy, but there was a protocol to follow, the commander in chief expressing the nation's sympathy to the family of those who had made the ultimate sacrifice.

But now?

Now I was expressing my own personal sympathy to a father and mother who lost their son because he was dating my daughter.

"Mr. Kenyon? Mrs. Kenyon? This is Matt Keating."

A tired male voice—"Hello, Mr. President"—and a fainter, woman's voice saying just "Hello."

"May I call you Bill? And Laura?"

"I guess," he says, and his wife doesn't say anything.

I close my eyes. We're all grieving in our own ways, but their grief is real and solid. Mine is the grief of an unknown outcome for my kidnapped daughter, each second filled with terrible thoughts of what might be happening to her.

I say, "Bill, Laura, I'm so sorry for what happened to Tim. I met him a few times during the last couple of months, and he was a great young man, very smart, very personable. I know Mel very much enjoyed being with him. I…"

I run out of things to say. What else? *Sorry your beloved son had the misfortune to date the daughter of the president, who made so many enemies, and died because he was collateral damage?*

I finally say, "The FBI, Homeland Security, and hundreds of police officers and other investigators are tracking down Tim's killer. I know that must be small comfort, but his killer won't escape. I promise you that."

A long silence ensues, and I wonder if we've been disconnected. Then I hear the sad sigh of Tim's father. He says, "Those are good words, Mr. President, and I appreciate it, but right now it's all words, isn't it? I mean, you look at the news, you read the papers, and what do you see? A lot of stories about your girl, and nearly nothing about my boy. And what little there is about my boy is just so much crap—misspelling his name, or getting his age wrong."

I hear a few sobs and then a *click,* and I imagine it's Tim's mother hanging up.

But his father continues. "Your girl has it all. Comfortable life, best schools she ever wanted, she could choose any life she desired. My Tim"—his voice struggles—"had to chase down scholarships, grants, and work after school and during the summer, to make enough to get to a school like Dartmouth. He had hopes, Mr. President, and Laura and I, we had hopes for him, too. Now he's gone. Because he reached too far, wanted to date your girl, and that got him killed."

I wait, not wanting to interrupt this grieving man, and he says, choking back the tears, "My wife and I, we're gonna pray tonight again for our boy. And then we're gonna pray for you, and your wife. Pray that you don't have to go through what we're experiencing right now, Mr. President."

He disconnects the call.

I put Maddie's phone down and stretch my back and look up at the white plaster ceiling, hoping that if God is in an answering mood tonight he will answer the Kenyons' prayers.

Mel.

Where are you?

* * *

When I was a kid growing up in rural Texas, hours to the west of Austin, I was fascinated by the Navy, even though there were no rivers or lakes of note near our small dusty town. But we were close to Fredericksburg, where famed World War II fleet admiral Chester Nimitz was born, and I must have gone to the museum marking his life a half dozen times.

Among the scores of books I read about the Navy in those years was one called *The Terrible Hours,* about the desperate attempts to rescue sailors trapped in the USS *Squalus,* a submarine that in 1939 sank off the coast of New Hampshire during a training accident.

A great book, a great title, and I mean no disrespect to those long-dead thirty-three rescued men, but I would gladly exchange their terrible hours for my own terrible hours during the glacial passage of time following the failed rescue of Mel.

The hours slowly pass, with meals half eaten, phone calls, visits from representatives from Homeland Security and the Secret Service, even some cryptic briefings from CIA officers. I have some comforting words with Samantha, each of us trying to buck the other up as the red numerals on the various clocks flip their way into the next day.

Maddie Perry is busy next door as well, juggling lots of phone calls and visits, an amazing number of them from psychics who claim to know where Mel is at this moment. Sometimes the "readings" are precise, with a street name and number, and other times it's a psychic thinking that Mel is near a railroad by a body of water.

One phone call that isn't received, however, is from Pamela Barnes, president of the United States.

At some point in the middle of the night, my body gives up and I fall into a troubled sleep on the unmade bed, Samantha cuddled up next to me.

* * *

A touch on the shoulder and I'm instantly awake. A chubby man is looking at me, and for a moment I don't recognize him in the low light of the suite's bedroom.

"Sir?" he says.

Now I know who he is. FBI special agent Burke, who's still dressed in his gray suit, though his white shirt is wrinkled and stained and his navy-blue necktie is undone.

I swing off the bed, trying not to wake up Samantha, but she's sleeping as lightly as I am, and she says, "What is it? What's going on?"

Burke says, "Sir, ma'am. Director Blair is coming here. She should arrive in about ten minutes."

Samantha says, "What time is it?"

I look at the bedside clock. "It's 2 a.m. Agent Burke, why is she coming here?"

Burke looks tired, troubled. "Sir, we've received word that Asim Al-Asheed is going to be releasing a statement within the hour."

CHAPTER 63

Family quarters
The White House

Among the several things that President Pamela Barnes hates about her job is knowing that her time is never really her own, that other people have demands upon her, and that at any minute or hour of the day or night, she will have to respond to some emerging crisis or disaster.

For years her predecessors ran TV advertisements during election season that claimed that *they* would have what it takes to answer the phone at three in the morning in case of an emergency, but the honest truth is that she's never been awakened by a phone call during the night.

Like now: it's just a gentle knock on the bedroom door, with a subsequent, louder knock. She switches on a bedside lamp and says, "Come in. I'm awake."

After her inauguration, Barnes made it clear to her husband, Richard, that her staff should never delay in waking her up in case something of national importance was occurring. She was remembering an observation from a famed *New York Times* columnist who quoted a White House aide as saying, "You can't be fired for waking the president; you can only be fired for not waking him."

Or her.

A familiar figure slides into the room from the corridor, where a Secret Service agent has apparently accompanied Felicia Taft, deputy chief of staff.

"Sorry to disturb you, ma'am," Taft says.

Barnes's chief of staff is deep asleep next to her, a pillow over his head. She's often gently teased Richard that he could sleep through an earthquake, to which he has jokingly replied, "Never been an earthquake in Florida as long as I've been around, so we'll never know, will we?"

She gets out of bed, puts on her old blue terry cloth robe, which has traveled many miles and years with her.

"Is it news about Mel Keating?" she asks.

"Yes, ma'am."

"What is it?"

Taft says, "Ma'am, the watch officers in the Situation Room have received word that Al Jazeera will be releasing a statement from Asim Al-Asheed within the hour. The deputy national security advisor is on her way there now."

Barnes slides her feet into soft leather sandals and says, "I'll be there shortly as well."

Taft goes out, softly closing the door behind her, and Barnes leans over the bed, shakes her husband and chief of staff awake.

He coughs, grunts, and sits up, bare-chested, wearing only a pair of blue pajama bottoms. "What's up, Pamela?"

"Get up, get dressed," she says. "Time to earn your salary. Asim Al-Asheed is going to announce something in the next hour. We need to get down to the Situation Room."

Richard yawns, scratches at the back of his head. "Do we know what he's going to say?"

"Something horrible and bloody," she says.

He moves to get out of bed. "For sure?"

Barnes says, "An educated guess. What, you think he's going to give up Mel Keating because he likes her, and is going to forgive all? Come along, Richard. No time to waste."

CHAPTER 64

Saunders Hotel
Arlington, Virginia

The suite is crowded again, with FBI director Lisa Blair and three more FBI agents, and they've set up another television screen, which has a direct feed coming in from Al Jazeera, in Doha, Qatar. The suite's own set is tuned to CNN. Even at this ungodly hour, Lisa is wearing a DC power suit—dark slacks and jacket, white blouse—and her hair is perfectly styled.

Samantha is on the edge of the bed, staring, hands clasped tightly in her lap, and I catch her attention, and the look in her eyes is haunted, both seeing me and staring a thousand yards away. I've seen that look before, on fellow team members or Army soldiers or Marines in the field who've been out too long and have seen way too much.

When that look comes to someone's eyes, he or she is perilously close to collapse.

I hug her but it's like hugging a store mannequin.

I step back and Lisa checks the time, and says, "Our FBI

liaison in Doha tells us that it's a video message, dropped off by a courier. Flash drive or thumb drive. We're trying to track down the courier but…"

Her voice trails off.

Sure. I know what she's about to say. Any American law enforcement agency in a foreign country works under tremendous limitations, trailed by the host country's intelligence agencies, not able to proceed with an investigation without the cooperation of the locals, and not able to work quickly or respond to developments.

Like fighting with ropes of taffy covering one's arms and legs.

The feed coming into the two television screens is the same, though the CNN feed is just a few seconds behind the one coming from Al Jazeera.

I sit down next to Samantha, hug her waist, and she slightly leans into me as we both wait.

The male Al Jazeera anchor is well-dressed, with black hair and a mustache. He's speaking fast, face lit up with the excitement of reporting a breaking story.

"Can we have the sound, please?" I ask. "From Al Jazeera?"

One of the male FBI agents obliges and steps back.

Others in the room include Secret Service agent David Stahl and my chief of staff, Maddie Perry, who's clasping a Bible to her chest and looks like she hasn't slept in two days. The chaos and the fear I'm feeling is intermingled with affection for this smart and strong-willed woman. She could have gone anywhere in the Barnes Administration or private industry but decided to follow me from the White House into exile.

In a crisp voice, the television announcer says, "We will now air the video supplied to us by Asim Al-Asheed. We have not reviewed this video because of its timeliness and newsworthiness. You and our valued viewers will be seeing this for the very first time."

The screen cuts away from the anchor desk, and there's a blue screen, bursts of lines of static, and the picture becomes clear.

A rough rock face, some moss and tiny plants at its base, which leads out to a rock ledge.

Asim Al-Asheed walks into the frame, seen from his waist up; he's wearing a black T-shirt and a smile on his face. He looks sharper, harder, deadlier without his beard.

He nods. "*As-salam alaykom,* Matthew Keating, Samantha Keating, President Pamela Barnes, and all who are viewing this. I apologize that this is not a...what you call a *live feed* but a recording, from several hours ago, after we departed the home of Mr. Macomber in your White Mountains, and here we are, in these mountains still. My thanks to Mr. Macomber for his unwitting hospitality, and my apologies for what happened to his home. I am sure the proper authorities will compensate him for the damages caused by your FBI."

The suite is quiet. Sam is firm against my side, my arm still around her waist.

Asim says, "And why have we come to this, Matthew Keating? A simple answer, for it is all due to your actions two years past, when you killed my wife Layla Al-Asheed and my sweet daughters, Amina, Zara, and Fatima. I am a jihadist, a warrior of Allah, and I knew it was my fate to die on the battlefield. But my wife? My daughters? They were innocents, and you killed them. Their blood is on your hands. Their blood will be on your hands until you die."

A long pause. It's like he's staring right at me.

"Here we are. According to the great lawgiver Hammurabi and the laws of the holy prophet Moses, and the laws of Islam, I am due compensation. I am due reparation. I am due...justice. I asked for all this, and I was ignored, I was mocked, and yesterday morning, armed men attempted to kill me."

He looks to his side for a second, like something is interrupting him, and he says, "And is what I asked for so unreasonable? I asked for a sum much less than what you pay for one of your F-22 Raptor aircraft. Is your daughter's life not worth the cost of one of your aircraft that bombs and strafes innocents?"

He smiles wider. The bastard knows he's making a point that will be accepted by many people here and around the world.

"I asked for the release of three of my comrades in arms," he says. "I know the excuse for not letting them go. 'This government does not negotiate with terrorists.' Oh, please. The United States government negotiates with terrorists whenever it suits their needs, their desires. The United States counts as allies governments who do the same as I do, only on a much larger scale. Ask yourself, then, Matthew Keating: Why is it that your government does not desire your daughter's release?"

Samantha is trembling against me, like we're in the middle of a blizzard with the heat off in our room.

"Finally," he says, "I asked for a slip of paper, a promise from President Pamela Barnes to ensure my safety. A reasonable request, I'm sure you understand, and a fair exchange for your daughter's safety. But what was her answer? Armed men trying to kill me and my cousin Faraj."

Asim shakes his head. "According to laws and tradition that I learned while growing up, all I sought was simple justice. And that was not offered to me. Alas, Matthew Keating, this is what I am forced to offer in return."

The next few seconds brutally bring me back to my first nighttime parachute jump while I was in SEAL training. My first half dozen jumps took place in the daylight, when I could see the landscape below me, the other parachutists, the distant horizon and overhead blue sky and clouds. But on that windy night, departing from a four-engine C-130 Hercules, I was stepping out into the darkness, into the unknown, hoping and trusting in my training and my equipment.

Now there is no trust—in anything.

Just blindly again stepping out into the unforgiving darkness.

For the camera slowly pulls back, revealing Asim Al-Asheed, and on her knees beside him is our daughter, Mel Keating, eyes wide with fright behind her eyeglasses, arms bound tightly behind her.

CHAPTER 65

East 33rd Street
New York, New York

In his home office in the Great Bay Condominiums, Jiang Lijun of the Chinese Ministry of State Security is smoking a Zhonghua cigarette and watching the scene videotaped from somewhere in the American White Mountains unfold before him on a small wall-mounted television set. The office is modest and has no windows, for Jiang doesn't want the surveillance cameras and snoopers out there keeping track of his activities. A light switching on at this hour of the morning would send a note of concern among the CIA that something is up with the Chinese.

Which is true.

A few minutes ago, his wristwatch vibrated, waking him, and in the darkness, he got out of bed without waking his wife, Zhen, or their daughter, Li Na. In his office he picked up the secure phone that connected him to the mission, which is only two blocks away, and the night-duty officer said, "You're advised to turn on one of the American cable channels, Comrade Jiang."

He takes another puff from his cigarette. His office has shelves of books, mostly historical and political works about the United States and China, and there is no computer terminal here to be hacked or filing cabinets to be pried open. Half of the floors in this building are owned by the mission to house its diplomats and staff, and Jiang uses this room for thinking, reading, and contemplation.

On the television set is a crisp video of Asim Al-Asheed, speaking clearly and confidently into the camera.

"...I asked for a sum much less than what you pay for one of your F-22 Raptor aircraft. Is your daughter's life not worth the cost of one of your aircraft that bombs and strafes innocents?"

Not a bad question, Jiang thinks, sitting comfortably in blue cotton pajamas topped with a red silk robe that once belonged to Father.

The man on the television is speaking plainly and truthfully, and Jiang has to admire how he holds himself. His words are powerful, and at any time and place, Asim Al-Asheed could have become a prominent political leader in his world, or, as Jiang knows, a medical doctor, the man's original dream and desire.

But he chose the bloody path of a terrorist, and even though there are millions of *bèn dàn*—stupid eggs—here and abroad who are now thinking kindly of him, Jiang remembers another Asim Al-Asheed.

Four years ago.

In a dusty, windswept collection of huts and dirt roads laughingly called a village in southern Libya, Jiang was tasked with overseeing the construction of a vital oil pipeline in this district, but the equipment supplied by the China State Construction

Engineering Corporation had been sabotaged, and oil workers hired from Georgia had been threatened and chased away.

The tribe that lived in this village and others in the area refused to cooperate with the pipeline's construction, even with the promise of money and laborer jobs for their men.

The pipeline was a month overdue.

And Jiang was told to fix it. No detailed orders, no suggestions, no recommendations.

Just fix it.

Jiang stood next to a battered yellow Toyota pickup truck with two personal guards from a Pakistan contract force that had accompanied him from Tripoli, and they watched as Asim Al-Asheed convinced the tribe to stop its actions against the pipeline project. A half dozen other pickup trucks were parked in a semicircle.

Gunshots. Shouts. A scream. Al-Asheed and his collection of fighters herded eight men and women into the dirt area in front of the parked trucks. They were forced to kneel. A crowd of about fifty villagers was clustered together, held in place by Asim's armed men. A number of young boys and girls were brought forward, and then Asim went down the line of kneeling men and women and shot each one of them in the back of the head.

The women villagers screamed and lamented in an Arabic singsong that chilled Jiang, and when a satisfied Asim Al-Asheed came up to Jiang, he said, "You will have no more problems in this village."

Jiang asked, "Why did you force the children to watch you?"

Asim looked surprised to be asked such a question. "Because they will remember forever what happened here, and will tell their children, and their children's children, of what happens when you oppose Asim Al-Asheed and your great and powerful China."

* * *

On his desk are day-old copies of *Reference News, People's Daily,* and *The Global Times,* flown in each day from Beijing. It's always good to keep abreast of what's going on back home, not rely on stories filed on the Internet, which could be reedited or disappeared in seconds. Jiang's phone is next to the newspapers, and a screen lights up, meaning an incoming call. He picks up the receiver. "Yes?"

His boss, Li Baodong, breathes heavily into the phone and says, "Your boy is speaking well on the television, isn't he?"

Jiang bristles at the tone of Li's voice, thinks, *One day, you fat man, you'll get what you deserve, and I'll be in your chair.*

Though when the time comes, I'll make sure to order a new one, for I don't want to sit where your fat sweaty ass has been over the years.

Jiang says, "He does have his talents."

"And stupidity and stubbornness as well," Li says. "A pity you could not convince him to release the president's daughter... ah, look, there she is now."

Not a pity, Jiang thinks. *Not a pity at all.*

Li says, "What will the *hún dàn* do next?"

With satisfaction, Jiang sees motion on the television screen.

"I think we're about to find out, Comrade Li," he says, leaning back in his chair.

CHAPTER 66

White House Situation Room

President Pamela Barnes yawns and desperately wants a cup of coffee but knows better, realizing that a shot of caffeine right now will result in her never getting back to sleep. She has on gray sweatpants and an orange long-sleeved Florida Gators T-shirt, and Richard is next to her, with Deputy National Security Advisor Sarah Palumbo on her other side.

Up on the main screen is an anchor for Al Jazeera, in Qatar, and Barnes glumly thinks that most of her predecessors went months without being shepherded into the Situation Room, and here she is now, in this basement area, two days in a row.

Richard says, "Aw, shit, there's the bastard."

Pamela looks at the smug and arrogant face of Asim Al-Asheed, who is standing in front of a blank stone formation somewhere in the White Mountains. Asim speaks fluently and forcefully in good English about justice and money and the cost of an F-22.

Barnes says, "Sarah, is there anything we can get from this, about where he is, how this footage got to Al Jazeera?"

Her deputy national security advisor says, "I'm afraid not much, ma'am. Unfortunately, he's good at his tradecraft. If this message was recorded some hours ago, then he has moved on to somewhere else. I would guess that he recorded this message onto a thumb drive or flash drive, gave it to some trusted courier, who in turn emailed it to another courier in Qatar, who hand-delivered it to Al Jazeera's studios."

Richard mutters, "Goddamn studio should have been taken out by accident years ago. Damn terrorist supporters. Royal pain in the ass, they are."

Barnes says to Sarah, "What's the read on Asim Al-Asheed? He seems so…controlled."

On the screen, Asim is now talking about her own actions, and she wishes that the useless military out there had his GPS coordinates down cold because even though she's always been opposed to extrajudicial drone killing, she would be so tempted to drop a Hellfire missile into that man's face.

"Ma'am," Deputy National Security Advisor Palumbo says, "the latest analysis we've received from psychologists on contract with the CIA is that Asim Al-Asheed is a classic narcissistic sociopath, who had a troubled and poverty-stricken childhood and who is now constantly seeking attention and reaffirmation of his importance."

Barnes asks, "Meaning?"

Palumbo says, "He loves the attention. Loves the spotlight. He doesn't want it to end. They predicted that if he were to make another appearance following the ransom deadline's expiration, he would add additional conditions, additional requests, to show off his importance and special nature. Keep his face and name in the news."

Barnes says, "But the man's a killer. Children, women, families... he's murdered them all, up close and personal."

The deputy national security advisor says, "That's part of his sociopathic tendencies. The more shocking the crimes, the more attention he receives. Like now. He's in his element. The entire world focusing on what he's saying, and what his next set of demands will be. That's all he'll do today."

The camera pulls back, and with a jolt that makes Barnes instantly awake, the daughter of Matthew and Samantha Keating becomes visible. She's kneeling on a rocky surface, arms bound behind her, and she's wearing khaki shorts and a dirty and torn light gray Dartmouth sweatshirt.

Mel Keating stares up, head trembling, eyes wide behind her glasses, her hair a tangled mess. Barnes remembers the last time she saw Mel Keating, on Barnes's Inauguration Day, when she looked like a typical teenage girl, a bit overwhelmed by what was going on around her, with all the pomp and ceremony.

Asim Al-Asheed says something in Arabic. Barnes gasps, sees what he's holding in his hands, and in a trembling voice over the next few horrible seconds, her husband, Richard, says, "With all due respect, Ms. Palumbo, those hired CIA experts are full of shit."

CHAPTER 67

❖

Saunders Hotel
Arlington, Virginia

On the screen is our daughter, Mel, staring up through her eyeglasses, eyes wide, and I see with a pang of memory that she's still wearing that Dartmouth sweatshirt she had on the last time I saw her, on that bright beautiful day, when she was about to leave on a hike with her boyfriend and offered to bring me back pastries from our local general store.

Oh, Mel.

Asim Al-Asheed steps out of the camera's view for a moment, returns, and displays what's in his strong hands:

A sharp-looking saber.

In the suite there are gasps and cries, and I stare, and think…

That blessed late night nineteen years ago in a room at Naval Medical Center San Diego, with a worn but smiling Samantha in a bed, holding a pink little baby against her and saying, "Oh, Matt, she's so perfect… she's so perfect."

* * *

Asim Al-Asheed's face hardens, and he barks out a phrase in Arabic.

Little Mel at five years old, face serious and with eyeglasses fastened with a band across the back of her head, chubby legs scraped and cut, pink T-shirt and white shorts, picking up the little two-wheeled bicycle and saying, "Daddy, I can do it this time, I know I can."

The sword rises up, up, and up. Light glistening off the blade. Mel kneeling still, eyes closed tight, lips pressed together.

At my side Samantha is moaning, the low heartrending sounds of a mother in despair.

Mel winning her first district track meet at twelve, jumping over the finish line, looking behind to see her nearest competitor meters away, turning and smiling, raising her skinny arms up, just so damn happy, Samantha and me clapping hard and with joy from the sidelines.

The sword held high up.

The entire world seems to stop.

I'm on the edge of that aircraft at night, ready to step out into the darkness.

In her bedroom on the second floor of the White House, Mel curled up in bed, covers almost over her head, her face red and eyes swollen from all the crying, and her saying, "Dad, why do they hate me? They were laughing at me! Laughing at me on television! And millions of people were laughing, too…Dad…what did I do wrong?"

And me, gently stroking her back under the covers, knowing I have no good answer.

* * *

The sword is moving fast, coming down toward my girl.

The TV screen on the left cuts away from what a producer in Atlanta knows is about to happen. The screen now shows the CNN feed with one of the shocked overnight anchors.

Al Jazeera keeps on broadcasting, though it looks like the anchor is shouting at someone off-screen, telling them to pull the plug as well.

I'm stepping out into the darkness.

Just three days ago—only three days!—Mel, happy and smiling, hair wet from just being in the shower, looking so damn happy, so alive, so ready for the day, and asking me if I wanted her to do something for me, and then laughing before walking away, me asking her to call me when she got cell service the next day.

And her reply:

Sure, Dad. You can trust me! I'll be safe and sound.

The flash of the descending sword, everything at a halt here in this room, and at the very last second, Mel opens her eyes and yells in a strong firm voice, "Mommy, don't look!"

I grab Samantha's head, pull her into my shoulder, as—

The sword strikes.

A burst of blood splatters against the camera lens.

A low, mournful "Ooooh" comes from someone in the room.

I hold Samantha tight, tight, tight.

I want to look away.

But I won't allow myself to do that.

A finger seems to smudge away some of the blood on the camera lens, smearing it but keeping the lens clear enough to show what's on the rocky surface.

A figure curled on its side, the word DARTMOUTH still visible on the dirty torn sweatshirt, khaki shorts, strong bare legs, dirty foot soles.

Some feet away, a—
I can't say what I see.
Just an oval shape with frizzy blond hair, the shock of blood.
And a pair of eyeglasses, alone on the rock.

I step out into the darkness and fall forever.

PART THREE

CHAPTER 68

Two weeks later
Lake Marie, New Hampshire

I'm sitting in a wicker chair on the enclosed porch of my home, staring out at the waves of rain pelting the lake and the nearby forested hills. There are two Boston Whalers out there on the lake, Secret Service agents in each, doubling the usual water watch. Out in the woods surrounding my home, members of the Secret Service CAT team are on aggressive patrol, and the New Hampshire State Police has set up roadblocks, redirecting traffic away from the entrance to my access road.

If there's been a better example of closing the barn door after the proverbial horse has escaped, I've not heard of it.

The rain continues to fall.

No matter the weather, it's been cold and raining here for two weeks straight.

Besides the Secret Service agents in and around the compound, also doubled in number, I'm alone in the house. Samantha went back to Maine last week and has again thrown herself into her archaeological dig. Our few phone calls have been polite and strained. Before she left, there were lots of tears, hugs, rages, recriminations, slamming doors, and more tears and hugs, and long talks into the night, sharing memories of Mel.

My chief of staff, Madeline Perry, has visited twice, both times bringing along a selection of sympathy cards and letters from all over the world, including one that was slipped in by mistake, with a scrawled note saying, "Good that your ugly girl is gone. Your bitch wife and you should be next, traytor."

Last week, Yvette Cloutier, a local French-Canadian woman who's been working as a house cleaner here for six months, burst into tears when she saw me in the living room. She held my hands in hers and prayed aloud in French, and only stopped when one of the new Secret Service agents gently led her away.

I feel like I'm trapped in a large funeral home, with no body to grieve over but lots of quiet mourners moving about, not daring to speak too loudly or laugh in my presence.

I've been trying to avoid the news coverage as much as possible, but what I've seen is both heartening and discouraging. There have been prayer vigils in Mel's memory at religious institutions across the nation, police and military raids on terrorist cells allied with Asim Al-Asheed here and in Canada, Britain, and France, and hundreds of people have clustered on roads leading to my home, bearing flowers and cards.

But there are those taking advantage of Mel's death to make their own points, from politicians blaming the Barnes Administration for allowing this to happen to others criticizing New Hampshire's governor for not immediately deputizing every gun owner in the state to assist in the earlier search.

There are also rumors that my successor is planning military action, but where? And how? And who knows where Asim Al-Asheed is now, having slipped back into the shadows as he's done so many times before. Is he in Canada, the States, or hiding among his supporters around the world?

About the only other distraction here was when, soon after Samantha went back to work, three FBI agents arrived from DC, intent on going into Mel's empty room to look through her belongings and pack up her laptop for forensic analysis.

I stood in front of her bedroom door.

"Not going to happen," I said, unable to stand the thought of strangers going through Mel's possessions, her papers, and reading her private thoughts and searches on her PC.

"Sir," the lead FBI agent said, "we need to see if there's any evidence your daughter had been in earlier contact with—"

I said, "Not going to happen. Nobody's going into Mel's room. Nobody's looking at her computer."

"Sir..."

"The only way any of you are getting into my daughter's room is through me, and the Secret Service might have something to say about that."

The FBI left, and that night, I slept on the floor in Mel's room, curled up in a blanket, just mourning, remembering, and mourning some more.

I rub at my face and the stubble. It's been a few days since I've shaved. The first few days back at Lake Marie were filled with lots of drinking and guilt. Then I shook that off and got to work, going for long runs along the access road and nearby trails—never alone, of course—and working out in a small shed near the garage that has some weights and other training gear. And I did other training, the type of training I've hidden away from my protective detail.

I check the time.

Five p.m.

I take out my iPhone and hold it up and start recording a short video message for my wife.

"Hey, Sam, it's me," I say. "Here's the weather at Lake Marie." I slowly rotate the phone so she can get a view of the dock, moored pontoon boat, and sodden beach. I bring the phone back and say, "Lots of rain. At least it's keeping the tourists and gawkers away. I hope the weather is better up in Maine, hope you're making progress, hope you're making history up there..."

I stop, thinking, *Idiot: Yeah, she's making history, all right, the sorrowful First Lady, away from her husband, the only First Lady to have her daughter murdered.*

"Anyway, if it's sunny out tomorrow, I'll take out the tools and get back to clearing brush. Nothing much else is going on..."

Meaning, *Yes, Sam, our daughter's body hasn't been found yet.*

"That's the news from Lake Marie. Love you. Miss you...call if you get a chance. Bye for now."

I switch off and email the message to Sam, wondering if she will call me back.

I look out once more at the rain, at the drawn-up canoes, and the memory of the canoe race and of seeing Mel for the last time comes charging back, and I wipe at my eyes.

The screen door opens and Agent David Stahl comes out, nods, and then looks out to the cold, dark gray waters of the lake. He's lost weight, his face is drawn and tired, and it seems like years ago when he and I were out there on those sunny waters.

I say, "Take a load off, David."

"Thank you, sir."

He drags over a wicker chair and sits down. He has on boat shoes, tan slacks, and a wrinkled dark blue polo shirt.

A few seconds pass, and he says, "Sir, you know we have some new agents here. I think tonight might be a good time to introduce them to your poker skills."

Any other time I'd smile and eagerly say yes, for one of the simple joys I've had is playing poker, sometimes nightlong sessions, with the agents stationed here, winning more often than losing.

But this isn't any other time.

"Maybe not tonight," I say, "and maybe not ever, if Agent Peyton is on shift."

David grimaces. One of the new agents assigned here is Agent Brett Peyton, who is brash and full of himself and who I guess is reporting directly to Faith Murray, the deputy assistant director in charge of the Presidential Protection Detail. She's preparing a purge and disciplinary action against my original detail.

"What's the latest?" I ask.

"The search is expanding into Maine and New York State, as well as southern Vermont, and southern Ontario and Quebec. There's been a lot of reports and tips about that floatplane, but unfortunately, nobody can recall a registration number, so we can't trace that. And with the number of isolated lakes, rivers, and ponds within the flying range of that floatplane..."

He stops, and we both know he doesn't have to continue.

The odds against Mel's body being found anytime soon are very high indeed.

I cross my arms, look at the canoes, wondering if I'll ever again race David out there on the lake.

I try very hard to speak the next several sentences in a firm and unwavering voice, like I'm giving a State of the Union address, and with the first words I fail.

"When she's found, no matter where, David...and it's time for her to be moved...I want you there, and five other agents from the original detail...I want you to take her home. All right?"

Tears are rolling down his face, and he says hoarsely, "Mr. President, we can't do that."

"Why?"

"Because we failed her...and you, and Mrs. Keating. It wouldn't be right."

I shake my head. "We all failed her. David, do it. All right? You take my girl home."

He just nods.

I nod in return.

After a few more gray minutes pass, I say, "I admire you, David, you and the other agents, for the job that you do, for keeping alert during long hours of boredom, traveling with me while hearing the same dull speech, over and over again, and putting up with us protectees. It's a hard job that most people know nothing about, only the bullshit they see on TV or at the movies."

He doesn't say anything, which is fine.

"My apologies in advance, David, because in this hard time, I'm going to make your life, and the lives of the other agents, very, very difficult indeed."

"How's that, sir?"

I look again at the sodden beach. Think of the volleyball net being up, Mel and her Dartmouth friends, laughing and playing, enjoying the best times of their lives, every day here a perfect day with lots of sun and no rain, no clouds, ever.

I say, "I'm going dark over the next few weeks. I'll be going places, talking to people. Some not so nice people, probably. And there will come a day when I find Asim Al-Asheed, and I'm going to look at him, face-to-face so he knows I'm there, standing in front of him, during those last few seconds."

I pause.

"Then I'm going to blow his goddamn head off."

CHAPTER 69

Lake Marie, New Hampshire

To Agent Stahl's credit, he doesn't blink, he doesn't protest, doesn't say a word.

I say, "Along the way I might find the floatplane pilot who helped Asim escape with my girl. I might find the man who sold him the rope that tied her up, and the man who gave Asim the sword he used to behead her. And if I come across these people, I'll kill every one of them."

I pause again.

No word from Agent Stahl.

I say, "At some point I'm going to leave here, without your approval, and without the knowledge of the director of the Secret Service and the secretary of Homeland Security. Do you understand what I'm saying, David?"

"Yes, sir."

"There's nothing on this earth that's going to stop me," I say, my voice even and not quavering, not like before when

I was talking about recovering Mel's body. "If you want to make your arguments to convince me to do otherwise, go right ahead. It'll be a waste of your breath, but I'll be polite and listen. If you and the rest of the agents here want to stop me from doing this, you're going to have to shackle me in the safe room."

David says, "All right, sir. Then please listen to what I have to say."

"I said I would."

He stares right at me with his tired face and haunted eyes and says, "I want in."

After a moment of surprise on my end, I say, "Hold on, David, hold on. This is going to be rough, rugged, and mostly illegal. If you come along—"

He shakes his head. "What? If I come along my career's over? It's already finished. All that's left are the congressional hearings and the disciplinary proceedings. I'll be lucky to keep my pension, and right now, I don't give a shit about that. I want to help you, Mr. President."

"David..."

He leans forward in the worn wicker chair. "Mr. President, let me rephrase what I just said. I *need* to come with you."

His eyes are still haunted but there's a pleading in there as well.

"What are you looking for, David? Redemption?"

A harsh shake of the head. "No, sir. Just like you, justice."

There's determination in his eyes, and I'm sure he's looking for justice, but I see what he means when he says he needs this.

We all do.

"All right," I say, clasping my tired hands together. "I'm going to need a lot of burner cell phones and prepaid debit cards set up under false email addresses. And I'll probably need a few trusted operators to join me. I'll be doing a lot of digging, a lot of off-the-grid research. I've got some cash in the bedroom safe. If you want to help, spend a day or two traveling to different stores in the area—make sure you're wearing a hat or something to hide your features. Get a Chrome laptop or something similar from Best Buy. The phones from different stores. You'll need to set up an encrypted email account to activate the phones and to purchase some prepaid debit cards. Then..."

I stop.

There's a slight smile on his face.

I say, "Sorry, David. I'm telling you your job, the ins and outs of tradecraft. You don't need to hear that from me. You know what I need, and how best to do it."

"That's all right, Mr. President," he says, getting up from the chair. "I'll be checking the perimeter here in a few minutes. If you have the cash when I come back, I can get to work."

"Thanks, David," I say.

"But I have to say, and with my apologies, sir, that I already knew what you were up to."

That surprises me. "How?"

"Because when you've been working out in the shed over the past two weeks, I knew that you had your weapons with you, and had been practicing dry firing, getting reacclimated to holding an automatic rifle or pistol. Pretty clear if you stand close enough to the shed and listen."

I should probably be upset, but instead I'm impressed. "Good job again, David. Thanks."

As he walks to the screen door, he does something very unprofessional and very un–Secret Service like.

A gentle grasp of my shoulder.

"No, sir," he says. "I'm the one who should be thanking you."

He goes back into the main house and I wait for a while, peering up at the cloudy skies where it looks like the rain has finally stopped, at least reducing the misery index for those soaked agents out there in the two Boston Whalers.

I rub my face and chin.

Time to get shaved, showered, and dressed in clean clothes.

It's time to get back to work.

CHAPTER 70

Lake Marie, New Hampshire

After checking the perimeter security—and finding out that a two-agent CAT team has just arrested a photographer from a supermarket tabloid trying to sneak onto the property to take photos of the grieving former president—Agent David Stahl goes to the kitchen, looking to grab a glass of cold water before heading out. A few minutes earlier he was in his small office in the barn, where he found a white business-sized envelope with twenty crisp hundred-dollar bills on his chair.

But Chief of Staff Madeline Perry is blocking his way to the stainless-steel refrigerator in the large kitchen, a hard and determined look on her face. She has on black slacks and a red pullover sweater with the sleeves rolled up, and she doesn't look happy.

"We need to talk, David."

"Okay," he says, not sure what the problem is, and hoping it's nothing major. David has had years of experience dealing with White House staff, and those folks have run the gamut from thinking Secret Service agents are servants at their beck and call, grim-jawed angels of death, or part of the background to be ignored. All in all, David prefers to be ignored. Being part of the background is what the job is all about.

When it comes to Madeline, David has found her to be tough but reasonable. She understands the Secret Service's job at this former president's home but isn't afraid to push back if she thinks some of the agents are too gung ho in enforcing the rules.

For the most part, he's liked working with her, but a few seconds later that observation goes down in flames, like a World War II bomber being taken down by fighter aircraft.

She says in a cold voice, "What in hell are you thinking, helping Harbor plan a kill mission for Asim Al-Asheed? That's nuts!"

How the hell? he thinks, and she says, "I know what you're thinking. I'm not proud of it, and I own it, but I was walking by the screen door to the porch when I heard you talking to Harbor. David, what the hell are you thinking?"

David is thinking furiously—that's what he's thinking. He knew that down the road he'd have to do some serious spinning and falsification to make this happen for the president and himself, but he didn't expect the damn thing to be compromised before anything even started.

He says, "It's not nuts."

"It sure as hell sounds like it," she says. "I know he's grieving, I know he's looking for revenge—we all are!—but this is lunacy. Let the professionals handle it. Not a former president with a bum hip who's overwhelmed with grief and guilt."

David says, "*Professionals?* The Barnes Administration didn't cover themselves in glory, now, did they? Especially with that bullshit story that the president really wanted to pay the ransom but was overruled by the FBI and others. You've seen the follow-up stories. Her spin was so much crap."

"We don't know that for sure, do we?" she says. "It's just one side spinning against the other. Typical DC bullshit, I know, but please: you know this should be left to the professionals."

"Well," he says, "the professionals have been looking for Asim Al-Asheed for years and they've come up empty, time and time again. Why is this time going to be any different?"

"And you think Harbor will be able to do it? Really?"

Stahl takes a breath, tries to ease things out and keep his cool. "Maddie... what's going on? You've worked with Harbor, his wife, and his daughter for years. Why this pushback?"

She looks away and David knows he's struck home. Something is behind this chief of staff's blustery attitude, more than just her wish to derail Harbor from doing what must be done.

Perry is now looking back at him, eyes wide, moistened. "I believed in him, David. And it sucked when he was denied a second term. And I thought I could do well by him by following him in his post-presidency, especially when he said he'd be setting up a charitable foundation for vets."

The tears start trickling. "Harbor doesn't know this, so please don't tell him, but one of my cousins served with honor in the Rangers. At the end of Harbor's term, he froze to death on the streets in Detroit, like other homeless veterans across the country. Harbor said that would never happen again, and that his foundation would take care of vets... all of their needs."

Now it all makes sense, Stahl thinks. "The foundation hasn't been set up yet, has it?"

Perry shakes her head. "On paper, yes. But where it matters, in the accounts, there's hardly any money in there. We were planning on him writing his memoir, covering everything from growing up poor in Texas to serving in the teams, and then a career in politics, and then the shock of being president. That book would earn him and his charitable foundation millions, and then the aid would start flowing, so never again would there be a homeless vet on the streets."

She takes a deep breath. "But he hasn't written a damn word! It's always, 'Tomorrow, tomorrow, or next week,' while I'm trying to help Robert Barnett, his literary agent, negotiate a good publishing deal without even a damn outline. Now…he wants to go out on a revenge mission. You know it's not going to work. It's going to end in humiliation."

"That might be," Stahl says. "But it doesn't matter now, does it? He's going."

"Yes, it does matter," Perry says, voice firm. "If it fails, and you know it will, the publishers will stop returning my phone calls, and those vets he wants to help will be ignored."

"Maddie, you're making good points, but it's above my pay grade. He's doing it, and we can't stop him."

"Please, David," she says. "Let the agencies hunt down Asim Al-Asheed. They have a lot more resources than Harbor could ever get on his own."

Stahl starts to turn away from the president's chief of staff, thinking he'll have to wait a bit longer before getting his cold water.

"But they don't have one thing, Maddie," he says.

"What's that?"

"A father who's going to get the job done, no matter what it takes."

CHAPTER 71

Lake Marie, New Hampshire

Alone in my office, which might make a good book title one of these days, the lights are dimmed, and I lean back in an old leather swivel chair that came with the place. The computer is off, and there's no view out my small window, which is fine. No distant lights over there on the lake, marking neighbors having fun and living life and laughing and talking amongst themselves.

The bookshelves in my small office are packed with histories, autobiographies, and reference books on military matters, and similar books are piled up on the floor. Samantha often teased me that I have too many books, and I retorted by saying, "No, the problem is, not enough bookshelves."

What little bare plaster remains displays framed family photos, some faded color shots of me growing up in Texas with Lucille Keating, my mom, who died ten years back from lung cancer. My dad was Gus Keating, who worked on a rig in the Gulf of Mexico, got drunk on smuggled Jack Daniel's, and fell overboard and drowned when I was five. There have been a number of books and studies concerning the SEALs, and one odd fact that has stood out is that most operators—like myself—either come from a broken home or were raised by single parents.

I've resisted the urge over the years to put up what I call a "See how great I am?" wall, with plaques, trophies, and framed certificates. That's a sign of looking back, and I've always been one to look forward.

On my desk with the silent computer are the photos that mean the most to me: of young Mel growing up, of me standing proudly next to Samantha after she got her doctorate, and one taken here a couple of winters ago, in the snowy front yard, with the three of us standing and smiling amid the whiteness, ready for whatever was ahead for all of us during my post-presidency.

I pick up a yellow legal pad from a pile that Maddie Perry got for me months back, to help me write my autobiography. I get a pen and get to work.

No time to worry about the past, I think.

At my feet is a white-and-blue plastic Walmart bag, and I take out the first of about a dozen charged and active Tracfones purchased at various stores around the county. Using my personal iPhone as a directory, I make my first call overseas. It rings and rings and then an irritated voice with a touch of a Brooklyn accent answers.

"Who the hell is this?" demands Danny Cohen, retired head of Mossad. "And how did you get this number?"

"Danny, please, don't hang up," I say. "It's Matt Keating."

Instantly the tone of his voice changes, and he says, "Oh, Matt, Matt, so sorry to answer like that. My phone said *unknown caller* and—"

Interrupting, I say, "I'm using a disposable phone over here. Is yours secure?"

"It is," he says. "Matt, again, Dora and I send you our deepest sympathies for the loss of Mel. Heartbreaking."

"I know," I say, the pen firmly in my grasp. "The card and the letter you sent us both were very much welcomed. But Danny..."

"Yes," he crisply says. "You're using a burner phone. This isn't a social call. What kind of help are you looking for?"

"Everything and anything on Asim Al-Asheed, his friends, associates, anything that will give me a good lead on his current whereabouts."

"You've got it," he says. "How long are you going to have that disposable phone in your possession?"

"A day," I reply, amazed at Danny's quick and affirmative answer. "I'll start with a fresh one tomorrow."

He says, "Then feel free to call me, anytime, no matter what, for updates. I'll get to work on this. I know your agencies are also looking for Asim, but we both know what happens when competing agencies are seeking the same information."

I don't need the reminder. The disaster of 9/11 could have easily been avoided if the CIA, FBI, Customs, and others had put aside their turf wars and if Congress had permitted cross-channel communications to allow these agencies to easily exchange data and intelligence.

Things have improved since that dark Tuesday, but there is still a ways to go.

I say, "Danny...this is incredibly generous. I was half expecting some pushback. Or a lot of questions."

"I have no questions for you," he says. "Because I know what you are planning. And it's not my place to argue with you, or to try to discourage you. You know our history, Matt. We know the importance of family, and the importance of settling accounts, no matter the time, no matter the cost. Again, call at any time. I'm honored to assist. *Shalom lekha,* my friend."

He disconnects the call. I rub at my eyes and get back to work.

The second call is nearly identical to the first, except the accent is a touch of Arab and British.

"Who is this?" is the sharp demand of Ahmad Bin Nayef, former deputy director of Saudi Arabia's General Intelligence Directorate. "Where are you calling from?"

"From New Hampshire, Ahmad," I say. "It's Matt Keating."

As with Danny, the tone of the voice changes. "Ah, Matt, so good to hear from you, and again, my deep condolences. How are you and Samantha doing?"

"Samantha is back at work, trying to get by, day by day," I say. "Me, I'm doing my best...Ahmad, is this call secure? I'm on a disposable cell phone."

"Yes, yes, quite secure," he says, "or my nephew will be in great trouble otherwise. Matt, please, what can I do for you?"

"Anything you learn concerning Asim Al-Asheed's whereabouts," I say. "It doesn't have to be one hundred percent. It can be anything that can be developed into a lead. Whatever you have that can be shared."

A moment or two passes. "Are you sure, my friend?"

"Absolutely."

"This is a dangerous task you are taking on."

I say, "Are you telling me no?"

"Oh, Matt, not at all, not at all," he says. "It's just...and please take this with my deep and true affection, and with the greatest respect, but this is a job for a younger man. Or younger men. More recent in their skills and not, alas, with a healed fractured hip."

"This needs to be done."

"Yes, of course," Ahmad says. "But let me offer you an alternative. If I am incredibly fortunate and somehow manage to get actionable information on Asim, I will personally do something with it. I could pass on the information to the responsible officials here in the Kingdom, but it may stay there and be analyzed and reanalyzed, and not be shared with your agencies. Some here in Riyadh, I am sorry to say, admire Asim Al-Asheed."

Hard to hear, but I know Ahmad is right.

He says, "As for me, though, if I know where he is, through luck and the kindness of Allah, I can send a squad of men, very hard, very tough, trained by your SEALs and the British SAS, and they will do this job for you."

God, what a tempting offer, but one I cannot accept, not if I hope to live with myself in the years ahead.

"Ahmad, I am touched and honored more than I could tell you," I say, "but I have to do this myself. For... my family."

He speaks briskly. "I entirely understand. You know how to contact me, and I promise I won't bark at you the next time I see *unknown caller* on my phone screen. But at any time, Matt, my offer remains. We can do this for you."

"Thank you again, Ahmad," I say. "But I have to see this through on my own."

"Very well," he says. "*Wadaeaan,* Matt."

After my second call ends and before I resume my work, I think of the oddity that just happened. Years ago, Danny's grandfather and Ahmad's grandfather no doubt hated each other, hated each other's country and people, and each in their own way would have been greatly pleased to see the other destroyed.

Now?

Not only do their grandchildren secretly work together in

that turbulent region to bring some form of peace and stability, but both are now working to help a former American president in his own personal mission.

Maybe there's still some hope out there, somewhere.

I go back to my phones and return to the task at hand.

CHAPTER 72

Lake Marie, New Hampshire

It's 2 a.m. in Montana when I make my third call. As the phone rings and rings, I wonder just who's going to finally answer this landline to an isolated farmhouse near the Beartooth Mountains owned by Trask Floyd, movie director and action star and former operator who supplied me with transportation to DC those long days ago. The phone rings for a long while and then a sleepy male voice answers, and says slowly and with distinction, "If you're some starlet convinced that you belong in my next movie 'cause you can giggle on cue, go away. And if you're a former operator looking for a handout, send your resume to my P.O. box. Other than that, you call again, I'm gonna chase you down and kick your ass."

I say, "How about the former leader of the free world?"

A quick expletive, and the wide-awake voice now says, "Mr. President! Jesus, I'm sorry. I didn't recognize the number."

I say, "That's for a reason, Trask. I'm using a burner phone, and I'm calling on your landline. And please: it's Matt."

A yawn from the other end of the call. "Sorry, Matt, just an instant reaction. And damn, I'm still so sorry about Mel. Good Lord."

"Appreciate it, Trask."

"How did you know I'd be home?"

"Saw a Google news story about you attending a film festival in Boise," I say. "I figured you'd probably bunk down after a romp like that."

He starts to talk and then stops himself and says, "Burner phone, huh?"

"Yes."

"What do you need?"

Good ol' Trask, getting right to the point.

I say, "Two skilled operators you know and trust. They have to be recently retired or on extended leave. They need to be quickly available and be able to drop out of sight for a while with no questions being asked."

Trask says, "Make it one. I'll be the second."

"Trask, a great offer, but—"

"Matt," he interrupts. "I'm in as good shape as I was when I left the teams. I hit the range almost every day, and with me, you've got funds and options."

I say, "But I also have Trask Floyd, actor and movie director. Extremely recognizable, with lots of weird fans following your every move."

"And you?" he says incredulously. "The former president?"

"The former president wearing ratty clothes, sunglasses, beard stubble, and a baseball cap," I say. "Just another guy out there in a car or catching a flight. Ex-presidents are recognizable when they're dressed well, surrounded by a group of Secret Service agents, making a speech, or appearing on a cable news show. That's not what I'm going to do."

He says, "Then we should make it three. Matt, I want in."

"You get me two operators and some additional funds and support when I need it, then you'll be in, Trask. Don't make this any harder."

A sigh. "Okay. You got it. Two operators. Where should I send them?"

"I'll call you at noon, your time, in two days. That work?"

"It'll have to, now, won't it?"

"Thanks."

Trask says, "Okay, and if I'm not going to be riding shotgun with you on wherever you're going, I'll still be behind you. And if you come back with that son of a bitch's head in a box filled with ice, we'll have a celebration at my ranch that they'll talk about for a hundred years. You be safe, Mr. President."

"Thanks, Trask," I say, disconnecting the call. I pry open the rear of the Tracfone, remove the battery and the SIM card, and then snap the SIM card in two. I get out of my chair, and a few minutes later I'm at the end of the dock, a quiet late night on Lake Marie.

The clouds have cleared the northern New Hampshire night sky. I take a moment to appreciate all those stars, and all those billions of galaxies out there. Some nights, a sight like this fills me with awe—to think of a Creator who put this all together. Other nights, it fills me with despair—to think of that grandeur out there, and yet on this little speck of dust, so much time is spent hating and killing.

I toss the broken SIM card and phone into the dark waters of the lake and stop looking at the stars. I reach into my pants pocket and touch Mel's ring, the one she left behind when she was kidnapped, and which was later returned to us by the FBI.

"Asim," I whisper, "I'm coming for you."

CHAPTER 73

Lake Marie, New Hampshire

Secret Service agent David Stahl is outside the garage at President Matt Keating's home, near Harbor's workout shed, ready to go into town to run a few errands this early evening, when a high-pitched male voice calls out, "Hey, David! Before you leave. Got a sec?"

Coming toward him with a big fake smile and happy eyes is fellow Secret Service agent Brett Peyton, and David keeps himself from sighing in disgust at the man's approach. Peyton looks like some Homeland Security hiring officer's dream agent: tall and well-built, tanned and toned, perfect brown hair that's never messed up, and with a charming way about him.

He's also a favorite agent of Faith Murray, deputy assistant director in charge of the Presidential Protection Detail; she's David's boss and the woman who told him months ago to stop providing unofficial protection for Mel Keating. And in addition, for long weeks now, David has been pushing to have a deputy special agent in charge to assist him, and Brett has been named to that position.

"Sure, Brett," David says. "What's up?"

"Going into town?"

No, you damn fool, David thinks, *I'm taking a drive to Cape Cod.*

"Sure seems that way," he says. "Can I get you anything? Some Green Mountain coffee? A cruller? Bottle of Moxie?"

"No, no, no," Peyton gently protests. "I just think it's odd, that's all. You're in charge of this protective detail, and yet here you are, doing something that a rookie agent should be assigned to do."

"I like to get out on occasion, see what's going on in the community, get a feel of the place."

"That's in your official procedures, then?" Peyton asks, and David is reminded once again why Peyton is really here: not to assist in protecting Harbor or to help David, as his deputy, but to gather information and intelligence on David and the detail, so they can be publicly and loudly humiliated and fired at the appropriate time for letting the president's daughter get kidnapped and murdered.

"No, Brett," David says, tapping the side of his head. "It's part of my field experience. You should try it someday."

Peyton keeps on smiling, and David climbs into one of the four black Chevrolet Suburbans belonging to the detail and heads off to Monmouth.

The access road is dirt but well maintained, and as he drives, he thinks about Harbor and what he wants. David is surprised at how thinking about this improbable mission has improved his mood, has charged up his batteries.

There's no way in hell it's going to succeed, he knows, not with so much attention out there, keeping track of Harbor, but by God, he and Harbor and whoever else Harbor recruits are going to give it their best.

Up ahead is a new wooden gatehouse, staffed by two of the new agents transferred here, and they wave him through, and he turns right, heading into the small village of Monmouth. He comes up against a roadblock maintained by well-armed troopers from the New Hampshire State Police, and they let him through as well. He spots the black bands around their badges—still mourning the death of Monmouth officer Corinne Bradford, who did so much to locate Mel Keating's place of captivity.

He notes with pleasure the reduced number of people crowding each side of the country road, ghouls looking for some sign of a sad and lonely Harbor. For more than two weeks, the town of Monmouth has been under siege from the news media and assorted losers, psychics, and attention seekers, and David wishes a winter blizzard would suddenly descend here, months ahead of schedule, to drive these people back to their sorry homes.

Rodney Pace walks back and forth, back and forth, in the crowded dirt parking lot of Cook's General Store, waiting, knowing that if he doesn't see Matt Keating today, then it will mean another night of sleeping in the back seat of his old Monte Carlo sedan, and he's not sure his back can survive that.

Three days ago, he made a momentous decision to drive up here from his crappy and cluttered studio apartment in Baltimore, to personally meet the former president and explain what's really going on, but his attempts to approach Keating's lakefront home haven't even come close to succeeding.

Too many roadblocks, too many police, and most of all, too many people.

In researching this rural place, Rodney learned that Monmouth is supposed to have a population of only six hundred or so, but in looking around the parking lot, he thinks it sure seems as though the town's population has doubled in size. In the dirt parking lot are news vans from various cable channels and local stations, rental vans and cars, and people just wandering around with coffee cups, chatting and gossiping, all waiting.

Not waiting for the search and rescue to end—no, those words have changed.

It's now a recovery.

The body of Mel Keating.

As if.

The store looks like a rehabbed two-story Victorian-style yellow house, with a wide-open wooden front porch. Hand-drawn signs outside announce church-sponsored Sunday pancake breakfasts, hay for sale by farmers, raffles to help pay for someone's kidney transplant. Inside, along the creaky wood floors that must be at least a hundred years old, boxes of cereal are for sale one aisle away from motor oil, and another aisle away from nail clippers and brushes for horses.

Rodney's stomach grumbles.

His plan was to see the president, be rewarded for his efforts, but he is out of money, with less than a dollar in change in his right jacket pocket.

What now?

A black Chevrolet Suburban pulls up across the narrow road, and a muscular man steps out, and Rodney stops walking back and forth, back and forth, awed by what he's seeing.

Secret Service agent.

That's who that man is.

Right over there!

Now all he needs to do is convince the Secret Service agent to take him to see President Keating.

Rodney starts walking to meet up with him and puts his hand in his thin cloth jacket's right pocket, grasping the butt of the Smith & Wesson .38-caliber revolver that belonged to his dad years ago when he was a cop in Baltimore.

One way or another, Rodney is going to see President Keating.

CHAPTER 74

Monmouth, New Hampshire

Secret Service agent David Stahl gets out of the Suburban, starts walking across the narrow country road toward Cook's General Store, shaking his head upon seeing the circus over there. Three weeks ago, he could have parked right in front of the store, maybe with two or three cars and a mud-splattered pickup truck or two in the gravel lot, and now there's no space for any other vehicles. The store's interior is always crowded as well, and instead of spending a fun few minutes chatting with Mrs. Grissom, the store's owner, or her two sons, Clay and Todd, now David just goes in, does his business, and heads back to the compound.

Today's business is getting some coffee for the evening shift, as well as a few other odds and ends, and David hopes he can get out without some journalist recognizing him and asking questions, starting with, *How did you let the president's daughter get kidnapped and murdered?*

The porch and the parking lot are filled with those damn reporters, hangers-on, mourners, and thrill seekers hoping to see Harbor make an appearance or—more exciting!—to see a dark green van from the New Hampshire medical examiner's office drive by, escorted by New Hampshire State Police cruisers, carrying the mortal remains of Mel Keating, age nineteen.

To hell with them all.

David changes his earlier wish for an off-season blizzard to strike these fools, and instead is wishing for Old Testament fire and brimstone to strike when he spots somebody coming at him who looks like an Old Testament prophet. Skinny, baggy jeans, torn tan jacket, scraggly beard, and thick greasy hair, one eye swollen, driven look on his face, and David thinks, *Great: another one.*

There are Secret Service groupies, hangers-on, who want to pass on news about UFO landing sites or alien lizard–occupied office buildings, and this one—

This one's right jacket pocket is weighted with something heavy.

Like a weapon.

The man puts his hand into the pocket and says, "Agent Stahl, Agent Stahl, I need to see the president, right away!"

The hand starts to come out, holding something, and David instantly responds.

My God, how fast and mean that agent is, his hand going to his side, whipping out a baton that instantly expands, and the baton is cracked against Rodney's hand, sending a bolt of pain through his entire right arm and shoulder.

Rodney yelps and drops the revolver, and the baton swings again, hitting him at the back of the knees, and he tumbles to the ground. Strong hands are poking and patting and prodding, and there's a *snap-click* as handcuffs are slapped around his wrists, and Rodney can't help it, he starts to sob, thinking, *Failed again, failed again, failed again.*

The agent is speaking into a radio, it seems—Rodney hears something like "...requesting a pickup at Cook's General Store, one in custody..."—and then he's rolled over onto his back.

The Secret Service agent is glaring at him in anger, reminding Rodney of his university's president staring at him with disgust throughout that damned hearing last year.

Agent Stahl says, "Who are you and what are you doing here?"

There's gravel and dirt in Rodney's mouth, and he spits it out and says, "Agent Stahl, it's me! Don't you recognize me?"

The agent is standing over him, and then leans down some. "I...no, I don't think so."

Rodney says, "It's me, Rodney Pace. From the University of Baltimore. You...when I was a professor there, I taught some seminars at your Rowley Training Center. You were in two of my seminars, I'm sure!"

Agent Stahl squats, looking closer. A ring of people starts to gather around, and Stahl says, "Professor Pace...it's really you? Forensic sciences?"

Sweet relief flows through Rodney. Maybe this will work out after all.

"Yes, yes, that's me," he says.

"You...what the hell are you doing here?"

"I need to see the president—desperately so," Rodney says. "I have vital information for him."

"What kind of information?"

Rodney tells him and Agent Stahl's angry face instantly changes, and he grabs Rodney's upper arm, pulls him to his feet, and then starts briskly walking him across the street to the Suburban. Just before they reach the parked vehicle, Stahl says, "Hold on a sec."

Rodney's wrists ache with relief when the handcuffs are removed, and Stahl quickly calls someone on his radio, speaking into his wrist microphone: "This is Stahl. Cancel my pickup request."

And then Rodney is put into the rear seat of the Suburban, and before he can even fasten his seat belt, Stahl is in the driver's seat, roaring the engine to life, and the Suburban makes a sharp U-turn, tires squealing, and heads away from the store.

CHAPTER 75

Lake Marie, New Hampshire

I'm on the porch of my lakeside house, legal pad in my lap, lots of scribbled notes recording my day's work. It's now evening and I'm sure close to dinnertime, but I'm not that hungry. I don't think I've been hungry in three weeks. The lights are on and various insects are battling and thumping against the porch screens.

These past few hours I've been sketching out an operations plan, and setting aside the fact that I have no official support, no operators as of yet, no transportation assets, no tactical equipment or stores, and definitely no actionable intelligence, it's been one hell of a productive afternoon.

The door squeaks open and Agent David Stahl steps in. I look hard in his direction and he gives me a quick, mournful shake of the head.

I don't have to ask him anything. He's just answered me. Mel's body has still not been recovered.

But it seems it's his turn to ask a question.

"Sir, will you come with me for a moment?" he asks.

"Can it wait?" I ask.

Surprise.

"No, Mr. President, it can't," he says. "I need to show you something in the furnace room."

I get up, keep my pad and pen with me—I usually trust my detail, but I don't really know the new agents yet—and follow David through the large and darkened living room, down a hallway leading to a bathroom and well-stocked pantry, and to a door, which David opens for me. We clomp down the wooden stairs, the lights already on, and emerge onto the dirt floor in this part of the basement. Lots of older homes up here still have dirt cellars, and I remember gently teasing Samantha that if she ever got tired of digging outdoors, she could start here and find out if there is anything interesting in our basement.

"Like a hidden Indian burial ground," I said. "That'll explain the weird creaks at night."

And she shot back, smiling, "That still won't explain the weird creak I share a bed with."

A happy lifetime ago, it seems.

Up ahead is the confusing mass of pipes, vents, and wires, and the furnace and the dark fuel tank. Earlier, slabs of concrete were placed over the dirt. A workbench filled with tools is on the far side of the stone foundation wall, and an odd-looking man is sitting on a metal stool, next to the bench.

On the bench is a large open laptop, its screen blank.

"Mr. President," David says, "this is Professor Rodney Pace. Used to be head of the forensic sciences department at the University of Baltimore."

The man smiles, nods. His thick dark hair is a greasy mess, and he's wearing dirty jeans and a tan cloth jacket that's torn and repaired with duct tape. He leans forward, offers a hand, which I automatically shake. The skin is cold and dry.

"Ah, Mr. President, a true honor, and I have to admit that I'm a former department head and, alas, a former professor." He sits back on the stool, shrugs, and says, "An unfortunate event involving a number of my students and a camping trip and certain illegal substances...well, a sordid story. Not enough time to discuss what happened to me and my career, but here I am."

I look in disbelief at David, and he says, "Sir, believe me, Professor Pace knows his forensics. Before he was forced to leave the university, he even lectured a few times at our Rowley Training Center, in Maryland. He's the best in his field, knows his stuff, and he wants to show you something."

I look at the blank screen of the open laptop, and I know what's hidden in there, in long strings of computer code, of ones and zeros: my daughter's last moment broken down into something that could be saved forever.

"I don't want to see it."

David says, "I know, Mr. President. Believe me, I know...but please. Listen to what Professor Pace has to say."

"And what's that?" I ask sharply.

David says, "Sir, trust me on this. You have to see it cold. No preconceptions."

My legal pad feels useless and silly in my hands. I'm a former president, former SEAL, and former father. Not much of a legacy.

"Go ahead," I say.

My visitor hops off the stool and goes to the keyboard. "It would have been best if I had the source video, could reduce the amount of pixelation and degradation for my examination, but we do what we can. Pay close attention, now." He taps a few keys.

A sound comes out, the anguished "Mommy, don't—" and

Rodney punches a key, and the audio goes silent, and there, in all their color and gore and excess, are the last few seconds of my daughter's life, and I don't look away, won't look away. In the teams and when I was president, I saw enough grainy and bloody death videos to last several lifetimes, but this video is the only one that has woken me up in the middle of the night, shouting and with fists clenched in despair.

"Did you see it?" the former professor asks. "Did you?"

I choke out the words. "Yes, I did."

Pace sighs, like I'm a student who will struggle to earn even a D in his class. "I don't think you did. The last few seconds. Pay attention."

The last few seconds...a burst of blood hitting the camera lens, a gloved finger smearing it, the shape on the rocks, the frizzy hair, and, alone again, the eyeglasses.

"There," the professor says with satisfaction in his voice. "Did you see it? Did you?"

"See what?" I ask, frustration and anger and sadness all roiling inside of me. "What am I supposed to see?"

He *tsk-tsks,* replays the video again, slowing it down, way down, from the sword descending—

Oh, Mel.

The flicker, the blood spurting out and splashing the lens.

"There," he says again, his voice filled with the impatience of some Cassandra, trying to share what he knows with the oblivious masses next to him who are ignoring God's word.

Agent Stahl plays intermediary. "Professor, please, it's been a long couple of weeks. President Keating has been under tremendous pressure. Can you explain, simply, what we should be noticing?"

"Ah, of course," he says. "My apologies. You see, when blood emerges from a fresh wound and strikes an object, like the camera lens here, you get a type of blood pattern and spatter, and it's observable in a certain way. But when the blood doesn't come instantly from its source, then it looks and acts entirely different. That's what I saw here, and that's why I was so insistent on seeing you, Mr. President."

Deep, deep inside of me, a little flare of something has just been ignited.

Oh, God, I think, *please make it so.*

Please.

I say, "Professor, are you saying what I think you're saying?"

A confident nod.

"The beheading video is a fake," he says.

CHAPTER 76

Lake Marie, New Hampshire

I'm standing so close to the disgraced professor that I can smell his clothes and his sweat, and I don't care. I say, "Explain it again. Slowly. With details I can understand. Please, professor."

And I think, *If you're crazy or bullshitting me in any way, there's a shovel in the corner and a dirt basement floor behind me.*

"Certainly," he says. "It's a study that I came up with a few years back, with assistance from a couple of my more intelligent grad students. It used to be that forensic investigators were just looking at the blood pattern, what's now known as spatter. You can examine a pattern at a crime scene, and most times, you can deduce where the victim was standing, or sitting, or if he or she resisted, and how the body was later transported. It's all there, if you know how to read the spatter."

He taps the side of his forehead, smiles. His teeth are yellow.

The professor says, "I took it to another level, by introducing the concept of fluid dynamics. When a fluid like blood is expelled, it makes a world of difference if the blood is fresh or stored. They act like two completely different sets of fluids. The consistency, the levels of oxygenation—all that comes into play. You can then determine if the blood spatter was part of the actual crime or an afterthought, to set up a crime scene that has a false message. I wrote two papers on this for the journal *Forensic Science International* that received very positive responses from my colleagues."

He taps again, this time on the screen. "This is not fresh blood. In fact, if I had a better version of this video recording, I could make a strong case that it's not even human blood."

The little flare of hope inside of me is growing hard and fast, threatening to overtake my common sense and skepticism.

"But the earlier part of the video," I say. "The…the sword and the beheading. Couldn't that be real?"

He shakes his head, sits back on the stool, crosses his arms. "For what purpose? A real beheading followed by a fake blood spurt? What would be the point? Besides, before I was forced to leave the university, there were already studies under way because of the concern over what's known as deepfake videos. Taking a real video recording of President Barnes, for example, and changing her business suit into latex and feathers, like a Las Vegas showgirl, to make it look like she was taking part in some naughty Vegas revue. Anyone with experience in filmmaking or special effects could probably come up with a way to take a real video of your daughter and then splice in a beheading scene."

Agent Stahl starts to say something, and I snap, "No, not now! Everybody just shut up, just don't say a word."

I close my eyes.

Trying hard to remember.

When I was president, each minute, half hour, and hour was scheduled down to the second, every day, even the weekends.

With meetings, briefings, and reports. Being asked to make decisions and judgments in areas from the economy to human rights to diplomacy to domestic issues and politics. A week into my presidency, not long after the funeral of my predecessor, I had a childhood memory. I remembered reading a paperback novel—with its cover torn off—that had been one of the few possessions of my father's that came back from the oil rig after his death.

The book, called *The Multiple Man,* was published in 1976, and it took place sometime in an imagined future when the world was so deadly and complex that the elected president had six secretly cloned brothers, each one an expert in one field. Working together, each was able to bring his own special expertise to their collective administration during a very challenging era.

It seemed fantastic and off-the-wall at the time, but later, in trying to remember all the details from that constant treadmill of meetings and briefings when I was in the Oval Office, it all made intriguing sense: some science fiction future, on the page or on the screen—

I open my eyes.

"Faraj Al-Asheed," I say. "Asim's younger cousin. I received a number of intelligence briefings on him as well, during the run-up to that raid. Before he joined jihad with Asim, he was in Paris. Attending film school. With an emphasis on fantasy, science fiction, and special effects."

I reach for the keyboard, pull my hand away.

I have this desperate desire not to spoil anything.

Trying to keep the growing excitement out of my voice, I say, "Professor, please: run back the video to the beginning."

"Certainly," he says. He gets off the stool, plays with the keyboard. The video speeds up in reverse—*Fake, fake, fake!* I want to scream out; *My daughter's death was faked!*—and then he plays it from the beginning.

The same stern-looking Asim Al-Asheed is now there again, and from the computer's speakers comes his voice. After the initial greetings, he goes on.

"I apologize that this is not a... what you call a *live feed* but a recording, from several hours ago, after we departed the home of Mr. Macomber in your White Mountains, and here we are, in these mountains still."

"There!" I say. "Run it back to the very beginning, before he appears."

Seconds later, the video starts up again, and I say, "Freeze it. Right there."

The professor is on my left, and Agent Stahl is on my right.

I gently trace the screen before me, which shows a rock wall and an adjoining ledge.

With a soft voice I say, "He says this is being recorded in the White Mountains. But look at that rock formation. In every hike I've done here with Sam or Mel, there's always vegetation, from lichen to grasses to scrub brush, among the rock formations. None of that is here. Can we be sure he filmed this here, in New Hampshire? Or someplace else?"

Agent Stahl says, "Mr. President... that's a hell of a good point."

I strike the screen with some force, making it vibrate. "We're going to find that out, right now."

And I think of last night, being on the dock out there in the darkness, and vowing, *Asim, I'm coming for you.*

Now, can I dare believe one more thing?

Mel, I'm coming for you, too.

CHAPTER 77

Enfield, New Hampshire

Trent Youngblood, associate professor of earth sciences at Dartmouth College, is drying off the last of his dinner dishes when there's a pounding at his front door, followed by the frantic ringing of the doorbell.

He takes a look at the small Bavarian cuckoo clock hanging in the cluttered kitchen, a souvenir his wife, Carol, bought on a river cruise they took in Germany last year. The clock looks old and hand-carved, but it's a silly piece of kitsch made in Cambodia and operated by a hidden battery.

Trent thinks the ridiculous thing is a good metaphor for his work: something that looks one way on the surface but is revealed to be quite different once you start digging.

The clock says it's almost 9 p.m.

Who the hell could be banging on his door at this hour?

Carol is off at a late-night tai chi class, and their son, Greg, is in California, attending the Stanford Graduate School of Business; the nearest neighbor is almost a half mile away. Instead of quickly answering the door, Trent checks his laptop on the kitchen counter, next to piles of mail, and sees the feed from the Nest Hello doorbell camera.

What's there disturbs him.

Three figures wearing jackets and caps pulled down low. The one in the lead hammers the door again, and Trent sees it's a Black woman.

Trent is *so* not a racist, but what's a Black woman doing out here, at this hour? In this part of rural New Hampshire? And what should he do? Call the police?

Right, he thinks. Imagine what would happen to him and his career if that bit of news got out: a white, privileged college professor calling the police on a Black woman knocking on his door at night. For all he knows, this trio could be lost and looking for directions.

But then again, who gets lost nowadays with everyone having a GPS-enabled cell phone?

The doorbell rings again.

To hell with it.

He'll answer the door.

As he goes down the front hallway, he stops for a moment, opens a closet door, and takes down a loaded Colt .357 revolver from the top shelf. He's been to dig sites in some sketchy parts of the world, and just over twenty years ago, two Dartmouth professors were murdered in their homes by two local teenage losers. Trent isn't going to be a victim tonight.

He switches on the outdoor light, gun partially hidden by his hip, unlocks the door, opens it, and says, "Can I help you?"

And then the Black woman yells "Gun, gun, gun!" and he's slammed to the floor of his own home.

* * *

He's brought to his feet, shaking with fear and anger, after being stripped of his revolver, and the Black woman and another man are standing next to him, and the third man comes in, saying in a familiar voice, "Professor Youngblood, I'm so sorry for that. But Agent Washington and Agent Stahl are true professionals. I hope you're not hurt."

The man removes his plain dark blue baseball cap, revealing the face of former president Matthew Keating. Trent blinks his eyes. It's no big deal having him live in the area—hell, he spotted Keating twice over the years at the local Whole Foods. But what's he doing here?

"Mr.... ah, well, how can I help you?"

The former president's face is drawn, worn, and his eyes seem sunken, and Trent suddenly feels a deep sorrow for this man, whose daughter was publicly executed just two weeks ago.

Keating says, "I need your help. We've done some research and found out you're one of the best geology experts at Dartmouth. I need for you to look at a rock display for us, tell me what you see. Can you do that?"

Holy crap, Trent thinks. He and his wife, Carol, spent countless hours two years ago working as volunteers to elect this man's vice president to the Oval Office: making phone calls, knocking on doors, and holding signs during the New Hampshire primary. There were political meetings at their house, with late-night drinks of wine and beer and determined vows to get that damn killer out of the White House. There were jokes about his Texas accent and his oh-so-smart-and-precious wife. Lots of snarky comments about his accidental presidency. They passed out bumper stickers saying DEFEAT KEATING: THE ERROR OF THE ERA.

Now the error of the era is standing right in front of him.

What would Carol think? What would their friends think?

Trent nods.

"Absolutely, Mr. President. I can start whenever you're ready."

Minutes later they're in Trent's crowded upstairs office, with workbench, shelves of books and binders, computer and filing cabinets, and shelves of rock samples from sites all over the world. The female Secret Service agent gets to work, and Trent is a bit miffed that she didn't apologize for tossing him violently to the floor. She opens a laptop she carried in, and in a few seconds, an image comes up.

Rock wall, rock ledge.

He's seen that before.

Oh, God, he thinks. *The place where this sad man's daughter was murdered.*

In a slightly strained voice, Keating says, "Professor, give that rock face a good look. I know it's not a great image, but can you tell us…is that from somewhere in the White Mountains?"

Trent bends over, gives the image a long hard stare, and says, "Absolutely not."

Keating's hand is on his shoulder. "Are you sure? What are you seeing?"

Trent feels a bit of childish pride, explaining his work to a former president of the United States.

He says, "If it was somewhere in New Hampshire—or even Vermont or Maine—that rock surface would be leucocratic, likely with crosscutting quartz veins and present surface fracturing, which is typical of the freeze-and-thaw weathering in granitoid rock you get in this part of the world. But you can see that rock surface is brown and shows the distinct bedding of a sedimentary rock. But there's a lack of distinct clastic grains, which means this rock is likely a limestone or dolostone."

Keating's hand slightly tightens on Trent's shoulder. "Can you tell us where it is?"

Trent says, "No, I can't."

There's a sense of disappointment from his three visitors, and he quickly says, "No, no, don't worry. I can't, but my grandfather can. Hold on. Give me a few minutes."

Trent goes to the binders in one section of his crowded shelves, finds the marker he's looking for, and hauls the old black file down. The former president and his Secret Service agents gather around him as he opens the book, revealing old black-and-white photos and handwritten field notes, the writing still clear decades later.

He says, "My grandfather Enoch was a great geologist, but instead of academia, he worked for the oil companies. That's where I learned to love geology—him bringing back rock samples for me. He traveled all around the world, jungles to deserts...but that rock formation you showed me: it triggered something *he* showed me years back. Ah, here we go."

He traces his finger up and down two photos stuck in glassine pages, side by side. "Here. Practically a double to the one on the computer screen, isn't it? See, like I said before, you can see the bedding of sedimentary rock, but the absence of distinct clastic grains means this rock is either a limestone or dolostone. Also, you can see the presence of the distinct chert horizons, which narrows it down considerably."

"Narrows it down to what?" the former president asks.

"Oh, no question," Trent says. "Libya. The Nafusa Mountains."

CHAPTER 78

Hitchcock, Maine

Samantha Keating wakes up in her motel room, someone firmly knocking at her door. She checks the time.

Just past 5 a.m.

She rolls out of bed, barefoot on the rough-surfaced light green rug, wearing loose shorts and a BU T-shirt, and turns on the nightstand light. It takes three tries before she gets it right because her fingers are shaking, and she knows why.

Only one reason somebody's at her door so damn early in the morning.

In seconds she's there, unchaining and unlocking, taking deep breaths, trying to stay calm despite the sudden chill in her hands and feet, thinking of her Mel, out there in some wilderness, her remains exposed to the elements, and birds, and coyotes, and—

Samantha gets the door open.

It's still dark outside.

From the utility lights in the motel's small parking lot she sees Matt standing in front of her. Instantly there's love and fear and lots of guilt, guilt from knowing that years back she could have ensured Matt's easy reelection and the safety of their girl but chose not to do so, guilt about how she's been coldly ignoring his desperately cheerful video messages from their lakefront home.

She leans on the doorframe for support.

"Oh, Matt, where?" she asks, voice choked.

He takes both of her hands.

"Sam," he says. "I think she's still alive."

She falls into his arms.

A minute later she's sitting on her still-warm bed, and Matt is sitting next to her, arm around her shoulders, his free hand grasping hers.

He says, "A forensic scientist came by yesterday, unofficially and on his own. He's well respected, knows his stuff, and Agent Stahl vouches for him. He's convinced the video of Mel's murder was faked."

"But…I saw it! You saw it!"

"The blood that struck the camera lens, near the end," her husband says. "The professor is convinced it's fake. The way it moved, dripped—it didn't have the consistency of fresh blood. He thinks there's a good chance it wasn't even human blood."

Samantha feels as though she's on one of those Tilt-a-Whirl carnival rides from when she was younger, going in all directions, up and down and sideways, not even sure what is true and secure. This unexpected visit, Matt dropping in here without warning, it seems too good to be true, a dream that she's in the middle of experiencing, a dream where Mel is still alive.

"Matt…are you sure? It looked so real!"

With confidence he says, "Faraj, Asim Al-Asheed's cousin, spent months in Paris, studying film and special effects. That's how it could have been faked. And there's another piece of information."

Now she's afraid that if she says anything, she'll burst into tears. Samantha just nods.

"If the beheading was faked, why not the location?" Matt goes on, still holding her tight. "Asim said he and Mel were still in New Hampshire. I found a geology professor from Dartmouth last night. He said the rock surface in the video isn't from New Hampshire, or even New England. The video was recorded in Libya, in the Nafusa Mountains, where Asim is from and where he likes to hide out."

"The floatplane," Samantha says, finding her voice. "It took her north. To an airport somewhere. That's why there was the delay in the videotape. They had to have enough time to fly her to Libya."

Matt says, "Exactly."

Samantha now feels incredibly light all over, as if she could float off the bed and gently bump into the ceiling if Matt wasn't holding on to her so tight. "Matt, do you have that forensic professor with you? Or the geologist?"

"No," he says. "It's just Agents Stahl and Washington."

"But..."

She stops. She knows what she's feeling, what she is about to say. *Evidence.* You need solid evidence before coming up with a theory, especially a theory like this one, so welcome yet so unsupported. *I want to believe,* she thinks. *I have to believe, but I need to see the evidence for myself. Before I start hoping again.*

I need to see the evidence.

Matt says quietly, "Sam? You were going to say something?"

She squeezes his hand right back.

Trust him. Trust your man.

She says, "Yes. This information. Do you think anyone else has it? Somebody from the FBI or Homeland Security?"

"No," he says. "Not right now."

"Good," she says.

Matt releases his grip to get a better look at her. "Sam? What did you just say?"

"You heard me," she says, feeling stronger, happier. "What are the chances that if someone in the government found this out it would remain secret? Somebody might want to leak it to impress their husband or wife, or to get a favor from a news reporter. They wouldn't care. It's just another headline, another deposit in somebody's favor bank. Or they would take their time, trying to confirm, and reconfirm, before doing anything."

Matt stands up, holding her hands, bending down to kiss her, and then breaking away, his hands still in hers.

"Sam, I'm going to get our girl back."

"I know you are," she says. "You get Mel, you get her safe and you bring her home. But you're going to do one more thing."

"What's that?"

She kisses his hand. "Once you get Mel back safe and sound, you kill that son of a bitch Asim."

CHAPTER 79

Lake Marie, New Hampshire

Secret Service agent David Stahl watches as one of the two Boston Whalers owned by Homeland Security motors out to the flat and clear waters of the lake, and he stifles a yawn. He's drunk three more cups of coffee than his usual daily ration, but he still feels as though he could close his eyes and sleep until the sun rises the next day.

A long, long night and early morning, driving straight through from Enfield to Hitchcock, Maine, and then back again to Lake Marie, traveling mostly on narrow country roads, twice dodging moose rambling out in front of the Suburban. On the way to Maine, Harbor briefed Agent Washington, and now she's part of the rescue mission planning. David is confident that she has Harbor's back.

Nice to trust your team.

He's still running down a mental checklist for Harbor's mission when he hears steps on the dock. He turns as Agent Brett

Peyton, his supposed deputy here on the detail, approaches. David has the irrational feeling that if Peyton was out as long as he was last night, the guy wouldn't look tired or even have a hair out of place.

"How goes it, Dave?" Peyton asks.

"It goes," David says.

He wants to get back to his barn office but Peyton gently steps in front of him. Smile still firmly secured, Peyton says, "Odd that during my brief time here, I think I've found the root cause of why this detail failed. Too comfortable, too loose. Like your travels all last night with Harbor. No planning, no logistics. Just saddle up and go."

David says, "Harbor was feeling stir-crazy, having been stuck here in the compound since he came back from Virginia. Agent Washington and I took him for a drive. His mood improved. Then he wanted to go see Harp. It's been a while."

Peyton still has that frozen, know-it-all look on his face, and he says, "Still. Unorthodox."

"You know how it is, Brett," David says. "You need to balance keeping the protectee safe with not keeping him or her stuck in a room, covered with bubble wrap. Keeping the protectee both safe and happy. A hell of a job, isn't it? If most of your career had been spent in the field instead of behind a desk chasing down cybercriminals, you might be more aware of that."

Peyton's smile fades. "It's an important job."

"True, but not as important as protecting POTUS, other government officials, and foreign dignitaries," David says. "That and counterfeiting were our original roles. Then some fools years back decided it was a good idea to do a power grab, get the Secret Service into areas it has no business being in, like cybercrime. Which seems to be the business you love."

Peyton steps closer and now the smile is gone. "It'd be better for you and the agency if you and this entire detail resign.

Within the week. I have it on good authority that the director and the secretary of Homeland Security would look favorably upon it."

"But nothing in writing, I'm sure."

"Of course not."

"Well, I'll certainly keep that under consideration, Brett. In the meantime, I've got lots of work to do."

"Including additional unorthodox trips with Harbor?"

Those words make David feel as though he's just had his feet nailed to the dock.

What the hell does Peyton know?

He keeps his voice controlled. "Within reason, certainly. Harbor's not under house arrest. If he wants to leave the compound, we'll make it work."

"Suppose it's another long trip? Like last night?"

David says, "Like I said, within reason."

"That's the situation, isn't it?" Brett goes on. "You have a protectee who's deep in grief, probably feeling guilt over what happened to his girl, guilt at knowing his actions as POTUS led to her death. It might pressure him to do something…unwise. And our job is to keep him safe and keep him grounded. Right?"

David knows he's about thirty seconds away from tossing Peyton into the lake.

Brett lowers his voice. "Resign, already. You're too close to Harbor. If he were to do something reckless, you might not want to stop him. David, you'd do him and the agency well by leaving. Sooner rather than later."

David slowly nods. "From your point of view, Brett, I'm sure that makes sense. Leave. Wash your hands. Put your head down and bail out. But from where I stand, where I'm continuing to stand until told otherwise, leaving is another way of quitting."

He walks forward, enjoying jostling Peyton as he passes him on the dock.

"If you had been in the Marines like me, you would've known I'm not a quitter," David says. "And if you haven't figured it out yet, neither is Harbor."

CHAPTER 80

First Congregational Church of Spencer
Spencer, New Hampshire

It's just past 11 a.m. on a Sunday in this plain white Congregational church that was built when America was still only thirteen colonies, and I'm enjoying every minute of being here. I grew up in a small crossroads town in the flat plains of Texas, and its history—Native Americans, first settlers, cotton farms, conflicts here and there, and the joy of Juneteenth in 1865 and additional long years of drought and deprivation—could be written on a pamphlet.

In this town, first settled in 1758, the history fills three leather-bound volumes, and a retired history teacher from the local regional high school is hard at work on volume four. One of my quiet hobbies is reading up on the history of my new home and surrounding towns and retaining quirky bits of knowledge, like the fact that in this county, there are five fake Underground Railroad stations for every real one that helped escaping slaves cross the nearby Canadian border.

And why are so many fake?

Because it usually adds 10 percent value to the sale of historic homes.

Earlier, the pews were unbolted and stacked in the corner while I worked with other members of the church in the small kitchen in the rear. My specialty is flapjacks, which these stubborn Northerners call *pancakes,* and it's good to be working hard in the small kitchen, with laughs and jokes and gentle ribbing as flapjacks, bacon, sausage, scrambled eggs, and French toast get passed out through a rectangular opening where church volunteers pick up the freshly cooked food and bring it out to the guests.

The church charges nothing for this Sunday feast, which is run by volunteers, and most of the food is donated, although there's a large glass mason jar at the entrance for contributions. Mostly it's a place to catch up with one's neighbors, pass along the latest family news or gossip, and just maintain that elusive sense of community. As I help wash dishes, I get a warm feeling in knowing that this tradition has been going on for more than two centuries.

I grab a plate of flapjacks and bacon—volunteers eat last—and Agent David Stahl steps in and says, "Looks like you worked up quite the appetite, sir."

"And I bet you've already eaten," I say.

"Good guess, sir," he says. "Here, this way."

I follow his lead across the wooden floor, the old planks creaking, and I'm pretty much ignored by the guests finishing up their breakfasts, lingering over cups of coffee and tea. Another reason I like living around here is that in the true Yankee sense, people mostly mind their own damned business.

I approach a small folding card table underneath a large black-and-white photo of some stern-looking minister from 1901. Sitting there are two men, early thirties, one with a mustache, the other with a neatly trimmed beard, both wearing jeans and polo shirts. The one with the beard is wearing a plain red polo and his mustached seatmate is wearing a black one.

They nod as I sit down, and I say, "Enjoy your meal?"

"Pretty damn good," the bearded one says, at my left. His companion nods.

An older woman volunteer smiles and comes by and drops off coffee in a chipped white mug, and I take a bracing sip. It's made just the way I like: black with two sugars.

The bearded man starts. "Mr. President, I—"

I dig into my flapjacks. "Stop that. From now on, it's Matt. All right?"

He knowingly nods. "Absolutely, sir."

"Damn it, and cut out the *sir* crap, too."

"Ah…" A pause, and then he says, "Habit. Sorry."

"Not a problem," I say. "Just as long as your buddy and you have kept other habits up to snuff."

His companion says, "You got it. We're ready to go wherever you need us."

"Your status?"

The bearded man says, "Both of us on fourteen-days' leave. And if that's not enough, we'll figure something out. We're also geared up."

I nod, continue eating. The flapjacks are delicious, of course, and despite New Englanders being New Englanders, I love their insistence on using real maple syrup. The first time I ever tasted the real stuff was when I moved up here eighteen months ago, and I've never looked back.

"Which teams are you with?"

The man on the right says, "Six. We're both with Six."

"And you know what you've volunteered for, right?" I say. "I'm sure you do, but I want to make sure there's a complete understanding. This is unofficial, off-the-books, illegal, and even if it's successful, prison time is a real possibility."

The SEAL on the left says, "We're all in."

His companion says, "We want to make it right, for what happened to your daughter."

My daughter!

I smile. "Since I've talked to Trask Floyd, the scope of the mission has expanded. It's not just a zap mission. It's also a rescue. That beheading video was faked. I'm pretty sure Mel is being held in the Nafusa Mountains, in Libya."

I enjoy seeing the shocked looks on both of their faces. There's a myth that SEALs are six feet tall with lots of ripped muscles on top of other muscles. The truth is, what counts in SEALs is the muscle between the ears. In BUD/S training, it was usually the overbulked and -exercised recruits who failed first. The ones who hung tough and kept their smarts about them were the ones who eventually got the tridents.

I reach into my coat pocket, pull out a slip of paper, slide it over. "A room's been rented at this motel in Contoocook. I'll see you there at noon tomorrow."

"Going to be tricky for you," the SEAL on the right says.

"Tricky is going to be our way of life over the next several days," I say. "But before we go on, I'm sorry, I should have asked your names."

The one with the mustache says, "Alejandro Lopez, bosun's mate first class. I go by Al or Alejandro."

"All right," I say, and the other SEAL is smiling widely, like he's keeping a wonderful secret, and by God he is.

"Chief Nick Zeppos," he says. "And Matt, you can just call me Nick."

His name. That familiar voice.

Me talking to him, more than two years ago.

From my chair in the Situation Room.

Now you squids body-bag that son of a bitch for the country, the SEALs, and especially for Boyd Tanner.

"Chief Zeppos," I say. "Damn it, you were lead on that mission to nail Asim, more than two years back."

He's still smiling, but it's not a friendly smile.

It's the look of a wolf, ready to hunt.

"That's why I'm here, Matt," he says. "This time, we're going to get it done."

CHAPTER 81

Mary's Diner
Leah, New Hampshire

Secret Service agent Brett Peyton is riding in the lead black Chevrolet Suburban as Harbor decides to have breakfast at a local greasy spoon about twenty minutes away from his compound. Another typical outing for a very atypical former president, and Peyton wishes the damn man would just stay in his compound and brood, mourn, and play poker—Brett's own favorite card game is cribbage, depending more on smarts than on just damn luck—instead of going out like this. The pathetic guy seems to need and thrive on mingling with the so-called plain folks in these small northern towns.

Agent Kelly Ferguson, a slim Black woman, is driving this Suburban, and behind them is the second Suburban, with Harbor in the rear and Agents Stahl and Washington riding up front. There was a small crowd gathered by the state police roadblock greeting the two-vehicle motorcade, and Brett wonders if Harbor waved back at them through the tinted glass.

And it's odd: Kelly seems to have read his mind. She says, "You think Harbor waved back?"

"Who knows?" he answers.

"Tarpon wouldn't," she says, using their code name for President Barnes. "Too busy reading, plotting against her enemies, or listening to her husband. But Harbor…he would. He's that kind of guy."

Brett laughs. "You've been here less than a month. Drinking the Kool-Aid already? He's just a former POTUS. Nothing else."

Kelly says, "That's your opinion, nothing more. And those folks at that suicide temple in Jonestown didn't drink Kool-Aid; it was Flavor Aid. Get your facts straight."

"Shut up and drive," Brett shoots back, and he's slightly surprised at how angry he's just gotten. The truth is that Agent Stahl and others on the original detail are getting under his skin. When he was transferred here, Brett expected a group that was shell-shocked about what happened to the president's daughter, nervous about the hammer that was going to soon come down on them.

But the detail acted nothing like that. They moved around and did their jobs and responded to Harbor's jokes and gentle teasing as though nothing had happened. It's an open secret that he has been sent here to collect information for the upcoming hearings and disciplinary action, but for the most part, he's been cheerfully ignored by the original detail.

And that earlier comment from Stahl at the boat dock about cybercrime also struck home, for most of Brett's career has been with the Secret Service's Criminal Investigative Division, in DC, working on cyber investigations and other financial crimes. A few years back he was transferred to Protective Operations as part of his crawl up the career ladder, and although he won't admit it to anyone, he's looking forward to getting out of fieldwork.

Mary's Diner comes into view on Route 115 as Agent Ferguson

flicks on the Suburban's directional, and Brett notes the battered pickup trucks and old Volvos and Toyotas parked in the dirt lot. Not much chance of any cybercrime happening here, and truth be told, that's why Brett is tired of being in the PPD. The long hours of just…standing around. That's it. Just standing around, wasting time. He'd much rather be in a cool and protected office somewhere, nine to five in front of a computer terminal, being a hell of a lot more productive than he feels standing in front of some out-of-the-way diner while the protectee is eating ham and eggs and shaking hands with the locals.

The Suburban comes to a halt and he and Agent Ferguson slide out, joining Agents Washington and Stahl as Harbor exits the Suburban's rear door, looking more relaxed and grungier than usual. Harbor is wearing a worn dark brown leather jacket, Dartmouth ball cap, blue jeans, and black sneakers, and it looks as though he hasn't shaved in two or three days.

Stahl takes lead and goes into the diner—a one-story brick and wood building with a pitched roof, abutting a river at the rear—with Harbor right behind him and Washington riding tail. Brett nods to Ferguson and says, "Okay, then," and Ferguson walks around to the rear of the diner while he maintains his post outside the front door.

He can't help it.

Brett yawns.

An early-morning mist is hugging the dark green of the forested hills around this part of the town of Leah. There's a gas station and convenience store across the street, a couple of smaller homes down the road, and, about a hundred feet away, a bigger, sagging yellow house that's known around here as a Colonial. Brett grew up in Phoenix, worked in the Arizona Department of Public Safety before joining the Secret Service, and one big surprise is seeing how *old* everything around here is. Hell, Phoenix didn't become an official city until 1881 or thereabouts, and folks here don't think it's a big deal to own a house that was built in the 1700s.

He yawns again.

Brett thinks that one day somebody should write a book called *Boredom: A Secret Service Agent's Memoir.*

From his earpiece, he hears from inside the diner, "Stahl here with Harbor."

Brett speaks into his wrist—"Roger that"—and there are echoing responses from Ferguson and one of the on-duty agents back at the former president's home.

"Lake Marie, acknowledged," says a woman's voice.

More than an hour later, Brett is pacing the dirt lot, no longer bored.

What the hell is taking Harbor so long?

Over the last hour, there have been quick updates from Stahl, all repeating the same thing: "Harbor is secure."

But doing what? Working on his third breakfast?

Brett brings the wrist microphone to his mouth and says, "Ferguson, is Harbor back there helping to empty the trash?"

"Only thing going on back here is a turf war between chipmunks and squirrels," she replies via his radio earpiece.

He says, "Stahl, this is Peyton. What's your status?"

An older couple walks out of the diner, the man saying, "Don't know why you have to overtip all the time, Jenny..."

No answer.

"Stahl, this is Peyton. Reply, please."

The older couple climbs into a dark blue Volvo sedan. She starts the engine, and they drive off on the narrow and empty country road.

What the hell?

"Ferguson, this is Peyton," he says, voice tight. "Something's wrong. I'm going in."

Ferguson says, "See you inside."

He slides his light jacket aside, hand on his SIG Sauer P229 semiautomatic pistol, and he quickly enters the diner.

Snapshot view.

Tables and booths to the left.

Counter with round stools in front, half or so occupied.

Everyone here turning their heads to look at him, and then to see Agent Ferguson come in through the kitchen area from the right.

No President Keating.

Nor Agent Stahl.

Nor Agent Washington.

A bone-thin white-haired woman wearing black slacks and a pink top comes by, expertly balancing a tray on her left shoulder, and Brett steps in front of her. "President Keating! Where is he?"

She shrugs. "He went down there a while ago."

"Where?" Brett demands. "Went where?"

She gestures with her free shoulder to the far corner of the diner, where there's a closed wooden door next to towering piles of cardboard boxes, and he gets to the door, throws it open, sees a staircase leading to a cellar.

Light switch on.

Agent Ferguson is right behind him.

Down the worn wooden steps to the cellar, low ceiling.

"Mr. President?" he calls out. "Stahl? Washington?"

There are two freezers, shelves filled with canned goods. Ferguson slides past, and there's a roaring in Brett's ears, hands cold, now holding his SIG Sauer, thinking, *An ambush? Another kidnapping? Why no gunshots?*

"Peyton! Over here!"

He goes around a set of shelves to an old brick and stone foundation, and there's a heavy wooden door set in the center.

Ferguson tugs the door open, steps through, flashlight in hand, lighting up the interior.

A brick-lined tunnel, going into the darkness.

Brett stands next to Ferguson. "Holy shit," he says.

A woman's voice behind them—"Nothing holy about it"—and there's a laugh.

Brett turns, and the older woman with the black slacks and pink top is there, wrinkled face smiling. He says, "What is this? A storage room? Root cellar?"

A firm shake of the head. "Nope. Smugglin' tunnel, back during Prohibition."

Ferguson says, "Where does it go?"

"About a hundred feet, over to the Trainor house. Back in the day, the boats would come down the Trinity River from Ontario, with all that fine Canadian whiskey and beer. They'd drop it off at the house, and then it'd get brought over here through that tunnel, back when this place was a roadhouse. Exciting times."

Ferguson says, "Peyton, we've got to get the word out."

Before Brett can reply, the older woman digs into her slacks, pulls out a folded envelope, and says, "You Agent Peyton, Secret Service?"

He nods.

"This is for you, then," she says, passing over the envelope.

The envelope is buff ivory, professionally made, and in the upper left corner is the seal of the United States, and under that the words OFFICE OF MATTHEW KEATING.

Brett's own name is handwritten in the center.

He tears open the envelope, quickly reads the single sheet of paper, knowing with a sharp clarity, like a lightning bolt nearby, that both his career and the former president are gone.

CHAPTER
82

Autumn Leaves Motel
Contoocook, New Hampshire

The largest room the Autumn Leaves Motel offers is crowded this morning, with myself, Secret Service agent David Stahl, and the two Navy SEALs, Alejandro Lopez and Nick Zeppos, who earlier undid the frame of one of the two beds and put it and the mattress and box spring up against a wall.

Piled in one corner are variously sized duffel bags containing our equipment, and on the thin blue carpet a large-scale topo map of Libya is spread out. We're drinking coffee from a local Dunkin' as our planning continues.

Hard to explain, but I feel pride, hope, and exhilaration being with these fellow warriors, preparing to go into the field one more time. The cliché of Shakespeare's famed Henry V speech before the Battle of Agincourt—

We few, we happy few, we band of brothers;
For he to-day that sheds his blood with me
Shall be my brother

—is a cliché because it's true.

These men here, no matter the outcome, will always be my brothers.

To the head of my Secret Service detail I say, "David, how long before the Secret Service gets mobilized and starts beating the bushes for me?"

"Never," he says.

Even the two SEALs seem to sit up and take notice. "Why's that?" I ask.

David says, "Once you left Secret Service protection, it became an FBI matter. The same when Mel was kidnapped. The FBI took control."

Alejandro smiles. "But he hasn't left Secret Service protection. You're still here, eh?"

David doesn't smile in return. "Official protection, not what we've got going on here. Once the…once Matt left, it became the FBI's responsibility. Word probably went right to the top, to Director Blair, and they're gearing up right now to start the search. It's going to be one intense effort, sir."

I say, "But the note I left behind at the diner—won't that buy us some time?"

David says, "Doubtful. The FBI can't take that letter at face value. They'll have to assume that this is part of a kidnap plot, maybe a follow-up to Mel's kidnapping, and respond appropriately."

"Good," I say.

Now all three of my fellow brothers-in-arms are staring at me. Nick says, "Sir?"

"Good," I repeat. "By now Director Blair has briefed President Barnes. Do you think she wants word to get out that I've disappeared? After the news leaks and columns about their botched response to my daughter's kidnapping? No, they don't want the added humiliation. That's the biggest reason governments keep secrets. Not because they're sensitive. Because the secrets are embarrassing."

Alejandro says, "It'll get out eventually."

"Sure," I say. "In a day or two. And by then, we'll be in North Africa, God willing and the crick don't rise. And if Agent Washington makes good distance before being picked up."

Secret Service agent Nicole Washington, devoted to her career and to protecting me. A Black woman from Anacostia in DC, and not the part of Anacostia that's being gentrified with cafés and brick sidewalks. When I asked her to do this one task that has a good chance of ruining her life and career—drive on back roads through rural Maine carrying my iPhone and David's Android and radio gear, in case our searchers can track those instruments—she just nodded and said, "It'll be an honor, Mr. President."

What did I and the country ever do to deserve such people?

I take a sip of strong coffee. "Back to the original question. Where do we insert in Libya? I can make some calls, get us private transport from one of my deep-pocketed donors…though it might take some time, finding a transatlantic jet to get us there."

David says, "Libyan customs might frown upon letting us in with all that gear we're carrying."

I say, "Then our air transport goes for a private strip. Money gets passed around, the Customs folks decide all at once to kneel down and tie their shoes as we depart. But what next? Steal or rent some ground transport and make a high-speed run to the Nafusa Mountains, hoping we get actionable intelligence by the time we arrive?"

Alejandro shakes his head. "Mr. President, I—sorry, *Matt.* I don't like it. I was there six months ago. Libya is damn fragile, especially once you get out of the coast cities like Tripoli or Misrata. There are pretty much only two major highways that run into the interior from the western part of the country, and you stand a good chance of running into armed checkpoints. Depending on who's getting paid and what day of the week it is, those checkpoints could be regular Libyan army, militia, or tribesmen looking for tribute. Too messy."

I nod. "Good point. Plus, I'm sure our Chinese friends are all over the place, still pouring money into their Belt and Road Initiative. They see four Americans show up at any airstrip, we'll have a ground asset or drone following us as soon as we leave the runway."

Nick leans over the large map, taps a finger, and says, "Tunisia. We get to Tunisia, at their air base at Sfax-Thyna, on the coast. They have a unit of the Groupe des Forces Spéciales—their Special Forces group—based there. Me and a platoon spent five months there last year, doing training."

I like what I'm hearing. "Go on, Nick."

"With some... encouragement, I bet we can get them spun up for a training mission. And if it goes cross-border into Libya, well, navigation accidents happen all the time. But that's a closed base. No civilian aircraft allowed."

"Then we'll get over there on a military flight," I say, staring at the detailed map of Libya while my mind sees a map of New England. "Vermont has an Air National Guard unit at Burlington, but only F-35 fighter jets are stationed there. No good. And Maine's Air National Guard base is up in Bangor, and that's at least a four-hour drive away, and gents, we don't have four hours. It's going to be Pease, over on the New

Hampshire coast. In Newington. Less than an hour away if we push it."

David says, "What's there, Matt?"

"Refueling tankers, both the KC-135 and the newer KC-46. Both have the range to get us there. But getting us on one of those aircraft..."

I fall silent, knowing that with the right phone calls, I can get the necessary information as to what refueling jets are stationed at Pease: *Are any leaving within the next several hours, and oh, by the way, are any of them going to the Mediterranean, and would it be any problem to take along four passengers with enough weaponry to go up against a squad of ISIS fighters?*

But making phone calls means leaving digital crumbs out there for the FBI or the White House to locate.

What to do, what to do, what—

A firm knock on the door.

We all look in the same direction.

The knock comes back, harder.

I say, "If that's the FBI, then I'm seriously impressed."

Nick says, "Hard to believe, sir. We paid for the room in cash. With black IDs. There should be no trace that we're here."

Another knock and I say, "Dave, answer the damn door. We don't need anybody out in the parking lot reporting a disturbance. Nick, fold up the map."

Alejandro says, "Maybe you should hide out in the bathroom."

The suggestion irritates me. I sit in the corner, pull a plain black baseball cap down on my head. "I'm not hiding, but Dave, get rid of whoever's out there."

Nick quickly folds up the map and Alejandro pulls a sheet from the disassembled bed, tosses it over the pile of black duffel bags containing our gear. Dave goes to the door, unlocks it, opens it.

A slim young woman is there, early twenties, wearing jeans

and a black T-shirt with a red anarchy symbol on the front. Her red hair is cut short and she's wearing plain black-rimmed glasses, and she says, "Oh, good, you haven't left yet."

Dave says, "Excuse me, what did you just say? And who the hell are you?"

She ducks down, picks up a computer bag and her own black duffel bag, and comes into the room seemingly without a worry in the world. She spots me, drops her stuff, and nods.

"Mr. President," she says. "Claire Boone. National Security Agency. I was here a couple of weeks ago as part of the response to help find your daughter, and that sure as hell turned into a goat rope of epic proportions, didn't it? Let's do it right this time, okay?"

I take off my baseball cap, stand up. "What do you mean, *do it right?*"

She dumps her computer bag onto the remaining bed, unzips it, and takes out a laptop, and then sits down on the bed next to it. "We need to get to the Med as fast as we can, and I think I've got an asset lined up."

The NSA woman powers up her computer and looks around at the four silent men standing in the room. "What, you can't speak? You want me to leave?"

"No," I say, stepping toward her and her laptop. "I don't want you to leave."

CHAPTER 83

❖

Autumn Leaves Motel
Contoocook, New Hampshire

As Claire's computer comes to life, I say, "I…how in the world did you find us?"

Nick says, "Yeah, I was thinking that, too. Damn it."

His SEAL partner adds, "Me, too, Chief."

My Secret Service escort says, "Sir, I know her. She is with the NSA. I was with her in the joint agency debrief after that raid on the house in Monmouth. The house where we thought Mel was being kept."

Claire glances up at David. "Gosh, doesn't that feel sweet? Being told by a man what I've already told you all a few seconds ago. Make you feel special? Smart?"

David seems at a loss, and I don't blame him.

She looks to her computer screen and says, "As to how I found you, it was all numbers. We all use math every day, even when we don't realize it. Predicting the weather, designing software, making money. Math is logical. It's rational. And it can't lie. When I found that a local airport has had an unexpected uptick in car rentals, as small as it was, I took notice. And a rural motel on the edge of bankruptcy makes a large cash deposit? That got my attention, too. And when the passenger manifest for said airport listed two passengers with too-perfect IDs and backgrounds, a little more digging revealed who they really were."

Claire sighs with pleasure. "Then there's you, Mr. President. Do you realize how many heads are exploding in DC because of your disappearance? Books will be written, news specials…that is, if you get to the Med and get Mel back."

My mouth dries right out. "You…they know my daughter is alive?"

She works the keyboard. "No concrete information, I'm afraid. Various theories and suppositions. It seems that there's digital evidence that the beheading video—ugh, I couldn't watch it—was a deepfake, and that the filming probably didn't take place in the White Mountains. But nothing actionable. There are meetings, debates, arguments, seminars…you know DC: it'll take a couple of weeks to make up their mind. And then they'll be wrong…ah, okay, here we go."

The room is quiet, save for Claire's fingers working the keyboard. "Pease Air National Guard in Newington. The 157th Air Refueling Wing. They're participating in a large-scale exercise in the eastern Mediterranean, centered at Naval Station Rota, in Spain. One of their aircraft was delayed in deploying for twelve hours because of a maintenance issue. This KC-135…looks like its call sign for the upcoming mission is Granite Four. It's departing in ninety minutes. I've done what I can, Mr. President. It's up to you to get us on that aircraft."

I feel like I'm on a dream movie set, with everyone else knowing their lines and roles, save for me. "Claire…why are you doing this?"

She smiles. "Don't you recognize me, Mr. President?"

A faint flush of embarrassment. "No, I'm afraid I don't."

Claire works her computer once more, rotates it, and a photo is in the center of the screen. With a jolt, I recognize Mel, another young lady, and a plumper Claire Boone, her hair black instead of red, and they're sitting on Mel's bed in her room in the family quarters at the White House. Her voice soft, Claire says, "I was friends with Mel, back when we were at Sidwell Friends. Ha. Nice name, not as friendly as they claim. I was in twelfth grade, she was in ninth, and I don't know why, but she warmed up to me. Maybe because I was getting bullied and teased all the time. I was fat, and as you can probably tell, I'm on the spectrum. Talk too fast, more used to numbers than people. But Mel stopped the bullying. When I heard we were being sent here to help in the initial search, I made sure I was on the deployment. And then I stuck around."

She rotates the laptop. "After Sidwell, I joined the Army, mainly to freak out my parents. Became one hell of an infantry scout. Took some additional tests, the NSA liked what they saw, and I joined their clandestine service, became a field operative. Good work, but hung out in too many Internet cafés in Berlin and Paris with lots of cigarette smoke, tracking down hackers and cybercriminals. Is that enough? Do you need to hear more? Or can you make a phone call or two, and get us on that refueling aircraft before it's too late? I mean, I'm raiding some restricted systems I shouldn't be in. Aren't you going to do your part?"

I say, "*Us?* You're coming along?"

She smiles. "Like it or not, you need me, Mr. President. Do you want to debate that or make that damn phone call?"

"I will," I say. "If you look up a phone number for me."

The smile gets wider. "Gosh, I think I've got the resources to do that."

CHAPTER 84

The Pentagon
Arlington, Virginia

Kimberly Bouchard, secretary of the Air Force, is sitting at her desk at the Pentagon, an uneaten corned beef sandwich at her elbow. She's working through a sheaf of papers explaining the procurement problem for one subset of one ongoing maintenance issue with the aging B-2 stealth bomber fleet when her office phone rings, blessedly giving her a respite.

"Madam Secretary?" her office assistant, Martin Hernandez, says.

"Yes?"

"Ma'am...there's a male caller on the line. Says he's Matt Keating. The—"

"President Keating?" She rubs at her eyes, the thought of numbers and part qualifications quickly leaving her mind. "Are you sure?"

"He said you'd recognize the phrase 'I might be concerned if it was some damn church bingo game.' Ma'am?"

My God, she thinks.

"Put him through," she says, and she remembers.

More than three years ago, sitting alone with President Matt Keating in the Oval Office, each taking a separate couch in the center of the room, him in black slacks and a blue oxford shirt, unknotted red tie dangling down the front. A minute earlier she was ushered in by Chief of Staff Jack Lyon, who gave her a look of disdain, for Kimberly had violated the first rule of Washington: Never, ever embarrass your boss.

Keating says, "Something to drink? Water? Coke? Something stronger?"

Kimberly shakes her head. She wants this humiliating and embarrassing moment in her life to be over as quickly as possible.

"Mr. President, I'm still very sorry that this information came out," she says. "I thought the vetting process was going to be confidential, but the news of my addiction…"

She sighs, removes a folded sheet of paper from her suit jacket's inner pocket. "When we're through here, I'll go out and make a statement, announcing that I'm withdrawing my name from nomination for secretary of the Air Force."

Keating leans back into the sofa, hands behind his head. "Remind me, Kimberly: the vetting process also noted that you grew up on a dairy farm in Pennsylvania, went to the University of Pittsburgh on an Air Force ROTC scholarship, then worked your way up the career ladder, became an expert in maintenance and parts procurement, and then, apparently bored, you also went to pilot training school at Laughlin Air Force Base in Texas. Correct so far?"

She nods, unsure of where this is going. The president says, "Eventually, you became a pilot of Lockheed EC-130 electronic countermeasures aircraft. Flew in some dangerous and dark parts of the world. Left the Air Force, worked at some think tanks and as a consultant at Lockheed. Along the way you developed a gambling problem, right? Your husband left you because of that, correct?"

She nods, lips pursed with shame. He goes on. "Eventually you joined Gamblers Anonymous. Paid back every dime that you owed to banks and people that you borrowed money from, including interest. You've been clean for at least four years. True?"

"Yes, sir, but—"

"You've made amends. You've paid everything back. You've been clean."

He smiles at her, and she feels utterly at ease. "Now, I might be concerned if it was some damn church bingo game you've been caught at or something, but that hasn't happened, has it? What did happen was some grudge-settling jerk up on the Hill decided to hurt me by releasing that confidential FBI background check, hoping it would force me to dump you. A minor skirmish and victory for whatever senator or staff member is seeking it, and if you got destroyed in the process, well, that's how the game is played here in DC. Let me see that little speech of yours."

Kimberly passes over the folded piece of paper, and without even looking at it, the president tears it in half, then into quarters, and then drops the torn paper on the coffee table.

He gets up, starts to retie his necktie. "Tell you what. If you're not busy, future Madam Secretary, let's go out to the Rose Garden and tell the press that I'm sticking with you, one hundred percent."

She doesn't know what to say. Keating adds, "And that's how I play the game, Kimberly. My people, my rules. Come along. We want to make sure we make the top of the hour for the cable networks."

Kimberly follows him out of the Oval Office, still unable to say anything, just feeling her eyes moisten as a smile starts to form on her relieved face.

On the phone, the ex-president says, "Kimberly, glad I got through."

"Mr. President, I'm so sorry—"

"Please, Kimberly, I hate to interrupt, but I need something. I need your help. And I don't have much time."

"What is it, Mr. President?"

The tone of his voice is nothing she's ever heard in him before: tight, hard, controlled.

He says, "There's a KC-135 departing the Air National Guard base at Pease in New Hampshire in under two hours. Call sign Granite Four. It's heading to Naval Station Rota. Kimberly, I need to be on that aircraft, with four others. And before it goes to Rota, it needs to make a stop in Tunisia. At their military airfield at Sfax-Thyna. Arrangements will be made on that end to allow Granite Four to land."

A few tense seconds. "Kimberly, I need to get there, with my folks. I'm putting you in a terrible bind, I know it, but—"

She interrupts him. "That's enough, Mr. President. I'm on it. You can count on me."

"Kimberly, I—"

She can sense the relief in his voice. "You're in a hurry. I think I know why, but I won't ask. Go with God, Mr. President, and do what has to be done."

She hangs up the phone, picks it up, connects with her admin assistant. "Martin."

"Ma'am?" he says.

"Get me on the horn, now, with the wing commander or the senior officer at the Air National Guard up at Pease, in New Hampshire."

“Yes, ma’am,” Martin says. “I’ll put you on hold for a moment, until I make the connection.”

While she’s waiting, she looks down at the dull paperwork about parts, procurement, and maintenance. She picks up the pages with one hand and tosses them in the air behind her.

Good to be doing something important for a change, she thinks.

CHAPTER 85

❖

Autumn Leaves Motel
Contoocook, New Hampshire

I put away my burner phone and look at my four comrades—now a band of brothers and one sister—and I say, "It's on. Let's get packing."

David says, "Well done, sir."

I think for a moment, pull out the burner phone, and head to this room's small and smelly bathroom. "Need to make one more phone call before we head out. Private, you understand."

"Of course," David says, and I call out, "And Alejandro and Nick, put that bed frame and bed back together. That's not how I roll."

I duck into the filthy bathroom, try not to breathe through my nose, and close the door.

Take out the burner phone, punch in the numbers, and it rings.

Rings.

Rings.

Where is she?

Then a breathless Sam answers: "Yes, who's this?"

"Sam, it's Matt," I say. "I just wanted to give you an update. I've arranged transportation. Refueling jet at Pease. We'll be leaving in under two hours. David Stahl is with me, along with two Navy SEALs and an NSA field operative."

"Matt…is that enough?"

"It's going to have to be, Sam," I say. "We need to be small, we need to move fast."

Then I realize what I've just done: for the first time in my life, I've told my wife what I'm about to do. Usually my deployments back in the day were announced with a quiet, "Hey, I'm going to be away for a few months, training," or, "I need to be away at work for a while. I'll email when I can."

But not now.

Sam knows everything: that I'm going overseas to get our daughter and kill anyone who gets in the way.

"You do it, Matt. You do it," she says, her voice strained yet fierce, and I hear noises in the background and say, "Sam, you okay? What's the noise?"

A light laugh. "We're both going on last-minute trips. I've been asked to present an award at the Society for American Archaeology's annual meeting at Georgetown. The original presenter got the flu, so here I am. So safe travels for the both of us, right? I'm at Dulles, waiting to get picked up."

"I love you, Sam," I say. "And I'm not coming back without her, safe and sound. I'll keep you advised, every step that I can."

"I love you, too, Matt," she says. "And I know you'll do it. Shit, my Uber's here. Bye, Matt."

"Bye, Sam," I say, and I switch off the call, take a breath, and hear sounds in the outer room as our duffel bags stuffed with gear get hauled out to the two rental cars.

I look at my burner phone.

One more call, I think.

One more call to settle accounts.

CHAPTER 86

Aboard Granite Four
Pease Air National Guard base, New Hampshire

Captain Ray Josephs of the 157th Air Refueling Wing of the New Hampshire Air National Guard is sitting in the cramped left-side pilot's seat of this old KC-135 refueling tanker, preparing for this late afternoon's flight across the Atlantic, one that should have taken place yesterday.

But a pump in the left-side hydraulic system on the aircraft failed and needed to be replaced, causing the delay, even though it shouldn't have been much of a surprise. This refueling aircraft and a few hundred others still flying first came into service in 1957—based on the Boeing 707 design of the 1950s—and the last one was delivered to the Air Force in 1965.

Ray knows a couple of tales about current KC-135 pilots flying the same airframe their grandfathers flew while in the Air Force, and he can believe it. This cockpit is still crammed tight with knobs, dials, and switches, with nary a computer touchscreen in sight. At Ray's right, less than a yard away, his copilot,

Lieutenant Ginny Zimmerman, is reviewing the stack of mission documents for their flight to Rota. Like Ray, she's wearing the standard green zippered jumpsuit and sage-green boots, a thick earphone and mic system over her short blond hair.

"Ginny," he says, "what's this I hear about you guys at Delta doing a slowdown?"

She shakes her head, starts flipping through pages. "Something's gotta bend, and it's not gonna be us."

He laughs, goes through his own binder. He's a pilot for United, Ginny is a pilot for Delta, and serving with this wing is part of their duties as New Hampshire Air National Guard members.

On the back cover of his checklist binder is an old cracked decal showing a flying Pegasus circled with the acronym NKAWTG, which means *Nobody kicks ass without tanker gas!*

Funny thing he learned way back when is that when it comes to military operations, amateurs discuss tactics, and professionals discuss logistics. And when it comes to warfare in the air, nothing gets done without the logistics of these old flying gas stations, which refuel everything from fighter jets to bombers, all around the world.

And the job of passing along the necessary fuel belongs to the third crew member, Technical Sergeant Frank Palmer, who operates the refueling boom at the stern of the aircraft. Right now he's at the aircraft's small galley, storing the meals for their half day's flight across the Atlantic.

Ray is about to ask his copilot if she's ready to start going through the preflight checklist when a voice suddenly comes to him via his earphones.

"Pease control to Granite Four," a woman's voice says.

He toggles the Reply switch. "Granite Four, go," he says.

"Hold on," the controller says.

Ginny looks at Ray and he raises his eyebrows, shrugs.

Then an unexpected voice comes through.

"Captain Josephs, this is Colonel Tighe." Ray momentarily freezes.

The wing commander? Right now?

"Yes, sir," he says.

Colonel Tighe says, "There's a party of five that will be boarding your aircraft within the next few minutes. Allow them every possible courtesy you can, within reason."

"Sir…" Ray is thinking furiously. "Are these Space A passengers?"

Under Air Force regulations, if there is availability on Air Force aircraft, certain personnel—active-duty or retired military personnel, dependent families, and even Medal of Honor recipients—can fly for free under what is known as Space A availability. But having such personnel come aboard so soon before takeoff is highly irregular.

"In a manner of speaking," Colonel Tighe replies, voice clipped. "They're traveling at the request of the secretary of the Air Force. I know it's last-minute and highly irregular, but I trust you'll make it work, Captain."

"And their manifest?"

"I'll take care of their manifest," Tighe says. "I vouch for their luggage and their identification. And this is last-minute, again, I know, but their destination is going to be the Tunisian Air Force base at Sfax-Thyna. The necessary arrangements have been made at that end to allow you to land and service. Any questions?"

Ray has about a hundred or so questions to ask but knows enough to salute smartly—in a manner of speaking—and keep his mouth shut. "No, Colonel," he says. "We've got this."

"Good," the colonel says. "Tighe out."

With the radio transmission ended, Ginny, who also heard the broadcast, is staring at Ray with wide eyes. "What the hell was that?"

He takes the headset and mic off his head, gets up from his seat. "I don't know, but I'm about to find out. In the meantime, calculate how much more fuel we'll need to get to Tunisia."

Ray scrambles out of the tight cockpit and goes aft, where there's nothing but a flat metal deck with built-in rings to hold down pallets and red webbed seating against each side of the fuselage. At the far end is the refueling compartment manned by their technical sergeant, or boomer, who's responsible for controlling the air-to-air refueling boom. Underneath the deck is where more than 202,000 pounds of JP-8 jet fuel is stored. Ray turns right, to the open port cargo door. With the lights from the near buildings and runway, he can spot the dark blue pickup truck with adjustable stairs on the rear, called the airstairs. Five passengers are trailing the airstairs, each carrying two duffel bags. Ray stands there, waiting, feeling a bit nervous and tingly, wondering how and why this typical and usual transatlantic flight has turned into something spooky and different.

Technical Sergeant Palmer comes up to him, black hair cut in an old-fashioned crew cut, his potbelly straining against his green jumpsuit. "What's going on, Captain?"

"Last-minute passengers, Frank," Ray says. "Mind marshaling in the airstairs?"

The movable stairway rises up to the open door, and his boomer fastens it in place.

The first three passengers come up the stairs, into the aircraft, and just nod at Ray and go aft. They lower the red webbed seating and fasten their duffel bags, as if they've done this before. While he's had no real experience with members of the Special Forces, Ray senses that these three are operators—or at least military—from the way they move smoothly and quickly, without any wasted motion.

The fourth passenger is a bit of a surprise: a tall redheaded woman wearing black-rimmed glasses. She nods and says, "No in-flight movie, am I right?"

Ray is about to reply when the fifth passenger gets on deck, and the pilot freezes, instantly recognizing the man.

President Matt Keating.

Holy crap on a cracker, Ray thinks. *What the hell is going on here?*

Keating says softly, "Sorry to be a disturbance, Captain, but I appreciate this more than you'll ever know."

Ray finds his voice. "Glad to help, sir."

The ex-president makes his way over to the other four passengers. The boomer, Palmer, catches Ray's eye, shakes his head, and quietly says, "Nearly fifteen years in this man's Air Force, and now I can say I've seen everything."

Ray returns to the cockpit, still stunned at who he just saw, and he puts his headphones and mic set back on as he squeezes himself into the pilot's seat.

In a demanding voice, his copilot asks, "Who's back there? What's the big deal?"

Ray says, "Ginny, you don't know, and trust me, you'll never want to know. Let's just get this bird up and running."

CHAPTER 87

The Oval Office
The White House

After FBI director Lisa Blair updates President Pamela Barnes about the search for Matt Keating—"We're flooding the area with FBI agents, we're working with local officials without alerting the news media, but he's done a good job covering his tracks, Madam President"—Barnes stares again at the printout of the handwritten note that Matt Keating left behind at the breakfast place in upstate New Hampshire.

To Director Blair she says, "What the hell does that last phrase mean?"

Blair glances at the older male FBI agent sitting next to her—both are directly across from Barnes, in front of the Resolute desk—and says, "I'd prefer Dr. Abrams to explain that, Madam President. He's the best forensic psychologist in the Bureau."

Barnes lifts a hand. "Just a moment. I want to read the damn thing again."

She looks once more at the clear and strong handwriting of

her predecessor, the message directed to the head of Homeland Security, who is ultimately in charge of the Secret Service.

Dear Secretary Charles,

I'm writing this of my own free will, under no duress or the orders of any outside agency. My decision to depart my residence at Lake Marie is personal and is being done against the strong advice and recommendation of my Secret Service detail.

No one in my detail should be blamed or reprimanded for my decision, and in fact, praise should be given to the head of my detail, David Stahl, who has decided to accompany me, knowing the irreparable harm it will do to his career.

As to why and where I'm going…

I am just going outside and may be some time.

Sincerely,
Matt Keating

Barnes shakes her head. That damn handwriting. That same damn arrogance from a year and a half ago, when she read that letter he had placed in this very same desk.

The letter in the Resolute desk from one president to another is a tradition to honor the peaceful transition of power, but that son of a bitch had to take it one step further on that January 20.

Barnes focuses on Dr. Clint Abrams, the FBI forensic psychologist, and says, "Tell me. Do you think he's telling the truth, that he's not under duress?"

Dr. Abrams, slim, well-dressed in a gray suit, and completely bald save for two bushy white eyebrows, says, "Yes, I do. Without a doubt. The handwriting is firm, not wavering or shaky. The voice he is using is strong, confident, and it's very unlikely he's written this with a gun to his head, or a knife to his throat."

Barnes taps the paper printout. "But that last line. The quotation. Where's it from? What does it mean?"

The FBI doctor says, "It's a historical comment. From British Army captain Lawrence Oates. He was on Robert Scott's expedition to the South Pole in 1912. They meant to be the first to get there, but they were beaten by Roald Amundsen, from Norway. By about six weeks."

Barnes says, "Damn fascinating, I'm sure, but what's Keating saying?"

Abrams says, "When the Scott expedition was returning to its base camp, it was slowed by vicious weather, and some of the expedition members became quite ill. Oates was one of them, with severe gangrene of his feet, and he knew his condition might end up killing everyone else. During a fierce blizzard, he left the tent and spoke those very words: 'I am just going outside and may be some time.' It's considered one of the great acts of self-sacrifice and an example of the legendary British calmness under peril."

Barnes says, "But Keating's not British, he's not sick with gangrene, and he sure as hell isn't walking out into a blizzard."

Blair says, "From my perspective, Madam President, it's a boast. Or a statement. Matt is saying he might be sacrificing himself for some greater good, and he doesn't care."

"Getting his daughter back," Barnes says. "But we don't know for certain if she's alive. Or where she might be. That's still being chased down."

"That's true, Madam President, and—"

There's a sharp knock on the door, and Barnes's husband and chief of staff strides in, face colored, looking incongruous in a tuxedo, dressed for a fundraising event later that evening.

"We've got him," Richard says. "He's trying to fly out of the country aboard an Air Force refueling tanker, at a base up in New Hampshire. Looks like he's got a couple of military folks with him. He's no longer missing, Madam President."

"Where's the aircraft headed?"

"Rota, in Spain."

She says, "Southwestern Spain, right? Just a hop and a skip to North Africa."

Her husband, Richard, nods. "Absolutely right, Madam President. With armed men accompanying him, it looks like he's conducting a search for his daughter."

Damn it, Barnes thinks, knowing what kind of media and political storm is about to descend upon her if word gets out that Matt Keating is starting a rescue mission on his own.

Who's in charge? Her or the former president?

Barnes turns to the head of the FBI. "Director Blair, he can't be conducting military operations on his own. You've got to send agents there and stop him."

The FBI director's voice is skeptical. "Stop him from doing what? He's ex-military and an ex-president. I'm sure he called in some favors to get aboard that Air Force aircraft. That isn't against federal law, Madam President."

Barnes gives it right back to Blair, cold gaze to cold gaze, knowing that at some point this damn Keating appointee is going to get her due.

"Very well," Barnes says, and goes to her phone, picks it up. No time to debate with this stubborn FBI director. Protocol for what she's about to do would be to go through her secretary of defense, but he's currently on a tour in South Korea and Japan, and she knows she doesn't have the time to make nice with the DOD bureaucracy.

"Madam President?" her secretary, Paul McQuire, says over the line.

"Paul," she says, "I need to be connected immediately with the National Military Command Center at the Pentagon."

"Certainly, Madam President," he says. "Hold on for a moment."

A brief moment of dead air. Barnes's husband, the FBI director, and the FBI forensic psychologist are all looking at her. Despite her inherent dislike for the military, damn it, some days it's good to be commander in chief.

Her secretary's voice returns and says, "Madam President, I have Army colonel Susan Sinclair on the line."

"Colonel Sinclair?" Barnes says.

"Yes, Madam President," says a woman's voice.

Barnes says, "There's an Air Force refueling tanker departing Pease air base up in New Hampshire. The flight is going to Rota, Spain. I want that aircraft grounded. It is not to leave without my express permission. Do you understand, Colonel?"

A brief hesitation, and Barnes imagines this colonel stuck somewhere in the bowels of the Pentagon with all the computer screens and equipment and memorized procedures and plans, and then getting a call like this.

So what? she thinks. *Do your damn job.*

"Yes, Madam President. I understand."

"Good," Barnes says. "I don't care if you have to contact the Joint Chiefs of Staff, the head of the base, or the pilot himself, but that plane is not to leave the ground."

"Understood, Madam President."

"Good," Barnes says. "Contact the White House Office of Communications when you have confirmation, so I'll know for certain that the aircraft has been grounded."

"Yes, Madam President."

"Very well."

Barnes hangs up the phone, and to Director Blair she says, "I don't care how you do it, or what laws get stretched or bent, but I want FBI agents to get to Pease and escort Matt Keating off that aircraft. Say we're doing it for his own protection, or because we have concerns about his current state of mind, or because we need to interview him about a criminal matter—I really don't care. Get Keating off that Air Force jet."

Blair says, "It might take some time, Madam President. We'll need to coordinate with base security and its commanding officers to allow our agents on that field."

Barnes says, "With that jet not going anywhere, I'm not concerned with how long it'll take."

She sees the approving look of her husband, Richard, and that makes her feel as though she's doing exactly the right thing.

A good feeling indeed.

Barnes adds, "But I want it done."

Director Blair starts to get up, joined by Dr. Abrams.

"Very good, Madam President."

CHAPTER 88

Aboard Granite Four
Pease Air National Guard base, New Hampshire

I'm sitting in the red webbed seating along the interior fuselage of the KC-135, fastening my seat belt, and next to me, Agent David Stahl says, "Not like the last time you flew out of Pease, am I right?"

I have to smile. David is right. The interior of Air Force One is like a luxury hotel, the communications system is world-class, the meals are gourmet, and the sleeping arrangements are comparable to those in a four-star suite, though one that gets bumpy every now and then.

And I was on Air Force One and at this base during that brutal primary season when my vice president was running an insurrection campaign against me. After I got my teeth kicked in at the Iowa caucuses, I flew here for a last-minute campaign blitz that resulted in a narrow win that gave me hope I could ride out Pamela Barnes's challenge.

That hope went nowhere, but I'm gambling my luck

will change on this bare-bones Air Force jet, where I'm drinking bottled water and eating energy bars while trying to be comfortable in this old webbed seating. No windows, no outside view, just green-gray insulation on the jet's airframe.

I make two quick phone calls overseas, to Danny Cohen of Mossad and to Major General Ahmad Bin Nayef of Saudi Arabia's General Intelligence Directorate, and I tell them of my plans.

And each wishes me luck, and each tells me that he's still working to locate Asim Al-Asheed.

Across from me are Nick Zeppos, Alejandro Lopez, and Claire Boone. Alejandro is leaning back in the uncomfortable seating, arms crossed, eyes closed.

Claire is playing a game on her iPhone.

Nick is talking urgently to someone on a satellite phone, and then he grins at me, switches the phone off, unsnaps his seat belt, and strolls over, still grinning.

He squats in front of me, lifting his voice as the jet engines whine louder and we begin to taxi out to the air base's sole runway. "Got great news, Mr.—ah, Matt. Great news."

"Give it," I say.

"Just got off the phone with a bud of mine serving in a Team Six platoon," he says. "They're on a training mission in Tunisia. Guess where they're stationed?"

I nearly can't believe what I'm hearing. "Sfax-Thyna."

A nod, a slap on my knee as he gets back up. "That's right, Matt. That's sixteen more operators coming along for the ride…and you know they'll be on board once we get there and brief them. Transport, communications, heavy weapons…our odds just grew a hell of a lot in our favor."

We bump fists and he goes back to his side of the aircraft.

David says, "That's a good break, Matt."

"I'll take every break we can get." The jet engines whine higher, and I know we're just moments away from takeoff.

I close my eyes, like my brother Alejandro across from me.

So many other times I've been on other military aircraft, eyes closed like this, listening to the whine of the engines—either jet or propeller—and getting ready for the upcoming mission. Highly trained, well equipped, going off somewhere for God and country, though the secret is, we never went out for God and country.

We went out because of our team members, our friends, our comrades in arms.

The same tonight.

And we're going out as well for my family.

The engines whine higher, and there's a slight surge, and I think, *Mel, we're coming…hang in there, we're coming…*

It's becoming real.

And in a few seconds, it all comes apart.

The engines whine down and the KC-135 eventually rolls to a stop.

David says, "What the hell?"

Even the dozing Alejandro opens his eyes.

We wait.

Claire still plays on her iPhone.

The metal door to the cockpit flings open, and a shamed-looking Captain Josephs steps out, comes over to me, and shakes his head.

"Sorry, sir," he says. "We've been ordered to stand down. We're not going anywhere tonight."

CHAPTER 89

Permanent Mission of the People's Republic of China
New York, New York

Jiang Lijun of the Chinese Ministry of State Security is walking along East 35th Street in New York, wondering why his boss, Li Baodong, has summoned him back to the mission. Jiang isn't giving in to the temptation to hurry his step. To his observers out there, a casual stroll would mean nothing, but hurrying would raise questions, increase attention.

He will not hurry tonight, even though he is angry. A few minutes ago, he was with his wife, Zhen, and their daughter, Li Na, during some rare free time, delighting in seeing the child make her first stumbling steps across the living room while he and Zhen clapped and cheered her on.

Then his watch vibrated, he went to his small office and made the phone call, and he abruptly said to Zhen as he left, "Work."

Just one word, but he saw the hurt expression in her eyes, and even Li Na seemed to note the change in her parents' moods.

Her little cries were the last thing Jiang heard when he left their condo.

As he gets to the mission's entrance, he wonders again if he's getting too old and has become too much of a father to continue in his position, being overseas, being sent out on a job within seconds.

How did his own father face these same challenges back when he was in service to his country?

Jiang frowns. He would be able to ask him if not for the damn Americans who killed him.

Eleven minutes later he's in the basement concrete-cube office of the fat man who is his supervisor. After Jiang sits down, Li Baodong blinks behind his thick gold-rimmed glasses and says, "You made good time, Lijun. That should serve you well, since you are shortly about to depart New York City."

"Comrade?" Jiang says, suddenly fearful. Is he being reassigned? Sent home in some sort of disgrace? Reduced in rank and humiliated here among his peers?

"Yes, you're off to Libya. Soon."

Jiang says, "But Libya…why? I haven't been there in two years."

The eyes of the fat mushroom across from him flash in anger. "Because your asset Asim Al-Asheed is back in Libya, and we have reliable information that Mel Keating, his kidnap victim, is still alive and with him."

"But the video of her execution…"

"The Americans believe it might be fake, a bit of video magic," Li says, drumming his fat fingers on his desktop. "Our experts agree. And our embassy in Tripoli has received reliable information that Asim Al-Asheed and his nephew are there. You're to go to Libya and get the former president's daughter out. No matter the cost."

Jiang is stunned at what he's hearing. "I doubt he will change his mind, considering our last meeting."

Li arches a thick black eyebrow. "Ah, yes. Your meeting with Asim, in New Hampshire. You reported that Asim wouldn't release Mel Keating into your custody, no matter how many entreaties you made, from threats to bribery."

Jiang nods. "That is correct, comrade."

Li stares and stares and Jiang is suddenly quite uncomfortable. He has seen that look from this *Pàng mógū*—fat mushroom—before, and he knows what it means: a trap is about to be sprung, and Jiang knows it's for him.

"Well, let's remember that," his boss says, and he goes to his computer terminal and keyboard, taps out a few commands, and then rotates the screen so he and Jiang can see what's being displayed.

An overhead video, showing a small body of water, then trees, a dirt parking lot, and—

A rental car from Canada.

Two figures standing outside, talking.

Jiang feels as though his arms and legs have gone dead.

"Look familiar?" Li asks with sweet contempt.

Trying to put confidence in his voice, Jiang says, "Yes. Williams Pond. Where I met with Asim Al-Asheed."

"Very good," Li says. "Can you explain this, then?"

Li depresses another key, and sound comes from the speakers, and Jiang's stomach seems to want to crawl its way up his tight throat as he hears himself talking to that Libyan creature a few weeks back.

"Congratulations, Asim. One professional to another, this has been one impressive operation. It must have taken years..."

Some static—thankfully!—but the videotape continues to play as Li sits back in his chair, hands crossed over his plump belly.

"Thank you."

"But what now, Asim?"

"You know of..."

More static.

Jiang's boss quietly says, "Did you think I was going to have you perform such an important mission without employing our own surveillance? Unfortunately, our drone program still has problems with its listening devices."

The videotape goes on, and Jiang feels sweat trickling down his spine.

Keep your face calm, he says to himself. *Show not an ember of emotion.*

Especially as the videotape goes to the final seconds of their meeting.

His voice: *"I can provide you with funds, means of transportation, weapons. Some intelligence..."*

"Why would you do this...?"

"My business. And I have put my career and life..."

"...I will consider your generous, and unofficial, offer."

More static, and then the video goes black, and Jiang's heavy-set boss sighs and reorients the computer screen back to his own private view.

"That doesn't sound like you were trying to convince him to return Mel Keating to you, now, does it?"

Jiang tries to stay relaxed, face impassive. "That recording...sections are missing."

"Ah, so the sections where you follow orders and try to convince Asim to release the president's daughter—those are the missing ones. How convenient."

Jiang slightly shrugs. *Don't wilt,* he thinks. *Make Li talk.*

His boss shakes his head, jowls quivering. "You're to leave at once and get to Libya, meet up with your old connections and assets, and get Mel Keating. Understand? Whatever it takes. Get her."

Jiang stays quiet, his emotions roiling, knowing how close he came to being executed for disobeying orders.

Li says, "Something concerning you?"

Jiang says, "I know it's coming from Beijing, but I hate aiding the Americans."

"Because of what they did to your family in 1999?"

"Among other things," Jiang says. "But yes, I hate them because they murdered my father."

"Would you think otherwise if the Americans hadn't murdered him?"

Jiang tries to keep his voice calm and collected. "But they did murder him, by bombing our embassy. It was an unprovoked attack by their Air Force, and the Americans tried to cover it up by blaming it on an inaccurate map."

Li smiles and scratches at his left ear. "Yes, that was a particularly stupid cover story, wasn't it? But many want to believe in the dumb, bumbling Americans raining bombs from the skies, so the cover story was mostly accepted. But what happened there, it wasn't unprovoked."

Jiang can only say, "Comrade?"

A sad shake of Li's head. "During those NATO bombing attacks to convince the Serbs to stop massacring their Muslim neighbors, the Serbs shot down one of the American stealth aircraft, their F-117 Nighthawk. The Serbs gathered up all the wreckage they could and made a deal."

"A deal?" Jiang asks.

"Yes, a deal," his boss says. "NATO was bombing the shit out of the Serbs' military communications systems. And the Serbs offered us the F-117 wreckage—giving us about a five-year advance in stealth technology—if we would allow them to transmit military orders and information from our embassy basement. We were never sure whether NATO tracked down the source of those transmissions, but the American bombing destroyed that Serb military facility in our embassy. They said it was a mistake, and we pretended to believe them. We lost three of our dear comrades, including your father, but we gained so very much in stolen American technology."

Jiang licks his dry lips.

Li leans over the desk, voice stern. "Put away your irrational hatred of the Americans over your father's death and do your job. Get the president's daughter back in our custody. Beijing needs something to thaw our relations with Washington, and this teen girl is the key. Now get out of my sight."

Jiang stands up, nearly stumbles over the chair, and walks to the exit, thinking of how many times he and his mother have burned joss offerings to the memory of his father, including elaborately created mansions of paper, to honor his spirit in the afterworld and to vow revenge for his needless death.

Now Jiang feels as though his entire life and drive have turned into a joss structure, intricately made and created, only to go into ashes with just one spark.

Time to do what is right.

Rescue the president's daughter for Jiang's party and country.

CHAPTER 90

❖

Georgetown University
Washington, DC

Samantha Keating is in her room at the Georgetown University Hotel and Conference Center in Washington, DC, about ten minutes away from attending a cocktail party and reception for the five-day annual meeting of the Society for American Archaeology. She feels tired but also excited, knowing that Mel is alive and that Matt and his crew are now on their way to rescue her.

She thinks, *Matt will get it done.*

Samantha won't allow herself to think anything else.

Even coming here is something she is surprised that she's done. She has a nervous energy these days: she'll move around, read a newspaper, put it down, look at a television program for a few seconds, and then switch to another channel.

But here in Georgetown, at least she will be busy with something, not sitting back at that motel in Maine, staring at her phone, watching the minutes ooze by, wondering when Matt might be in Libya.

Waiting, always waiting.

No.

Better to be doing something, even if she's back in the city she has hated for years.

At the annual meeting's official opening tomorrow night, she is to present the Gene S. Stuart Award for the best article on archaeology that appeared last year in a newspaper or magazine, and she's feeling a bit giddy, hoping that by the time she gives that award, another award will have been presented to her half a world away.

The safe return of Mel.

Her quiet, hopeful mood is disturbed by the ringing of her iPhone.

She picks it up, seeing the digits of the incoming call and recognizing them as coming from Matt's burner cell phone.

Sam looks at her watch.

Shouldn't they be in the air by now, over the Atlantic?

Oh, God, something's wrong.

She answers the phone. "Matt?"

"... grounded."

The reception is awful.

She walks to the window, puts a finger in her left ear. "Matt, I can't hear you! What did you say?"

"... flight has been grounded. We're still at Pease."

"Who did that?"

The reception suddenly clears up. "The order came straight from the Pentagon," her husband says, voice tight with anger. "Which means the secretary of the Air Force was overruled. And that means the White House, Sam."

She closes her eyes tight. "What now?"

He says, "I'm working through options, Sam, but it's not looking good..."

The reception dies for a few seconds.

"…I'm not giving up. Trust me, Sam. I'm not giving up. Hold on. The pilot's coming out again…gotta go."

He disconnects the call, and she lowers the cell phone.

Not giving up.

"Me, neither," she says.

Sam rummages through her luggage for a moment, gathers up her purse, a light wrap, and then leaves her room behind.

She waits and waits in front of the elevator.

Waiting.

Ding!

An older couple, well-dressed and looking as though they're going out to dinner, joins her as she finally enters the open car. She punches the button for the lobby, stares at the door sliding shut, thinking, *Hurry, hurry, hurry.*

The elevator starts moving.

"Excuse me?" the man says.

Samantha ignores him, watching the floor indicator lights flicker.

The White House grounded Matt's flight.

Somehow President Barnes or her husband found out about Matt's flight.

"Excuse me, ma'am," the man persists. "Aren't you…"

Ding!

The door slides open.

"No," Samantha snaps, and then quickly moves through the lobby, staying focused, not catching anyone's eye, ignoring the few calls of "Hey, Dr. Keating! Dr. Keating!"

Blessedly outside.

A well-dressed doorman. "Ma'am?"

"A taxi," she says. "Please."

He lifts his arm, a green Diamond cab rolls up, and she

fumbles in her purse, slips two one-dollar bills into the doorman's hand.

In the cab.

"Yes, lady?" the driver asks.

"The White House."

He turns to her, grinning, the look of a DC resident who knows a lot more than this woman from out of town.

"Lady, it's late," he says. "No tourists allowed."

"Fine by me," Samantha says. "Get me to the White House gate at 15th Street Northwest. And make it quick."

The taxi driver pulls out onto West Road and Samantha sits back, hand up to her face, hoping she has the courage to do what must happen next.

CHAPTER 91

The Oval Office
The White House

President Pamela Barnes steps away from the Resolute desk, picks up the soft leather dispatch case that carries her evening reading, which is done up in the family quarters. Memoranda, email printouts, and briefing papers. The evenings of sitting back, sipping her whiskey, and leafing through the *Washington Post* or the *New York Times* are long gone.

Richard, lured by his love of racehorses, is at a charity event in Georgetown for the Equus Foundation. Since Pamela has always been allergic to horses and really wants to spend the night here, Richard is off on his own.

Which is fine.

After finding out about Matt Keating's mad plan for a rescue mission overseas—the latest news is that FBI agents are en route to the halted aircraft—Barnes thinks that a quiet night is just what she needs.

She shudders to think of what might have happened if he actually made it overseas. Suppose he was killed? Or captured?

And she tries to forget what Richard told her just before he left: *Pam, imagine he succeeds…that would be worse than him being caught or killed.*

True, as much as she hates to admit it.

The curved door to the Oval Office opens, and one of her staff members, Lydia Wang, dressed in a black pantsuit, steps in, looking concerned.

"Madam President?"

"Yes, what is it?"

She says, "Ma'am, the Secret Service is reporting a situation at the 15th Street Northwest gate."

"What, a trespasser? Somebody making a threat?"

"No, ma'am," Wang says. "It's Samantha Keating. She says she needs to see you, right now, and she won't take no for an answer."

A few minutes later, Barnes is back in her chair, hands clasped in front of her on the desk. The dispatch case is on the floor.

Cold anger is flowing through her, like a harsh mountain stream pushing everything aside.

The door opens and Samantha Keating walks in. She's dressed nicely but her hair is in disarray, and her face is taut, making her prominent nose seem even larger.

"Madam President," she says, approaching the desk. "Thank you for seeing me on such short notice."

"Glad to do it," Barnes lies, thinking, *How dare you threaten me, how dare you come back to a place where you don't belong, how dare you…*

Barnes knows with 90 percent certainty why Samantha is here, but she's damned if she's going to make the first move.

Let her work for it.

Barnes motions to one of the chairs in front of the desk. She doesn't get up, doesn't offer a hand or an embrace.

"Have a seat," Barnes says, not bothering to offer a drink or anything else. "And please, can you make it quick? I have a stack of official papers to review and sign off on before I can even have dinner sent up."

Samantha sits down and says, "I'll make it quick. There's an Air Force plane about to fly from a base up in New Hampshire. My husband and others are on it. Please allow it to leave."

Barnes offers a chilly smile. "Why in the world would I want to do that?"

"Because it's the right thing to do, Madam President. Matt is on a mission. Please let him do it."

Barnes firmly shakes her head. "No. Not a chance."

"Please," Samantha says.

"No," Barnes quickly replies. "This country has one president, one foreign policy, one Department of Defense. I can't allow your husband to go out on a rogue mission, grieving as he may be. Trust me, Samantha, we're doing all we can to bring Mel's killers to justice."

Samantha says, "That's just the point. Matt thinks she's still alive."

How the hell did he get that *information?* Barnes thinks.

"Perhaps," she admits aloud. "Our own intelligence and military professionals are exploring that possibility. But that doesn't mean I'm going to allow an armed former president of the United States to fly on a military aircraft on a personal matter. No matter how much he is grieving. I can't allow it to happen."

"Pamela..."

She says, "*Madam President,* if you don't mind. And besides everything else I've said, I can't have a former president expose himself to possibly being wounded, captured, or killed."

Barnes makes a point of looking at her wristwatch. "Now Samantha, as I said before, I have a lot of papers to review and sign tonight. I'm sorry I can't allow Matt to fly overseas. I have to ask you to trust the professionals in this. If there's evidence that Mel is alive, we'll track her down and find her. We won't let anything get in our way."

Samantha's voice is so slight that Barnes has to strain to hear it: "Like when you refused to pay the ransom? Is that what you mean by not letting anything get in your way?"

Barnes stands up, reaches down, and picks up her dispatch case. "Don't believe everything you read in the newspapers or on the Internet. I thought you would have learned that when you were in the White House."

Samantha remains seated. "And there's nothing I can do to change your mind?"

Barnes is standing behind her desk, wondering how in God's name she can get this woman out of here without having the Secret Service grab her arms and drag her out.

"Nothing," Barnes says.

Samantha reaches into her purse, pulls something out, and gently drops it in the middle of the Resolute desk.

"How about something that can destroy your presidency in the next forty-eight hours?"

CHAPTER 92

The Oval Office
The White House

Samantha Keating feels a sharp sensation of satisfaction upon seeing the president look at the thumb drive and then slowly sit down behind the historic desk that was once Matt's.

She remembers all the times she's seen Matt defeat his home Secret Service detail while playing poker through the night, even when the cards weren't in his favor. Once he said, *Sam, it's all in the way you handle yourself. If you can stay calm and collected, you can win with a pair of deuces. But if your opponent sees your eyes flicker, your hands tremble, or you look away…they'll go through you like a buzz saw.*

High stakes poker, Samantha thinks.

That's what she's playing tonight.

"What is that?" Barnes asks.

"A thumb drive," Samantha says. "With a video on it."

Samantha keeps her mouth shut.

Whoever folds and talks first, she thinks, *has lost.*

She stares at Barnes, and Barnes stares right back.

"All right," the president says. "What's on the video, and why should I care?"

Samantha coolly presses on.

"Three years ago next week," she begins, starting to utter the sentences she practiced, over and over, on the fifteen-minute taxi ride to the White House, "your husband flew to Macau, to attend a reception and eightieth birthday party for one of his casino investors. You were serving as vice president then, so Richard flew over there alone."

Barnes shakes her head. "I don't remember that. Sorry."

Samantha says, "Oh, he went there, all right. There are news accounts, and photographs, and a number of blog postings, including some criticizing your husband for spending time in a Chinese-controlled territory."

Barnes attempts a bit of humor. "What's on the video, then? Richard singing 'Happy Birthday' in Mandarin to some Chinese Communist Party apparatchik?"

"No," Samantha says. "The video shows your husband engaged in sexual congress with three individuals in his hotel room, none of whom appear to have reached the age of puberty."

The president's face pales, and she says, "I don't believe you. What, that thumb drive magically appears in your mailbox at BU? After it was made at some cyber facility in Moscow or Beijing? Utter bullshit, Samantha. You should be ashamed of yourself."

Samantha planned for this reaction. She says, "When Richard was staying at the Golden Palace Macau, a former grad student of mine was in that same building, working for a respected international firm updating security software. He saw what was going on—despite the surveillance jamming instrument Richard was carrying; the Chinese know how to get around that—and was so shocked at what he saw that he recorded your husband's activities. I'm sure he'd be happy to testify as to what he saw and recorded."

"And he just gave this to you now?" Barnes demands.

Stay calm, Samantha thinks. *Stay right on target.*

"No," she says. "He gave it to me right after you declared you were running against Matt for the nomination."

Barnes's eyes flicker down to the black thumb drive, and she looks at it as if it were a poisonous reptile, ready to scuttle across her desk and bite. "But..."

"But why didn't I use it back then, during the primary season?" Samantha asks. "Because I'm not like you. Or your Richard. I wasn't going to use this to win an election. That was too disgusting to even consider."

Silence for a few seconds.

Samantha gently taps the thumb drive. "But I will use it to save my daughter. Make the phone call, allow that aircraft with Matt and his crew to depart, and I won't release the video."

Barnes says, "Go ahead. Release the video. Who will believe you? No one will touch that. It's too..."

"Repulsive. Horrible. Oh, I'm sure the major news media won't touch it. But there are some Internet news sites that would love to run the story. It'll be worldwide news within a day. The so-called legitimate news organizations will be forced to report on it. The pictures will be everywhere."

There's another pause. She can see Barnes's face struggling with emotions, and Samantha says, "That's the deal. Make the call now, and I'll never release the video."

In a tight voice, Barnes says, "Not good enough. I want that thumb drive, and I want your promise no other copies exist."

Samantha says, "No other copies exist, and this thumb drive isn't leaving my possession."

With that, she scoops it up and puts it in her suit jacket pocket. "Pamela. Make the call."

Poker face, Samantha thinks.

Silence.

The ticking of an antique clock in the Oval Office.

A far-off siren on the street.

Barnes picks up the phone. "Paul," she says, "connect me again with the National Military Command Center."

Barnes waits.

Samantha waits.

"Colonel Sinclair? This is President Barnes. I'm reversing my earlier order grounding that National Guard flight at Pease. Contact the wing commander. That flight is to leave immediately."

She slams the receiver down. "Done. Happy now?"

Samantha stands up and says, "Good night, Madam President. Glad we could sort this out."

Ten minutes later, Samantha Keating is out on 15th Street Northwest, the White House and its compound behind her, her legs shaking, her insides violently rolling around, as if she's about to vomit.

She pulls it together, does her best to wave down a cab in the heavy traffic.

As she waits, she puts a hand into her purse, gently caresses the thumb drive—the one that contains a backup of her remarks for tomorrow night.

Matt, she thinks, *thanks for the poker lesson.*

Now go get our girl.

CHAPTER 93

Aboard Granite Four
Pease Air National Guard base, New Hampshire

The cockpit of a fifty-year-old KC-135 is crowded as it is, but with Palmer and me trying to shove ourselves in with the pilot and the copilot to get an update on what the hell is going on, it's like those old *Life* magazine photos of crazy frat boys in the 1950s trying to shove themselves into a telephone booth.

On the runway below us are three men, one wearing an Air Force jumpsuit and two wearing business suits. There's a lot of arm waving from the two civilians, but the Air Force officer—wearing a dark blue garrison cap with a colonel insignia—is standing there, arms crossed.

I say, "Mind ID'ing the colonel down there?"

"That's Colonel Tighe, our wing commander," Captain Josephs says.

"And the other two gentlemen?"

"They are FBI agents from the Portsmouth field office. They

are demanding access to the aircraft to ensure you're here of your own free will and are not being held captive. Colonel Tighe says that's not possible."

"Why?"

Captain Josephs says, "Remember the truck carrying the gangway you used to gain access? We call that the airstairs. Apparently, the airstairs is not functioning at the moment. Flat tire, engine won't start—something like that."

I say, "Isn't there a ladder from the fuselage that the crew uses?"

"Sure," Josephs says, face widening into a smile. "We call that the entry chute. Aircrew only. The FBI wants to use that to access the aircraft and interview you. Colonel Tighe says non–Air Force personnel can only use the entry chute if they take part in a four-hour safety training module."

His copilot is grinning as well. Josephs says, "As you can see, they are having a frank and open exchange of views as to other methods of getting aboard this aircraft."

The argument continues. I say, "Captain, back when I was in the teams, we used to call you folks the Chair Force."

I slap his shoulder, start to maneuver my way back aft in the aircraft. "I take that all back, and then some."

The captain calls out, "Appreciate that, sir, but this is just a delaying action. Eventually the hammer's gonna come down on Colonel Tighe, and those FBI agents are going to get inside."

"Roger that," I say, and back into the interior I go.

My four team members are standing in a group, midway down the largely empty interior. I say, "The Feds are here, wanting to get aboard and make sure I'm alive and well."

David Stahl says, "And in the meantime, make sure you don't take off."

Claire says, "Isn't there any other way out of here?"

Nick Zeppos says, "The cargo door that we came through, and the crew ladder up forward. That's it."

Alejandro adds, "We take the aircraft's fire ax, we could probably break through the fuselage at an emergency fire access point, but that would really piss off our hosts. And even the FBI would eventually notice somebody chopping their way out."

Nick says to me, "And what then, sir? We get out and make a run for it?"

I say, "If we have to…okay, forget the fire ax. We'll dump our way out through the crew ladder in the entry chute and—"

The technical sergeant suddenly comes out of the cockpit. "Hey! What are all you passengers doing, standing around like this? Sit down and buckle up. This bird is taking off in a few minutes."

I stare at him for one blessed second. "What the hell just happened?"

"Way, way above my pay grade, sir," he says. "All I know is that Pease control contacted Captain Josephs, told him he was cleared to take off. Straight from the Pentagon. And that's all she wrote."

One and then two and then the other two engines start whining to life.

Agent Stahl says, "What do you think, Matt?"

"I think we need to follow the tech sergeant's orders."

I go back to my spot in the red webbed seating, buckle up, and Agent Stahl sits next to me, does the same. Across from me Nick Zeppos and Alejandro Lopez are fastening themselves in as well, and Claire Boone of the NSA is strapping in with one hand while still playing a video game with the other.

The technical sergeant checks all of our belts, nods, and says, "Looks like you still know what you're doing, Mr. President."

"Too bad most Americans didn't believe that a couple of years back," I say.

"Their loss," he says, going to his own seat. "Our loss, sir."

The old aircraft starts moving, taxiing along, and then there's a turn, and a pause.

I can imagine the conversation up front between the pilot and copilot, professionally doing their jobs but no doubt thinking in the back of their minds, *Is this what we signed up for? This black-ops-and-orders-from-DC nonsense?*

The engines howl louder.

Close.

But…

Another order from Pease control could shut us down.

One of those old engines could throw a turbine blade right now, causing it to explode.

The two FBI agents could go all J. Edgar Hoover and drive their official vehicle out onto the runway, forcing the pilot to abort.

Faster now.

The surge of speed is pushing me sideways into the webbed seating.

The plane arches its way up.

Airborne.

Whine-clunk as the landing gear retracts, and my eyes swell.

We are go.

Mel, we're coming for you.

I check my watch.

About a twelve-plus-hour flight to Tunisia.

In those hours, it will be pretty much silent over the Atlantic, but my friends in Israeli and Saudi intelligence will be working to find Asim Al-Asheed, who's now back in North Africa, in their neck of the woods.

We were lucky in getting off the ground in America.

Will our luck hold upon landing in North Africa, with actionable intelligence from the Israelis and Saudis?

I look at my watch once more.

Airborne now about ten minutes, heading east.

Mel, I think. *Where are you?*

PART
FOUR

CHAPTER 94

Somewhere in northwest Libya

Mel Keating is in the rear of a dirty white van, parked somewhere in a very small village in what she's pretty sure, upon assessing her situation, is Libya.

The back of her neck still aches from being struck by a dull sword blade more than a week ago. She's certain that her parents have believed her dead since then. She grieves for the pain and agony that miserable shithead Asim has inflicted on them even more than she hurts for herself.

She was ashamed to realize that she soiled herself when she thought she was about to have her head cut off. At a little muddy stream, she was able to hand-wash her clothes and put them back on after they dried in the sun, laid out on a boulder, but that was just a rinse job.

She feels filthy, her hair is a mess, and her ankles and wrists ache where they're bound tight by plastic flex-cuffs. But there was a bright spot earlier that day.

She asked one of her captors to move her bound hands from her back to her front. The guy—she didn't know his name but called him Alpha, for he was the first person she met after they filmed that fake execution scene—knew a fair amount of English, and after she sobbed and said her wrists ached and her back was itchy, he said, "A kiss. You give me a kiss, and I'll do that for you."

She was horrified at the prospect of kissing him on the lips—she would be tempted to bite down and tear off his lower lip—but Alpha offered a bearded cheek. She pretended that she was kissing a grungy coyote, and he cut off the flex-cuffs at the rear and applied a fresh set at the front.

"Welcome to Libya," he said, laughing, as if he was amused to grant her this small favor.

Idiot. His small favor was going to bite him on the ass.

She looks around the van's interior again. Bare rusted metal, old blankets and pillows here in the rear. Up ahead, an empty passenger seat row, and in front of that, driver and passenger seating.

It's the middle of the night, and in the driver's seat is the captor she's named Beta. He's armed with an AK-47—the weapon of choice for revolutionaries and losers around the world, Dad told her years back, and Beta is definitely a loser.

He's asleep.

Her other captor, Alpha, was in the passenger seat until about twenty minutes ago, when a woman apparently came up and started talking to him through the open window. Mel didn't see her, but she heard her voice and saw the results: Alpha whispered to Beta, and the door opened, and Alpha was gone.

Now it is just the two of them.

Although it's the middle of the night, there's a flickering streetlight out there illuminating the van's interior. She moves around, sees that Beta is still fast asleep, snoring.

Now's her chance.

Mel moves around until she's in position. She's remembering back to when Dad was just thinking of running for Congress, and he had some friends over from the teams, and along with the drinking and storytelling and hell-raising in their small flat backyard, they played some rough-and-tumble games, also known as grab-assing.

One game involved trying to tie up or bind someone, and whoever broke free quickest won a case of Lone Star.

Mel, a young girl at the time, hid in the backyard and watched.

And learned.

Right now she's on her knees, next to the metal hub over the right rear tire. She brings her bound wrists to her face, sees the lock mechanism on the right side. Mel bites the free end of the plastic flex-cuffs, pulls and tugs and pulls until the flex-cuffs rotate around her wrists and the lock mechanism is in the middle.

Mel raises her arms, high as she can, arches her back, and brings her bound wrists down hard on the metal hub.

The pain rockets right up her arms and she falls back, trying to keep as quiet as possible.

Ouch, damn it!

She tugs the flex-cuffs.

Still fastened.

One more time.

Again, the arms up, fingertips grazing the metal ceiling, and again—

The pain is worse than before.

She bites her lower lip. Tears come to her eyes.

Why isn't it working?

It should work.

It has to work.

Her wrists are throbbing hard with the fiery pain.

Just a few yards away, Beta is deep asleep, and the music from a radio outside gets louder.

In addition to the radio, Mel hears a woman and a man laughing. She thinks it's Alpha, having a good time, and she remembers kissing that gristly, smelly face, feeling scared and humiliated, and she takes a deep breath, sore arms up again, and—

Slam!

Mel falls back again, breathing hard, her wrists free.

She rubs at them, pulling off the broken plastic flex-cuffs.

Mel nearly whimpers with joy. *My wrists and arms are free.*

Mel moves around, her bound feet in front of her, and she checks out a jagged piece of metal near the rear door. She inches forward, rubs the plastic on the metal, rubs it and pushes down and rubs it—

A quiet *snap.*

She wastes a few seconds, rubbing her sore ankles.

Now?

There's a hot fury inside of her as she thinks of her kidnapping, Tim's murder, being manhandled, pushed around, drugged—oh, yes: that's why she fell asleep after eating that breakfast back in New Hampshire—and being slapped awake in some stone and brick building close to the ocean, which she could smell.

Then in the trunk of a car, bumpy drive, and—

That dull sword blade across her neck, crumpling her in pain.

The AK-47 is right there. Just scramble over the row of passenger seats, grab it, make sure the safety is off, work the action, and she'll put Beta away forever.

Then out of the van, find Alpha, do the same to him…

And then what?

One armed teen girl? How many fighters are out there? Where is Asim and his cousin Faraj? What would they do if she were to suddenly jump out and start shooting? And how many rounds? The standard magazine for an AK-47 is thirty rounds. Are there any spare magazines up there?

Shut up, she thinks.

Wasting time.

She moves to the rear of the van, finds the latch, gives it a twist.

Clicking open.

Open!

It feels cold out there. She grabs a blanket, wraps it around her shoulders and head, steps out—

Damn it!

The road seems to be just dirt and rocks, and she twists her right foot. A pulse of hot pain explodes in her ankle.

Some damn easy escape, she thinks.

Mel moves as quietly as she can, finally seeing her surroundings, some sort of small village. Groupings of one- and two-story stone buildings. Dirt road and alleys. Two streetlights, flickering. The van she was in and two SUVs, maybe Suburbans. Lights on in the near buildings. A dog barking somewhere.

Knock on a door, ask for help?

No, not here!

To knock on a door and have Asim answer it?

She pulls the dirty blanket around her, starts limping away from the parked vehicles, trying to hurry along, knowing that at some point Beta is going to wake up, or Alpha is going to return, and then all hell is going to break loose.

Mel tries to speed up, trips, and falls.

She closes her eyes tight, rolls to the side of the road, and starts quietly weeping. She's just got on her shorts and sweatshirt from the States, socks, and the smelly blanket around her shoulders.

Dad, she thinks. *Dad, please find me.*

Keeping her eyes closed, she stops the crying.

Waits.

* * *

Minutes pass.

Mel opens her eyes.

Now adjusted to the dark.

Overhead is an incredible view, the desert night sky. So many constellations pop into view. Mom taught her the history of the stars and how their human ancestors had named them, and Mel looks and finds friendly old Big Dipper—Ursa Major—and she follows the two pointing stars in its bowl until she crosses the sky and locates the Little Dipper, Ursa Minor.

Polaris.

The North Star.

Mel gets up, not looking at where she was lying.

Looking only to the north.

To the north is the Mediterranean Sea, and along the sea are cities and villages, and there will be some people who speak English and will help her, she's sure of that.

Mel starts moving again, seeing the outlines of the dirt road from the starlight, and even though her right ankle throbs and her wrists ache, she's smiling through the tears.

She's free.

CHAPTER 95

Somewhere in northwest Libya

Asim Al-Asheed is sitting comfortably on a padded couch, a glass of sweet tea in his hand, a plate of dates and grapes and small cookies on a table in front of him, and he's smiling graciously at his host for the night, Omar al-Muntasser.

Omar is fat, bearded, wearing loose white cotton pants and shirt, and working a series of worry beads in his pudgy fingers. If this was any other night, Asim would gently get off this overstuffed couch, walk around to Omar's rear, grab his hair, and slit the fat man's throat.

Omar is smiling, his words seem to be dipped in honey, but he is not bending.

"My dear friend Asim, I apologize again, but it will be impossible for me to find lodgings for you and your friends tonight," Omar says. "I will feed you, and fuel your vehicles, and prepare meals and drinks for wherever your journey may take you, but I cannot offer you lodgings. My apologies."

The man's receiving room is filled with rugs, tapestries, framed photos of Omar Mukhtar, Libya's most famous resistance leader and Asim's own personal hero, and of Ahmed Al-Trbi, Libya's greatest footballer.

Three of Omar's sons are standing against the wall, armed with pistols, staring at Asim with anger, knowing that the man's presence here is putting their father and their families in danger. Earlier, Omar "excused" Asim's cousin Faraj to check on how much gasoline would be needed for Asim's two Suburbans and the GMC van, and Asim knows that the ruse was used to leave him alone with this tribal leader, once an ally.

Asim says, "My blessed friend Omar, again, I am honored to be under your roof and with your strong and devout sons, but I wonder: what kind of example are you providing them by refusing an old friend such simple hospitality?"

A wave of the fat man's hand. "Ah, but these are not simple times, are they, like when you started your jihad? Then you could live and regroup here, with few concerns, and your neighbors would always be willing to help. Today? The Russians, Turks, and Chinese all crawl around our lands, with money and influence and weapons, and now the Americans are coming."

"The Americans are always coming," Asim says. "Until they get bloodied, like in Somalia, Iraq, and Afghanistan, and then they leave."

Omar's smile is still there but seasoned with a brisk shake of the head. "This time is different. You murdered the daughter of the former president. The Americans are a soft people indeed, but when you go against their children like this, especially one so prominent, they will not give up until you are dead."

"A risk I've always been comfortable to meet," Asim says, the anger growing harder inside of him.

"Your risk, yes, is quite admirable. But your presence here

is putting my family at risk, and my people." Omar points to the ceiling. "At this very moment, an American drone could be circling overhead, and CIA agents could be reviewing its video footage, watching you walk inside…and then missiles will rain down on us. Many of us will die, women and children as well, but do you think the Americans would care? No. They would only care that they had killed you. My family and I would be, as they say, collateral damage."

"Omar, my friend—"

"No," he says, heaving himself out of his chair. "Enough. Your vehicles have been refueled, you have been given water and food. Leave. Now."

Asim slowly stands up, gives a quick nod in Omar's direction, and says quietly, "I am in your debt for offering me shelter, even if it was for a short time. But the Chinese, Russians, Turks, and even the Americans will someday leave. And you will remain, and so will I. And we will meet again, dear friend."

Omar says, "If you are alive at that time, I shall look forward to it."

The door outside opens and Asim passes by the angry-looking sons and approaches a concrete stairway, which empties into a modest tiled courtyard. Small electric lamps light the way outside, and Faraj is standing in the courtyard, along with the two men who were guarding the president's daughter.

From the looks on all three of their faces, Asim knows what's happened.

"How?" he asks.

Faraj starts to speak and Asim changes his mind.

"No, later," he says, knowing that Omar's sons are looking at him, and not wanting to give them any satisfaction or gossip to be taken back to their father, and thus to the tribesmen here, and to others in these mountains.

* * *

It takes only a few minutes for his three-vehicle convoy to depart Omar's village, and from the lead Suburban, he tells his driver, Taraq, to pull over, and then he assembles everyone in the glare from the vehicle's headlights.

There is a confusing conversation lasting two or three minutes during which the two men tasked with guarding Mel Keating blame each other for her escape, and when they pause in their weeping and pleading, Asim takes out his 9mm Beretta pistol and shoots the first one in the head. The man slumps to the ground and his companion makes a run for it. Asim fires twice, catching him in the back, and then he goes to the figure on the ground and finishes him off with a bullet to the forehead.

He takes a deep breath.

The anger is still roiling within him.

To his cousin Faraj, Asim says, "Take these two and drag them into the desert. Leave their bodies to the birds and the rats."

Faraj barks out the order to the group of men, comes over to Asim, and says, "Then, Asim?"

He puts the still-warm pistol in his hidden waist holster.

"We find Mel Keating," Asim says, "and finish it."

CHAPTER 96

Family quarters
The White House

President Pamela Barnes is alone in a living room that is part of what's known as the family quarters on the second floor of the White House, a tumbler of Glenlivet and ice in her hand. She takes another sip, the biting taste refreshing, and she pushes away the temptation to knock the drink back and make herself another.

Just one, she thinks. That's all she'll allow herself, despite the day she's just had. Before her is a large-screen TV, muted and set to the History Channel. Tonight's documentary is about the very building she's living in, and when and how it was built.

Another small sip, trying to ration it out, and she thinks sourly of her long-ago predecessor, John Adams, whose words were carved into the stone mantel of a fireplace in the State Dining Room back in 1945:

I Pray Heaven to Bestow the Best of Blessings on This House and All That Shall Hereafter Inhabit It. May None but Honest and Wise Men Ever Rule Under This Roof.

She lowers her glass and whispers, "Guess you never imagined us ladies ruling here, eh, Johnny?"

The door opens and her husband and chief of staff, Richard Barnes, comes in, still wearing his tuxedo, but with the tie undone and dangling down the front of his starched white dress shirt. He rubs at his face and says, "Man, what a night. I could go for another drink."

"Take a seat, Richard," she says.

"Sure, in a sec," he says. "I got a thirst that needs to be quenched."

"Now, Richard," she snaps, and she waits, and like a chastened boy, he comes over and sits down on the couch adjacent to her comfortable chair. The History Channel keeps on broadcasting in silence.

Quiet.

Richard finally speaks. "Is Matt Keating in custody?"

"In a matter of speaking," she says, staring at the television, the program now showing the interior redecorating done by Jacqueline Kennedy, the colors and the ache of the history still so strong.

She adds, "He's in custody, all right, but in the custody of the New Hampshire Air National Guard, heading across the Atlantic, just as he wanted."

Richard shifts in his seat, anger rising to his face. "How the hell did that happen? What Air Force officer disobeyed orders? Who let this happen?"

"You," she says. "You let it happen, Richard. You."

He looks angry and confused. "I'm sorry, Pamela. I don't know what you're talking about."

She reaches down and picks up her dispatch case. "Here are my daily set of papers, briefings, and analyses of various world problems. But there's not one single document in there telling me the details of a trip you took to Macau nearly three years ago. When I was vice president. When you had recently sold that cattle land for a casino development. And you flew off to Macau to celebrate one of your investors' birthdays. True?"

He starts to rub his hands together. "It's…been a while, Pamela. Three years."

"That's all right," she says. "While you were out partying tonight, I was unexpectedly debriefed on what happened during your trip. To the Golden Palace Macau. You had a wonderful time. But at some point, at about 2 a.m. local time, you received three visitors. Three young visitors."

His face darkens even more. His chin appears to be quivering.

Barnes says, "I'm sure you thought you had it covered. I'm certain you brought along a certain toy you had showed me back then, a military-grade jamming device that blocked the recording of any voices or images in a room. But the device didn't work, Richard. There's a recording of your…activities that night."

His hands are rubbing each other faster, almost frantically. "How…how does this have anything to do with Matt Keating?"

"I'm disappointed—again—with you, Richard," Barnes says. "Can't you see what's obvious? In exchange for that video not being publicly released, I had to let Matt Keating go."

His once-strong voice is shaky. "Who had that video?"

"Samantha Keating," she says. "She came here about three hours ago, told me that she had received a thumb drive containing the video from a former grad student working in Macau who saw you, Richard. He was there at the same time, updating the hotel's security software. Samantha offered me a deal. Let her husband go, and the video never gets released."

Richard says, "But letting Matt fly out like that…you should have bluffed, Pamela. Demanded more time, asked to review the video and verify—"

Barnes nearly drops her glass. "Verify? For God's sake, Richard, do you think I wanted to see even five seconds of that video?"

He doesn't answer. He looks down at the room's carpeting.

She sighs. "Tomorrow afternoon you're announcing your resignation as my chief of staff for medical reasons. I, of course, will accept it with tears and sorrow, given that your health is so very important to me. We'll have a brief press availability out in the Rose Garden, you'll say some nice words, I'll say some even nicer words. It'll be a wonderful send-off, Richard, but before we do that, I want your office belongings packed and on the way out of the White House."

He chokes out the words, "But…but I'm not sick, Pamela!"

"Oh, yes, yes you are, where it really counts."

She rattles the ice cubes in her glass. "But you get to stay on as First Gentleman. You'll smile and keep your mouth shut, and you won't talk to the press or anybody else in the government. You're going to find yourself traveling a lot in the months ahead, as we plan for my reelection. But when it comes to day-to-day politics here, Richard, you're through."

"But…Pamela, please…"

On the TV screen is Pat Nixon. Poor old Pat Nixon…a First Lady who never really seemed to thrive in this so-called People's House.

"Richard, I can't have you as my chief of staff. Too much risk that you might be compromised one of these days, if Chinese intelligence has the same video that Mrs. Keating has."

He slowly stands up, wipes at his eyes with a rough right hand. "Is that it, Pamela?"

Barnes takes a sip of the whiskey-flavored ice water left behind. "Almost. Tonight... you're not welcome in my bedroom."

"But... where do I go?"

"There are sixteen bedrooms in this house," she snaps. "Go find one."

CHAPTER 97

Somewhere in northwest Libya

From the lightening of the horizon, Mel Keating can see that the sun is about to rise and the last stars above will eventually fade out. Her feet hurt, her right ankle is throbbing something fierce, and she is desperately thirsty. She knows that the rising sun will make the day even hotter, but at least she'll be able to *see.* Since escaping from Asim Al-Asheed's men some hours ago—how long, she has no idea—she has stuck mainly to the dirt road, thankful that it runs mostly north, according to Polaris. During rest breaks, she'd leave the road and go into the sands, where once something crawled over her legs and she shrieked loud enough to be heard for miles.

And twice during the long night she heard the sounds of a loud, speeding vehicle coming her way, the headlights illuminating far ahead, and both times she raced into the desert and flopped down, pulling the dirty blanket over her, praying that scorpions and spiders wouldn't crawl in with her.

Once a vehicle stopped nearby, close enough that she could hear distant voices and the rumble of the engine idling, and a handheld spotlight shot out, sweeping both sides of the road. Mel closed her eyes, remembering the times when she was younger and afraid of ghosts in her bedroom and would think, *If I close my eyes, I can't see them, and they can't see me.*

If I close my eyes, I can't see them, and they can't see me.

She kept her eyes closed until she heard a disappointed shout, then the roar of the engine and the vehicle leaving.

Still, she didn't move, and that was a smart thing, for the vehicle—maybe a pickup truck?—suddenly stopped and the spotlight kept racing, as if it wanted to catch her coming out from her hiding spot.

It's getting lighter.

Her thirst is growing, and she chews on her tongue and inner cheeks, trying to get some moisture started.

Nothing.

She picks up a pebble, puts it in her mouth, starts chewing on that. A bit of saliva starts to emerge, but God, it really doesn't help.

Mel knows that the traditional way to survive in the desert is to move at night in the coolness and hide out and conserve energy and water in the daylight. Find a shaded place. Look for a depression in the sand, where plants might be growing. Dig into the soil there, find water. Find a piece of shiny metal, flash an SOS to any overhead aircraft.

All wonderful ideas, but only worthwhile if you're lost on your own out in the desert, she thinks. Not if brutal killers like Asim and his followers are out there, chasing you. Hiding in these sands and rocks means not moving, and she has to keep moving, has to find water, shelter, and, hopefully, people.

People who can help her.

Who speak English.

And have a truck or a car or a motorcycle to put more distance between her and Asim.

With the sun starting to rise, the landscape comes into clearer focus. Sand, exposed rocks, low scrub brush. Dirt road that she's walking on, with occasional ruts where tires have worn through. Low mountains and mesas all around her. Good places to hide; no wonder Asim brought her here.

Wherever *here* happens to be.

Getting lighter.

She starts looking carefully at what's on either side of the road, sees empty cans, some flattened cardboard boxes, and white plastic trash bags, which will probably last for another thousand years.

There.

A broken wooden box, some nice slats. Mel kneels down, tugs out the longest slat. In a flat patch of dirt, she shoves the slat in about a half foot or so, and then sits down, looks at her feet.

What a goddamn mess.

No sneakers or boots since her kidnapping, leaving her with only strong hiking socks. Over the days the socks have taken quite the beating, gotten torn and worn. Her feet are blistered and cut, but there is no point in taking the socks off without water and soap to wash them and bandages to wrap around her feet.

Mel retrieves two of the plastic trash bags, puts her feet in them, wraps them tight. With long threads torn off the edge of her blanket, Mel ties the bags as tight as she can.

Hot, miserable, but at least her feet will have more protection.

The sun is higher now.

Mel goes to the slat of wood she's stuck into the dirt. A shadow extends from the wood, marking west, since the sun is in the east. Meaning...north is that way.

Mel spots an oddly shaped piece of rock jutting out from a near peak. *There. Head toward that rock, and you're heading north.*

North, to the sea and villages and towns.

Mel starts walking again, limping on her twisted ankle, blanket around her head and shoulders, and then the dirt road splits into left and right.

Now what?

The left is closer to north.

North it shall be, and she starts moving again, stomach grumbling, mouth oh so dry.

Dad, she thinks. Oh, if he was still president, imagine what he could be doing right now. Every FBI and CIA agent in the world would be looking for her, and every drone and overhead satellite would also be hunting for her.

But so what? she thinks.

Asim didn't have to say anything, but Mel knows that with her fake execution, Asim wanted Dad and others to think she was dead.

Dad and Mom…probably together at Lake Marie, mourning her—hell, maybe even preparing some sort of memorial service.

How creepy: a memorial service when she's still alive.

She keeps on moving, hurrying as much as she can. The only sign of life she's seeing is a distant uncaring bird or two.

Sound travels far over this dry land, and when she hears the noise of the engine growing louder behind her, she gets off the dirt road, huddles behind some crumbled boulders. A cloud of dust erupts, extends maybe a hundred feet or so, and then a battered small white Toyota pickup truck appears, the front holding four people, squashed inside, and the rear overflowing with cardboard boxes and cloth bags, tied down with a series of ropes.

The truck roars by and the tailgate is down, and two women and two children are sitting there, feet dangling over the side, laughing as they try to stay in place with every bump and jostle.

Mel makes a quick decision.

She jumps up, hollers, waves her arms.

Waves her arms, takes off the blanket, and flaps it up and down, up and down.

"Help!" she screams.

The truck keeps on moving, disappearing into a cloud of dust.

The sound of the engine starts to quiet.

Mel kicks at a rock, starts to dry sob, wondering what she'll do, how she can survive, how much longer she can keep on trudging along like this.

She swings the blanket over her shoulders.

The engine sound returns, whining, and the pickup truck comes back, in reverse. The two women and two children, clad in dust-covered tan and black robes, are looking at her with amazement.

Mel thinks of the many things she's learned from Dad, one being, *Always be aware of your surroundings—always.* That's how she instantly knew back at Mount Rollins—when she was bathing in that isolated pool with Tim—that the two men approaching were trouble. They didn't fit.

But this group…men, women, children, a truck bed filled with packages and belongings.

Mel doesn't think they're jihadists.

She limps forward, her dry mouth cracked, and she loudly whispers, "Please…help…Can you help? Please…"

The women quickly start speaking in a language she doesn't understand—and which doesn't sound quite like Arabic—and one puts a child on her lap, and the other woman does the same, and both gesture for Mel to come forward.

Mel gets in between the women, squeezing in on the metal tailgate, and the woman to her right yells something to the driver, and the Toyota spurts forward.

She nearly falls out, but the strong hands of the women keep her in place, and they laugh at her, and Mel laughs right back, now not feeling any pain at all.

CHAPTER 98

Al Sheyab, Libya

Asim Al-Asheed is sitting in the shaded section of a small courtyard in the home of a local tribal leader who is willing to have Asim and his comrades rest there during the hot desert day, unlike the disloyal Omar al-Muntasser. Asim's vehicles are parked nearby, covered with a canvas awning, and substitute vehicles will be coming here soon from the larger village of Badr so he can continue his travels.

Asim is dining on a late breakfast of coffee, two eggs, and *sfinz* when his cousin Faraj comes up, tugging a young woman by her wrist. Asim looks up, wipes his fingers on a tan cloth napkin, and says, "Well?"

Faraj pushes the woman in front of him. She is wide-eyed, fearful, wearing a black robe across her body and over her head. Her feet are clad in dusty black Nike trainers.

"Take the cloth off her head," Asim says.

Faraj tugs off the covering and the woman cries out, and Faraj slaps her face, forces her into place.

Asim stares and stares. The woman lowers her eyes. The body, the face, the bone structure… yes, it will work. She looks to be in her late teens, and Asim says, "You've done well, cousin."

"Thank you," Faraj says.

Asim can't help but think of his wife, Layla Al-Asheed, and his three girls, Amina, Zara, and Fatima—now no doubt in paradise—and how when they were alive he would never allow himself to be in a room alone with another woman, no matter the age, to avoid the temptation.

Now?

He does what he must to get his revenge.

"Where did you find her?" he asks.

"At a special market south of Brak," Faraj says. "She is French, once married to an ISIS jihadist from Syria. He was killed and… here she is."

"Very good, indeed," Asim says. "And the hunt for Mel Keating?"

Faraj frowns. "It's continuing. I am sure we will find her, cousin."

Asim returns to his breakfast. "So am I. But not with you standing here with this sad girl. Get back to the hunt… and I want her found by this evening."

He senses that Faraj is angry, but so what?

Faraj knows his job, and more importantly, Faraj knows his place.

"Yes, Asim," he says, leaving, pulling the teen girl along with him, and she starts quietly wailing as they head to the door, speaking in French, the tone begging and pleading.

Asim shrugs, returns to his meal.

CHAPTER 99

On Highway 19, Libya

Jiang Lijun of the Chinese Ministry of State Security is sitting in the rear seat of a crowded Land Rover Defender, bouncing along this potholed road, heading south and to the Nafusa Mountains, trying hard to keep his tired eyes open. Two other Defenders are in front of this one, bouncing and jolting along, raising clouds of dust.

A hard jolt nearly cracks his skull against the roof, and next to him, Walid Ali Osman laughs. Walid is a longtime asset of Jiang's, and Jiang has hired him, a tribal leader, and ten tribesmen to go into the Nafusa Mountains to find Asim Al-Asheed and free the president's daughter.

Walid, a skinny bearded man, is wearing tan camouflage fatigues, as is Jiang, who's also wearing a bullet-resistant vest. He has a Chinese-made QSZ-92 9mm pistol holstered at his side, with four spare magazines. He tries not to yawn again. It's been a brutally long day, beginning back in New York City, where he didn't even have time to return home before grabbing a Turkish Airlines flight that eventually got him to Tripoli.

A long day, with no end in sight, and when he got to Tripoli, his first thought was that his boss had sent him on a suicide mission. Sent alone to Libya to rescue Mel Keating with no support! But Jiang had to obey the man's orders; otherwise, he'd be led to a small steel room with a raked dirt floor in the embassy's basement, where he'd take a bullet to the back of his head.

Walid laughs again at another jolt as they speed through a dull landscape of dirt, rocks, and brush, the rugged mountains and mesas coming into view. In good English, Walid says, "Seems there are many places yet for my Chinese friends to spend on your Road and Suspenders plan, eh?"

"Belt and Road," Jiang says. "That's what it's called."

The tribal leader laughs. "However you want to call it, it's just a way for a wealthy nation far away to sprinkle riches around, trying to buy influence and friendships." A slap to Jiang's knee. "How is that working for you, friend?"

Jiang says, "You're here with me, aren't you?"

That results in another laugh. Yes, after arriving in Tripoli, good fortune smiled upon Jiang, because he was able to make contact with Walid, and now here he is. Maybe, just maybe, this suicide mission has become something less deadly.

Another hard jolt. Even with doors and windows firmly secured, dust is finding its way inside the Defender. Up ahead, the driver is murmuring and cursing while his seatmate holds on to an AK-47 with one hand and is yelling into a sat phone with the other.

Jiang should be thinking and planning what will be done when Asim is located, but he is still haunted by that last conversation with his boss, Li Baodong, back in the basement of the Chinese UN mission building in New York.

Jiang's father died for his country.

Now Jiang is alone with these desert barbarians, bouncing and racing in this wasteland, to retrieve the daughter of an American president, and he feels as though he should have screamed at his boss back there in New York.

You stupid fat mushroom: if you had told me the truth about my father months ago, I would have gotten Mel Keating rescued back when she was being held in New Hampshire!

Then Asim and his cousin would be dead or in Guantánamo Bay. Mel Keating would be safely back with her parents.

And Jiang wouldn't be here, in the middle of this wasteland, speeding off to a possible lonely and bloody death up in those approaching mountains. Shudder, bounce, rattle. This time his head does strike the padded roof.

If he lives, this is his last field mission.

No more.

Even if it means returning to Beijing in disgrace, getting shuttled off to some distant office, placed in the middle of ungrateful Tibet or among the restless Uighurs, Jiang is through. He wants to live and be a good father to his own daughter for years and years to come.

The man with the sat phone turns and rattles off a number of urgent words to Walid, who claps his hands with joy.

"We have done it!" he announces. "A small family compound, less than an hour away, *inshallah*. Rumor has spread that a teen American girl is now in one of the houses there, being taken care of, a guest."

Jiang says, "Faster. We need to go faster."

Walid pats the shoulder of the driver, tells him something, and then repeats a similar string of words to the armed man with the phone who's sitting up front. The two Land Rovers up ahead speed up, and this one accelerates as well.

Maybe I will survive the day after all, Jiang thinks.

CHAPTER 100

Abrika family residence, Libya

Mel Keating takes another satisfying drink of the slightly cool water from a metal cup and decides once again that it's the finest liquid she's ever swallowed. She's resting in a small room inside a cool stone and plaster house, lying on a pile of carpets and pillows, while an elder woman—perhaps the grandmother of this family?—oversees two young women who are washing and now gently drying off Mel's sore and abused feet. All three are wearing loose black robes with colorful scarves around their heads, and the younger two seem to be about Mel's age. They chat and laugh in what she guesses is an Arabic dialect.

The water! Never has she tasted anything so delicious, so refreshing, so filling. The water seems to gently wash away the dust and thirst and dryness that made her mouth feel as though she was chewing cotton balls. Her feet still hurt but it's a pleasing hurt, part of being cleansed and healed.

Still, as comfortable as she is, Mel is jumpy, fearful, turning at every noise or disturbance. She knows that Asim Al-Asheed is out there looking for her, and being here isn't like trying to hide in Georgetown, with all its buildings, streets, and alleys. She's on a rocky desert plain at the foot of these mountains, and she imagines there's not another collection of houses for miles around.

As refreshed as she is, Mel needs to get out of here.

Earlier she had a moment of panic, as one of the young women took off Mel's glasses, making her instantly blind, but the woman came back a minute or so later, having carefully washed and dried them, and Mel was ashamed at her fear.

Another woman comes in, her head covering a bright blue, and she puts a ceramic platter in Mel's lap. On it are small light brown cakes that look like the flapjacks Dad makes—and that makes her tear up, thinking of Dad—and there's honey drizzled over them, and she eats one, and then two, and after another drink she says, "I'm sorry, does anyone here speak English? Please?"

The woman serving the cakes smiles. "Yes, I do…some. For two years I went to university in Tripoli…"

"Oh, my God, thank you, thank you so much for picking me up," Mel says. "I was so thirsty…and lost."

The woman steps back. "My name is Tala Abrika. What is yours?"

Mel hesitates. All right, she's been rescued, but who are these people? Can they be trusted? Are they friends of Asim Al-Asheed?

The taste of the water is still in her no-longer-dry mouth.

"My name is Mel," she says. "Mel Keating. Thanks again for rescuing me."

Tala smiles, nods. "It is what we do."

Mel nibbles on another of the delicious cakes while the other women in the room chat amongst themselves. "I've heard that the Libyan people are kind and gracious to strangers," Mel says to Tala.

Tala's smile fades some. "We are not Libyans. We are Amazigh, what some call Berber."

Mel sees something haunting in Tala's dark eyes, and senses she's made a mistake. "I'm sorry," she says. "I didn't mean any disrespect."

"Don't worry," Tala says. "We Amazigh, who live here and in the Nafusa Mountains, we were hunted, killed, and oppressed by whatever evil men were ruling Libya, for the crime of being different. Only in the past few years have we had any semblance of peace."

The other women, still laughing and chatting, leave the room. Now Tala is alone with Mel. She stares at Mel with her sharp dark eyes.

In a firm voice, Tala says, "How did you come to be lost, Mel Keating? A young American like you, wearing the wrong clothes, wearing no shoes, on our land?"

Mel recalls the times she's heard Dad swapping stories and tall tales with his SEAL buddies about how—despite the years of training and experience—sometimes you just have to go with your gut, what it's telling you, what you're feeling.

Mel goes with her gut.

She trusts this woman.

"I was kidnapped in the United States by terrorists and brought here," she says. "I escaped last night. Please: can you help me? Do you have a cell phone?"

Tala's face is solemn. "We do, but there is no…what you say, coverage. Here. One needs to drive up to Miraz, before it works."

"Please…"

Tala's face breaks into a smile. "My cousin, Abu Sag, is coming here within an hour or two. He will take you to Miraz. There you can make your phone call. And you will be safe, Mel Keating. *Mushiiyat Allah*, you will be safe."

Mel is wearing soft black slippers that the elder woman slipped onto her bandaged feet, and she even dozes for a while. She is awoken when Tala comes back in and says, "Quickly now. My cousin Abu is here."

Tala helps Mel get up. Holding Tala's arm, Mel is led outside, into a dusty dirt courtyard. She sees the old truck that picked her up, and now a dark gray Toyota Land Cruiser is parked nearby. A squat young bearded man wearing blue jeans and a white buttoned shirt gets out of the front seat, smiles, and gives a quick wave in her direction.

The other women are standing near the entrance to the one-story home. There are three other similar homes, built in a semicircle. Goats and chickens scramble around, and on two of the homes there are satellite dishes.

Tala grasps Mel's hand, gives it a squeeze.

"Safe travels, Mel Keating. I hope we meet again."

Mel chokes up, remembering Mom once saying, years ago, *Most people are nice people, Mel. It's our curse that it's the evil ones who get so much attention.*

"Me, too," she says.

Abu waves a hand. "Come. Let's go, miss, let's go!"

The inside of the Land Cruiser smells of incense and cinnamon, and beads and trinkets dangle from the rearview mirror. Abu is a wild and reckless driver, and Mel finds that the seat belt mechanism doesn't work, so she ties the belt across her waist with a square knot, hoping for the best.

The radio is loud, and Abu sings along. The road isn't much

of a road, just a wide dirt lane, with lots of ruts, but Abu drives as if he could do this with his eyes closed.

The sun is high up and the sky is a deep blue, not a cloud in sight, and Abu says, "We get to Miraz, I let you use my phone, true?"

"That's right," she says.

He slightly leers. "Will you give me something in return?"

Great, Mel thinks. "We'll make the deal after I make the call."

"Ha ha," Abu laughs, and they keep on driving, the road wide and empty through the desert. Then Abu says, "Ah, look. Look there. Up ahead."

The windshield is smeared with dirt and dust, and Mel can't see what Abu is seeing until they are almost upon it.

Three SUVs, parked in a row, a huddle of men around the first one, examining a map on the hood.

Abu speeds by. "Did you see that? Did you?"

"What?" Mel asks. "What's there?"

"A man from Japan. Or China. Standing there, with the others." Another barking laugh. "So lost, eh?"

Mel says, "I know the feeling."

Some minutes later, Abu seems to curse in Arabic and taps the display above the steering wheel. "Ah, so damn stupid. I forgot to refuel. We're running low on petrol."

Mel puts one hand on her seat belt and the other on the door handle. She thinks, *If this clown is going to try the "We're out of gas" bullshit line, I'm bailing out the moment he slows down.*

"No worries," he says. "Up there. The crossroads. The Dajout family. A service station, a little store. Mel, would you like a cold Coca-Cola? Would you?"

Would she!

"Yes," Mel says. "That would be great."

He whistles, slaps her on the knee—okay, she'll let that one go—and says, "It will be my delight. And unlike the phone call, no charge."

The road widens and Mel sees two pickup trucks cross before them, both raising clouds of dust, and there are three one-story buildings in a row, with other trucks parked nearby and men in long white robes or pants and shirts standing outside, talking amongst themselves.

Abu pulls into a narrow alleyway and says, "Just a few minutes, young lady. I will refuel, will get you the promised drink, and soon enough, you will be making that phone call."

A laugh, and then he gets out, shuts the door, and goes into the rear entrance of the nearest building. Another truck roars by on the main road. Mel gently rubs one sore foot against the other.

Who to call? How to call?

Sure, 911 won't work.

But there is a phone number that Agent David Stahl had her memorize back when Dad was in the White House.

Use this number and we'll find you, he said.

But will it work overseas?

Maybe, if she can figure out how to dial international from Libya.

What is the overseas code for calling the States?

She doesn't know, but maybe Abu can find out.

Mel unties her seat belt and is reaching down to rub at her feet again when the driver's door opens.

She looks to her left and freezes.

A smiling and satisfied Faraj Al-Asheed is looking in.

Standing beside him, calmly sipping from a bottle of Coca-Cola, is Abu.

"Do you think, young lady," Abu asks, "that I will risk my family's safety for you, a foreigner?"

Faraj reaches in and grabs Mel's shoulder, hard.

“Come along,” he says. “Asim is eager to see you.”

Mel slaps his face—hard!—and breaks free, opening the passenger door, jumping out, nearly crying aloud from the jolt of pain in her right foot. She moves as quickly as she can up the alleyway, sees a road out there. Maybe she can wave somebody down, or scream for help, or—

Two men with pistols are blocking the end of the alley.

Mel turns.

Faraj and Abu are coming toward her, looking relaxed and confident.

She says, “But I don’t want to see Asim.”

Faraj laughs and grabs Mel’s shoulder, and as she is brought past Abu, she lashes out with a free elbow and shoves the hard glass bottle into the man’s face.

CHAPTER 101

Aboard Granite Four
Mediterranean Sea

We're about fifteen minutes outbound from the Tunisian Air Force base at Sfax-Thyna when Claire Boone—Mel's friend and an operative for the National Security Agency—comes out of the KC-135's lavatory and walks over to me, squats. Next to me, Agent David Stahl is fast asleep, earplugs in his ears, arms folded across his chest.

"Matt?" she says.

"Yes?"

She leans in so I can hear her better.

"We're going to be kinda busy once we get on the ground," she says. "And I know I'd never forgive myself if I don't use this opportunity to ask about a mystery that's been bugging me for years. What did you say in the letter to President Barnes? The one you left in the Oval Office desk on Inauguration Day? Usually the text is always released, but not this time. Why?"

I feel like snapping at her, *With all that's going on, you're worried about* that?, but I'm saved when Technical Sergeant Palmer comes through and says, "Okay, folks, we're coming in. Take your seats, buckle up."

Claire gets up and notes the look on my face, and scurries over to her side of the fuselage.

The aircraft banks here and there, the engine noise changes pitch, and I feel the KC-135 dip and drop altitude as we approach the landing strip. There are no windows or portholes to allow me to judge our approach, and like so many other times in my previous military career, I put my trust and faith in the aircrew.

The landing gear whines and clunks into place, one more shift in the approach, and the KC-135 lands smoothly, the reverse thrusters kicking into action, the jet rapidly slowing down.

My small band of warriors either stir awake or come to attention as the aircraft slows, and Technical Sergeant Palmer approaches us and says, "Welcome to Tunisia, folks. If you unbuckle and bring your gear forward with me, we'll get you on the ground. There's no airstairs available, so we'll get you out through the entry chute."

We follow in a single line to the crew compartment up front, and the tech sergeant gets to work, lifting up part of the flight deck and revealing a yellow metal grid, which he removes. He lowers a metal ladder and fastens it in place. Then the tech sergeant climbs down and opens a small hatch in the lower fuselage. Our pilot stands up, and Nick Zeppos goes down first, followed by Alejandro Lopez, and David passes our duffel bags to the two SEALs below.

As this goes on, I move from one foot to the other, trying to bide my time, just knowing I need to get on the ground and get to work.

Patience, I think. *Get some patience or you'll move too quick and screw it up.*

I make my way to the ladder and Captain Josephs reaches out and offers his hand, his copilot checking some paperwork. I give his hand a quick shake.

"Good luck, sir," he says. "We'll be praying for you and your squad."

"Thanks, Captain," I say.

I take in the landscape of Sfax-Thyna's air base, and there's not much to see. We're at the end of a commercial airfield that belongs to a small detachment of the Tunisian Air Force, with a handful of hangars and support buildings clustered in one corner. There are four single-engine trainer aircraft and a collection of helicopters, a mix of older Hueys and newer Black Hawks. A scattering of one-story buildings stands beyond the airfield's fences. The landscape is flat and brown, and the air is humid but not too hot.

I've been in worse.

Nick Zeppos is talking to a man wearing dark green fatigues, black boots, and a tan baseball cap, and they both laugh, and Nick slaps him on the shoulder. Then Nick says to me, "Temporary quarters all set up. This way."

We begin quickly walking and a fuel truck starts racing over to the KC-135. I see the flight crew of Granite Four clustered around the front of the plane, stretching their legs and waiting for the craft to be serviced.

Move, move, I think.

Nick leads us into a small concrete and metal building that looks to be a maintenance facility, with workbenches, pallets, and tools hanging from the walls. It's hot and stuffy inside, with no air-conditioning. Alejandro and David start clearing off the workbenches and Nick says, "Hold tight, Mr.…ah, Matt. I'm going to hook up with the SEAL platoon, see if we can't have a briefing within the hour."

"Sounds good, Nick," I say. I open my duffel bag, take out a bottle of lukewarm water, take a long gulp.

David says, "The SEAL platoon here... what can they bring to the table?"

I say, "First of all, sixteen professional operators. Probably two Black Hawks, and if we're lucky, they're the latest stealth version, which will mean that crossing the border unnoticed will be a hell of a lot easier. Night-vision gear, small arms, sniper rifles, grenade launchers, explosives for breaching doors or barriers, and at least one corpsman. David, we can't do it without them."

With workbenches clear, David and Alejandro get to work, opening their respective duffel bags, taking out weapons and various pieces of equipment. I bring my own duffel bag over, start doing the same thing.

I check my watch.

One p.m. local time.

"Claire," I say. "What time is sunset?"

"Hold on, sir," she says. While the three of us are unloading our weapons, Claire has been getting her NSA-issued laptop up and running.

Priorities.

She says, "Local sunset is... 7:41 p.m., Matt."

I start thinking it through. No way we're going on a cross-border raid during the day.

And not right after sunset, either.

No, the best time is always the same time: middle of the night. Bulk of your enemy are asleep, drugged, or drunk, and those on guard duty are usually bored or sleepy.

The good news is that we have at least four hours—a good half day—to prep and practice with the heavily armed SEAL platoon for tonight's action.

The bad news?

Lots of bad news. We still don't know where Mel is, only that she's somewhere a hundred miles to the east, in the Nafusa Mountains of Libya.

And if she's at one location right now, where will she be five hours from now?

So much to worry about, so much to plan.

The door opens, and Chief Nick Zeppos comes in, face drawn, and I know the bad news is about to get worse.

"Sorry, Matt," he says, eyes haunted. "The SEALs were called out to help a French para unit to the south."

We all go silent. I think of what I just said to my Secret Service agent.

David, we can't do it without them.

Nick says, "They're gone, and won't be back for days."

CHAPTER 102

Nafusa Mountains, Libya

Jiang Lijun's bones and muscles are aching from the rough drive he's put up with for the past half hour. He's in the sole Land Rover Defender that's climbing deeply up into these mountains, and he's sitting in the rear, next to Walid Ali Osman. The driver and another gunman are up front, and the two other Land Rovers are parked about a half kilometer behind. The gunmen who were in those vehicles are quickly climbing ahead to provide cover for when Jiang and Walid finally reach the cluster of buildings inhabited by Asim Al-Asheed and his followers—a bit of information that one of Walid's tribesmen passed along an hour ago.

The Land Rover bounces, sways, lurches. This dirt road makes the previous dirt road they were riding on seem like the G45 highway south of Beijing. Since his briefing back in New York, Jiang has sent three email messages to Asim, telling him that he is en route, but none of the messages have been answered.

Another hard jolt.

Walid displays a handheld radio. "My men are on their way. When we get to Asim's residence, I will contact them, and the fighting will start, and we will rescue the American girl."

The engine whines louder as the incline becomes more steep. The rock walls are so close that if the windows were open, Jiang could touch them.

Jiang says, "You think Asim and his men are going to stand still while you talk into your radio?"

Walid laughs. "I know what I'm doing. The radio will be in my pocket. When we're in position, all I do is touch the Transmit button three times…sending out a signal. That's all it will take."

"And they know enough not to hurt any women they see, correct? We don't know how Mel Keating is dressed, or where—"

The Land Rover tops a crest.

A man is blocking the path, an AK-47 slung over his shoulder. He's wearing a dark green fatigue jacket, white trousers, and a black scarf around his head.

The vehicle slows and stops.

The man comes forward.

It's Faraj Al-Asheed, Asim's younger cousin.

For the first time since he's landed back in this cursed country, Jiang feels a bit of optimism.

Asim is a fanatic, a jihadist, one who is ice-cold when making a decision and seeing it through.

His cousin Faraj is more of a follower, more educated, and, on some days, open to listening to reason.

His presence here is a gift, and Jiang is rethinking the strategy he's developed with Walid over these past few hours.

Jiang unbuckles his seat belt. "Let me go talk to him. I might come up with a solution that doesn't involve gunfire."

"If you say so." Walid sounds skeptical. "But I still expect to be paid, even if there is no fighting."

Jiang says, "If I convince Faraj to release the American without fighting, I will pay you and give you and your men a bonus. Stay inside."

He steps out onto the firmly packed dirt and raises both arms to Faraj as he starts walking toward him. Jiang's pistol is still with him, but it's holstered and visible. He wants to put Faraj at ease, to show that his visit here poses no threat.

Faraj grins. "It's you, isn't it! Jiang Lijun—what a surprise!"

Asim's cousin comes toward Jiang, both arms held out, and Jiang thinks, *Oh, no, not a smelly hug,* but no, Faraj just grasps both of Jiang's hands, gives them a squeeze.

He says, "Asim told me earlier that you were coming here, up to our little remote home. What an honor! What a delight! What brings you here, then?"

Jiang forces a laugh in reply, and quickly lowers his hands. "Business, of course…business I wish to talk to your cousin about."

Faraj steps back, smiling, shakes his head. "Yes, Asim. He is always open to talk…except when he isn't. He told me he wasn't going to reply to your latest emails. He said, 'If that Chinaman wants to talk to me, let him come to my mountains.' So here you are. In his mountains. How did you find him?"

"My guides," Jiang says, "and my own intelligence."

Faraj says, "Lucky for us, the Americans aren't as wise as you. And your business…it has to do with the president's daughter, correct?"

"True," Jiang says. "I want to offer him an…agreement. An understanding. Something that could possibly serve both our interests. Perhaps you could convince him to consider my offer: to free Mel Keating to me in exchange for various compensations."

Faraj scratches at his chin, where a beard is slowly growing back in. "I don't know about that, Lijun. As I said earlier, he is always open to talk." He pauses. "Except when he isn't."

Faraj lifts his right arm, makes a circling motion with his hand, and from the rocks above and to the left of him, there's a hard blast of an explosion, a slight *whoosh,* and a hard explosion behind Jiang.

Jiang automatically falls to the ground, covering his head and ears, as the explosion echoes and reechoes behind him.

He tries to get up and Faraj takes Jiang's pistol from his side, and then grabs his shoulder, gets him to his feet.

Jiang turns his head.

The Land Rover is on its back, burning brightly, black clouds of smoke rising up, the flames crackling and roaring, even the tires ablaze.

Faraj is next to Jiang, arm around his shoulder.

In the distance are a number of rapid gunshots, and Jiang knows that Walid's fighters are being cut down, one by one.

Now he's alone with Faraj, save for the fighter coming down the rocks behind him, holding the spent RPG-7 rocket launcher in his hands. Jiang's chest aches, and not from landing on the ground.

It might have been easier, he thinks, *to have been in that destroyed vehicle.*

Faraj gives Jiang's shoulder a squeeze. "Ah, now that we've taken care of your…guides, as you call them, it's time to meet up with Asim. I'm sure the two of you will have a lot to talk about."

Jiang blinks at seeing the roaring flames. There's a brief scream from inside the shattered vehicle.

"If you're lucky," Faraj adds.

CHAPTER 103

Nafusa Mountains, Libya

Mel Keating is on her second bout of exercise this afternoon, and while she's pleased to have been given this small indulgence, her right ankle is still hurting like hell. She drags it along the dirt as she is shadowed by two men in tan trousers, fatigue jackets, and caps, each holding an AK-47 automatic rifle. The men are young, with scraggly beards and nervous eyes. Dad would say they both had lousy trigger discipline because their fingers are inside the trigger guards, meaning a trip, stumble, or hard sneeze could loose off a shot.

Mel's wrists are manacled at her side and tied to a wide leather belt secured at the rear. No more plastic flex-cuffs, and even with this additional binding, her two guards seem nervous, and for good reason. Mel is their responsibility, and she's sure that Alpha and Beta back there weren't given just an unsatisfactory performance review when she turned up missing.

Probably two taps to the back of the head, she thinks, or something similar.

She continues her dragging walk directly away from the one-story stone building that's her current prison. There are five other stone buildings in this little village, compound, or terrorist training camp, depending on one's point of view. All are one story, though in various shapes and sizes. There are about a dozen or so fighters in this place, no women, and no children. At a small building next to the one where she's being kept, there's a cluster of satellite dishes and antennas, disguised by overhead netting and canvas. The same kind of camouflage is over four small Nissan pickup trucks, all black.

Maybe they got a dealer discount on the color, she thinks sourly.

At the end of her walk, she turns around, resumes her slow pace back to her jail. The buildings are in a flat stretch of land, with steep rocky slides behind and to the right, the narrow dirt and stone road to the left, and, up ahead, a chunk of hollowed-out and crumbling wall of rock, rising up to a flat mountain. Two men are stationed up there, armed and with binoculars to their faces. The air is cold and the sky a crisp blue.

There's a shout. Asim Al-Asheed emerges from the largest of the stone buildings, accompanied by two of his lackeys, and there's laughter and chuckles. Mel wishes her arms were free so she could tackle her near guard, strip him of his AK-47, and cut them all down.

Asim comes directly to her, still smiling, and she's chilled, remembering the reception she got hours ago, when Faraj brought her up here. She thought she would be beaten, punched, or even worse, but Asim was in a good mood, smiling, and gently tapped her cheek. "What a naughty girl you were," he said, and she wishes now that she had had the presence of mind to bite his fingers.

He speaks rapidly in Arabic to the two guards, who step back, and Asim says to Mel, "Let me walk with you, back to your quarters."

Mel resumes her slow pace. "Some quarters. Looks like it was once stables. Still stinks."

"Yet we gave you the best room in there," Asim says. "For that, why aren't you grateful?"

Mel keeps her gaze straight ahead, not wanting to look at her captor. "You want my gratitude? Have a couple of your guys drive me out of here and drop me off at the American embassy in Tripoli. I'll be so grateful I'll put you on my Christmas card list."

He laughs, although she continues to ignore him by not looking at him.

Asim has started to speak when the sound of a far-off explosion thuds in the distance.

Mel stops, looks to the narrow road leading out from the encampment. She's not sure, but it sounded like a few rapid bursts of gunfire.

Her chest gets tight and she squeezes her handcuffed hands. Could it be? Is somebody coming for her? Now? A rescue attempt? Should she start running away from Asim?

Asim says, "Ah, there you go." He checks his watch. "Fairly on time."

Mel struggles to control her voice. "What's happening?"

"Oh," he says, lightness in his voice. "Didn't you hear? A rescue party was on its way. My cousin and a number of my warriors dispatched it before it arrived."

Mel turns away, not wanting Asim to see the tears in her eyes, the disappointment in her face, but it's too much, it's all too much, and she sobs.

So close!

Asim says, "Ah, don't cry, Mel Keating. It wasn't the Americans.

Or the British. Or the French. If you can believe it, someone from China, your powerful rival, tried to grab you from me. The strange ways of our world, when a rival nation tries to save you. Now, no more tears, all right?"

They come to the guarded main door of the stone building, and he says, "Resign yourself to your fate. You are here, with me, forever. Daddy isn't coming for you. And Mommy isn't coming for you. No one is coming for you. We believe that Allah wrote down in the *al-lawh al-mahfooz* all that has happened and will happen, and which will come to pass as written. That means that our respective fates and destinies have already been determined by Allah."

Mel decides to ignore that last bit of blather. She shuffles her feet in place and Asim says, "What is that?"

Mel says, "I may be living in a stone barn, but I didn't grow up in one. Just getting the dirt and dust off my feet."

Two armed men flank the heavy wooden door, and Asim opens it, nods, and says, "After you, Mel."

She walks into the darkness.

CHAPTER 104

Sfax-Thyna air base, Tunisia

After Chief Nick Zeppos announces the departure of the SEAL platoon they were depending on, the hot and smelly room falls silent, and Matt Keating seems to stiffen and grow a few inches. With his beard growth, the clothes he's wearing, and the look in his dark eyes, the man doesn't look like a former president of the United States to Nick: Nick sees a fellow SEAL operator.

"Chief," Matt says, the word hard and sharp, "you promised us transportation. We don't have it. You're going back out there to get it."

"Yes, sir," Nick says.

Matt says, "I don't care if you bribe a pilot, threaten a pilot, or hijack an aircraft. Or rent one. And if there isn't a helicopter or fixed-wing aircraft out there, get a truck. Or a four-by-four. Because one way or another, Nick, we're crossing into Libya tonight and going to the Nafusa Mountains. I'm not waiting on intelligence, and I'm not waiting on transport. We're going out tonight to get my daughter back."

"On it, sir," Nick says, and he quickly leaves the building.

Outside, Nick walks to the small collection of aircraft at the end of the runway and starts running through options and possibilities. Transportation is a given, he knows, but what's the point without actionable intelligence? He knows that President Keating's friends in Mossad and the Saudi intelligence service are working hard to locate Asim Al-Asheed, but Nick also knows from bitter experience that good intelligence comes organically. It can't be forced, or hurried, because then you end up with crap intelligence that leads to a crap mission and casualties.

The low roar of jet engines comes to him, and the New Hampshire Air National Guard KC-135 that brought them here takes off, heading to its original destination of Rota, Spain, and Nick feels a bit jealous of that crew. They're military, they have a job to do, and while it may be challenging, they never have to stretch rules and regs to get it done.

Nick recalls a vital sentence of the SEAL creed: "We expect innovation."

So innovate, already, he thinks.

As he gets closer to the assembly of aircraft, another, fainter engine noise reaches him, and he scans the clear Tunisian sky. Two Black Hawk helicopters are approaching from the south, looking to come in for a landing. They move nearly as one, and Nick admires their pilots' skills as one aircraft and then the other lands swiftly and carefully. Their fuselages are painted black, with a white roundel with a red crescent moon and a star.

A handful of flight crew members run from the nearest hangar and approach the helicopters as their rotors slow down, and as the crews emerge, removing their flight helmets, Nick stops, amazed.

He recognizes one of the pilots from his training visit last year.

Talk about innovation!

He resumes walking as the tall pilot with the thick black mustache sets off, joking and smiling with his copilot and two aircrew members. Nick yells out, "Joe! Is that you, Joe?"

The man he calls Joe stops, looks over, and grins as Nick gets closer.

"Chief Zeppos?" he asks. "What the hell are you doing out here?" His English has traces of both Arabic and French accents.

Nick extends a hand, which is promptly shaken by Youssef Zbidi, also known to the SEAL trainers as Joe, a captain in the Tunisian Army's Groupe des Forces Spéciales. Joe's free hand holds a leather dispatch case and his flight helmet. He's wearing a dark green flight suit, his name on his name patch in Arabic script. Epaulets on each shoulder display his rank: three stars.

Nick says, "I'm on a job."

"Really?" the captain asks. "That's a surprise. I surely would have been briefed that you were coming here. You're not here to join up the SEAL platoon that's been here for three weeks, are you? I'm afraid they're far away from here, assisting a unit of French paras to the south."

"No," Nick says. "It's something else. Highly classified. Off-the-books. Joe, I really need your help."

"Is it important?" he asks.

"Very," Nick says, thinking, *We got this, it's going to work out, we got this.*

But in just a second, Captain Zbidi's mood changes, his eyebrows narrow, face darkens. "When we last met, Chief Nick, you told me that my flying skills, as you say, suck. You said I belonged at one of your kiddie rides at an American amusement park. You said not only did I fly like a swine walking on ice, you said I fly like a drunken swine walking on ice."

Nick thinks, *Oh, shit,* and Captain Zbidi spits on the pavement between them.

"Why in hell should I help you with anything?" he says.

CHAPTER 105

❖

Sfax-Thyna air base, Tunisia

With Nick out seeking transportation, I put that problem away and get back to work. In the teams you quickly learn that you have to depend on your teammates to get their job done, while you concentrate on your own part of the mission. Nick is in charge of transporting us to Libya.

I have to focus on the job at hand: getting my gear ready.

From my two duffel bags I pull out my disassembled Colt M4 automatic rifle and begin putting it back together, starting with inserting the bolt into the receiver. Other parts and components follow, and it's almost comforting as my muscle memory takes over, letting me put this weapon back together. I can do it in the rain, in a jungle, in pure darkness, and the satisfying clicks and snaps seem to calm me down.

Alejandro Lopez and David Stahl are engaged in similar activities, and Claire Boone—quicker than the rest of us—has her own M4 assembled, and she's working her primary weapon, her NSA-issued laptop, wireless earbuds in both ears.

After pairing up and connecting the upper receiver of the M4 to the lower receiver, I test it by pulling back the bolt and squeezing the trigger.

Click.

Time to prepare the ammunition.

I break open boxes of 5.56mm ammo and start loading up thirty-round magazines, forcing each round into the spring-loaded metal magazine. I decide to have one magazine in the Colt M4 and six in pouches.

Next up is my SIG Sauer 9mm P226 pistol, and I'm going in with one twenty-round magazine in the pistol and four more in other pouches.

"Matt," Claire says from the other side of the hot and smelly room.

"Yeah," I say, trying to find the pouches for the pistol ammunition inside my duffel bag. "Give me a sec."

Claire raises her voice. "You don't have a sec. Get your butt over here."

I lift up my head. "What?"

Claire pulls the earbuds out and says, "CNN International says Asim Al-Asheed is about to release another video, this time live."

I drop what I have in my hands and quickly go over to Claire as she says, "And it's going to have Mel on it."

I'm behind the sitting Claire, and Alejandro is on my left, David on my right. Claire taps on the keyboard and the female news anchor from CNN International in London says, "…breaking news now, CNN has learned that in just a few moments, a live presentation is being made by terrorist mastermind Asim Al-Asheed to the Al Jazeera network…and…hold on…"

The anchor looks away and then the following words nearly make me gasp with relief, as she returns to looking directly at the camera and says, "It now appears that the president's daughter, Mel Keating, is in fact alive and well…and that the execution video from a few weeks back was a fake. And…here is the broadcast…"

My hands are on the back of the chair that Claire is sitting in, and my fingers clench the metal as a picture comes into focus:

My daughter, Mel Keating, face tired, smeared with dirt, wearing her eyeglasses, a black robe around her head and shoulders, some of her frizzy hair sticking out. The live video is grainy, not as crisp as the first one I saw back at the Saunders Hotel in Virginia.

She's holding a newspaper in her dirt-covered hands, and the paper is slightly shaking in her trembling grasp.

"Oh," is all I can say.

But inside I'm yelling to myself, *She's alive, she's alive, no more hoping, there she is, she's alive.*

The calm and happy voice of Asim Al-Asheed becomes audible as he narrates the live video. "Ah, good day, Matt Keating," he says, "and as you can see, I have very good news for you. Mel Keating is alive and well."

Claire says, "Matt, she's holding a copy of today's *Daily News Egypt,* an English-language paper out of Cairo."

Asim laughs for a sick second. "So I fooled you, did I not? Like the West has constantly fooled my people over the years, from the Sykes-Picot Agreement during your First World War that carved up lands not belonging to you among the British and French, to the Balfour Declaration that allowed the Zionists to invade and expel the Arabs, up to and including your so-called war on terror and invasions based on fantasies of weapons of mass destruction."

I'm hearing Asim's words but I'm still staring at Mel, seeing her look out at the camera, looking like she's fighting to keep calm. The newspaper continues to tremble in her hands.

Asim says, "So I lied to you. I made you and your wife live in mourning for a few weeks...to give you just the slightest taste of what I have been feeling since you, Matt Keating, killed my wife and daughters. Now my lies are over. Now is the time for truth, to tell you what will happen next."

He pauses and then says slowly and with firm clarity, "You took away my family. And as the law permits, I am due compensation, and that compensation, Matt Keating, is that your daughter is now mine."

David whispers, "What the hell?"

Asim says, "Your daughter is now *my* daughter, to repay me for what you did to my family. Soon she will receive a new name and will join me, for the rest of her life, as I raise her as my own. And you must consider this. Are you now in such a hurry to find me? To kill me? To drop one of your bombs or rockets on me? Think that through, Matt Keating, because if you do that, the collateral damage, which you so often like to use as an excuse, will be your teenage daughter. Leave me alone. Let me live. For in doing so, you will let your daughter live. *Masalama*, Matt Keating."

The sound cuts off, and I see my daughter for just a few more seconds before the screen goes blank.

Alejandro whispers, "Fuck," and that one word explains everything.

The bastard has put me into a tight corner, a very tight corner.

With Mel no longer his captive but his so-called daughter, Asim will have her close by his side, for now, for tomorrow, and for years to come.

Daring me to rescue her, and attack him, and put Mel in immediate danger.

Damn the bastard.

A phone starts ringing, and I yell, "Will somebody answer that damn thing? I'm trying to think over here."

David says, "Matt, it's your phone."

I go back to where my duffel bags and gear are located, pick up my burner phone—BLOCKED CALLER, says the ID screen—and I answer by saying, "Yes?"

"Matt?" says an excited voice.

"Yes," I say, recognizing Danny Cohen from Mossad. "Danny, what's going on?"

With joy in his voice, Danny says, "We found her. We know where Mel is located. No doubt about it."

CHAPTER 106

Nafusa Mountains, Libya

Jiang Lijun of the Chinese Ministry of State Security is in a small room with stone walls and ceiling, sitting in a wooden chair, ankles and wrists chained to it. There's a locked wooden door about two meters away, and on either side of the door, small square windows in stone open outside, blocked by metal bars. The floor is dirt.

He sits quietly, calmly, not knowing if there's a surveillance camera somewhere keeping tabs on him. He won't give anyone out there the pleasure of seeing him rattling or testing his chains.

To keep his mind off what will no doubt be his last hours alive, he recalls the history of Admiral Zheng He, who more than six hundred years ago set out with huge fleets of explorers and traders aboard ships that would overwhelm the European ships of the time. In his journeys, he became among the first Chinese to land on and explore Africa.

Not this part of Africa, of course, but if the rulers back then had followed up on Admiral Zheng's journeys—the fifteenth-century equivalent of the current Belt and Road Initiative—oh, how history would have changed.

The door is unlocked, opened, and Asim Al-Asheed strides in, smiling. Standing outside are two of Asim's armed men, who are staring at him as if they have never before seen a man from China.

"Lijun," Asim says. "I admire your dedication and persistence, to come all this way, through so many hardships, to talk to me."

Jiang says, "It's my job."

"Oh? And was it your job to bring along a squad of assassins, to attack me and my followers?"

Jiang says carefully, "You know how dangerous these lands are. I was only being cautious, with what resources were available to me. No plan to attack you was even considered."

Asim smiles. "I am sure." He turns, barks out an order, and a metal folding chair is brought in. He sits down. "Well, here you are. The last time we spoke, back in America, you said you admired what I had done, and that you were prepared to offer me assistance. Does that offer still stand? Do you still wish to assist?"

"Circumstances have changed," Jiang says. "And so has my offer to you."

"I see," Asim says. "Anything else?"

Jiang says, "The fact that I am here is clear truth that you can be discovered. If the Americans believe Mel Keating is alive—"

"They do now," Asim interrupts. "I just broadcasted a live video demonstrating she is alive. And thank you for your warning. I do not plan to stay here in these mountains much longer. Do go on."

Jiang says, "Knowing she is alive, the Americans won't stop looking for her and trying to kill you. Turn her over to me, and I will return her to American custody. My government will offer you a generous reward, fulfill any desire or need you have. Just return the girl to me."

Asim seems to be pondering this, but Jiang isn't fooled. There's a mocking look in those dark brown eyes.

"Ah, yes, you and your mercantile country, always willing to trade, to deal, to make profits," Asim says. "I'm sure that's what you mean by *reward,* correct? Lavish sums of money. Safe relocation to another country. A life of leisure, comfort, and wealth. Only if I release that teen girl to you."

Asim quickly stands up, grabs the chair. "But there are people in this world, my friend, who have no need for wealth or luxury. Who answer only to God. Later this day I will show you what I mean, in greater detail. And then you will be safely released, to return home, to tell your masters that you have finally met a man who couldn't be wooed or bribed against his beliefs."

Asim leaves, the door closes behind him, and the lock is reengaged.

Jiang sighs. Alive for now, but he doubts Asim is telling the truth.

Why should Asim release him?

He's alone.

But he doesn't remain alone for long.

Just a few minutes later, the door is unlocked and opened again, and this time it's Asim's cousin Faraj who comes in. In his right hand is a khaki-colored square satchel that he sets on the dirt floor.

He closes the door behind him and says, "You made an offer to my cousin. Repeat it to me."

"Mel Keating is released safely in my custody, and you will be amply rewarded."

"Specifics," Faraj says. "Give me specifics."

Jiang says, "Twenty million euros, in any confidential numbered bank account you may have or that we can set up. Safe transportation to any place in the world, and free lodging. New identification so the American, British, and Israeli services never find you."

Faraj nods. "Is that deal for Asim, or anyone else?"

Jiang is pleasantly stunned. "Anyone who will release Mel Keating to me and give us safe transport out of Tripoli."

"Then I will do it," Faraj says. "Not my cousin. I'm tired of jihad, of rotten food, of sleeping in caves, always fearing a drone will fire a missile at me. You and I, we will make this deal."

Fascinating, but Jiang is not sure if he's being set up for something. Could these two cousins, who have spilt so much blood between them, actually be having a falling-out, or is something else being planned?

Is Faraj setting a trap for him?

Time for caution.

Jiang says, "I'm not sure I can trust you. And I'm not sure if I feel right in betraying Asim."

Faraj crosses the dirt floor, squats so that he is eye level with Jiang.

"You will cooperate with me, you will pay me, or I will tell Asim that you were the one who murdered his family three years ago," Faraj says. "And not the Americans."

Jiang is frozen in place, not able to say a word.

"How do you feel now?" Faraj asks.

CHAPTER

107

Sfax-Thyna air base, Tunisia

To the former head of Mossad, I say, "Danny, please tell me more. What do you have?"

"That video of Mel: it was a live feed," he says, his voice triumphant. "It wasn't a recording. Our Unit 8200 was able to decrypt the feed when it started and found where it was being transmitted, to an Asim sympathizer in Qatar who was able to pass it along to another sympathizer with connections to Al Jazeera. But Matt, better yet, we were able to pinpoint where the transmission was coming from."

The Israeli Unit 8200. Their equivalent of our National Security Agency, professionals in every manner when it comes to signal intelligence, codes, and decryption. After I was sworn in as president and brought up to speed on the globe's various problems and hot spot areas, I was told that Unit 8200 was just as good as the NSA, and in some areas better.

"Danny, where did the transmission come from?"

"In Libya, the Nafusa Mountains," he says. "Coordinates follow, Matt: thirty-one degrees, fifty-four minutes, thirty-six point seventy-eight seconds north, and eleven degrees, nineteen minutes, three point sixty-six seconds east."

I find a pen, scribble the vital numbers on the palm of my hand. "Reading back, Danny: coordinates thirty-one degrees, fifty-four minutes, thirty-six point seventy-eight seconds north, and eleven degrees, nineteen minutes, three point sixty-six seconds east."

Danny says, "Perfect. That's where she is, Matt. God bless."

I disconnect the call to find that Chief Nick Zeppos and another man have come into the small maintenance hangar.

"Matt," Nick says. "This is Captain Youssef Zbidi, a Black Hawk pilot with the Tunisian Army's Groupe des Forces Spéciales, their Special Forces. I had the…honor of working with Captain Zbidi last year in a training assignment."

I take a quick moment to write the coordinates on a slip of paper and pass it over to Claire Boone, and then I go to Nick and nod in his direction.

"Captain Zbidi," I say.

The pilot is wearing a flight suit and is muscular, dark-skinned, with a thick mustache, and his face slowly goes from skepticism to slight awe. Nick says, "I talked to Joe—that was our nickname for him back then—and told him what we were up to. Naturally, he didn't believe me, but I convinced him to at least come over here and see for himself."

Right then I see an abrasion under Nick's left eye and notice that the Tunisian Army pilot's right cheek seems swollen.

Some convincing.

"Captain Zbidi," I say, "then you know what we're up to. Can you help?"

Zbidi nods and says, "Only for one thing. Do this thing…and it'll be fine."

The tired, overworked, and mercenary part of me wonders what the pilot is looking for—money, citizenship, gold bullion—and I give him the only answer I can.

"Absolutely," I say. "What is it?"

He steps forward, slightly smiles, and extends his right hand. "For the honor of shaking the American president's hand."

I give his hand a quick shake. He grins at both me and Nick and says, "For you, sir, and to rescue your daughter, my aircraft and crew are yours."

A few minutes ago, I was so dog-tired and depressed it felt like my butt was about to start dragging on the ground, but no more. I'm quickened, energized, and then Claire says, "Got it. Got it right here."

I'm walking over to Claire when my phone starts ringing again. I'm tempted to ignore it but since so few people know this burner phone's number I answer it.

"Keating," I say.

Another familiar voice comes on the line. "Matt. Are you well? Can you speak?"

It's Ahmad Bin Nayef, former deputy director of the General Intelligence Directorate of Saudi Arabia. I say, "Ahmad, of course. What is it?"

Then it feels like Christmas in June, for he says, "We have her location. We know where Mel is."

I'm almost giddy with relief. Just a few minutes ago I had no idea where my girl is being held, and now I have two of the finest intelligence services in the Middle East coming through for me at the very last moment.

Two sources, confirming where she is.

Intelligence doesn't get any better than that.

"Is it the Nafusa Mountains in Libya?"

"It is," he says. "There is a courier who brings special supplies for Asim's cousin, Faraj. Contractors working for us found him just as he was leaving Asim's compound. He was…interrogated and came up with the location. He says the word in the camp is that a very important prisoner is there, a young girl, the daughter of the former American president. Matt, I am so pleased for you."

"Ahmad, thank you so much," I say, my throat thickening. "Samantha and I are eternally in your debt."

"Do you require any other assistance?" he asks. "I might be able to get a force of men for you within the next twenty-four hours."

I say, "We don't have the time, Ahmad, but thank you. We're heading out tonight."

"Then *adhhab mae allah,* friend," he says. "Here are the coordinates where she is being kept. Twenty-five or so fighters are also there, so be careful."

Ahmad slowly and efficiently gives me the coordinates, and I write them down on a slip of paper, and—

Something is seriously not right.

"Ahmad, can you repeat that?"

"Certainly."

He does that, and I write down the coordinates once more. Phone still in hand, I go to Claire and hand her the slip of paper.

"Claire, Saudi intelligence is saying these are the coordinates where Mel is being kept. Key them in, will you?"

"Certainly," she says, and she works the keyboard. By now we—including the Tunisian pilot—are standing in a quiet semicircle behind her.

On her laptop screen is a topographical map of the rough and rugged Nafusa Mountains. With her keyboard input, a blinking red triangle appears.

I'm not an expert on computer mapping by any means, but I also see that there's an earlier blinking red triangle.

"Claire?" I say.

She swivels around in her chair, looks up at me.

"I'm sorry, Matt," she says. "The coordinates don't match. The Israelis say she's in one place, the Saudis in another. About twenty klicks apart."

CHAPTER 108

Nafusa Mountains, Libya

Jiang Lijun remains seated and quiet, not daring to say a word, or to move, or to otherwise do anything that will attract Faraj's attention even more, but Asim's cousin stands up and says, "Let's make progress, shall we? Let's stipulate you've just spent ten or so minutes denying everything I've said. Very well. Now it's my time to speak."

Faraj goes to the satchel he brought in and starts unzipping the top. "Three years ago, Asim's family were killed when the American SEALs attacked the small village where they were living. I'm sure you recall this…especially since you were serving at your embassy here when the raid occurred."

He halts in opening the satchel and says, "Horrible, wasn't it? A woman and her three children, innocents all, killed in an explosion. Worldwide news, with Matt Keating going on television later to apologize for this botched military operation."

He pauses. "But suppose it wasn't the Americans who did it?"

Jiang finally says, "I don't know what you're talking about."

Faraj laughs. "Oh, don't insult me, dear Lijun. Let me finish, and then you can insult me. After the raid was over, and the bodies buried, I was bothered by the news. I talked to survivors who were there the night of the attack. They all agreed as to what happened. The Americans arrived, fighting began, but before they reached the house where Asim's family was residing, it exploded."

Jiang says, "A Hellfire missile, I'm sure."

"Oh, no, not sure," Faraj says. "Why would the Americans use a Hellfire missile with so many of their soldiers nearby? Unnecessarily exposing them to danger? And when I went later to investigate with a good friend of mine, a man we call the Engineer, well, the first thing we learned was that the explosion came from inside the building. Not outside. Easy to see if you are standing there."

Jiang remains quiet. Sweat is starting to trickle down the back of his neck.

Faraj opens the top of the satchel. "The Engineer…he is an expert student in all things electronics and explosives and graduated with honors from the American University of Beirut. Ironic, eh? But he told me that we were fortunate that the explosion took place inside the building, because important clues and components would still be there. And he was right."

Jiang is fearfully focused on the satchel Faraj has brought in. What could be in there? A blowtorch? Pruning shears? Sharp knives?

Faraj says, "You should have seen him at work. Very methodical, very slow, but after two days of searching, he found it. An electronic triggering device was inside a shipment of 82mm mortar rounds that were temporarily being stored there. Mortar rounds that were shipped to Asim from…you. And the device would be triggered by a cell phone call."

Faraj reaches into the satchel, pulls out one, and then two—

Cans?

Jiang's eyes widen as he sees the familiar blue and white logo of a mountain climber ascending a peak, and the Chinese characters written on the side.

Snow beer.

Jiang says, "How…"

Faraj deftly opens one can, brings it over to Jiang, and with Faraj holding the can to his lips, Jiang takes a deep, refreshing swallow of the cold beverage. Faraj steps back, opens the second can, and takes a long drink as well.

Faraj says, "My cousin knows nothing but Allah, jihad, and revenge. I, on the other hand, appreciate the technologies that the West has afforded us. Like this." He gently nudges the satchel with his foot. "A battery-powered cooler. Ingenious, eh? Like that explosive device you attached to those mortar rounds."

Jiang says, "Thank you for the beer. It's quite refreshing."

Faraj laughs. "My, nothing seems to bother you. No wonder you make such a good intelligence man. You would probably continue to deny everything even if I was sawing your balls off. But it makes sense—it all makes sense. Asim was an asset of yours, for many years, but there always comes a time when an asset becomes a burden, an embarrassment. He must be retired. And somehow that night, three years ago, you learned the Americans were going to attack Asim. And the thought came to you, my intelligent friend, that a single phone call from you could retire your asset and also kill or humiliate the Americans. What they say, a *win-win.*"

Jiang says, "You tell a good story, Faraj."

Faraj approaches and offers the can of beer one more time. Jiang thinks of the drinking games he endured back when he was at Columbia, and he swallows.

The can finished, Faraj steps back and says, "But Asim lived.

His family died. And your actions probably caused the election defeat of Matt Keating. All in all, a good trade-off, am I right? But here is tonight's trade-off. Later there will be an opportunity for me to kill Asim. When that is finished, you will make the arrangements for my pay, new identity, and new home. Then you will get the girl."

Jiang says, "It will take some time to do that."

Faraj finishes his own beer. "I have all the time in the world. But just remember: you don't."

"What?"

Faraj places the two empty cans in the cooler, zips it shut, and stands up. "You betray me in any way, and Asim's other relatives and friends will be told of what you did, and you will not live out the week."

CHAPTER 109

Nafusa Mountains, Libya

Mel Keating is sitting on the dirt and stone floor of her cell, knees drawn up, arms across her lower legs. She's thinking and observing, and damn it, she doesn't like what she's seeing.

Or not seeing.

The stone room has a lightbulb hanging from a black cord run through a drilled hole in the doorframe, a wooden shelf with water bottles and various crackers and fruit snacks, and…

That's it.

No latrine.

And more importantly:

No bed.

Which means Asim doesn't plan on keeping her here for any lengthy amount of time.

But he has said that she will be his "forever."

Lots of ways to interpret that, none of them good.

Mel struggles to get up because her damn ankle is still throbbing something fierce. Tears come to her eyes, and it's not just the pain.

Trapped.

Oh, my God, she is so trapped.

Once she's on her feet she goes to the shelf, drinks some water, eats some dry crackers and then some fruit snacks. One snack appears to be made of some kind of cherry slop, and she gets red juice all over her fingers.

Interesting.

She keeps the juice on her fingers and plays with it for a while, and then licks them clean, and takes another swig of water.

Mel takes a deep breath, tries to ease the shakes in her arms and legs because she knows no one's coming for her. Mom and Dad think she's dead. Asim is a murderous terrorist, but he's right about something: she's on her own.

Time to get out of here.

But how?

She walks around the small interior, fingers on the bare rock, looking and evaluating, and—

It's bare rock.

Only way in and out is through that heavily locked door.

Sure, she thinks, *I'll break through the door and overwhelm the armed guards outside, and then limp my way to freedom.*

She kicks at the door with her good foot, and then starts hammering away with her fists, yelling, "Hey, hey, hey!"

Mel steps back. *Great: now both feet are aching.*

Wait.

Hold on.

The door is being unlocked!

It swings into the cell and there are two armed men there, peering at her, both maybe nineteen or twenty, thin beards, white pants, brown vests over dark blue shirts. The one who's closer has an AK-47 hanging from his shoulder by a strap, and his companion standing a few yards back has his AK-47 pointing straight at her. Beyond them is a corridor leading to the main door outside. The corridor is flanked with old stone stables filled with rations, bottles of water, boxes of ammunition and weapons.

"Yes?" the first man asks.

Thinking quickly, Mel says, "You know who I am, right? The daughter of the former president. Whatever you're getting paid here, he'll pay a lot more, a hell of a lot more to free me."

The first man turns to the second one, laughs, and, back to her, says, "Yes?"

"Right, right," Mel says. "My dad will make sure you two can come to America... with your families. Start a new life. Safe and secure. And he'll pay whatever you want, I promise you. Just get me out of here."

"Yes, yes," he says, and Mel thinks, *Really? Will it be this easy?*

He steps forward, unshoulders his weapon, prods at her with the muzzle end of the AK-47, and, laughing again, steps back through the door, draws it closed, and locks it.

No, she thinks, turning away, her eyes brimming with tears, *it won't be this easy.*

Again, she looks around the room. No bathroom or sleeping arrangements.

With a cold feeling in her gut, Mel knows that forever is coming very soon for her.

CHAPTER 110

Sfax-Thyna air base, Tunisia

Back on the phone, I say, "Ahmad, something's not right. Are you sure on these coordinates?"

"Positive, Matt," he says. "I was there during the interrogation, and we verified it with the courier by going over satellite maps and other resources. Those are the coordinates."

"But did he see Mel?"

Ahmad says, "No. Just heard the stories in the camp. About a very important young girl being kept there, the daughter of the president. Matt, what is wrong?"

I rub at my forehead and continue staring at Claire's computer screen and those two damnable blinking icons, so far apart.

"What's wrong is that Mossad is telling me she is being held at another place in the Nafusa Mountains, about twenty kilometers away," I say. "The video that Asim Al-Asheed sent out earlier was a live feed. The Israelis were able to track down where the broadcast originated. It's not the same location that your source told you."

Ahmad sighs. "The constant struggle, correct? Human intelligence versus signal intelligence."

"Can you talk to the courier again? Just to make sure?"

A second of hesitation. "I'm afraid I cannot do that, Matt. The courier…is no longer available."

In that one sentence, Ahmad just told me the courier is dead. Either died under questioning or was shot while trying to escape, or because a rival of Ahmad's and a supporter of Asim's spirited him away, and then killed him to prevent him from talking anymore.

"I understand," I say. "Is there anything else you can tell me?"

"No, I cannot, Matt," Ahmad says. "My apologies."

The call is disconnected.

The room is quiet, everyone looking at me, in the middle of making the proverbial life-or-death decision. Despite the self-serving stories from presidential aides or what happens in popular movies, there aren't that many presidential decisions that are truly life-or-death. In fact, most presidential decisions are already made by the time an order or memorandum comes to one's desk. Decisions are made in work sessions, cabinet meetings, briefings up on Capitol Hill, and when they get to the Oval Office, it's almost perfunctory.

But not now.

The two blinking icons seem to mock me.

"Sir…" Nick starts, and then he stops.

I know what he's thinking, what everyone else is thinking. We don't have the assets to make two missions tonight.

Just the one.

But which one?

Ahmad is right. Human intelligence versus signal intelligence. HUMINT versus SIGINT. Left or right. Heads or tails.

Where do we go?

All up to me.

On my shoulders.

The burden of command.

What now?

"Claire," I say. "Rerun the video of Mel, but no sound, please."

Her fingers move fast, and the video comes back up, and I stare at Mel's sad face, her soiled fingers holding up today's Egyptian newspaper, her gaze nearly exhausted, her tired eyes staring out from her eyeglasses, the image grainy.

An old memory pops up.

After my dad died in the Gulf of Mexico, his two brothers—my uncles—decided to help Mom raise me, and usually that meant hunting trips, drinking beer while underage, and learning how to play poker. The ins and outs of dealing, betting, and, most importantly, the all-vital tells. Reading your opponent. Sensing if he or she is bluffing. It all comes down to—

The eyes, sport. Always look to the eyes. If they're ice-cold, they're not bluffing. But if they're blinking, shifting, looking down, then they got squat in their hands.

The eyes.

Mel's gaze, steady and even, and even with the poor quality of the video, it all becomes clear.

"It's not Mel," I nearly yell. "That's not my daughter!"

Some murmurs from my crew, and I say, "David, get over here. Take a look. Tell me what you see."

Secret Service agent David Stahl, who's been at Mel's side for more than four years, steps forward, leans over Claire, stares at the screen. I so desperately want to tell him what I see, but I need to keep my mouth shut.

I need him to look without preconceptions.

David steps back. "Matt, you're right. That isn't Mel…the eyes…"

To everyone else I say, “Mel has myopia in one eye and astigmatism in the other. Due to the corrective lenses she wears, if you’re looking straight on at her, one eye would appear larger than the other.”

I tap the screen. “This girl…she looks like Mel, but it’s not her.”

I almost feel dizzy from the range of emotions I’ve gone through during the past few minutes.

I say, “This girl’s eyes are perfect. My daughter is at the other site. And we’re going there, soon as we can, to get her.”

CHAPTER 111

Nafusa Mountains, Libya

Mel Keating is sitting in darkness, for a little while ago—with her moistened fingers—she unscrewed the sole lightbulb in her cell, leaving it in the socket. Glasses in her hand, she is forcing herself to relax, to listen, to think and be quiet.

Once Dad said, *Whenever you feel trapped and helpless, take a deep, deep breath, and look at everything fresh. You might be surprised at what comes into view.*

She tears up.

Dad, I'm doing my best, honest to God, she thinks. *But I'm trapped and I'm scared, and I know what's going to happen to me tonight, for real. No more fakery.*

Help me, please.

Something flickers against the back of her neck.

Mel yells, slaps at the back of her neck, and puts her glasses back on.

Spiders.

Bugs.

Scorpions.

What the hell was that?

She fumbles in the darkness, her hand up above her—*God, suppose there's a rat up there, ready to bite my fingers?*—and she finds the still-warm bulb, twists it tight, and blessed light comes back into her cell.

What the hell was on her neck?

There's nothing on the floor.

She looks up. Nothing seems to be flying around.

But something was on her neck. She's positive about that.

Mel really wants to keep standing but forces herself to go back to where she was sitting.

She sits down, both the light and her glasses on, and waits.

Low talk on the other side of the door from some of Asim's men, who also use these old stables as living quarters.

A bit of music.

A muffled *pop-pop-pop* as someone fires off a rifle.

Mel freezes.

A slight tickle at the back of her neck.

She slowly brings her hand up there but doesn't feel a thing.

But the tickle is still there.

Mel quickly stands up, walks to the wall behind her, and reaches for an area up near the ceiling. She licks her fingers and holds them up against the stone and dirt and—

A bit of a draft.

A slight breeze.

Mel frantically starts digging at the stone and dirt, and a trickle of soil begins to come out. The rock here is loose, and she digs and digs.

More dirt falls.

The draft increases.

Oh, God, please, she thinks.

Mel goes to the wooden shelf and takes everything off, and then works the wood free from a couple of metal stanchions. She balances the shelf on a rock and jams her good foot down, breaking it into pieces.

She picks up the largest piece, with a sharp jagged edge at the end, and goes back to work.

The earlier trickle of stone and dirt nearly becomes a flood. An old chimney, water stanchion, or feed trough was once there and had been sealed up.

Mel slams the wood into the widening opening, again and again.

The door to the room is so thick she's sure she can't be heard.

Good.

She's getting the hell out of here.

CHAPTER 112

Sfax-Thyna air base, Tunisia

To our NSA rep, I say, "Claire, we need anything and everything you can pull up on that site."

"On it, Matt," she says, and her fingers fly across the keyboard.

Our little group is clustered behind her, and there are whispers and I hold my hand up and say, "Shut your damn traps. Claire is working. Don't disturb her."

Silence, then, as Claire whispers to herself and toggles various screens and links, and at about the time I realize what she's looking at, she's already moved on to something else three links down the line.

"Here," she says.

"Here" is an overhead shot of a mountain terrain, boulders and narrow gorges, two flat areas separated by what looks to be a rock wall, and slides.

No vegetation.

Or vehicles.

Or buildings.

"Claire, what's the date and provenance?" I ask.

"Sorry, Matt," she says. "Ten years old. Defense Mapping Agency. Best I can do."

I say, "Damn it, there has to be more out there than just this."

Nick says, "Have you tried—"

Voice sharp, she says, "You got a better idea? Do you? Any of you? Anybody want to sit in front of my keyboard?"

Crap, I think.

"Sorry, Claire," I say, wanting to keep her straight and focused. "You're the expert here. Everybody, back away. Let her do her job."

She exhales in a loud sigh of frustration, goes back to work on the keyboard, and I see:

Lines of code.

North Africa maps.

Global orbital elements.

More lines of code.

Claire says, "I need a sat phone. Now."

Nick ducks away, comes back, and gives his sat phone to her. She takes it, chews on her lower lip for a moment, and starts pressing in a series of numbers while we speak in hushed voices behind her.

"Guys?" she says. "Love you all, but shut the fuck up, okay?"

We all shut up.

The phone is apparently answered, and in a flat voice, Claire says, "Access."

A second or two pass. She says, "Bravo, Oscar, Oscar, November, Echo. One, four, niner, four."

I hear a plane take off nearby. I can hear David breathing next to me.

"Extension twelve."

A few more seconds, and Claire's tone instantly changes. "Hey, Josh, how's it going in Cheyenne? Missing daylight? No?

Well, your complexion is so fair you'd probably burst into flames if you went to the beach."

She laughs.

Nick looks to me and I shoot him a glance to keep his stance, and to keep his mouth shut.

Claire says, "Hey, Josh. Need a favor. Off the books. It—"

She stops.

"Josh," she says. "Josh...c'mon, look, do I have to remind you that you owe me one? Do I? You would have never gotten to the twelfth level of Universal Conflict without me..."

She waits, rubbing her eyes and forehead.

"Josh, don't make me beg...okay? Don't..."

Waiting.

Waiting.

Mel, so damn close...so damn far away.

She sits up, looks to me, smiles. "Josh, perfect. You're a dear...honest. Okay, I need a full sweep of the following location, all angles, all spectrums."

Claire slowly reads off the coordinates provided to us by Ahmad Bin Nayef.

Then repeats them.

Waits.

"Thanks for the read-back, Josh," she says. "You've got a Jason that will be able to give us a good live view in about ten minutes. That's all I need."

Another pause.

"Sure, but you can get away with it, I know," she says. "The damn thing still has stabilization problems. I know you've got a calibration schedule for that bird. Just do it ahead of schedule. Say this is just a test run, that's all."

She laughs again. "How do I know that? Do you forget where I spend my time? Okay, I'll let you get to work...and I owe you big-time. Really big-time."

Claire disconnects the sat phone, hands it back to Nick, and then bends over at the waist. "Man, I feel like I'm going to hurl... wow."

She sits back up, rubs her eyes, and says, "Okay, let's see what's what."

On the screen it suddenly goes black.

A line of green letters and numbers appears at the top of the screen and—

Crisp overhead view of mountains and valleys and ridges in faint green illumination. The view slowly slides up to the top of the screen and I get a funny feeling at the base of my skull. As president, you often get a "behind the curtains" look at what our military and intelligence systems can deliver, and this is definitely one of those times. It's like we're hovering maybe fifty or sixty feet above the ground.

Live.

At night.

"Buildings," Claire says. "Here we go. There's been a lot of changes from ten years back."

Alejandro whispers, "God."

There are six buildings in a semicircle, apparently stone or brick, various shapes and sizes. A flat area in front, fuzzy white shapes moving about, what looks to be a stone wall to the south, and a flat stretch of mesa before it drops off.

"People," she says. "And look... road leading up from the left. Which is west."

Those shapes down there. Could one be Mel? I squeeze my hands.

"Vehicles," she says. "Four trucks."

Nick says, "I got a head count of twelve."

Alejandro says, "Down the road. Two guards, one on each side. Flanking."

I say, "Claire, you're recording this, right?"

"Uh-huh," she says.

I look at the buildings, seeing how they seem to glow from the night-vision capabilities of the overhead surveillance satellite.

Six buildings.

But where is Mel?

We can probably hit one building, maybe two, without getting overwhelmed. But in the event of firepower and attack, does Asim have a plan to spirit Mel away? Or shoot her before she's rescued? Do we have time to maintain surveillance on all six buildings to find the one that's holding Mel?

Where—

"What's that?" I ask.

Claire says, "What?"

I lean over her, gently tap at the screen.

"Right there," I say. "That."

Claire minimizes the live broadcast and goes to a video recording.

Plays it back, enlarges it, sharpens it.

David says, "I'll be damned."

From the largest building, one that seems to have been built right into the base of a rocky peak, a faint line seems to extend out to the flat stone and dirt in the middle of the compound.

And at the end of the line, going right up to the building's entrance, an arrowhead shape has been scraped away.

Someone's made a straight arrow in the dirt, pointing right to the center building.

Like with a stick or by dragging a foot.

My smart daughter.

Good job, Mel.

"Mel's there," I say. "That building. Time to get to work, people."

PART FIVE

CHAPTER

113

The raid on Nafusa

After an hour of briefing, planning, and more planning, we go out into the night in a quick moving line, down the runway to the Tunisian Army's Black Hawk helicopter, its rotors already in motion. We're all geared up and armed, pretty similar in terms of what we're carrying, but each of us has our own little quirks and preferences in how we've prepped.

When it comes to arms, I'm carrying a fully automatic Colt M4 5.56mm rifle with an infrared laser sight, and holstered at my side is a SIG Sauer 9mm P226 pistol; extra magazines for each gun are secured in pouches. On my head is a level III high-cut ballistic helmet, with an ATN PVS14 night-vision device extended up into the air. I'm also wearing Point Blank level III body armor, and on my tactical vest I have a variety of other gear: water bottles, IFAK (individual first aid kit), QuikClot combat gauze for bleeding control, spare batteries, an Ontario

MOD Mark 3 knife, a Gerber multi-tool, and a small rucksack with a couple of other key items.

Funny thing: the gear is heavy and bulky, but there's a muscle memory in putting it back on, and I don't feel burdened at all, walking along this runway pavement.

I feel like I can walk all night.

We all have Motorola SRX 2200 single-band handheld radios, frequencies already keyed in, and Peltor ComTac headsets so we can talk to each other on the ground.

The communications tonight will be easy, first names only, and our Black Hawk helicopter pilot is going by his SEAL-issued nickname of Joe.

KISS: Keep it simple, stupid.

Claire is carrying an extra weapon, a .308 bolt-action Remington rifle with mounted scope, since she's our sniper tonight. After a brief but heated discussion back at the maintenance shed, it turns out she's a better shot than all of us.

It's two hours after sunset. In usual times, we would go in at 2 a.m. or 3 a.m., the best time to hit when there's a minimum of awake and alert bad guys, but this isn't a usual time. I know where Mel is. I'm taking a gamble, going in early.

Closer to the helicopter, bits of dirt and gravel are tossed our way, we're bending our heads, and I remember the last couple of hours back in our temporary quarters.

Looking at the screen of Claire's laptop in hopes of determining means of entry and exit, Joe pointed to a small area to the west of the compound and said, "This wadi here. I can drop you here. It's about a klick and a half away from Asim's place. It's narrow enough and a thousand meters lower. That should mask the noise enough that you won't be noticed."

I nodded and said, "Here. This flat area in front of the buildings, just beyond that low stone wall…we'll mark it with

IR glow sticks when it's time to exfil. Prepare to pick us up within forty-five minutes after you drop us off. We can't stay there any longer."

Joe said, "Oh, I wish I had a door gunner."

Nick, Alejandro, and I kept our mouths politely shut. We were all glad he didn't have a door gunner because we haven't trained with one, and we don't know how good Joe's door gunner might be. It'd be a hell of a thing to get to the exfil area and be cut down by friendly fire.

Nick said, "These two guard locations. Alejandro and I will leap ahead, eliminate them before the final staging."

I checked my watch.

It was time.

David said, "Matt, just so there's no confusion. Rules of engagement?"

I said, "This is a rescue. Nothing else. I don't care if we stumble across documents or piles of hard drives or blueprints for a dirty bomb. Mel is our sole objective. No prisoners are coming back with us. Nor bodies."

They all nodded in acknowledgment, and I was struck by the composition of this odd group: a Tunisian Special Forces pilot, two SEALs, an NSA field operative, a Secret Service agent, and a former POTUS. Band of strange brothers and a sister indeed.

I added, "Except for Mel, there are no innocents up there. Armed or unarmed, running away or running toward us, kill 'em all."

As I get close to the Black Hawk helicopter, a spasm of doubt hits me, just at the last moment. Am I doing the right thing? Is this really a rescue mission, or is it an attempt by an angry and humiliated dad to get payback for what's happened to his daughter?

A quick phone call by me, Nick, or Alejandro to JSOC, the Joint Special Operations Command, telling them where Mel is located would get the professionals up and running.

But that's the key point.

Up and running.

Unlike what some History Channel programs might have viewers believe, Special Forces aren't stored somewhere, geared up and ready, straining against a leash, ready to head out at a moment's notice. No, there would have to be activation, planning, preparation, phone calls up the chain of command, and maybe—just maybe—as the sun rises tomorrow, a unit might be on its way to the Nafusa Mountains.

Too late.

One by one, we climb up into the helicopter, take our positions along the canvas seats. Overhead is a dangling headset with a mic, and I take my helmet off, put the headset on, and say, "Joe, Matt here. We're all on board."

"Thanks, Matt," he says, and the helicopter's crew chief slides the door shut, gives us a smile and a thumbs-up, and we wait.

And wait.

And wait.

"Joe, what's going on?" I ask over the intercom.

"Ah, Mr. President, a slight problem," he says.

"What is it?"

A little hiss of static. "It seems the tower isn't satisfied that this is an unannounced night training flight. And a colonel is racing over here right now to stop us."

Nick Zeppos is the only other one here who's wearing the Black Hawk's comm gear, and he catches my eye, looks concerned.

I say, "Joe, what are you planning?"

He chuckles. "I'm planning a communications problem, that's all."

The pitch and sound of the Black Hawk's engines increase, and there's a slight sway as we take off and head out into the night, to the east.

Mel, I think, *just a few more minutes.*

Just a few more minutes.

CHAPTER 114

Mel Keating takes a quick break, eyes her progress. By working with the jagged piece of wooden shelving, she has widened the hole so that she can put her head and shoulders up into it, but her hands are blistered and cut.

So what?

Mel takes a long swallow of warm bottled water and then stands on the pile of dirt and rock so she can work with the wood up higher.

Shove, shove, shove.

Scrape, scrape, scrape.

Rocks and dirt and bits of stone shower down, getting into her hair and mouth, and she keeps on frantically digging.

Scrape.

Shove.

Mel waits.

What's that?

Voices, from beyond the door.

Mel's breathing quickens.

If the door is unlocked and someone comes in, what can she say? That she was suddenly struck by inspiration from Mom's career and decided to start an archaeological dig in the last hours of her life?

No, Mel thinks, stepping off the fresh dirt and rock pile and going to the door.

If the door opens, she's going to take this piece of jagged wood and shove it into the throat of the first guy to come through.

No begging, no crying.

Going out like a badass.

She waits.

No more voices.

The faint sound of music being played on a radio.

"All right, then," Mel whispers.

Back to the dirt pile.

Shove, scrape, shove—

The piece of wood slides up unexpectedly, and a burst of cold air comes down and caresses her dirty and sweaty face.

She's broken free to the outside!

Mel coughs, wipes her face, and quickly goes back to work.

So close.

So very, very close.

More rocks and dirt trickle out and tumble down.

She pushes up and—

Falls.

Her right ankle screams at her and the pain just radiates up her leg and spine.

Mel rolls over, clenches her fist, tries to take deep breaths.

Get up, she thinks. *Get up.*

You're the daughter of two tough and determined parents.

Prove it.

Mel gets up, hopping on her good foot, gets the piece of wood, and starts hammering away again.

Nothing is going to stop her now.

Nothing.

CHAPTER 115

The first nearly one hundred miles of our journey goes over flat water, the famed Gulf of Sidra, and Joe quietly says over the intercom, "Feet dry, Mr. President. We're in Libyan airspace now."

"Copy that, Joe," I say, and look to my fellow warriors inside the Black Hawk. As with so many other missions I've been on, each person here is in his or her own world. There's no rah-rah, no speeches, no words of derring-do. We all sit quietly, a couple of us drinking from water bottles, others just staring out or trying to sleep.

The steady roar of the engines, the red-lit interior, the straps and webbing and gear—it's all so familiar to me. I've been inside Black Hawks like this countless times, either on training missions or real ops, and it's like being with an old friend, save for one thing.

This isn't an official operation or a training exercise.

It's the real deal. We're out to rescue my daughter.

And while failure in training or in a real-life op can be expected, or even excused, not tonight.

No failure.

It cannot happen.

I will not allow it.

We speed along into the night, above the rocky desert and landscape of nighttime Libya.

My earphones crackle.

"Two minutes, Mr. President," Joe says. "Two minutes."

"Copy that," I say. I take off the headset, rearrange my Peltor ComTac headset, and hold up two fingers to the rest of my crew.

"Two minutes!" I call out. "Two minutes!"

We put on our respective helmets, lower the night-vision gear, switch it on. Instantly everything inside the helicopter has a ghostly green glow. I yell out, "Move tight, move quick, let's get this done!"

The Black Hawk's angle of approach and speed change, and the crew chief for the Black Hawk joins us, toggles free the near sliding door, pushes it open.

Cold night air rushes in and the ground is coming up close, rock walls dangerously near, and then we lift up and go down, and there's the narrow wadi that Joe picked out earlier, and the helicopter's speed changes again, we lower, lower, hover—

Off we go, one by one.

Nick Zeppos is the last one off and we huddle, our heads lowered, as the Black Hawk zooms up and out, and we're alone.

I stand up.

"Comm check," I say. "Matt's here."

"Claire."

"Nick."

"Alejandro."

"David," says the last voice.

"All coming in, loud and clear," I say, scanning in all directions, checking out the overhead rocks and flat cliffs.

Nothing.

I say, "Nick and Alejandro, you're up. We'll be following in ten minutes."

"Copy that," Nick says.

"Copy that," Alejandro says.

They move up the rocks like young mountain goats, skipping up and ahead, and the tightness in my chest eases some.

We came in cold. No shots, no mortar rounds falling, nothing. The sound of the Black Hawk is a distant humming noise. There's no moon tonight but the sky is so clear and cold that even the starlight is giving us pretty good visibility, even without our NVGs.

I check my watch and its glowing numerals.

Ten minutes have passed.

"Saddle up, folks," I say, and we start climbing.

After another fifteen minutes of climbing and hiking, pausing every few minutes to check our surroundings, we get to the narrow dirt road leading up steeply to Asim Al-Asheed's compound. We all take a knee under cover of nearby rocks and boulders.

I give the area a slow 360-degree observation.

All quiet, all lifeless.

The M4—with safety off and a round in its chamber—is firm in my gloved hands.

My headset remains quiet.

Up the road, Nick and Alejandro are on the job, and I know enough not to bother them. I look up the steep and narrow road.

A couple of days ago, Mel traveled up here, saw these very rock walls, breathed this same mountain air.

So damn close.

My earphones come to life. "Matt, this is Nick."

"Nick, go," I say.

"Matt, we're good here. Waiting on Alejandro."

And that is that. One man or teen boy, dreaming of glory and jihad and heaven, sitting in the cold dirt, working his shift as a guard for one of the most wanted terrorists in the world, quietly got a sound-suppressed 5.56mm round between his eyes.

"Copy that, Nick," I whisper. "Good job."

Next up: Alejandro.

We wait.

Nothing moves, nothing calls out in the dark night.

Just everything bathed in green ghost light.

I wait.

I check my watch.

Slow minutes pass.

"Nick, this is Matt," I say. "Status?"

"Matt, this is Nick," he replies. "Waiting on Alejandro."

Aren't we all.

Waiting.

I shift my weight, impatience starting to gnaw at me.

Let him do his job, I think.

But so many things could have gone wrong in the short time since we've landed.

Alejandro being ambushed.

Or stumbling and falling into a crevasse.

Or not finding the guard, who's moved his position.

Who might be seeing us now.

Reporting back to Asim via his handheld radio that an armed party is coming his way.

I toggle my Transmit switch. "Alejandro," I whisper. "This is Matt. Status?"

No reply.

Again: "Alejandro, this is Matt. Status?"

Nothing.

I feel like it's all slipping away.

CHAPTER 116

❖

Jiang Lijun looks up as the door is unlocked and Faraj enters, holding a small flashlight in his right hand.

"It's time," Faraj says, coming to him, kneeling down to undo the locks holding Jiang's chains to the chair.

Jiang asks, "Why so late?"

Faraj says, "Asim had to wait for his meal, and then he wanted some private time with his driver, Taraq. He's planning on packing up everyone and leaving later tonight, after he finishes his task."

Jiang rubs at his hands and ankles, stands up. "What task?"

Faraj steps back, drops the chains and locks on the dirt floor. "He wants you to witness him killing Mel Keating, so you can go back to Beijing and tell your masters that you've met a true man of God, who cannot be bribed or tempted by the riches of this life. Then he plans to use a body double in the years ahead, releasing a videotape here and there, to torment Matt Keating that his daughter is still alive. At some point, decades from now, after years of Keating's mental anguish, my cousin plans to tell the truth and reveal the location of Mel Keating's bones. His final means of revenge."

Jiang steps up. "But…you can't allow that."

Faraj gestures with the flashlight. "I won't. Come along. I'll take care of my cousin, and then we'll get Mel Keating."

Jiang thinks quickly. "My pistol. Return it to me, please."

Faraj shakes his head. "Be thankful we let you keep your protective vest. That's all you'll need."

Jiang follows Faraj out to the darkness of the compound, happy that, yes, he is keeping his protective vest, and also knowing that hidden away in the vest are a few items that will prove useful in the next few minutes. Thankfully, these brave and stupid warriors didn't take the time to closely search him when he was captured.

Still, he thinks, he wishes he had his QSZ-92 9mm pistol at his side.

But he will go ahead.

In planning, wishes don't count.

It takes just a few minutes to come to a large building in the center of the compound. It's a starlit night, and there are two flickering fires in old oil drums, and Jiang shakes his head at the carelessness of Asim's fighters. No discipline at all.

Ahead, Asim calls out, "Ah, cousin. Glad to see our Chinese friend is with us. Please, come along. What a historic night!"

Asim is in front of a heavy wooden door and Jiang again takes in the cold mountain air. A lovely night to do what must be done and, most of all, to live.

Jiang allows himself the hope that he will live out the night. And he decides to try once more, no matter what Faraj has offered.

He says, "Asim, I'm again pleased to see you…and again, I have to ask…will you let the girl free in my custody? And no payment will be made nor offered. Then I will return to my superiors in Beijing and tell them of you, not only a man of God but also a man of mercy."

In the dim light, Jiang sees Asim's face widen into a smile, and he mentions something to one of the two men guarding the entrance, and a laugh is shared.

Jiang thinks, *Well, it was worth the effort.*

Asim says, "A good try, but don't be afraid, Jiang. You will survive tonight. I give you my vow. You and the West, sometimes you forget the importance of God, of vows, of self-discipline. Like my dear cousin Faraj."

Faraj looks concerned, and Jiang takes one careful step back.

Asim goes on. "Faraj is loyal, smart, and a good fighter to have at your side. But he is always tempted by the technologies. Like drones. Or battery-operated coolers for forbidden drinks. Or listening devices."

He quickly steps next to Faraj, flings an arm across his shoulder. "Even if you don't need any of these technologies. Like when a good man with good ears listening through an open window can tell you all you need to know."

Faraj moves quickly but Asim is faster, pulling a knife from underneath his vest and plunging it into his cousin's chest.

CHAPTER 117

And then, like a voice from above, Alejandro comes through.

"Matt, this is Alejandro," he says.

"Alejandro, this is Matt. Go."

He says calmly, "Sorry for the delay, Matt. My guy left his post, went to water a rock. I took him out midstream."

Sweet relief courses through me. I say, "Nick, Alejandro, proceed. We'll meet you at the jump-off points."

We three stand up as one and resume our pace, the only sound being the gentle *crunch-crunch* of our booted feet on the dirt road as we climb. We don't hurry but we don't move slowly, either. Just methodical and on point, our heads swiveling around, always looking, seeing, evaluating.

The road widens.

Rocks and boulders are clustered at either side.

The land flattens out.

We move to the right, going in and around the rocks and scree.

I hold up a hand.

We pause.

Voices.

We move slower, spreading out.

I look through a gap of rocks, see the buildings come into view.

Two oil drums burning.

Armed men moving around, in small groups of two or three.

Laughter.

A flapping sound as the large tarpaulin covering four pickup trucks moves in the breeze. I quietly join Nick and Alejandro there as David and Claire keep moving and go behind the low stone wall, heading to the front of the center building.

That building, close up against the rise of rocks, is now in clear view.

Mel is in there, I think.

My daughter is there.

Right there.

Just a few seconds more.

All that's gone on during the past few weeks, from her kidnapping, to the murder of her boyfriend, Tim, to the dark horror of that beheading video and the hopeful hints that she was still alive, to my own journey here—all of those memories and thoughts roar through me as I rest on this cold stony ground in Libya.

Now, less than fifty meters away, my daughter waits.

I check my watch.

Almost time.

CHAPTER 118

Mel Keating bends over in her cell, coughing and choking after a big burst of dirt slams into her mouth and nose.

She stands up, grabs her last bottle of water, takes a swallow.

Close.

Mel caps the water bottle.

Puts the bottle under her shirt, starts working her way up the hole.

Head through.

Shoulders.

Squirm.

Elbows to the side, digging in, digging in…

She stops.

Plugged.

Damn it!

She worms her way back down, nearly losing her glasses

in the process—damn it again!—and she's back on the floor, breathing hard.

Picks up the length of wood.

Digs some more.

More rocks tumble down.

There.

Should be enough.

Has to be enough.

Mel goes back, stands on the little mound of dirt.

Voices, getting louder and getting closer.

She looks up the hole and convinces herself she sees the night sky and stars up there.

Freedom.

Someone starts unlocking the door.

Out of time.

CHAPTER 119

Asim leads Jiang Lijun into the single-story stone building, glad to see the Chinese intelligence officer being quiet and humble. For too long this foreigner had his hands on the proverbial purse strings, dispensing money and weapons and supplies when it suited Jiang and his masters, but now Asim is in charge. He will show Jiang the most sought woman on the planet—Mel Keating, the president's daughter—and will show Jiang the power of his hand and blade.

Then the Chinese man will be let loose.

Asim has lied many times over the years during his jihad, but at least this time he is telling the truth.

"Come, come," Asim says, "and in a very few minutes, you will be free."

Asim goes past the old stalls, stocked with supplies and piled weapons and lit from above by single lightbulbs, and past two of his warriors, squatting, sipping cups of tea—he frowns upon recalling how much Faraj enjoyed the infidel's alcohol—and he stops at the locked wooden door to Mel's cell.

Another of his armed warriors nods and steps aside.

Asim looks to Jiang.

The Chinese intelligence officer's face is blank.

Asim produces the key, unlocks the door, and pushes it open.

It halts.

He pushes again.

It grinds a bit and stops again.

What is going on? Asim wonders.

"You," he says to a warrior. "Help me get this door open."

The warrior slings his AK-47 over his shoulder and joins Asim in pushing the door open. It takes a few long seconds, and then something breaks free and the door swings in.

Asim quickly sees what happened.

Mel inserted a piece of broken wood under the bottom of the door, blocking it.

"Didn't work, did it, Mel?" Asim says, walking in.

The cell is empty.

Mel isn't there.

"What?" he shouts, stunned.

He sweeps the room and sees a pile of dirt and something wiggling, and a pair of feet are disappearing up into a hole.

CHAPTER 120

Shoving that piece of wood underneath the door gave Mel a few precious seconds, and yes, it worked, it worked, it worked.

She kicks with her feet, uses her elbows again, and her head is through, hands up and on the loose rock and dirt part of this roof, and she squirms and feels like a damn cork popping out of a champagne bottle.

Mel rolls to her side, flattens out, takes a few quick breaths.

Out.

Now what?

The mountain here is nearly a sheer cliff.

And the road is out. Too easy to be spotted. And that flat place over there with the stone wall: no, too exposed.

There's a mess of broken rocks and boulders off to the other side of the compound, and it looks easier to get there. Lots of places to hide and maneuver. She has the bottle of water stuck in her clothes, and she still has slippers on her feet from that sweet old woman who took her in.

Mel crawls to the edge of the roof, peers down, sees nobody moving around, though that's going to change in less than a minute or two, when Asim races out and starts raising hell.

She moves around, lowers herself down as quietly as she can, dangling, her hands on the sharp stone edge of the roof.

Mel drops to the ground, happy that she remembers at the last second to drop on her good foot, not her injured one.

Then she starts running to freedom.

CHAPTER 121

❖

Jiang Lijun steps forward into the cell. Ahead of him is the guard with the AK-47, and in front of the guard is Asim, reaching up with both hands, trying hard to grab Mel Keating's quickly disappearing feet.

Jiang takes it all in and moves quickly.

Hand under his vest and shirt, past two energy bars and a water flask, he grabs a ceramic tube, invisible to metal detectors.

Pulls it out, places the butt end against the base of the skull of Asim's guard, quickly pulls a plastic ring on the end of a nylon cable.

Thump.

The single-shot weapon fires a .32-caliber slug into the man's head, instantly killing him.

He drops.

Asim starts turning around.

Jiang tugs at the dead man's AK-47.

The sling is tangled up.

Asim doesn't say a word, just reaches into his vest and pulls out his knife.

Jiang gets the AK-47 free but it's in the wrong position, the muzzle end facing Jiang, the butt facing Asim, who is coming at him.

One of Jiang's training officers, many years ago:

Run to a gun, run away from a knife.

Jiang punches the wooden stock end of the AK-47 into Asim's forehead, and Asim stumbles back, falls down.

Jiang races from the cell, closes the door, wishes he had the key.

Wastes two seconds looking for something to tie off the door or block it.

Nothing.

He lowers his head, puts the AK-47 over his shoulder, starts walking down the corridor, past the stalls, past the piles of supplies, past the two armed men sipping tea who thankfully ignore him.

Outside into the cold night air.

Looks as though someone has hauled away the body of Faraj, and Jiang is happy about that, for Faraj is—was—one smart fellow who figured out what really happened when Asim's family was killed.

Good he's gone.

But where is Mel?

She wouldn't go to the road. Too far away, too many men walking around, and she is slight and small and would stand out as she's not carrying a weapon.

There.

To the east, where there's a mess of boulders and rough rocks, leading down into an incline.

Jiang moves out.

Also hidden in his vest is a transponder.

Once he grabs Mel and flips the switch, a contract team with a helicopter will be heading out to pick them up and fly them both back to the Chinese Embassy, and to safety.

He pulls out one more tool, a small night-vision monocular, and he puts it up to his left eye and—

There she is, just as he thought.

Heading to the rocks.

CHAPTER 122

After the weeks of fear, sadness, and terror, I'm in place, I'm in position. I'm with Alejandro and Nick near the four pickup trucks, keeping watch on the west side of the building where Mel is being kept.

The two oil drums are still ablaze, three or four armed men clustered around them, trying to stay warm. Other men walk in and out of the three stone buildings nearby, all carrying weapons.

No innocents here, I think, *save my girl.*

"Matt, this is David," he says over the radio.

"David, go," I say.

"Claire and I are in position," he whispers. "Just to let you know, there's activity at the main door. Armed tangos going in and out."

I say, "David, is Mel visible?"

"Negative, Matt," David says. "No sighting of Mel."

"Copy," I say. "Crew, light 'em up."

We all switch on our infrared lasers, which are invisible to the naked eye but visible with our NVGs and deadly useful for pinpointing our targets. Instantly five thin rods of light flare out and target five armed men near the building.

I say, "We go in three, starting… now."

"Copy" is repeated to me four times, in four different voices.

"Three," I say.

My little girl, Mel, five or six, screeching because she fell into a fire ant nest, running at me with arms held out: "Daddy, Daddy, Daddy!"

"Two," I say.

Mel at twelve, falling off a horse while taking lessons, lying motionless on the ground for long cold seconds until I see her start to move as I run across the dirt corral.

"One," I say.

Mel swimming at Lake Marie with heavy dark clouds on the horizon, and a bolt of lightning strikes a tree across the way, and me getting into a canoe and frantically paddling to her, with her laughing as I get to her: "Dad, what's the worry?"

I say, "Go."

We attack in a standard L-shaped ambush, with Claire and David eliminating any threat by the main door, and with us three current and former SEALs taking out everyone within the kill zone to the west of the building. There's muffled *thud thud thud*s for we're all using sound suppressors on our M4s.

Five men fall and then two more, and David says via my earpiece, "Main door clear, Matt."

"Copy that," I say, and Nick and Alejandro join me in moving quickly across the open rock and dirt field, Claire and David providing us with cover as we get to the door.

Technically and morally speaking, we've just killed seven men, and all I can think is, *Better you than me and my crew and my daughter.*

We get to the heavy wooden door with large hinges and Alejandro gets to work quick, and we ignore the two bodies sprawled on the ground.

He slaps a breaching charge on the lock, and we turn away as it snaps and flares to life, and then Nick grabs the door handle and pulls it open.

Alejandro is right behind Nick and tosses in one flash-bang grenade and then another, and the heavy *thump thump* seems to explode right out of the front door.

No doubt whoever's still alive out there in the other buildings will come running out to investigate and will be cut down by David and Claire.

Nick goes in, pivots left.

"Clear!"

Alejandro pivots right.

"Clear!"

I move down a stone hallway, smelling the burnt firecracker odor of the flash-bang grenades, proceed past piles of weaponry, pallets of weapons, one or two lightbulbs still burning after the blast of the flash-bangs, and—

A man comes out from one of the stalls, blinking his eyes, dragging an AK-47.

Training, experience, and memory all come back.

I shoot him in the forehead and twice in the chest.

I pivot left. Blanket and rations and teapot.

"Clear," I call out.

Nick and Alejandro follow me, and there's another three rounds fired off nearby, and Nick says, "Clear!"

Up ahead is another door.

It's ajar.

Alejandro throws his shoulder against it and the door opens wide, and *shit shit shit,* and I cry out "Mel!," seeing a body on the ground, blood around the head, thinking, *Too late, too late, oh, shit, we're too late!*

Nick kneels down, says, "Matt, it's a guy. No worries."

I give the room a quick glance.

Dirt in a corner.

I walk forward, look up.

A chimney or sluice pipe or something has been cleared free.

Was Mel here?

Or has she been taken away?

Alejandro says, "Sir, over here."

He's pointing to a flat rock, about a meter in width and height, part of the far wall.

Letters and numbers have been painted there.

MK
603

Nick says, "Her initials, maybe...but the numbers?"

"Six oh three," I say. "New Hampshire's area code."

I touch the letters. They feel sticky to the touch. Fruit or berry or something.

My clever, clever girl.

"Looks fresh," I say. "Guys, she was here, she was here just a while ago. Let's get moving."

We move in a single line, Nick taking the lead, me in the middle, Alejandro pulling up the rear.

I say, "Claire, David, this is Matt."

"Go," they both reply.

"Mel was here, but it looks like she might have escaped," I say. "David, work the stone wall to the south. Nick and Alejandro will work the buildings and area to the west. I'll head east, to that rocky area. Claire, get on top of this building and give us overwatch."

A chorus of "Copy"s and then we burst outside, and we split up to find my daughter, and I think again, *Clever girl.*

But please, God, not too clever.

We've got to find her in the next few minutes, before our Tunisian pilot comes back to retrieve us, because I'm not boarding that Black Hawk without her.

CHAPTER 123

After it happens, about thirty seconds after getting off the roof of the old stables, Mel Keating thinks it's her damn lousy night vision that screws everything up. She hasn't gotten far when she freakin' bumps into somebody walking in the darkness, and she tries to spin around and keep on strolling, but the guy says something.

She ignores him, keeps on walking.

Another burst of Arabic, and then *crap crap crap,* a second armed guy joins the chorus, and they grab her and feel her up, and one and then the other realizes who they have.

She struggles, squirms, tries to kick them both, but they are strong and hold her and start dragging her back to the buildings, and one starts yelling, *"Alshaykh! Alshaykh! Alshaykh!"*

And just like in those damn horror movies where the monster comes out of the darkness to get you, an angry Asim Al-Asheed strides into view, carrying a small tactical flashlight, an armed guy following him. He speaks in quick Arabic to the two jerks holding her, and then he says, "Mel Keating…you are about to get what you deserved since your miserable birth."

Two explosions echo out and startle them all, and there's muffled gunfire, and Mel yells to him, not knowing for sure but wanting to taunt the bastard, "Speaking of getting what you deserve…hear that, asshole? It's my dad and his buds, coming to get me and kill you all."

And like magic, she hears at the same time a *whizz-splat-grunt,* and the man holding her to the left drops, and then another *whizz-splat-grunt,* and the guy behind Asim falls to the ground, and she falls and rolls and starts crawling away from all the gunfire.

Those rocks, she thinks.

Good place to hide out until Dad, or the SEALs, or the Rangers, or whoever's out there makes their presence known.

Mel continues to crawl on the rough dirt and rock, keeping her head down.

CHAPTER 124

❖

Nick Zeppos and Alejandro Lopez work their way around to the west side of the building, and Claire announces through their respective earpieces, "Eyes open, guys. Two nearest buildings to you: lots of tangos running out."

Nick says, "Copy," and the NSA chick sure isn't fooling, because the three buildings nearest to where Mel was kept—damn, the place is swarming with armed guys coming out of doors and side entrances and even one open window.

Best cover they can get is a slight dirt berm, and they drop down and get to work. It's not much cover, because every time they take out a guy running out of one of the houses, yelling *"Allahu Akbar"* and spraying widely with machine-gun fire, two others fly out, taking up positions around the rocky ground near the buildings. These tangos start firing, and bits of dirt and rock fly up as they strike the berm that Nick and Alejandro are hiding behind.

Thud thud thud.

Thud thud thud.

He and Alejandro keep up a steady and calm fire. Nick says, "Changing mags!" when his bolt action snaps back, and he pops out the empty magazine, slams a full one into the M4, releases the bolt, and resumes firing, following the thin guiding rod of his infrared laser sight.

A few seconds later, Alejandro echoes Nick's actions, saying "Changing mags!," and Nick keeps focused, lasing one target after another, hearing a loud *crack* as Claire on overwatch takes down one of the tangos.

Initially, the fighters out there come running out in the typical spray and pray pattern, holding up their AK-47s and emptying the entire magazine in one frightened trigger pull, but a few over there know what they're doing and are firing back with hard, disciplined fire.

Alejandro says, "Would love to have a Warthog up there."

"Yeah, make it two," Nick says.

He spots something sparkling coming at them and yells "Grenade!" and huddles up, holding his helmet down, and—

Blam!

He looks up, sees another set of sparkles.

Blam!

"Shit," Nick says, resuming his position, returning fire, taking down one and then another tango trying to rush their positions.

It's too quiet at his right.

Nick whirls. Alejandro is curled up on his side. Nick rolls over and says, "Al, you okay? You okay?"

He groans. "You *estúpido,* do I look okay?" Alejandro groans again. "Piece of shrapnel nailed my right wrist. Feels like the fucker's broken. Help me get my SIG Sauer out."

Nick works quickly, tugging out Alejandro's pistol from the

holster, hands it over to his partner. He gets his M4 back up in time to take down two tangos who were only two meters away.

Thud thud thud.

Nick says, "Claire, this is Nick. We need more cover fire."

Two more shots from his M4. A sharper sound as the wounded Alejandro uses his 9mm pistol.

"Claire, we need help over here."

But Claire doesn't answer.

CHAPTER 125

❖

Jiang Lijun stays low, moving zigzag, knowing that the Americans are here, but he's still determined to grab Mel Keating first and bring her to safety, for the benefit of his country and his career.

But he has to be careful because there's a huge firefight breaking out over to the west, and he doesn't want to be caught up in any cross fire between the Americans and Asim's men. The Americans would shoot him because he's a male carrying an AK-47, and Asim's men would shoot him just because they are scared now and shooting at everything that looks threatening.

He takes cover behind a pile of scrap metal and crushed oil barrels, and he scans and scans with his monocular NVD, and yes, there she is, hiding behind those two cracked boulders.

Now.

Jiang squirms ahead, and with the pile of scrap metal behind him, he gets closer and calls out, "Mel! Mel Keating! US SEALs! Come on up, I can see you!"

Years back, Dad let her and Mom observe a night exercise, and man, that sure as hell seems like what's going on over there. Lots of gunfire, somebody's using a heavy-caliber bolt-action fire—easy to identify because of the hard *crack!* that's fired in a slow pattern—and now grenades are being tossed around over there.

"Mel!" a strong voice calls out. "Mel Keating! US SEALs! Come on up, I can see you!"

Oh, what a wonderful flood of relief and joy rushes through her upon hearing her name, hearing who's here to rescue her, and it must be Dad's buds, ones who'd go anywhere at any time to rescue one of their own.

"Coming!" she says, and she scrabbles up the rocks, seeing a squatting shape, slightly outlined by the fires breaking out on the west side of the area.

"Hurry, hurry," the man urges. "We need to get you out of here."

"Don't I know it," she yells back, nearly laughing. "Almost there!"

And here she is, Jiang thinks.

The president's daughter, after all this time, all the setbacks and travel, emerging from the broken boulders and rocks.

"Here," he says, grabbing her hand. "This way."

He holds her hand and she laughs and then—

She digs in.

Tugs her hand free.

"Who the hell are you?" she demands.

Jiang says, "Navy SEALs."

"Which team?"

"What?"

"Which team?" she says, quickly backing away. "And that's an AK, not an M4 or an HK. And you don't have the right gear. Where's your helmet? Your NVGs?"

Jiang grabs her collar as she tries to run away and wrestles with her, and she bites his hand and he says, "Damn it, girl, I'm trying to rescue you!"

Up on the roof of the building where Mel was kept, Claire Boone of the NSA is having one hell of a good time, although she'd never admit that to anyone at the agency, especially at the debriefing that's coming her way when this unauthorized op wraps up.

But this is like being the baddest, meanest cosplayer in the world, shooting evil guys from up on high. One of her problems with being on the spectrum is that her mind is always working, always racing, and she's thinking of the gamers she knows in the community, and maybe she could go to a couple of them with an investment and an idea for a single-shooter game, called Overwatch, of course...

She sweeps the southern side of the area, sees Secret Service agent David Stahl behind that small and crumbling rock wall, and he looks okay, and then she sweeps over to the west, and boy, those two SEAL guys are really in a hole, and she fires off three rounds, the spent brass tinkling on the rock roof.

Claire wants to keep pouring fire on those jerks threatening Nick and Alejandro, but she has responsibilities up here, she sure does, and she rolls herself around so she's facing east, and she easily makes out the IR laser sight coming from Matt Keating—the former president; she still can't believe she's with him—and she scans and stops cold.

A guy holding an AK-47 in one hand is fighting someone smaller, lighter, and, God be praised, with long hair.

She carefully aims her way to the slug and there are voices in her earpiece, and she ignores them as she gently pulls the trigger, as she's done thousands of times before in practice and in real life. This crazy cold night in the mountains of Libya is as real as it gets.

CHAPTER 126

Claire's calm voice in my earpiece stops me cold in my search, which has been going on for long empty minutes spent scanning, kneeling down, looking behind and in front of me, all the while trying to tamp down the fear that's saying to me, *Suppose you can't find her?*

Claire says, "Matt, just took down an armed tango who was holding Mel. She's about thirty meters to the east of where I'm located, near a pile of scrap metal. Go get her."

Go get her!

I turn my head and spot the scrap metal Claire's pointed out. About a second ago I was tired, hip aching, frustrated and fearful, and now I feel like I'm twenty years younger as I race toward where Mel is.

Go get her!

Those words will burn in joy inside me forever, along with memories of the instructors yelling out, "Congrats, gents: Hell

Week is over!," of Samantha saying, "I do," of the doctor calling out, "She's a girl, and she looks fine!," and of Samantha kissing me hard one late night in Texas and whispering, "Congratulations, Congressman."

I run and run, my weapon still in my hands, and I'm scanning and looking, and as I get closer to that scrap metal pile, I yell out, "Mel, it's Dad! Stay put! I'll be there in a second!"

Go get her!

I round the pile of rusted metal and oil drums and there's a body slumped over to the far left, and someone else hunched over near me, like she's trying to burrow into the ground, and I race up and just a few feet away I say, "Mel, it's Dad, let's go. Mel, it's me."

The shape pops up and whirls around and it's Asim Al-Asheed, and as I raise my M4 to fire I feel his knife stab deep into me.

CHAPTER

127

Secret Service agent David Stahl hears the firefight going on about seventy or so meters away, but he focuses on his job, which is sweeping this long and slow crumbling stone wall, and so far, there's nothing.

Through his headset he hears the calm chatter of the two SEALs and Claire, the NSA woman up there coolly firing off .308 full-metal-jacket rounds at the terrorists trying to get to Nick and Alejandro. In about one minute, David is calling off this search and going back to the compound.

Claire's calm voice brings a smile to his face and sends a warming joy throughout his cold and tired body.

"Matt," she says, "just took down an armed tango who was holding Mel. She's about thirty meters to the east of where I'm located, near a pile of scrap metal. Go get her."

David toggles the Transmit switch on his radio. "Matt, this is David, do you need me?"

He keeps low, starts going back up the stone wall, still taking cover because he doesn't know how many jihadists might be out here in these mountains, coming in to lend a hand to Asim Al-Asheed and his fighters.

"Matt, this is David. Can I assist?"

Still no answer.

He stops.

"Claire, this is David. Do you have visual on Matt and Mel?"

She instantly replies, "Not at the moment. Last I saw, Mel had hit the dirt, and her dad was approaching. Both are behind a pile of scrap metal. I—"

"Break, break," says the strained voice of Nick. "David, could really use your help over here."

David is torn. His Secret Service responsibility is over there, with the former POTUS and his daughter. He really should move over there.

But tonight he's a Marine.

Once a Marine, always a Marine.

You never leave anybody behind, never refuse a request for aid.

"Nick, on my way," he says, and he starts running toward the sound of the guns.

Asim feels strength course through him as he knocks down the former president, the man's weapon flying out of his hands, even his radio gear tumbling away. Asim also feels the quick joy of having his knife cut into the man who killed his family.

They are struggling near a mound of old metal and oil barrels, and being on top of the man, Asim quickly gauges he's old and out of shape. Oh, the weak infidel is struggling, holding on to Asim's wrists, but Asim is certain a few more seconds will end it. Even with his head throbbing from the attack from that damn Chinese spy—and Asim plans to take a week to kill him once he's found him—Asim feels the strength of righteous rage flowing through him.

He pushes down on Matt Keating's wrists, and in the dark he says, "Just you and me, Matt Keating, and you have no Secret Service, no Army, no drones, no satellites. It's like the days of old, the strong versus the weak, and after I kill you, I will go find your girl and kill her, too."

Asim pushes again, his entire weight on top of the president, knowing he's only moments away from breaking the man.

CHAPTER 128

My left wrist is burning something awful and a small rational part of me knows that Asim has cut me right down to the bone, but the larger rational part of me is realizing the son of a bitch has me and has me good. He's muscular, he's been living in Spartan conditions these past few years—while I've grown soft in politics—and he has a burning rage coming down on top of me.

My comm gear is off, my M4 is over there somewhere, and there's a knife and a SIG Sauer pistol by my feet, but both weapons could be back in the States for all the good they can do me.

I have my left hand on Asim's right wrist, right hand on his left wrist, and maybe I'm woozy or adrenaline-fueled, but I'm sure starlight is glittering off that sharp knife in his right hand.

I try pushing, kicking, sliding, but he matches me, move for move, as he pushes down harder on me. He's murmuring words of revenge and destruction and Allah and I'm not paying attention to what he's saying, and I'm definitely not answering him, because I can't spare the strength and the oxygen.

It's easy to see what's going to happen.

My cut left wrist is going to fail me in a few seconds, and with his knife hand free, he's going to go for my throat, and when he's sure I'm dead, he'll go hunting for Mel.

I finally decide to yell out, "Mel! Run for it! Get out of here! Head to the rock wall to the south!"

Oh, damn, that drew some strength from me, and Asim laughs, starts spouting again about revenge and death, and yes, my left wrist is weakening, it's hurting, and I know I'm just seconds away from calling it a night.

It's almost peaceful.

It'll be quick, and Mel will join up with the others, and she'll be safe.

But I keep on fighting.

Wonder if I'm going to get a state funeral, the first ex-POTUS not to die in bed.

Asim whispers, "Give up, Matt Keating, give up…I promise to make it quick…quicker than when you killed my wife and my daughters…"

I try twisting and pulling his other hand away, but his strong wrist barely moves. If I pull away now and try to put both hands on the hand holding the knife, he'll just use his other hand to throttle me.

A younger me would be able to lift up with my legs and throw him off balance, but I'm no longer the younger me.

Soon I'll no longer be me.

"Mel!" I yell for the last time. "Run!"

Blood is streaming down my wrist, which wobbles, weakens, and it's close, very close to bending.

Thud!

Asim gasps and falls back. Freed, I quickly sit up, pull my SIG Sauer, and I'm on top of him now and press the muzzle end of my pistol right under his chin, and I say, "You talk too much."

And I pull the trigger twice, blowing off the top of his head.

I sit back, exhausted.

A shadow comes forward.

Holding a long piece of metal.

A tentative voice. "Dad, is that you?"

I say, "Oh, Mel, yes, yes, it's me."

And we hug and both sob and the dad part of me just doesn't want to let her go, but the SEAL part—*Are there more bad guys out there? And Jesus, my wrist hurts!*—says, "C'mon, hon, let's get you out of here."

CHAPTER 129

Mel helps me get my gear back, and with my comm set secure again, I say, "Break, break, this is Matt. I've got Mel. Pull back to the exfil point. Pull back to the exfil point."

She starts to move, and I say, "Hold on. Get that rucksack off me, will you?"

"Dad, are you hurt?"

"Just a scratch," I say. "C'mon, Mel, hurry."

The rucksack falls to the ground and I say, "Open it up, put what's in there on, and then we'll get out of here."

She unzips the top, pulls out a bullet-resistant vest, which I help her put on, and then a small ballistic helmet, which she gets on without my help. Now that she's dressed for a fire zone, I put my bleeding left arm around her and start moving as quick as possible, still keenly aware of my surroundings, my M4 in my right hand.

The amount of gunfire has sharply dropped, meaning that

most of Asim's men are dead, wounded, or have headed up into the mountains for safety. I spot our exfil point, and through my NVGs I see movement there and two IR laser beams probing out, exploring for emerging targets.

"Matt, coming in," I call out as I clamber over the lone stone wall, and Mel is with me, and she instantly says, "My dad's hurt. Can someone help him?"

David comes over and Mel closes in, and says in an excited and credulous voice, "Agent Stahl? Is that you?"

He kneels in front of me, starts cutting away my BDU shirt-sleeve, and says, "Of course, Mel. Just because you're halfway across the world doesn't mean we won't come to protect you." Then, to me: "Jesus, Matt, what did you do to yourself?"

I say, "Got cut by Asim."

David pours water over my wound, and I wince and turn away, and he says, "Where is he now?"

"In another place, trying to explain what he's been doing these past years." I'm tired and my wrist is hurting, feels red-hot, but Mel is sitting right next to me, protected, and I look down the length of the wall and see that Nick is keeping watch on the compound, a bandaged Alejandro is doing the same, and Claire Boone is…

Checking out another person?

"David," I say. "Who's that with Claire? We're not taking prisoners."

He presses a wad of QuikClot combat gauze to my wrist to stop the bleeding, and then starts tightly wrapping a compression bandage against the wound. "You'll need some serious stitches once we get back to Tunisia."

"Yeah, I'm sure, but who's the guy with Claire?"

David laughs. "A Chinese national. Claims to be a field rep for the China State Construction Engineering Corporation. Complete with business card and official ID. Claire says she saw him tussling with Mel a few minutes ago, thought he was a bad guy. Shot him but he was wearing a vest, managed to break a few ribs. Claire heard him calling for help as she was coming back here."

I flex my wrist.

Still hurts.

I check my watch.

We've been on the ground for fifty-five very long minutes.

Where in hell is our Black Hawk?

I work my Motorola and switch frequencies, and call out, "Joe, Joe, Joe, this is Matt. Come in, please."

Nick fires off a shot.

"Joe, Joe, Joe, this is Matt. What's your status?"

No reply.

I say, "Damn it."

Mel says, "Who's Joe?"

"A Tunisian Special Forces pilot. He brought us in, and he's supposed to take us out. He's just a little late, that's all." To David I say, "If we have to, we'll take one of their trucks."

With regret in his voice, he says, "Sorry, Matt. We, uh... well, they're pretty shot up now. A bunch of the fighters tried to take shelter behind them. The three of us pretty much ventilated all of them."

Great, I think. *Just great.*

What now?

I put my uninjured arm around Mel, give her a quick squeeze.

Then, as the wind shifts, I faintly hear the finest sound an operator amidst enemy territory can ever hear: the thrumming sound of helicopter rotors.

Rescue coming in, courtesy of Sikorsky Aircraft.

"Prep for exfil!" I call out, and take out two infrared chem lights, break them to activate the chemicals, and toss them out into the small, flat, stony area. Invisible to the naked eye, to Joe and his copilot's NVGs they'll be a beacon they can't miss. Nick and Alejandro do the same as me, and for the Tunisian Special Forces guys up there, it must look like Times Square at night down here.

"A few minutes more, hon," I say to Mel. "Just a few minutes more."

Mel doesn't say anything, and I quickly become worried, but I listen harder and just hear my daughter sobbing into me.

CHAPTER 130

Faraj Al-Asheed knows he's dying, but he also knows he has bought himself several more minutes on earth due to having quickly moved after his cousin stabbed him, that filthy dog. Instead of instantly killing Faraj, the wound is just an eventually mortal one—mortal despite how much he has tried to bandage himself.

He's crawling to where he thinks the Americans are hiding, for their insolent voices are loud indeed, carrying easily in this cold thin air. He doesn't dare stand, and he doesn't dare move quickly, but move he does, dragging an AK-47 in his right hand.

Oh, Allah, how it hurts in his chest!

As he crawls along the rough ground, closer to the stone wall, final memories come to him: of his childhood in Tripoli, of staying alive during the civil wars and militia drive-bys, of getting that film school scholarship, of living in Paris and learning so much, and of committing *Haraam,* fornicating with the willing whores and drinking and eating forbidden foods.

Jihad, to which his cousin felt called, seemed like a road to redemption, something to eventually save his soul, but after years of bloodshed and combat, Faraj was tired of it, wanted to escape. But Asim—that *Ya Ibn el Sharmouta*—stopped him.

Oh, it hurts so much!

The sound of the helicopter grows louder. The aircraft is ready to rescue the Americans and perhaps even Mel Keating, take them back to their comfort and their secure lives.

One more memory comes to him before he leaves this world for the dark unknown out there.

He remembers the training classes for the raw recruits who found their way to his cousin's many camps and compounds. The first things Asim showed the young men were videos of the many jihad attacks over the years, from the USS *Cole* attack to the American embassy bombings in Africa and the sweet success of the fall of the Twin Towers in Manhattan, and subway and bus attacks in London, and other attacks in Brussels and Paris and Berlin…

Faraj watched the rapt expressions of those young men and heard their laughter and cheers at seeing civilians being torn to pieces or falling to their deaths from the tall buildings, and he didn't see holy warriors then or now.

Just young men with no future who took delight in breaking things, killing people, stomping on creatures. What Faraj learned in Paris as a young and vulnerable man, what is called nihilism.

It now makes sense.

He picks up the AK-47, ensures that the safety is off, and as the helicopter descends, he gets to his feet and pulls the trigger, enjoying those very last moments of being a killer.

CHAPTER 131

Our exfil flight is late but at least it's here, and I raise my voice and say, "Get Mel in first, then Alejandro and the Chinese guy, and we'll follow."

The light sticks scatter as the Black Hawk descends, dirt and gravel fly at us, and then it all goes to hell.

Gunfire erupts from the grounds beyond us and I turn and so does Nick, and through my NVGs and infrared laser spotter I see a wobbly man firing off an AK-47, and Nick and I shred him to pieces as Mel screams, "Daddy, I'm hit!"

Bodies tumble here and there, and the gunman gets off a few more rounds before he falls into the dirt, and Mel is pulled from underneath someone, and she's pushed into the helicopter. Claire helps the Chinese man aboard, and I shove Alejandro inside, and David is on the ground and Nick and I drag him in, and then the helicopter flares up and out, and the Tunisian crew chief slides the door shut.

Our pilot, Joe, yells from up front, "So sorry we're late…comm problems for real, tried to fix them, and then we gave up and came in."

I don't answer. I'm stepping frantically over extended legs and arms, getting to Mel, her face pale behind her eyeglasses. Claire is tearing off Mel's worn and filthy Dartmouth sweatshirt—I ache, thinking of the last time I saw this shirt, that sunny impossible day back at Lake Marie when Mel was safely heading off for a hike—and Claire looks and prods and says, "It's okay, Mr. President…I mean Matt. Shit. She's going to be okay. It looks worse than it is."

Mel turns and says, "Claire Boone…what the hell are you doing here?"

Claire paws through an open first aid kit from the Black Hawk. "Taking part in the rescue of your perky butt, it seems."

The helicopter gains altitude and speed, and I have to smile at seeing Mel and Claire together. I turn and I'm not smiling anymore.

David Stahl is on his back, helmet off, eyes open, mouth slowly working, his skin graying out. Nick is frantically trying to run an IV into David's bare arm, and Alejandro is desperately trying, with just one hand, to stop the bleeding from the large wound to David's neck.

I kneel and nudge Alejandro aside, and after Nick gets the needle in and stands up and hangs the IV bag from an overhead cable, he sees me and says, "I saw it all, Matt. The shooting started and David tossed Mel to the ground and threw himself on top of her. Just like the Secret Service, for sure."

I push a wad of QuikClot combat gauze against David's wound, and press another one on top, and that quickly soaks with blood, and I put another one on, and another one on, and they all soak through within seconds.

Alejandro whistles loudly toward the cockpit and says, "Joe! Get this bird moving! Any town or village nearby with a hospital! Get us there! Haul ass!"

Nick helps me with putting additional bandages and compresses on David's wound, but we exchange a look, and we know with cold certainty what's going to happen shortly, as David's skin color starts to fade even more.

His flickering eyes focus on me, and he whispers, "Hope, Hope, Hope..."

Nick says, "That's right, don't give up, keep hoping, pal, we're gonna get you to a clinic real soon now. Hang on, David, keep hoping."

My eyes tear up and I say, "No, he's using Mel's Secret Service code name. I'm Harbor, my wife is Harp...and Mel is Hope." I look up and yell, "Mel, get over here, now!"

She tries her best to keep her balance, her upper arm bandaged, as the helicopter increases its speed. Claire follows her, the chopper jumping and jerking, and Mel kneels down next to David, and I say, "David, look. She's here. Mel is safe. Hope is safe. You did your job."

Mel starts quietly crying and takes his right hand, squeezes it, and I take his left hand and do the same.

I say, "David, good job. You saved my daughter. You saved Hope."

His eyes flicker.

He smiles.

He whispers, "Good."

Then he dies.

CHAPTER 132

Georgetown University
Washington, DC

Rollie Spruce is a grad student at Georgetown, studying at the Georgetown University Law Center, but tonight he's working a double shift as a bartender at a convention being held at the university's hotel and conference center.

His feet hurt, his mouth is dry from last night's partying, and his hands shake a bit as he mixes cocktails and draws various beers for the convention attendees crowding the joint tonight.

Thing is, though, these guys—archaeologists and other types of dirt diggers—may be experts in their fields, but they're also experts at nursing drinks for hours and then tipping as if they, not him, were impoverished grad students.

Years back, in Vermont, Dad told him, "Rollie, learn a good trade like bartending. You'll always find work. In good times, people like to drink, and in bad times, they like to drink even more."

Good advice, and some nights he really does rake in the tips, but this night sure looks like another bust.

He's taking a minute to wash and rinse some cocktail glasses at his station when a woman sitting at the table in the near corner starts screaming loudly.

"What the..." he says, and he leans over the bar to see what the hell is going on, and then there's yells, shouts, applause, and the woman who was screaming just a moment ago is being hugged and kissed by a hell of a lot of people.

One of the guys breaks away from the table and comes rushing up to Rollie and says, "Quick, bud, a bottle of champagne. Best you got! Send it over to our table...hell, champagne for everyone. Drinks on the house!"

Rollie doesn't need to be told twice and gets to work as there's more cheering and applause. He sees that lots of people are standing, looking at the television set up above the bar. A few minutes ago, it was showing a Washington Nationals baseball game, but now there's a news anchor from one of the networks, smiling and talking into the camera.

Rollie doesn't know what the hell is going on, but on the TV screen behind the news anchor is a photo of Mel Keating, the former president's daughter—whom Rollie always thought was cute in a nerdy kind of way—and based on what Rollie sees, it looks as though she's alive and was rescued somewhere in North Africa.

Cool, Rollie thinks as he kneels down before the small refrigerator to check how many champagne bottles they have on ice.

Looks as though it's going to be a good night after all.

EPILOGUE

CHAPTER 133

Bangor International Airport
Bangor, Maine

We're flying home on a US Air Force Boeing C-40 passenger jet, provided to us following a happy phone call to Air Force secretary Kimberly Bouchard, who quickly dispatched it to Sfax-Thyna in Tunisia to pick us up.

As we descend into Bangor, we remain short two passengers: first, the Chinese man who claimed to be from the China State Construction Engineering Corporation, innocently caught in the cross fire.

Mel told me otherwise aboard our Black Hawk flight out of Libya, and I made sure that when we got back to Tunisia, the quiet and injured Chinese citizen was placed in the custody of a hard-looking man and equally hard-looking woman who were supposedly State Department representatives from our embassy in Tunisia.

They were to provide aid and assistance, of course, prior to his being brought to his country's embassy in Tunis.

The other missing passenger, the remains of one brave and dedicated Secret Service special agent David Stahl, is flying several hours behind us on a C-17 transport plane, heading to the Air Force base in Dover, Delaware.

It's been a quiet, long flight, with rows of empty seats beside us. Nick and Alejandro have slept a lot and ate the Air Force in-flight food, standard fare, and Mel and Claire have spent a couple of hours catching up and playing who's-gone-where and what-is-so-and-so-doing.

Now Mel is stretched out across two seats, a blanket draped over her, her head in my lap, as she sleeps and hopefully doesn't dream.

I've stayed awake most of the time. It's traditional among Special Forces to have a debrief following the end of a mission, but not this time. The only debrief is taking place in my memory, as I go over what happened, how it happened, could it have gone better? For though I'm grateful beyond words that my daughter is asleep in my lap, a terrible price was paid.

The pilot comes over the intercom. "Passengers, prepare for landing."

A uniformed female senior airman comes through and wakes up Nick, Claire, and Alejandro, tells them to fasten their safety belts, and she comes to Mel and me and smiles and shakes her head.

"You're fine, Mr. President," she says.

"Thanks."

After we land, we taxi some and the jet comes to a halt, and Mel wakes up, yawns, and I give her another hug and say, "Hold on. I nearly forgot to give this back to you."

From my pants pocket I take out her gold ring, her sixteenth birthday gift from her mother, and I slip it on her finger and her eyes tear right up. "Dad…God, I was dreading telling Mom that I might have lost it."

"Well, now you don't have to."

The forward door is opened, and a mobile stairway is rolled up. Nick and I try to help Mel down the stairs but she shakes us off—"I'm hurt, guys, not crippled." She goes down to the tarmac by herself, holding tight to the guardrails.

A black Chevrolet Suburban with tinted windows is waiting nearby, engine running. Nick, Alejandro, and Claire walk over to it, carrying their black duffel bags, and Mel and I follow them. Hugs and handshakes are exchanged—my wrist is aching but doing okay—and I say to them, "I can't tell you how much my wife and I owe you. We're in your debt. Forever."

Nick says, "No worries, sir. It was good to settle accounts for Boyd Tanner's capture and crucifixion. A few years late, but we took care of it, didn't we? Besides, we were never here. Or there. Alejandro and I were on leave. He hurt his arm doing something. Officially, that's what happened."

One more round of handshakes. "Safe travels," I say. "And for you, too, Claire."

To my daughter, Claire says, "You going to the Sidwell reunion this fall?"

Mel says, "God, no."

"Good. Neither am I. Keep in touch, okay?"

"Okay, girl."

They enter the Suburban and drive away, and Mel slips an arm through mine, and we head to the few structures that make up Bangor International Airport. Around the quiet airport are a lot of pine trees. A knot of people come running out of the near building, clapping and cheering, and leading the race is my wife, Samantha, and in seconds she's smothering Mel, and then me, and then the both of us, and so a precious and tearful few minutes pass.

A wheelchair is brought up and Mel says, "No, I don't need that," and her mother says, "You're sitting in that right now, young lady, and don't you say no."

Mel shrugs and sits down, and winces as her bandaged and slippered feet are put on the metal stands, and I see that the smiling people around me are my Secret Service detail from Lake Marie: agents Stacy Fields, Ron Dalton, Paula Chin, Emma Curtis, and Nicole Washington.

Agent Washington, who accompanied David Stahl and me when we escaped from Mary's Diner, and who sped out with our cell phones to lead FBI agents away from our trail, comes forward. I give her a hug and say, "You okay? You get caught?"

She laughs. "No. And I'm disappointed I wasn't. Guess the FBI didn't track a thing."

The agents all have black ribbons on their lapels, and it strikes me again, the sacrifice and duty of David, over in Libya, a long, long way from home, where he could have stayed safe.

But that wasn't David.

Madeline Perry, my chief of staff, comes through and hugs me, then Mel, then Samantha, and with tears running down her cheeks, she says, "Oh, Mr. President, you did it…you did it…welcome home, welcome home, sir."

I smile at her and say, "Sure as hell didn't do it by myself."

She says, "Sir…you probably weren't expecting this so soon, but there's a huge media presence in the terminal."

Samantha, standing behind Mel in her wheelchair, hands on Mel's shoulders, says, "How huge?"

"More than a hundred…Sir, could you give a brief statement? Please? Give them something now and they might leave you alone for the rest of the day."

Mel is frowning and Samantha looks toward the terminal, shrugs, and says, "Oh, why not?"

We start moving toward the terminal, Samantha holding Mel's hand and me pushing the wheelchair, and we get into the lower part of the building, and there are Maine state troopers and Bangor police officers to escort us in, each with a black band across his or her shield.

I catch the eye of Agent Washington and say, "Nicole, do me a favor: will you take over these pushing duties? I want a moment with my chief of staff."

We switch off and I spot an empty office behind a pile of luggage, and I lead Maddie inside and we both sit down, and she's still smiling.

"Sir, welcome home. I can't wait to hear how you pulled this off, and what happened over there."

I say, "I still can't believe it myself."

Maddie says, "I have to tell you: I've been getting texts all day from every major publisher in New York. Your book…an instant worldwide bestseller the moment you publish it."

"I'm sure," I say. "But Maddie, just one thing before we start talking book deals."

"Certainly, sir," she says, obviously happy, her eyes lit up. "What is it?"

I say, "Maddie, why did you sabotage me?"

CHAPTER 134

Bangor International Airport
Bangor, Maine

I have to give my tough chief of staff credit. She doesn't argue with me, or deny it, or say anything.

But the light is gone from her eyes.

She sits with me in this heavy silence in this small office.

I say, "Just before we left to catch that tanker flight from Pease, I made two phone calls. One to Samantha, and one to you, because I thought you deserved to know what I was doing. When we got to Pease, we almost weren't allowed to leave. The White House ordered the aircraft to stand fast. Who did you call? Richard Barnes?"

The color seems to slowly drain from her face. "No," she says. "Felicia Taft, his deputy. I…told her."

I wait.

"Why?"

Her eyes swell up, moisten. "I was afraid for you, sir. Afraid you were going to get wounded, captured, or killed. That the mission might be a failure. That you might end up…killing Mel. Instead of rescuing her. I didn't want your name, your legacy, to be a failure. If Mel was still alive, I thought…the professionals would be called in."

"That was my decision to make, wasn't it?" I say.

"Yes, sir, but I was also thinking about the future…the foundation you wanted to set up for vets. Without you…it would never happen. Thousands of vets would continue to suffer or die every year."

I want to make this quick.

My reunited family is waiting for me.

I say, "Then make the book deal, Maddie. Best you can. And then after the contracts are signed and I start writing it, I want you to run the foundation. We're going to call it the Boyd Tanner and David Stahl Memorial Fund, and you'll be in charge."

Maddie is confused. "But sir…"

I stand up. "That means you're out as my chief of staff. I can't trust you anymore, Maddie, but I can trust you to run this foundation. Do a good job in their memories."

She just nods. "I'm sorry, sir."

"Me, too," I say, and then I leave.

I follow a helpful Maine state trooper to where my family is waiting, in a hallway outside the main terminal, and I can hear the hum of voices nearby. To Mel and Sam I say, "Ready?," and they both nod.

We go out into the terminal, which has the ugliest black-and-white tiled floor I've ever seen, and as we become visible, loud applause and questions roar out. There's a small table with a forest of microphones set in the middle. Samantha wheels Mel up to the table, and I stand to Mel's left while my wife takes the other side.

Finally, I raise my hand and say, "Quiet, please, quiet. I'll answer as many questions as possible…but you have to realize my family is pretty tired." I point to a news anchor from one of the local Portland stations. "Go ahead."

"Mr. President, who joined you in this rescue mission? And can we talk to them?"

I say, "Well-trained friends of mine who helped me with the intelligence gathering, planning, and its execution. They've asked to remain anonymous, and I'm going to respect their wishes. Next?"

The brusque questioner is a male reporter from one of the cable networks, and he built his career on hunting down Keating Administration scandals and not finding one, which made him even more suspicious.

He asks, "Sir, isn't it true that by performing this risky and unauthorized mission, you're expressing your dislike and distrust of the Barnes Administration?"

That question silences the room, and after a few seconds pass, I say, "No. Next?"

"Sir, it appears you're injured. How did that happen?"

I lift my wrist. "Cut myself—that's all."

"Sir, is Asim Al-Asheed dead? And did you have a hand in his killing?"

I say, "Asim Al-Asheed is now in a position where he won't hurt or kill any more innocents. And that's all I'm going to say about that."

"Did you ask the Barnes Administration for permission before heading out to rescue your daughter?"

I smile. "Didn't have the time. One more, then, please."

My pompous cable reporter friend butts in loudly again and says, "Sir, aren't you concerned that the Barnes Administration will prosecute you under the Logan Act?"

I give them all a good smile and say, "Jake, you know as well as I do that the Logan Act only applies to citizens conducting unauthorized diplomacy with a foreign power." I pause. "Whatever I was doing in Libya was definitely not diplomacy."

Lots of laughter at that, and when it dies down, I say, "How about some questions for my daughter? She's the real hero here."

The media instantly picks up on that, and I expect Mel to be Mel, and she doesn't disappoint.

"Mel, how are you feeling?"

"Tired. Achy. My feet are a mess and it looks like a bullet scraped my upper right arm."

"Were you scared?"

"Every damn second."

"Did you say thank you to your dad?"

Mel waits for a moment and says, "Boy, that's a dumb question. Anybody got a smart one?"

A few titters at that, and someone yells out, "What food did you miss the most?"

"Cheeseburgers," she says. "I'm dying for a cheeseburger."

"Whose?" says a voice from the back. "McDonald's? Burger King? In-N-Out?"

"C'mon," Mel says. "There are no In-N-Out Burger chains on the East Coast. And besides, my dad makes the best cheeseburgers in the world. I'll wait for his."

Then it's Samantha's turn, and an anchor from a Boston channel says, "Mrs. Keating, what are your plans now?"

That seems to catch Sam off guard because she lowers her eyes, gives her head a quick shake, and looks at me while answering.

She's quietly weeping but smiling, and with a shock, I realize I'm doing the same thing.

They say politicians should never cry in public, but now I don't care.

We made it.

“I think it’s time for a sabbatical, to spend a lot more time with my family,” Samantha softly says.

A follow-up question: “But we understand that just a few weeks ago, you made a historic find in Maine, revealing the first Basque village ever to be found in North America. Don’t you want to go back to your work?”

Again, her loving and calm look, right at me, a few tears rolling down her cheeks. I look right back, loving her forever one more time, both of us holding on to our daughter with love and gratitude.

“No,” she says. “That’s what weekends and grad students are for.”

CHAPTER 135

Permanent Mission of the People's Republic of China
New York, New York

In a crowded dining room in the mission building, Jiang Lijun is feeling stuffed and achy. His stomach is full after an eight-course meal given in his honor, though the truth is, he doesn't feel very honorable, not after what happened in Libya. He has two cracked ribs at his back, where the American sniper's bullet struck his bullet-resistant vest, and only with the luck of having turned at the last moment did the bullet merely glance off him and not kill him.

The room is filled with red banners and decorations, and plate after plate has come out, from appetizers of bean curd and jellyfish to bowls of illegal shark fin soup and slices of Peking duck and vegetables and noodles. Overseeing the entire banquet is Jiang's boss, Li Baodong, who takes a smiling interest in Jiang's wife, Zhen, and their daughter, Li Na, who gurgles and laughs at all the attention.

There are about two dozen mission members here, and smiles

and waves come his way, and finally, when it seems as though Jiang and his family can go back to their condo, Li Baodong comes over and says to Zhen, "Sweet one, if I may, I need a few minutes alone with your hero."

Zhen is bouncing Li Na on her lap and feeding her tiny slices of tangerine, and she nods with pleasure. Jiang gets up and follows his boss, who goes through the mission's kitchen area and into a small, undecorated office with two chairs and a metal desk.

Li Baodong winks as he settles down heavily in the chair behind the desk, pulls a bottle and two glasses from a lower drawer, and pours into each glass a dark-colored liquid.

"A special Huangjiu," he says. "Very expensive, very rare. Smuggled here via diplomatic pouch. Have a good swallow. You deserve it."

Jiang does just that, and when he puts down the empty glass, Li says, "Enjoying yourself?"

"Yes, but..."

"But what?"

"It's uncomfortable," Jiang says. "Considering..."

"Considering how you fucked up everything you touched?" Li demands. "Weeks ago you were given a simple task: go to those New Hampshire mountains and retrieve Mel Keating. Instead, you disobeyed my orders, went rogue on a personal mission of vengeance...and when you had a second chance to do your job, you screwed up that one as well. You damn fool: you were supposed to rescue that girl and put the Americans in our debt and thaw our relations."

"But I—"

"But instead, you put *us* in debt to the Americans, by allowing yourself to be captured and *treated* by their intelligence agencies in Tunis before being released to us. A laughingstock you are, boy. That's what you've done."

"But I didn't say a word to them!"

Li says, "You didn't have to...no doubt they took high-quality photos of your facial features, not to mention gathered your fingerprints and DNA samples. Right now they are busily running all of that information through their data banks, and in a few hours, they'll be rolling up whatever networks you've established here and elsewhere."

The ache in Jiang's rear ribs continues to throb. His stomach is roiling with nausea.

"The Americans are making demands," Li says. "They say you interfered with the rescue of the president's daughter. They say no talks, no movement on improving our relations until your status is settled, Jiang Lijun."

He's starting to sweat. His mouth has a metallic taste.

"Settled how?" he asks, surprised at how weak his voice sounds.

"Permanently," his boss quickly replies. "Sorry to say, you will never leave the United States."

Aghast, Jiang says, "You're turning me over to the Americans?"

Li shakes his head. "Of course not. I would never do anything like that to one of my officers."

Jiang's vision is getting blurry. He looks at the desk.

Li's drink remains untouched.

Softly, his boss says, "Not bad for a fat mushroom, eh? Think of this, my dear Lijun: when this is all settled, you will be a hero, like your father, and the party will take care of your wife and your daughter. That I promise."

Jiang tries to speak, but his tongue, jaw, and, soon, everything else won't work.

CHAPTER 136

Family quarters
The White House

President Pamela Barnes is alone in the living room area of the White House's family quarters, bare feet up on a hassock, sipping her daily Glenlivet on ice, watching the news coverage this late afternoon on MSNBC, the sound off.

The past several hours have been grueling. Barnes refuses to watch any news coverage with the sound on because she can't stand the joyful and congratulatory words coming from the weasel mouths of the news anchors and the military and Special Forces experts who've come on to discuss in awed tones the unauthorized yet successful mission by Matt Keating to rescue his daughter.

And what of the Barnes Administration?

Hell, what else can she do but issue a cheerful press release praising Matt Keating and his crew of unnamed warriors, including that dead Secret Service agent?

Who's about to come home.

Up on the screen is live footage from Dover Air Force Base

in Delaware. An Air Force jet has just landed, and six Marines in dress blues have marched up into the rear of the aircraft and are now marching down, carrying the flag-draped metal coffin of former Marine and deceased Secret Service agent David Stahl.

She takes another bracing sip.

Some hours earlier today, word came to her deputy chief of staff, Felicia Taft, from Stahl's parents and his congressman from California that no member of the Barnes Administration would be welcome at the Dover Air Force Base ceremony.

Instead, standing with the head of the Secret Service—and not the secretary of Homeland Security—are Matthew Keating, Samantha Keating, and Mel Keating, sitting calmly in a wheelchair. Beside them are various members of the Secret Service and the Stahl family.

What an image, what a sight, as the casket is solemnly taken out.

Richard, she thinks, *I sure could use your advice today.*

But Richard is out in Iowa, trying to make nice with some dairy farmers who are upset with her administration's latest trade policy. The Iowa caucuses are coming up sooner than anyone thinks, and she needs to get ready for the challenges of running for a second term.

Barnes gets up and goes to a small desk. She looks back at the television screen. There's a graphic of northwestern Libya depicting a raid by Army Rangers on the compound where Asim Al-Asheed lived, and the news is that a number of important documents, blueprints, and computer drives have been seized.

Good news, all right.

But not particularly for her.

She opens the center desk drawer and takes out the buff-colored envelope she found in the Resolute desk on Inauguration Day, more than eighteen months ago. She slips out the handwritten note on White House stationery and rereads once more the words from her predecessor, following an Inauguration Day tradition nearly forty years old.

Dear Pamela,

My sincere congratulations on your victory following a historic political battle, well fought in the tough arena of today's heavily partisan environment.

Today you become the president of a proud and good people who are truly decent in their hearts and actions. They long for an America at peace, that knows prosperity, and that is a leader in the world.

You have my prayers, support, and good wishes for the challenging months ahead. You are starting an incredible journey experienced by very few over the years, and you should feel honored that the American people have chosen you.

God bless you and your family.

Sincerely,
Matt Keating

Barnes pauses.

Oh, if that damn SEAL had just stopped there.

But he didn't.

P.S.

Notwithstanding the above, Pamela, I plan to see you again, face-to-face, in four years.

Barnes takes the historic note, crumples it into a ball, and drops it on the floor.

She finishes off her drink.

Decides it's time for another.

ACKNOWLEDGMENTS

For their invaluable assistance and expertise, the authors wish to thank First Sergeant Matt Eversmann (Ret.), 75th Army Ranger Regiment; Captain Joe Roy, KC-135 pilot, US Air Force; former White House Chief of Staff John Podesta; and Richard Clarke, national coordinator for security and counterterrorism in the Clinton and Bush (43) White Houses.

Special thanks as well to Tina Flournoy, chief of staff for the office of Bill Clinton; Steve Rinehart; Oscar Flores; Deneen Howell; Michael O'Connor; and Mary Jordan.

ABOUT THE AUTHORS

BILL CLINTON was elected president of the United States in 1992, and served until 2001. After leaving the White House, he established the Clinton Foundation, which helps improve global health, increase opportunity for girls and women, reduce childhood obesity and preventable diseases, create economic opportunity and growth, and address the effects of climate change. He is the author of a number of non-fiction works, including *My Life*, which was a number one international bestseller. With James Patterson, he is co-author of the number one international bestselling novel *The President is Missing.*

JAMES PATTERSON is one of the best-known and biggest-selling writers of all time. His books have sold in excess of 400 million copies worldwide. He is the author of some of the most popular series of the past two decades – the Alex Cross, Women's Murder Club, Detective Michael Bennett and Private novels – and he has written many other number one bestsellers including non-fiction and stand-alone thrillers.

James is passionate about encouraging children to read. Inspired by his own son who was a reluctant reader, he also writes a range of books for young readers including the Middle School, Dog Diaries, Treasure Hunters and Max Einstein series. James has donated millions in grants to independent bookshops and has been the most borrowed author in UK libraries for the past thirteen years in a row. He lives in Florida with his family.